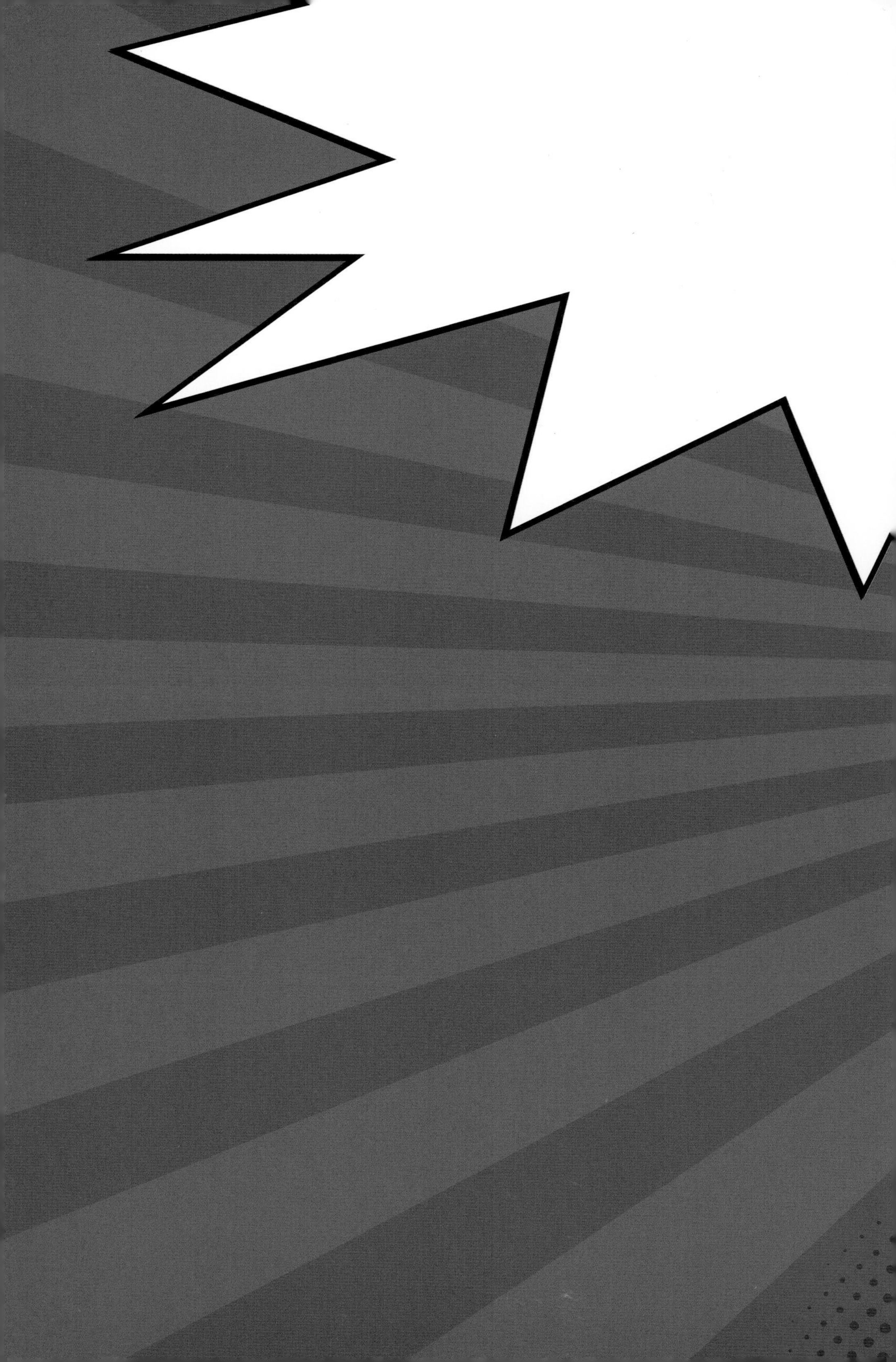

SUPER TURBO★

SAVES THE DAY!

WRITTEN BY **EDGAR POWERS**
ILLUSTRATED BY **SALVATORE COSTANZA**
AT GLASS HOUSE GRAPHICS

LITTLE SIMON
NEW YORK   LONDON   TORONTO   SYDNEY   NEW DELHI

LITTLE SIMON
AN IMPRINT OF SIMON & SCHUSTER CHILDREN'S PUBLISHING DIVISION
1230 AVENUE OF THE AMERICAS, NEW YORK, NEW YORK 10020
FIRST LITTLE SIMON EDITION FEBRUARY 2021 * COPYRIGHT © 2021 BY SIMON & SCHUSTER, INC. ALL RIGHTS RESERVED, INCLUDING THE RIGHT OF REPRODUCTION IN WHOLE OR IN PART IN ANY FORM. LITTLE SIMON IS A REGISTERED TRADEMARK OF SIMON & SCHUSTER, INC., AND ASSOCIATED COLOPHON IS A TRADEMARK OF SIMON & SCHUSTER, INC. FOR INFORMATION ABOUT SPECIAL DISCOUNTS FOR BULK PURCHASES, PLEASE CONTACT SIMON & SCHUSTER SPECIAL SALES AT 1-866-506-1949 OR BUSINESS@SIMONANDSCHUSTER.COM. THE SIMON & SCHUSTER SPEAKERS BUREAU CAN BRING AUTHORS TO YOUR LIVE EVENT. FOR MORE INFORMATION OR TO BOOK AN EVENT CONTACT THE SIMON & SCHUSTER SPEAKERS BUREAU AT 1-866-248-3049 OR VISIT OUR WEBSITE AT WWW.SIMONSPEAKERS.COM. DESIGNED BY NICHOLAS SCIACCA * ART SERVICES BY GLASS HOUSE GRAPHICS * ART AND COLOR BY SALVATORE COSTANZA LETTERING BY GIOVANI SPARADO/GRAFIMATED CARTOON * SUPERVISION BY SALVATORE DI MARCO/GRAFIMATED CARTOON * MANUFACTURED IN CHINA 1120 SCP * 2 4 6 8 10 9 7 5 3 1 * LIBRARY OF CONGRESS CATALOGING-IN-PUBLICATION DATA NAMES: POWERS, EDGAR J., AUTHOR. | GLASS HOUSE GRAPHICS, ILLUSTRATOR. TITLE: SUPER TURBO SAVES THE DAY! / BY EDGAR POWERS ; ILLUSTRATED BY GLASS HOUSE GRAPHICS. DESCRIPTION: FIRST LITTLE SIMON EDITION. | NEW YORK : LITTLE SIMON, 2021. | SERIES: SUPER TURBO, THE GRAPHIC NOVEL ; BOOK 1 | AUDIENCE: AGES 5-9 | AUDIENCE: GRADES 2-3 | SUMMARY: SUPER TURBO LEARNS HE IS NOT THE ONLY SUPERHERO PET AT SUNNYVIEW ELEMENTARY. IDENTIFIERS: LCCN 2020024872 (PRINT) | LCCN 2020024873 (EBOOK) | ISBN 9781534474468 (PAPERBACK) | ISBN 9781534474475 (HARDCOVER) | ISBN 9781534474482 (EBOOK) SUBJECTS: LCSH: GRAPHIC NOVELS. | CYAC: GRAPHIC NOVELS. | SUPERHEROES—FICTION. | HAMSTERS—FICTION. | PETS—FICTION. | ELEMENTARY SCHOOLS—FICTION. | SCHOOLS—FICTION. CLASSIFICATION: LCC PZ7.7.P7 ST 2021 (PRINT) | LCC PZ7.7.P7 (EBOOK) | DDC 741.5/973—DC23 LC RECORD AVAILABLE AT HTTPS://LCCN.LOC.GOV/2020024872 LC EBOOK RECORD AVAILABLE AT HTTPS://LCCN.LOC.GOV/2020024873

CONTENTS

CHAPTER 1 . . . 6

CHAPTER 2 . . . 18

CHAPTER 3 . . . 30

CHAPTER 4 . . . 42

CHAPTER 5 . . . 56

CHAPTER 6 . . . 72

CHAPTER 7 . . . 84

CHAPTER 8 . . . 98

CHAPTER 9 . . . 112

CHAPTER 10 . . . 126

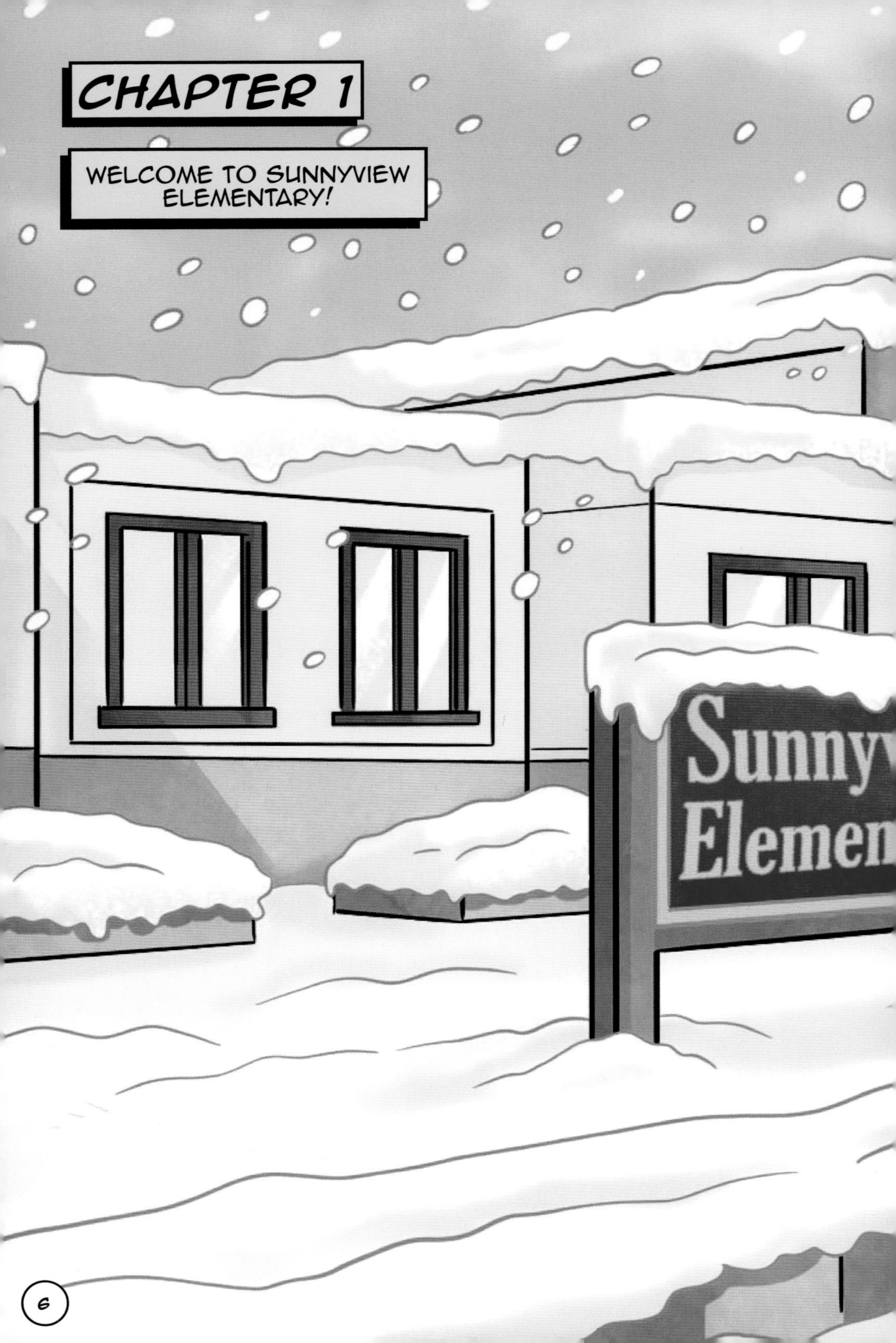
CHAPTER 1
WELCOME TO SUNNYVIEW ELEMENTARY!

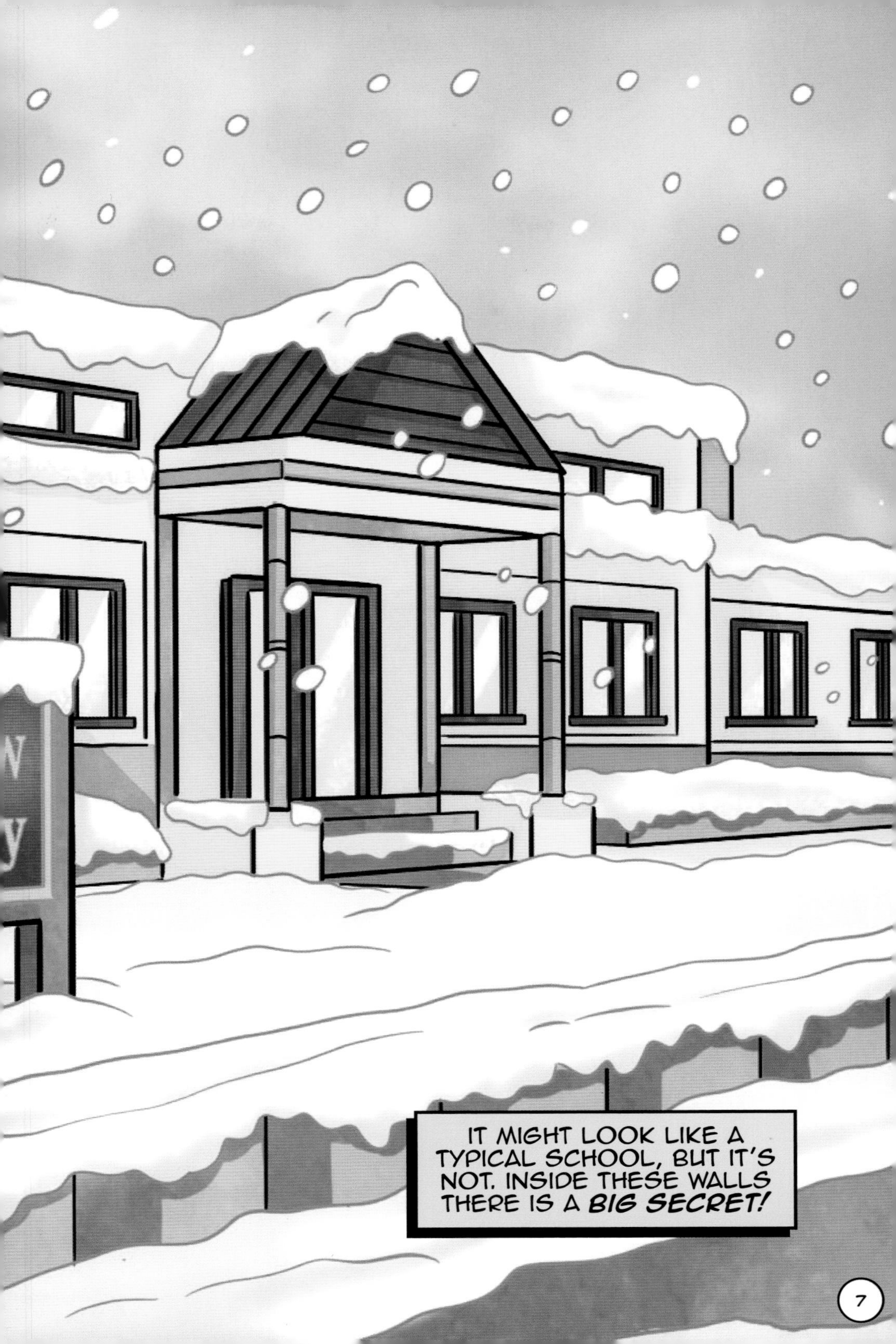
IT MIGHT LOOK LIKE A TYPICAL SCHOOL, BUT IT'S NOT. INSIDE THESE WALLS THERE IS A *BIG SECRET!*

BUT MORE ON THAT LATER. FIRST, THIS IS TURBO! HE IS A HAMSTER.
THIS IS TURBO'S CAGE.
I PREFER TO CALL IT MY "PALACE." CAGE JUST SOUNDS... WRONG.

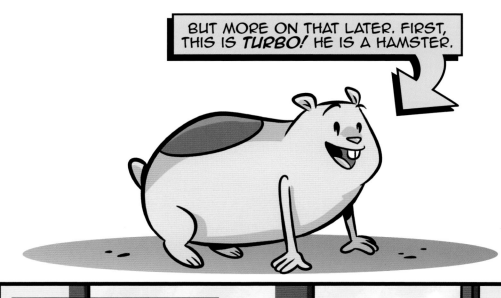

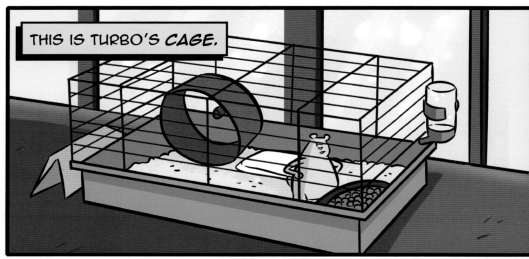

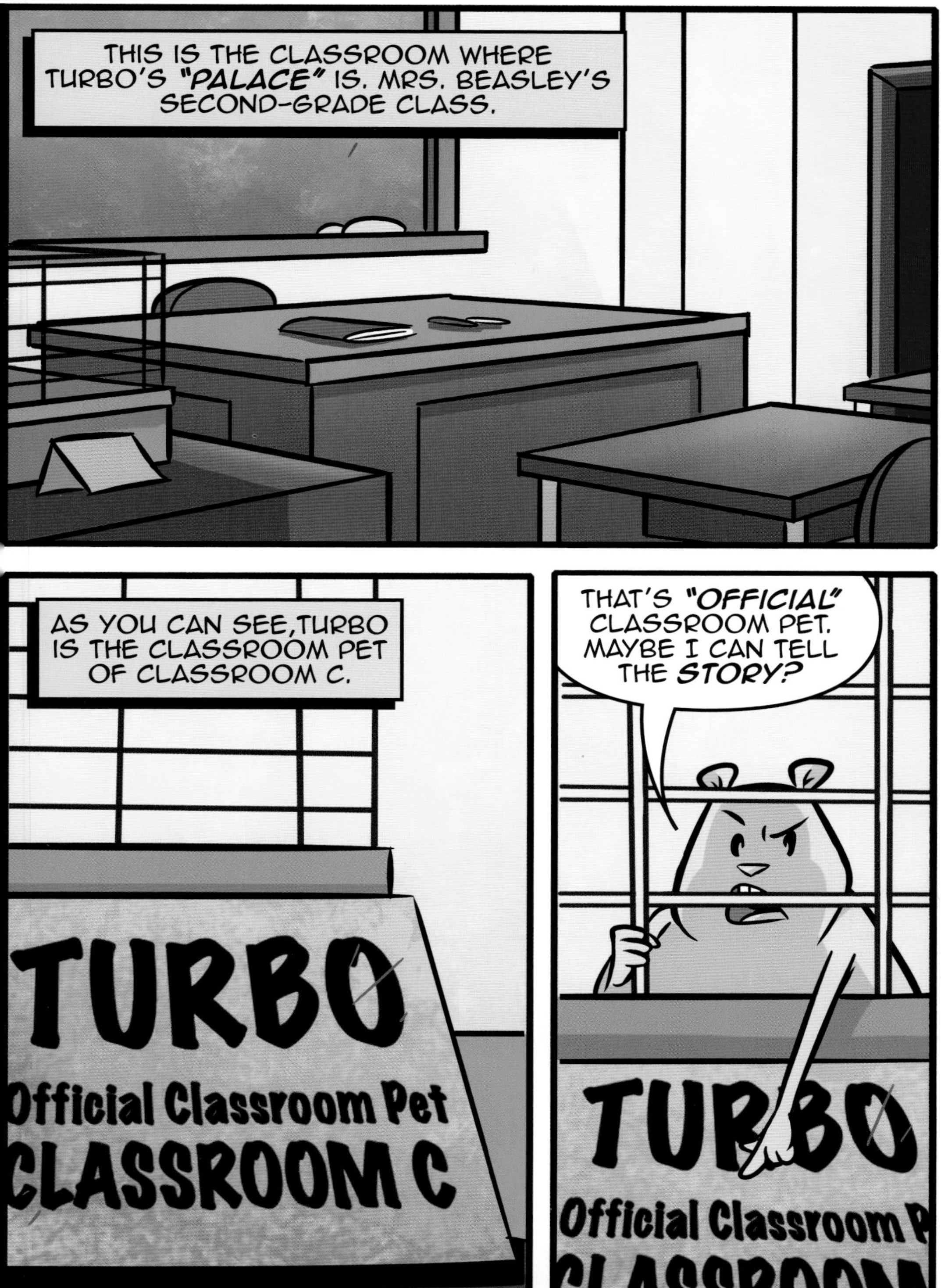
THIS IS THE CLASSROOM WHERE TURBO'S "PALACE" IS. MRS. BEASLEY'S SECOND-GRADE CLASS.
AS YOU CAN SEE, TURBO IS THE CLASSROOM PET OF CLASSROOM C.
TURBO
Official Classroom Pet
CLASSROOM C
THAT'S "OFFICIAL" CLASSROOM PET. MAYBE I CAN TELL THE STORY?
TURBO
Official Classroom P
CLASSROOM

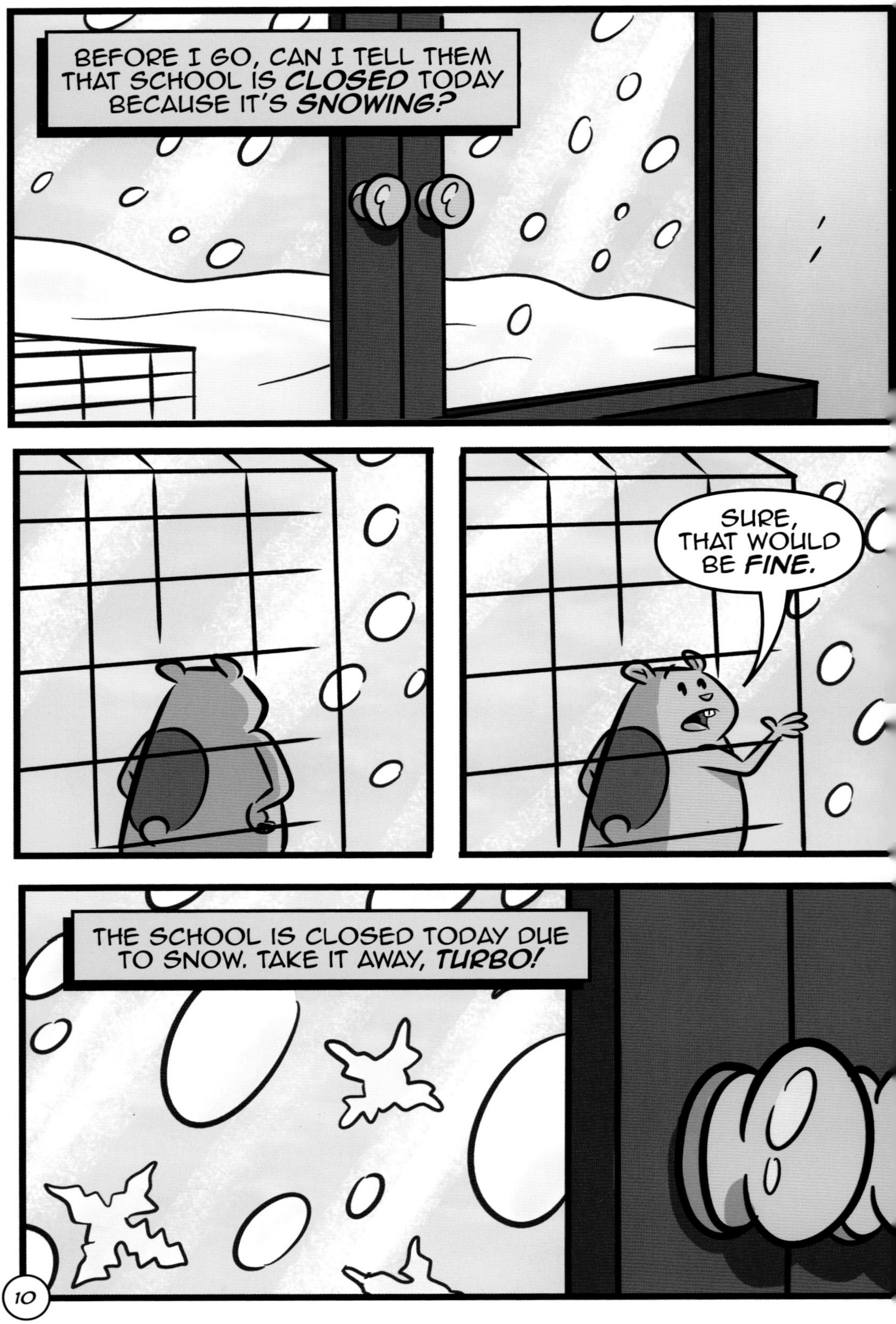
BEFORE I GO, CAN I TELL THEM THAT SCHOOL IS CLOSED TODAY BECAUSE IT'S SNOWING?
SURE, THAT WOULD BE FINE.
THE SCHOOL IS CLOSED TODAY DUE TO SNOW. TAKE IT AWAY, TURBO!

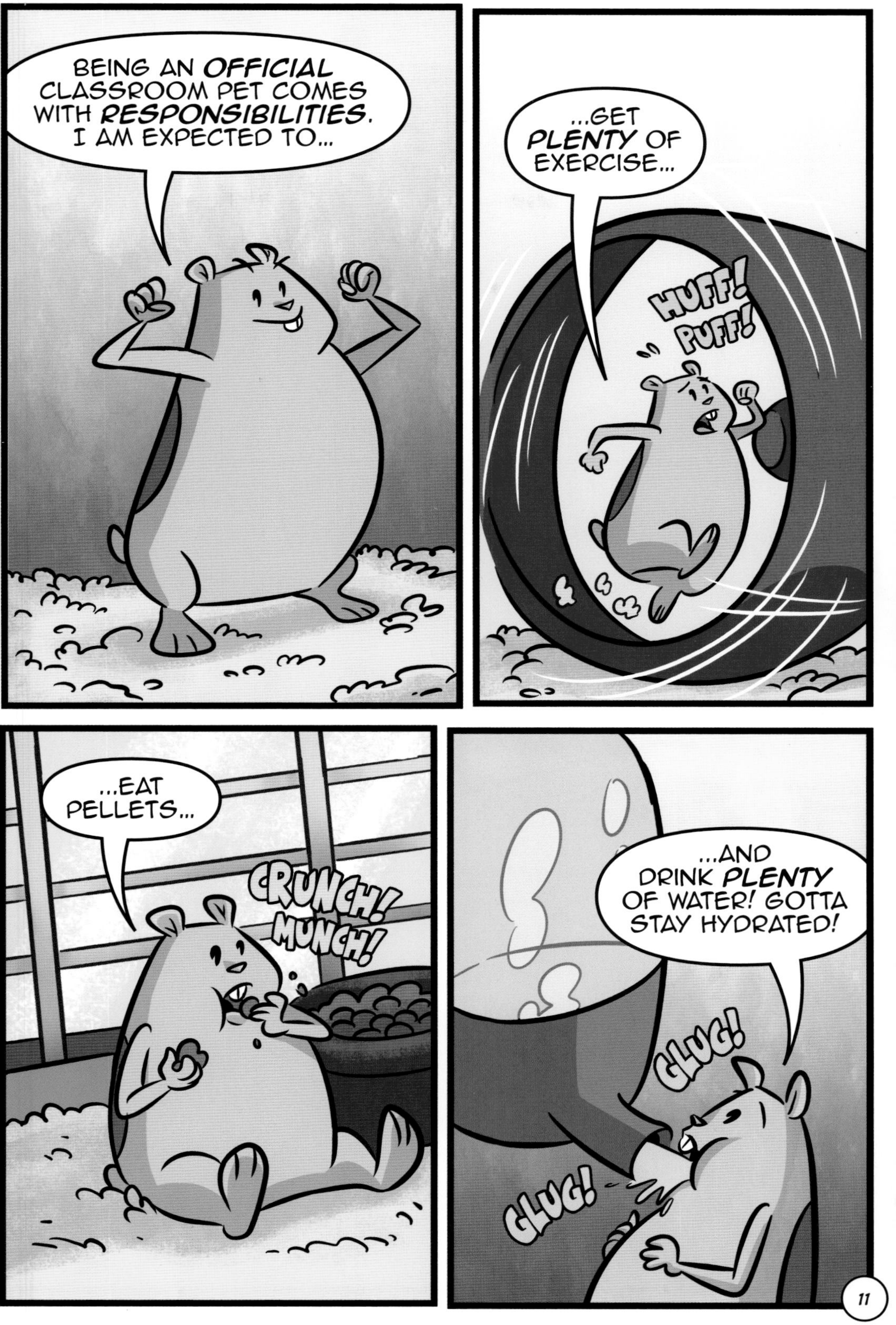
BEING AN OFFICIAL CLASSROOM PET COMES WITH RESPONSIBILITIES. I AM EXPECTED TO...
...GET PLENTY OF EXERCISE...
HUFF! PUFF!
...EAT PELLETS...
CRUNCH! MUNCH!
...AND DRINK PLENTY OF WATER! GOTTA STAY HYDRATED!
GLUG!
GLUG!

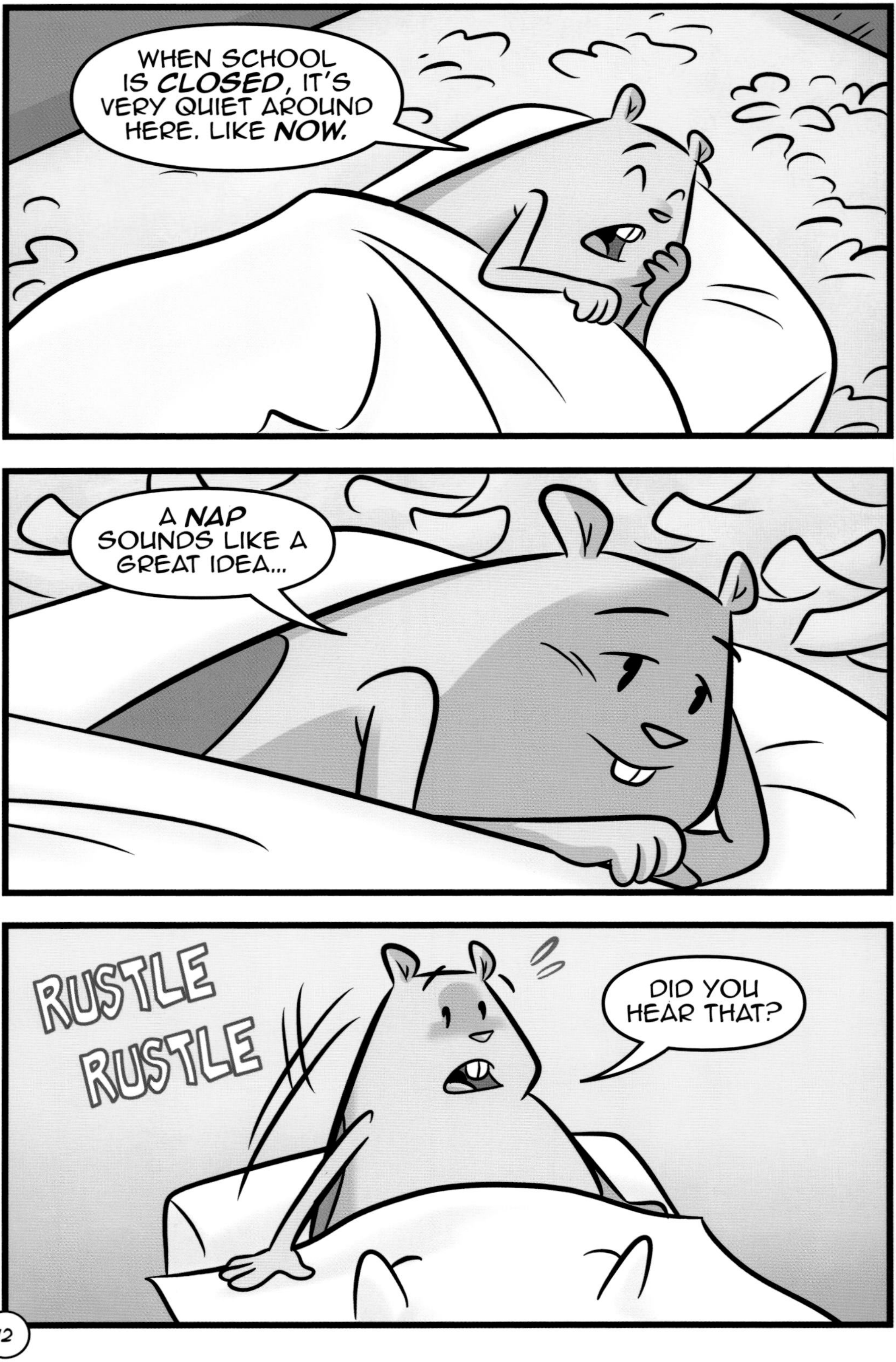
WHEN SCHOOL IS CLOSED, IT'S VERY QUIET AROUND HERE. LIKE NOW.
A NAP SOUNDS LIKE A GREAT IDEA...
RUSTLE RUSTLE
DID YOU HEAR THAT?

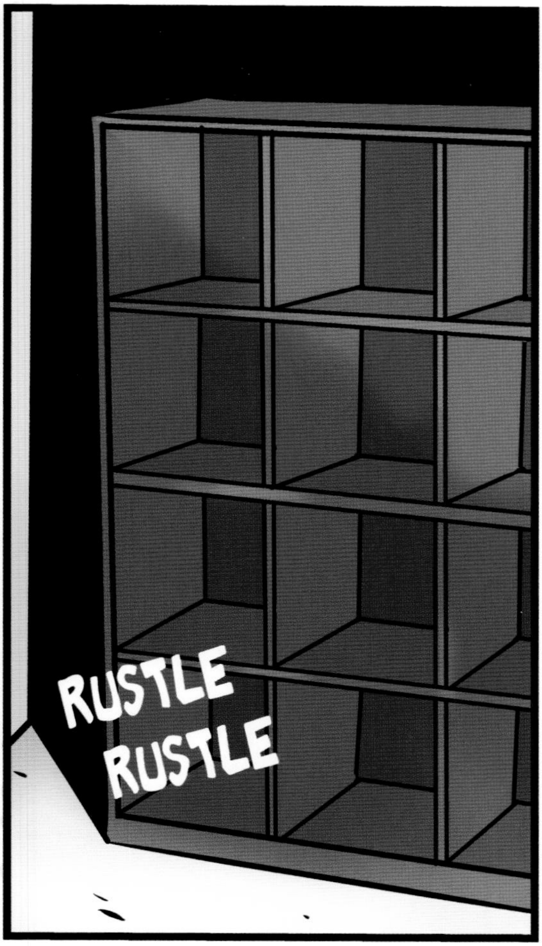
RUSTLE
RUSTLE

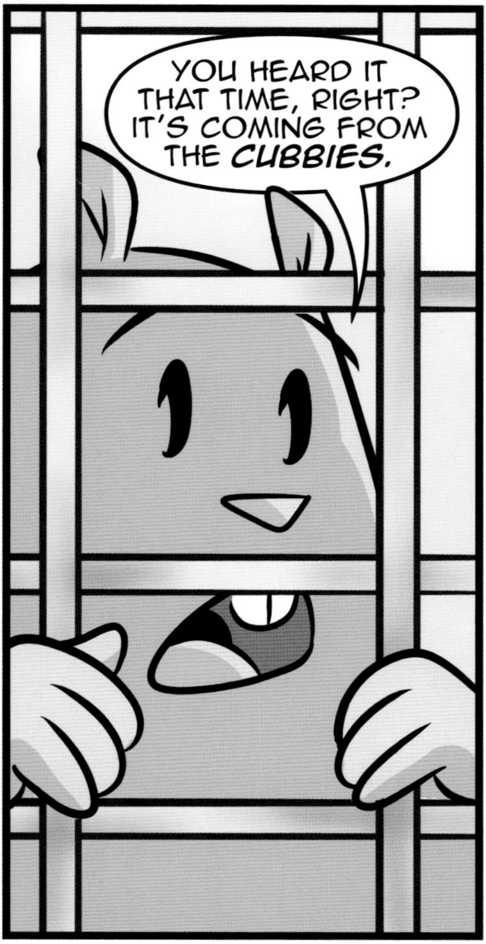
YOU HEARD IT THAT TIME, RIGHT? IT'S COMING FROM THE *CUBBIES.*

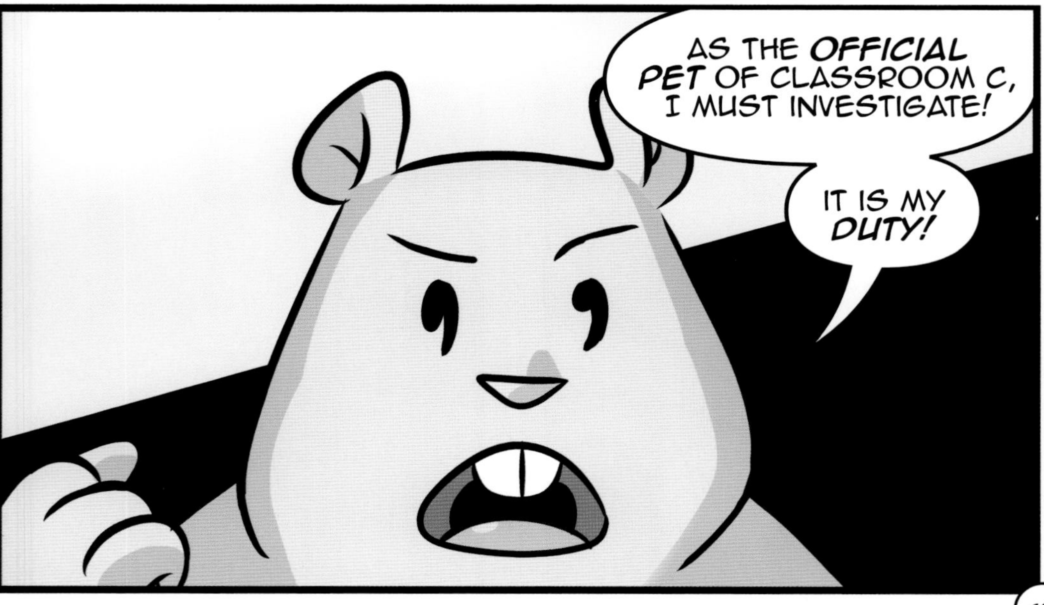
AS THE *OFFICIAL PET* OF CLASSROOM C, I MUST INVESTIGATE!
IT IS MY *DUTY!*

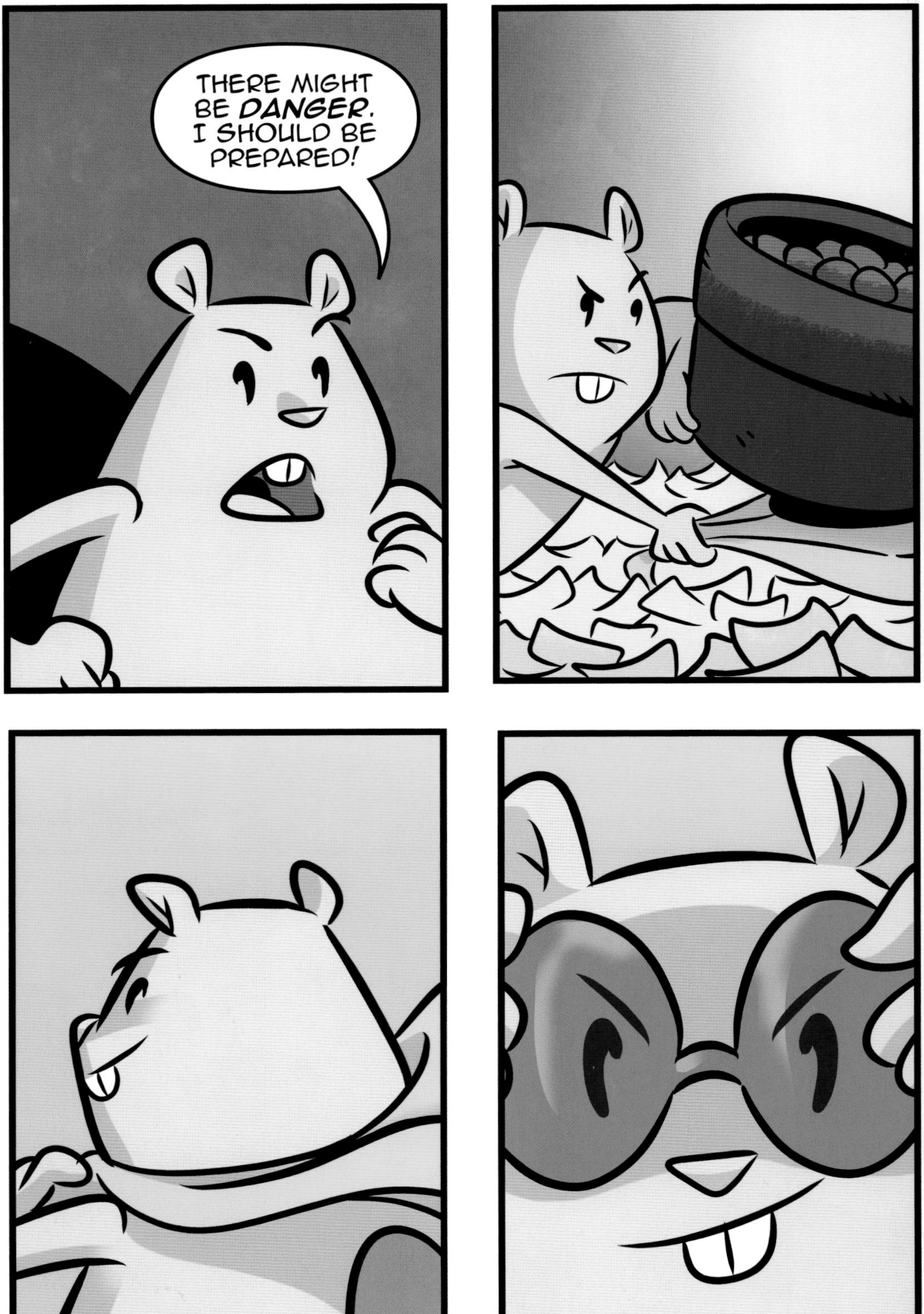
THERE MIGHT BE DANGER. I SHOULD BE PREPARED!

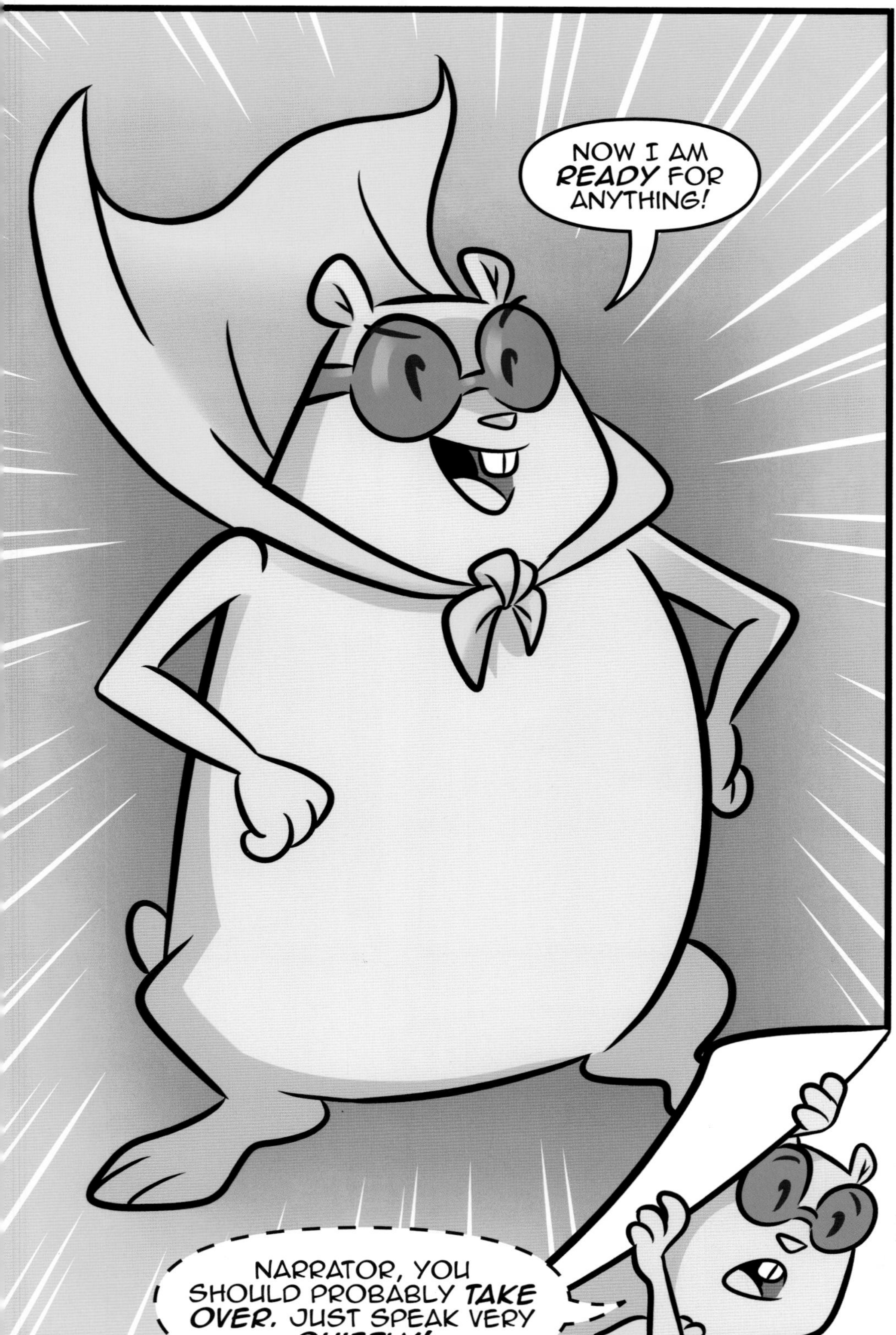
NOW I AM *READY* FOR ANYTHING!
NARRATOR, YOU SHOULD PROBABLY *TAKE OVER.* JUST SPEAK VERY *QUIETLY!*

TURBO SILENTLY EXITED HIS *"PALACE"* AND MADE HIS WAY ACROSS CLASSROOM C TO THE SOURCE OF THE MYSTERY NOISE.

HE WAS SNEAKY, SO YOU MIGHT NOT BE ABLE TO SEE HIM. SO HERE'S SOME HELP.

THERE HE IS.

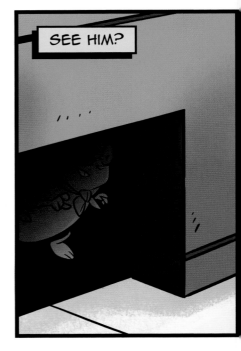

SEE HIM?

MAYBE?

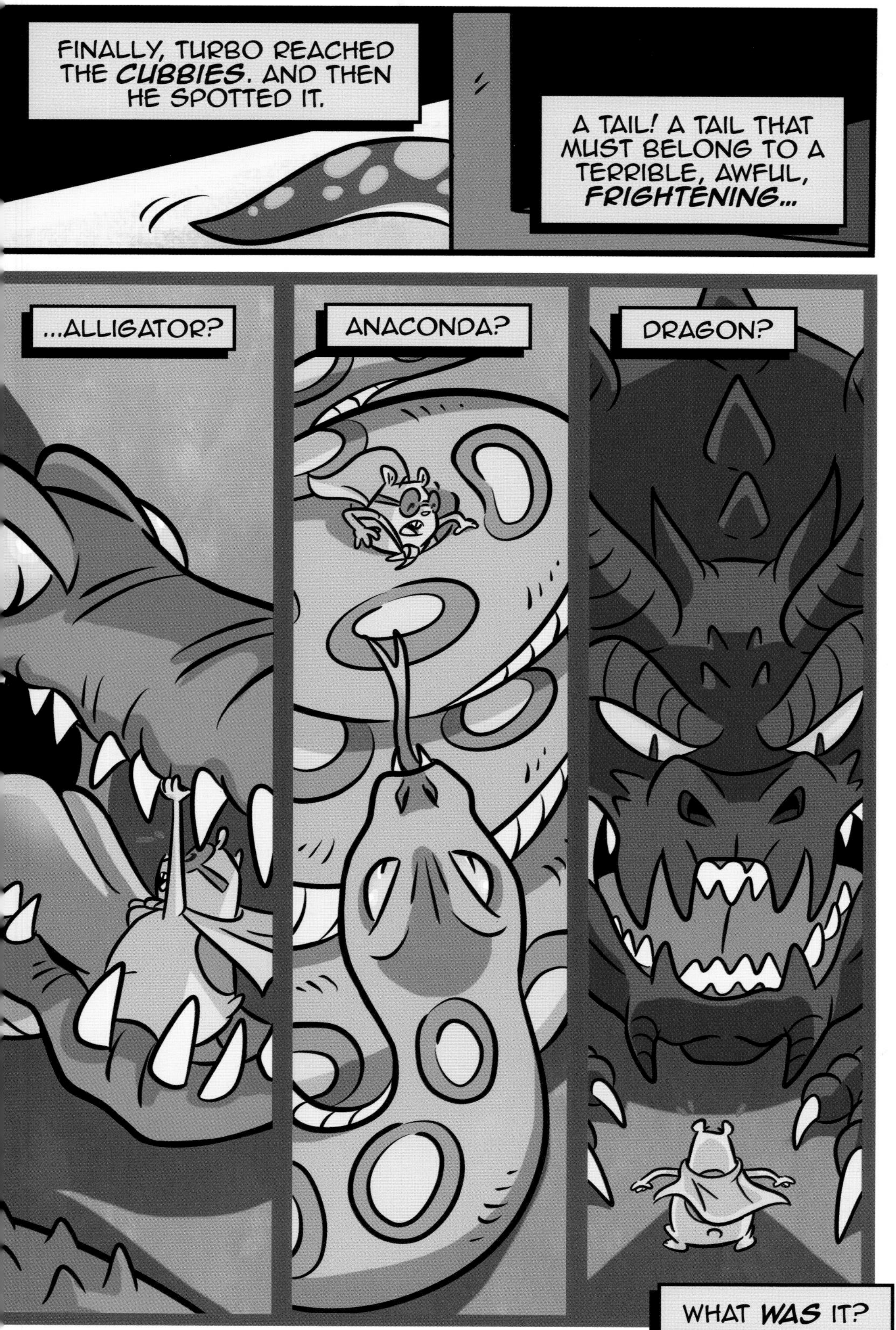
FINALLY, TURBO REACHED THE CUBBIES. AND THEN HE SPOTTED IT.
A TAIL! A TAIL THAT MUST BELONG TO A TERRIBLE, AWFUL, FRIGHTENING...
...ALLIGATOR?
ANACONDA?
DRAGON?
WHAT WAS IT?

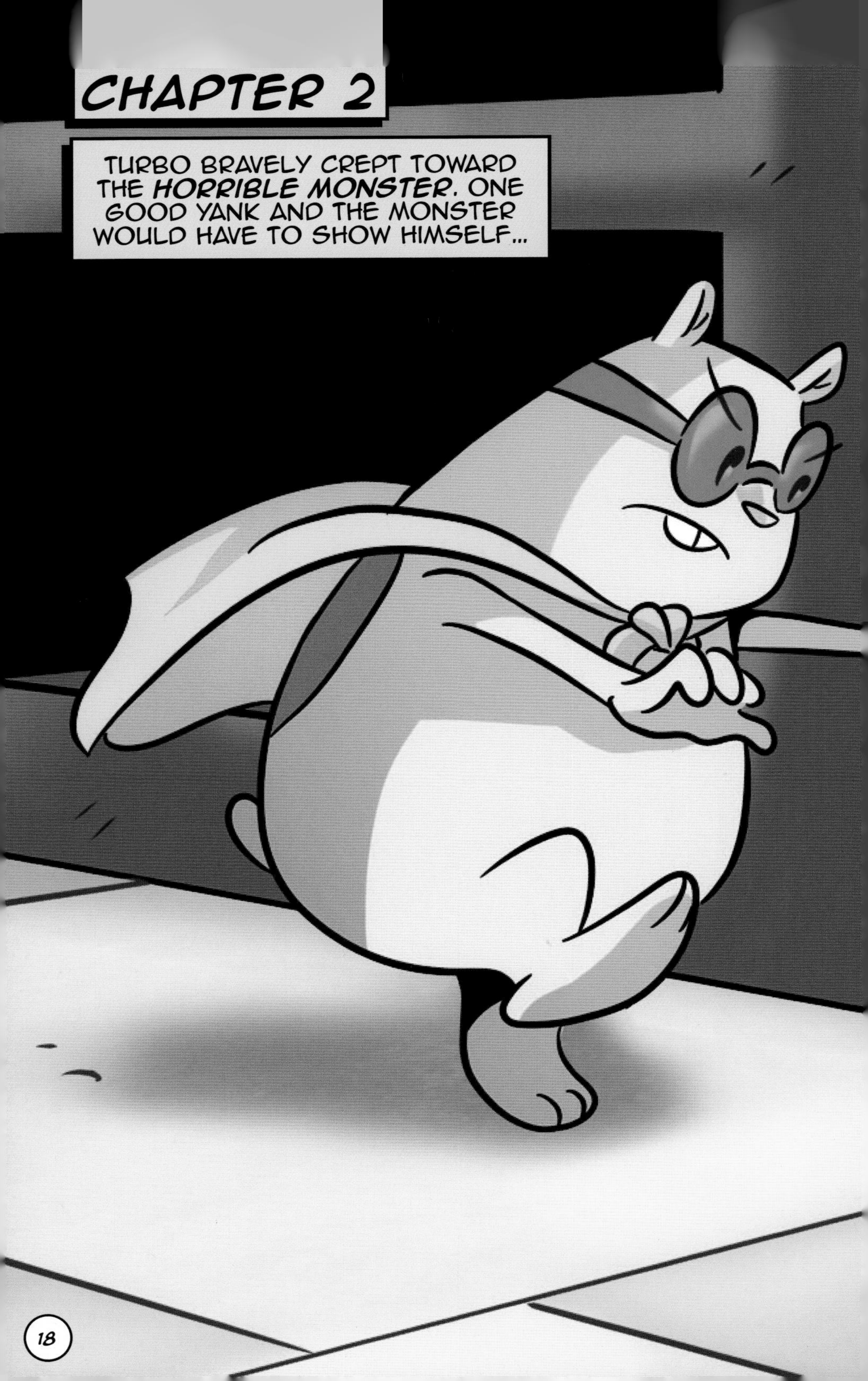
CHAPTER 2
TURBO BRAVELY CREPT TOWARD THE HORRIBLE MONSTER. ONE GOOD YANK AND THE MONSTER WOULD HAVE TO SHOW HIMSELF...

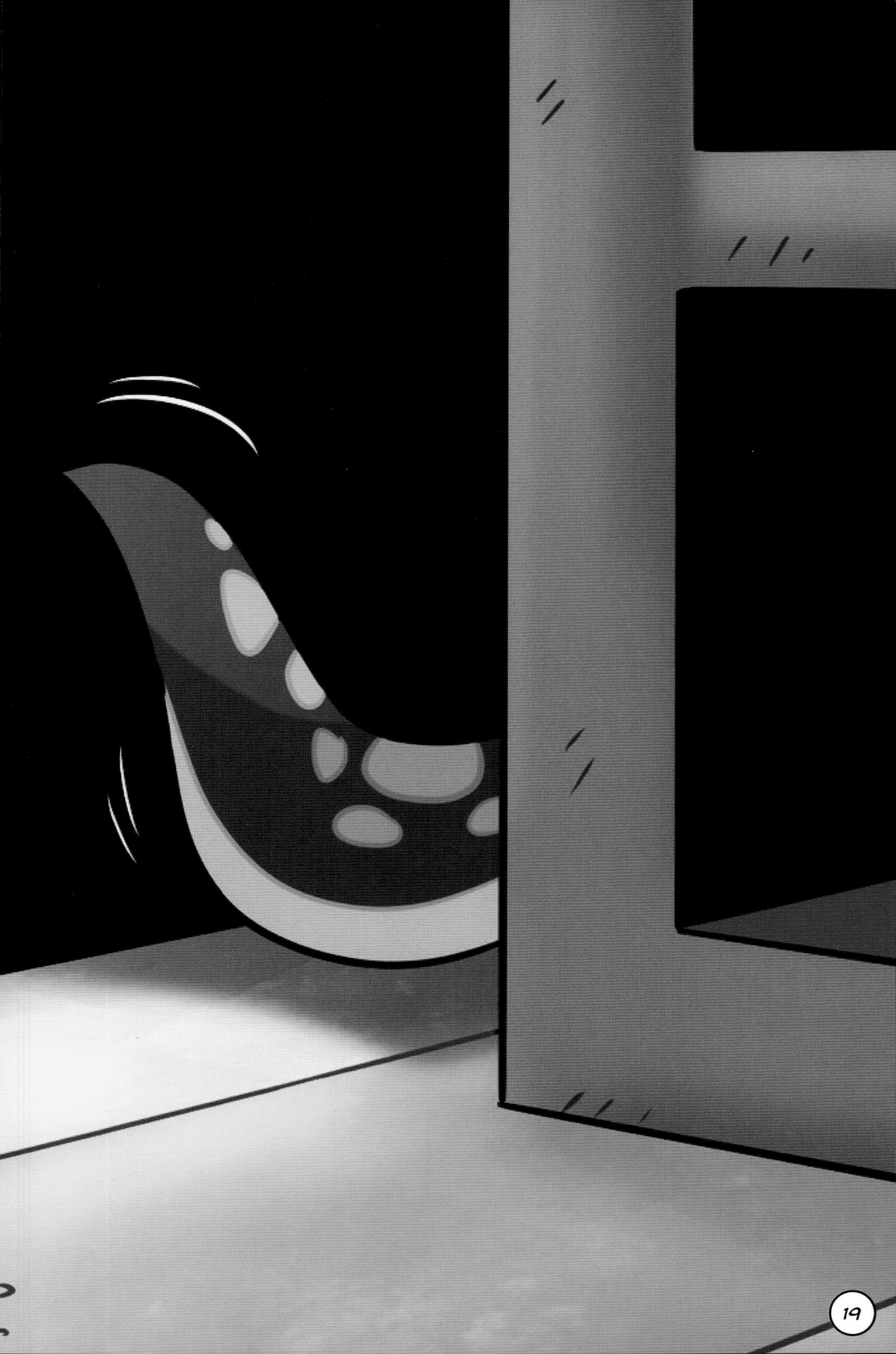

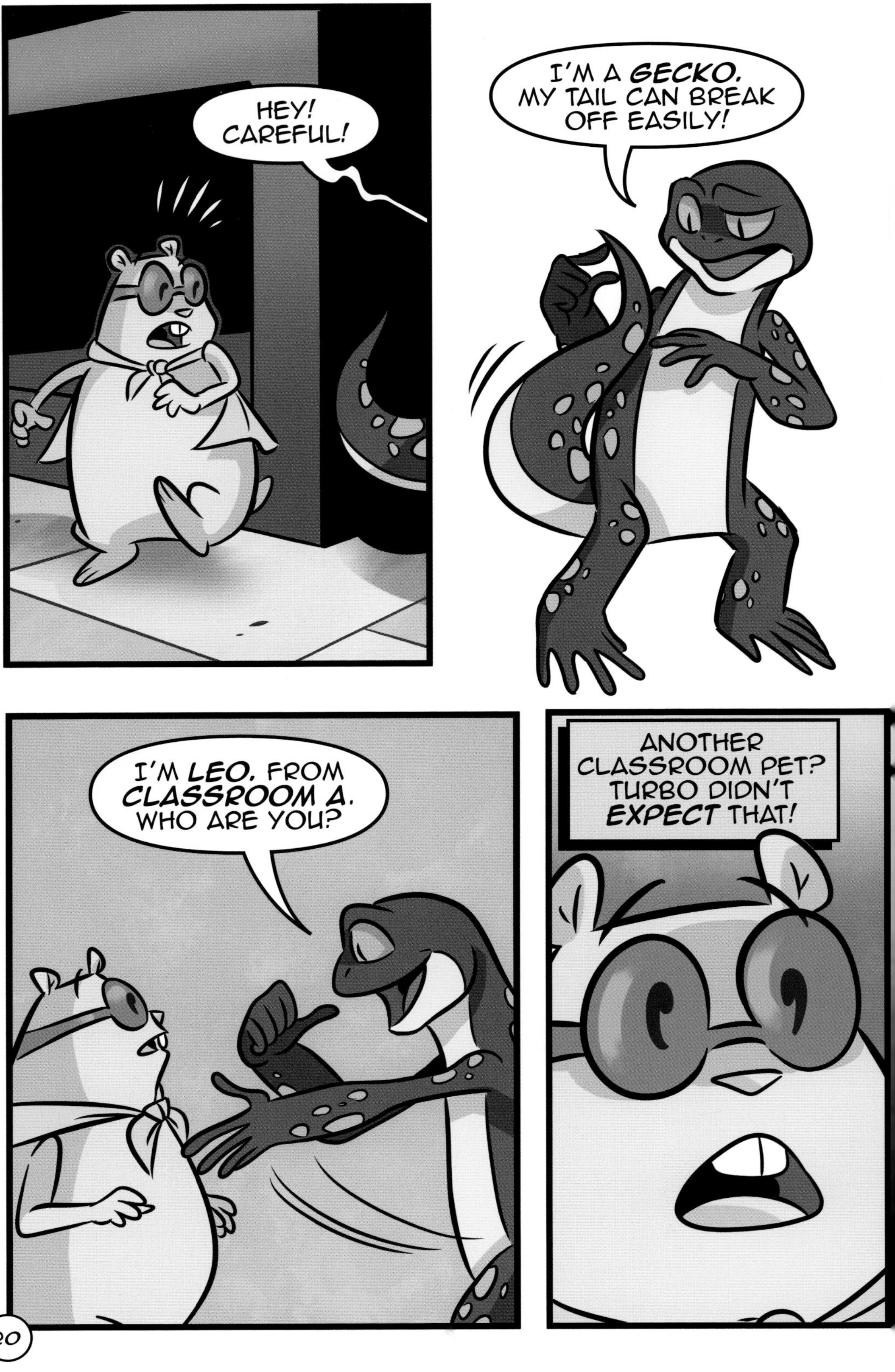
HEY! CAREFUL!
I'M A GECKO. MY TAIL CAN BREAK OFF EASILY!
I'M LEO, FROM CLASSROOM A. WHO ARE YOU?
ANOTHER CLASSROOM PET? TURBO DIDN'T EXPECT THAT!

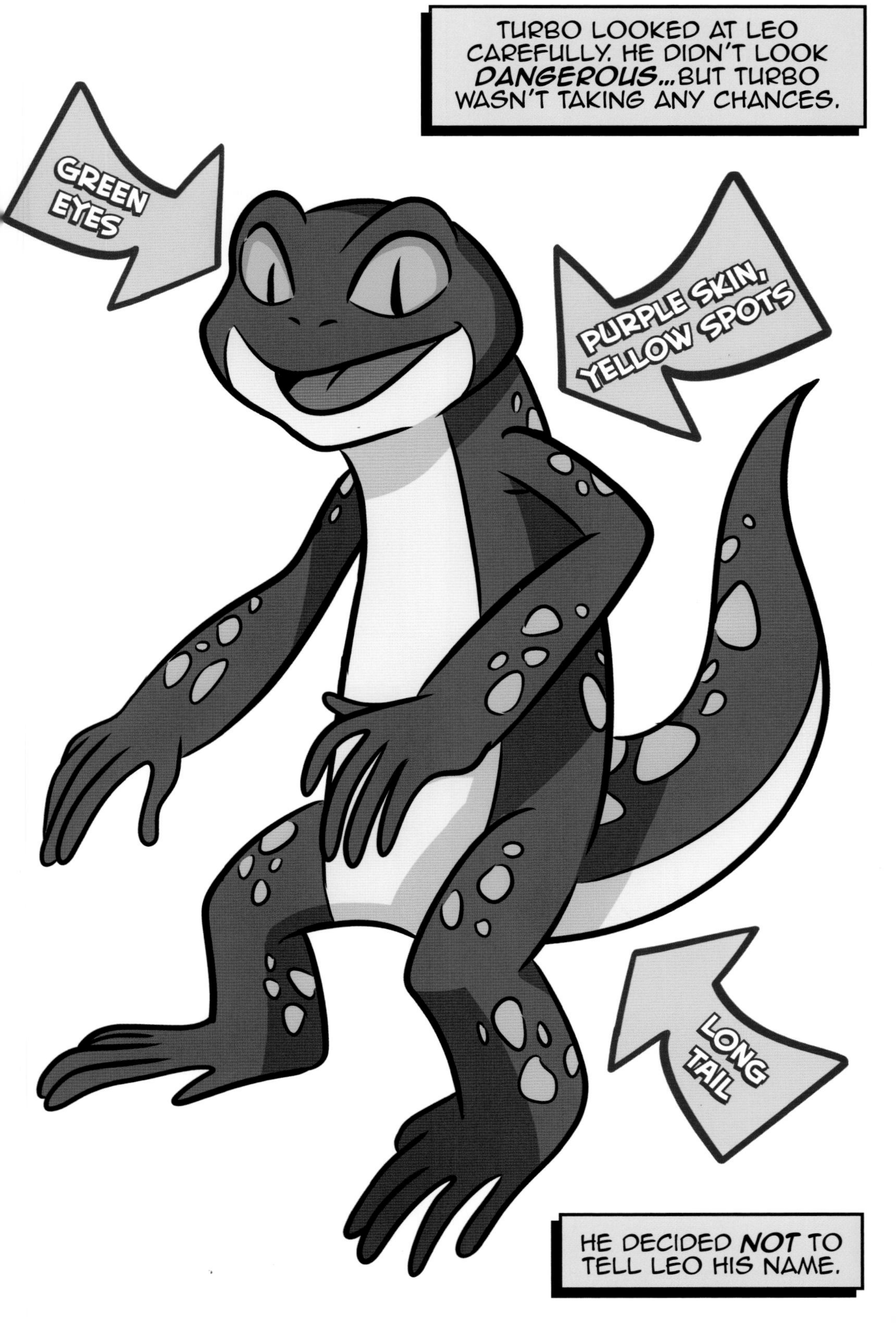

TURBO LOOKED AT LEO CAREFULLY. HE DIDN'T LOOK *DANGEROUS*...BUT TURBO WASN'T TAKING ANY CHANCES.
GREEN EYES
PURPLE SKIN, YELLOW SPOTS
LONG TAIL
HE DECIDED ***NOT*** TO TELL LEO HIS NAME.

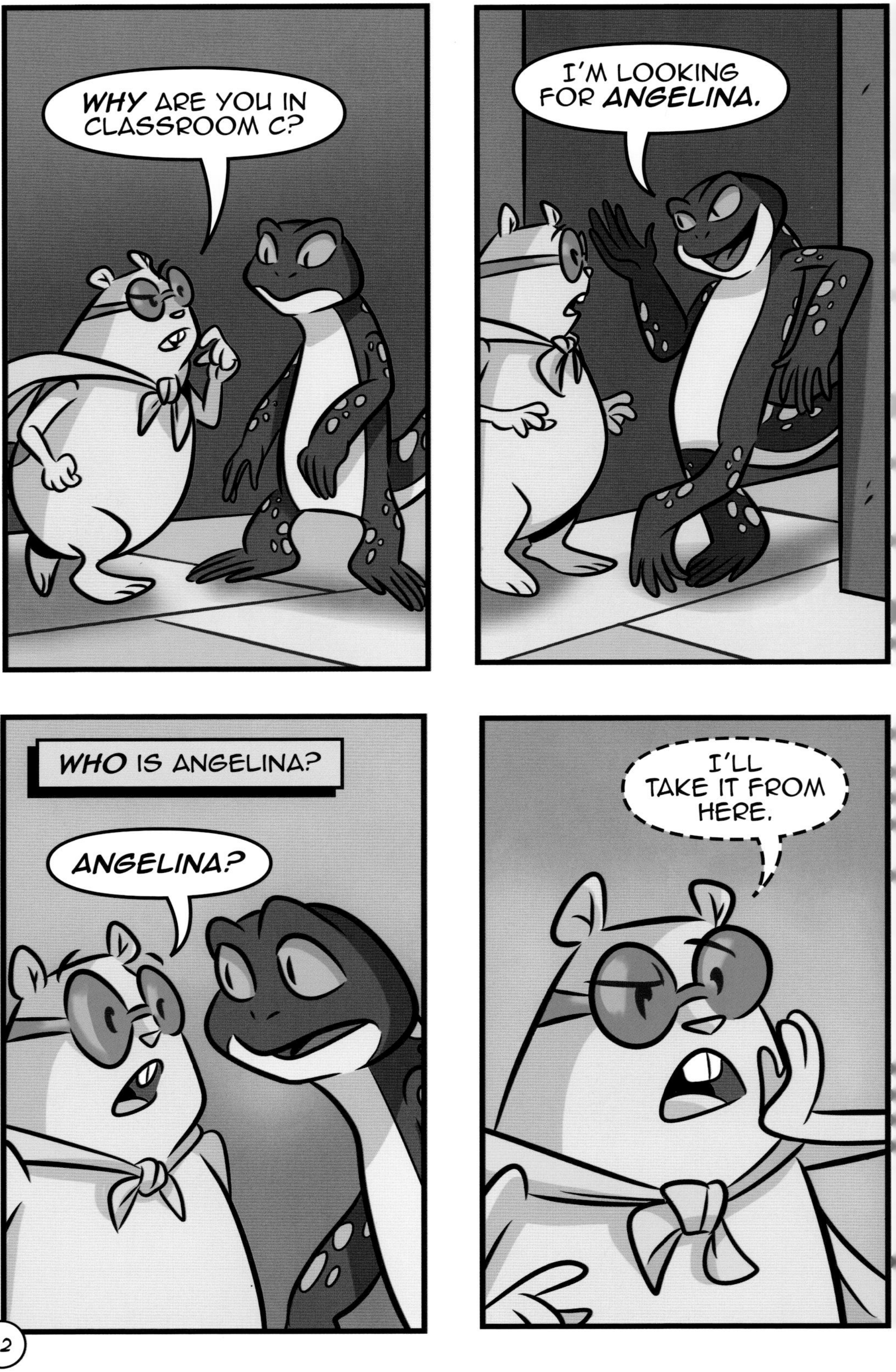
WHY ARE YOU IN CLASSROOM C?
I'M LOOKING FOR ANGELINA.
WHO IS ANGELINA?
ANGELINA?
I'LL TAKE IT FROM HERE.

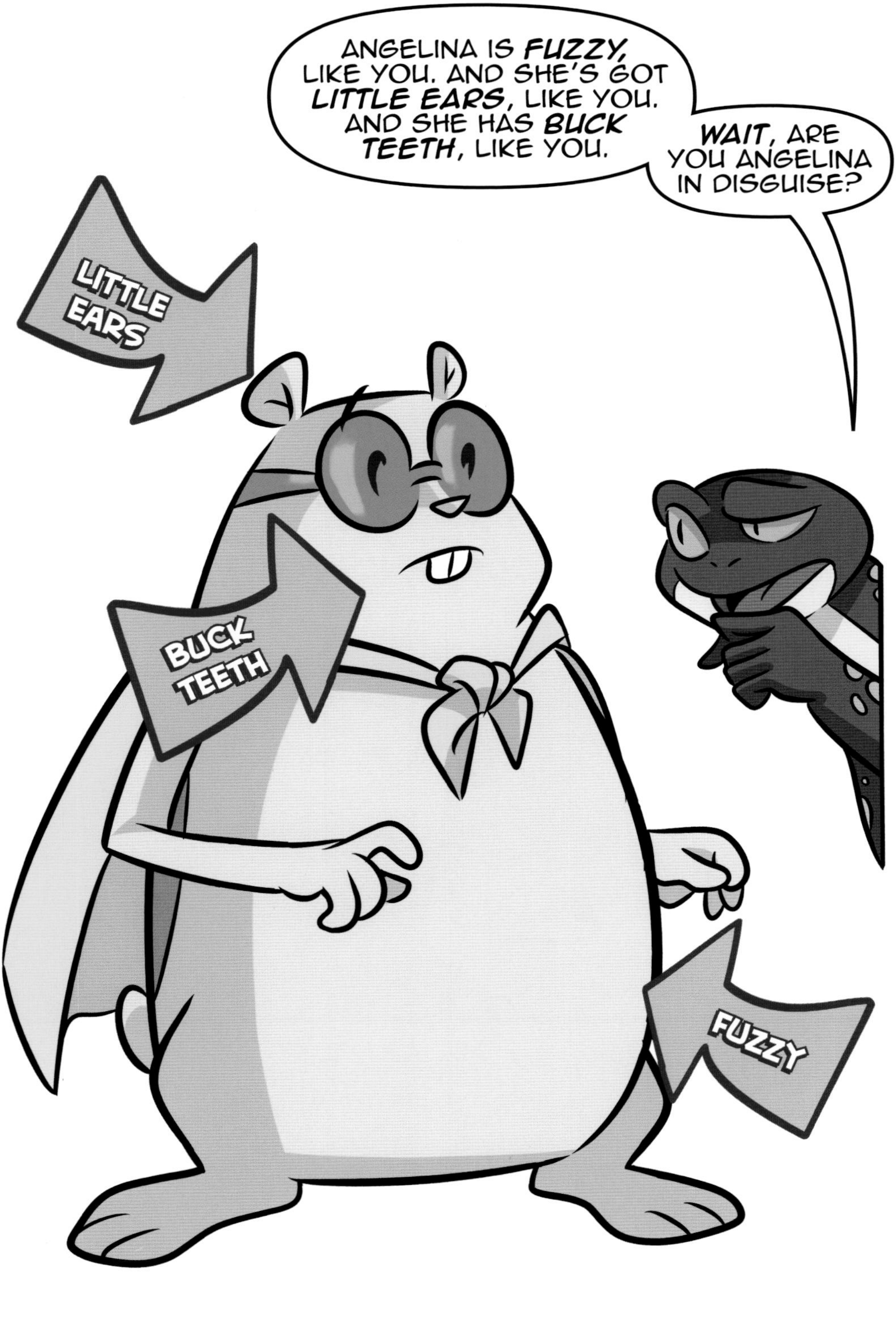
ANGELINA IS *FUZZY*, LIKE YOU. AND SHE'S GOT *LITTLE EARS*, LIKE YOU. AND SHE HAS *BUCK TEETH*, LIKE YOU.
WAIT, ARE YOU ANGELINA IN DISGUISE?
LITTLE EARS
BUCK TEETH
FUZZY

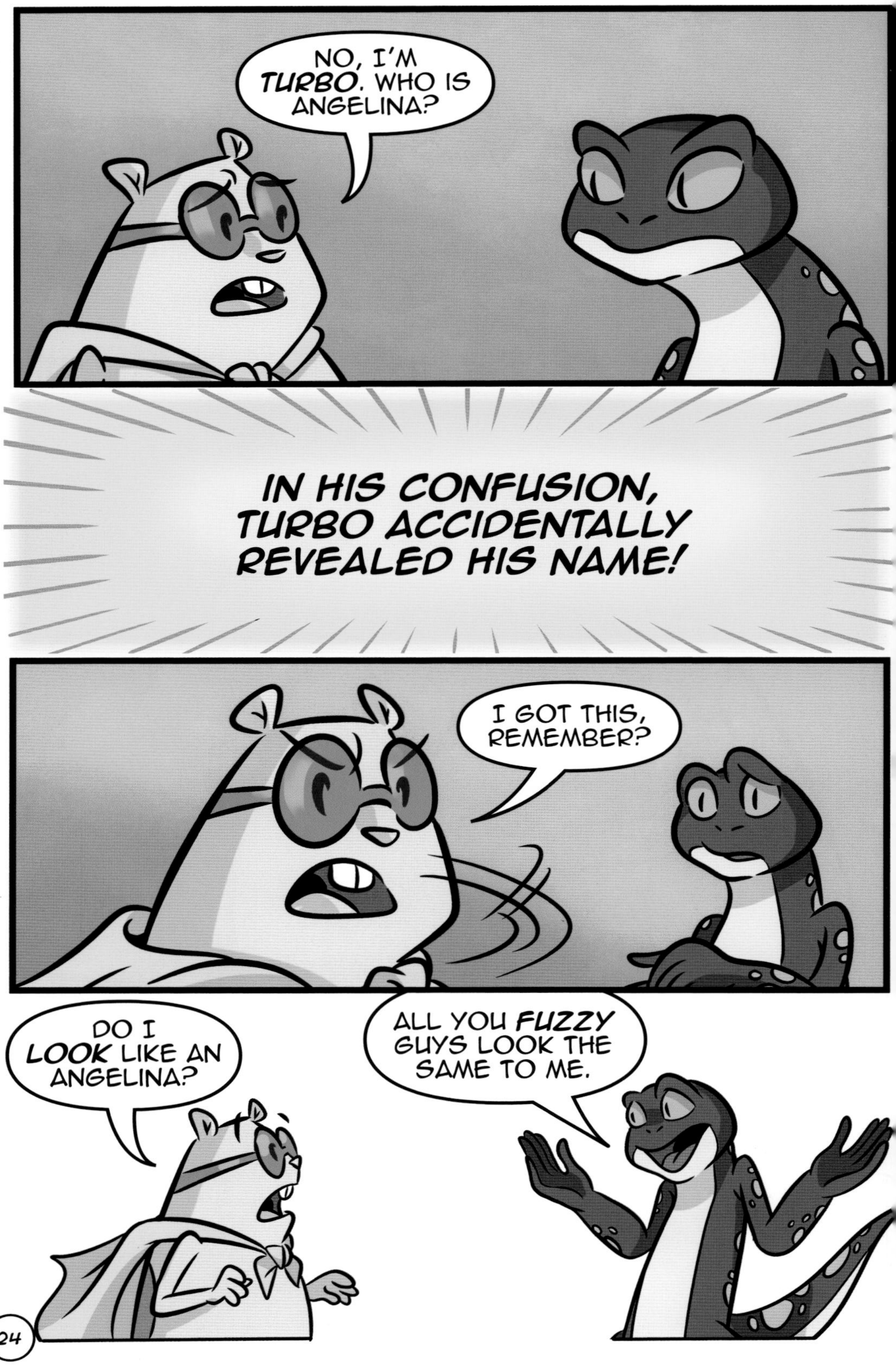
NO, I'M *TURBO*. WHO IS ANGELINA?
IN HIS CONFUSION, TURBO ACCIDENTALLY REVEALED HIS NAME!
I GOT THIS, REMEMBER?
DO I *LOOK* LIKE AN ANGELINA?
ALL YOU *FUZZY* GUYS LOOK THE SAME TO ME.

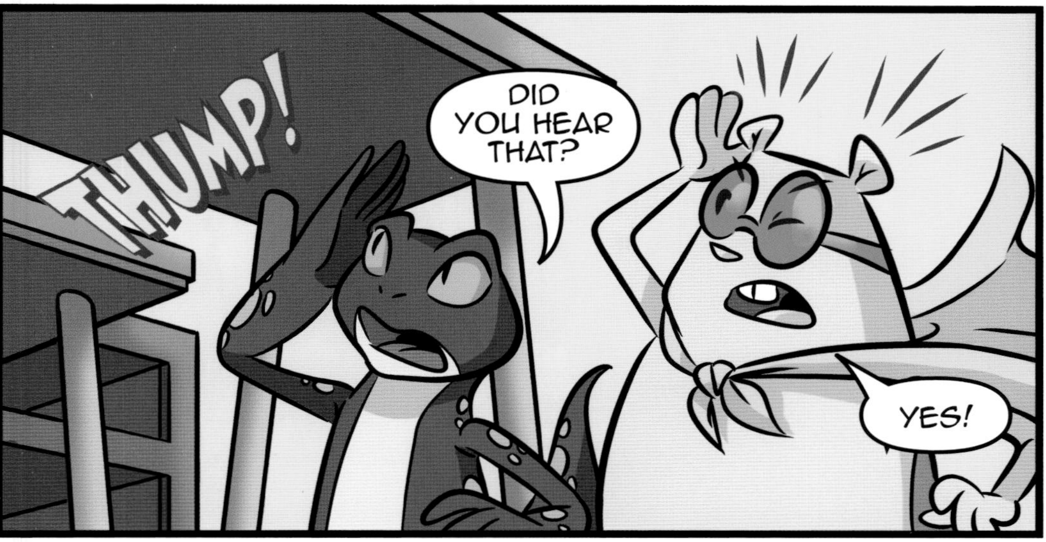
THUMP!
DID YOU HEAR THAT?
YES!

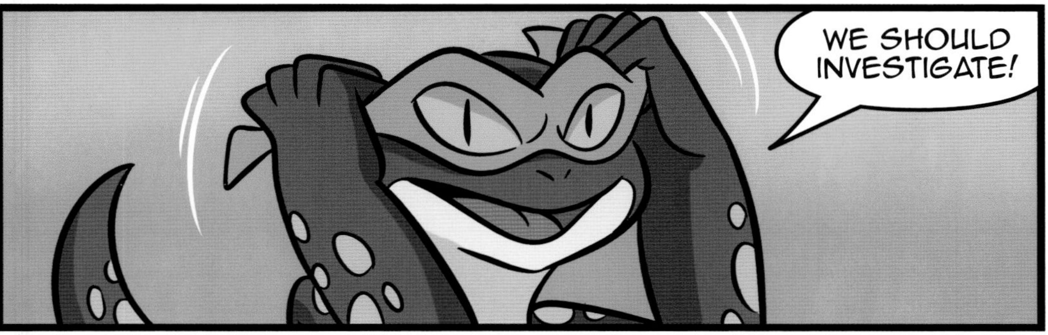
WE SHOULD INVESTIGATE!

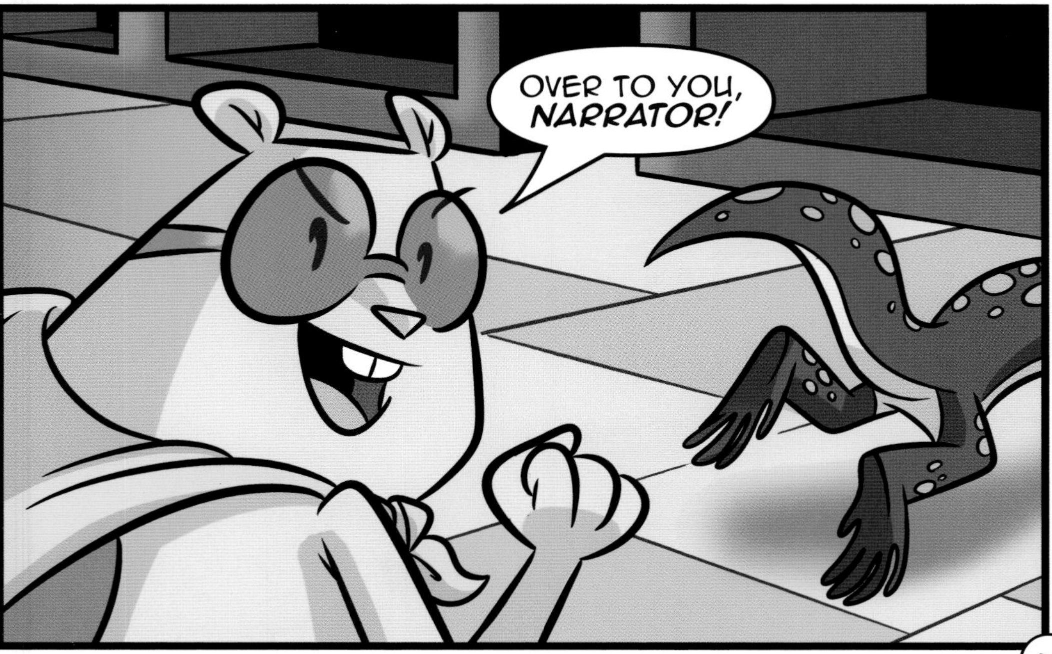
OVER TO YOU, NARRATOR!

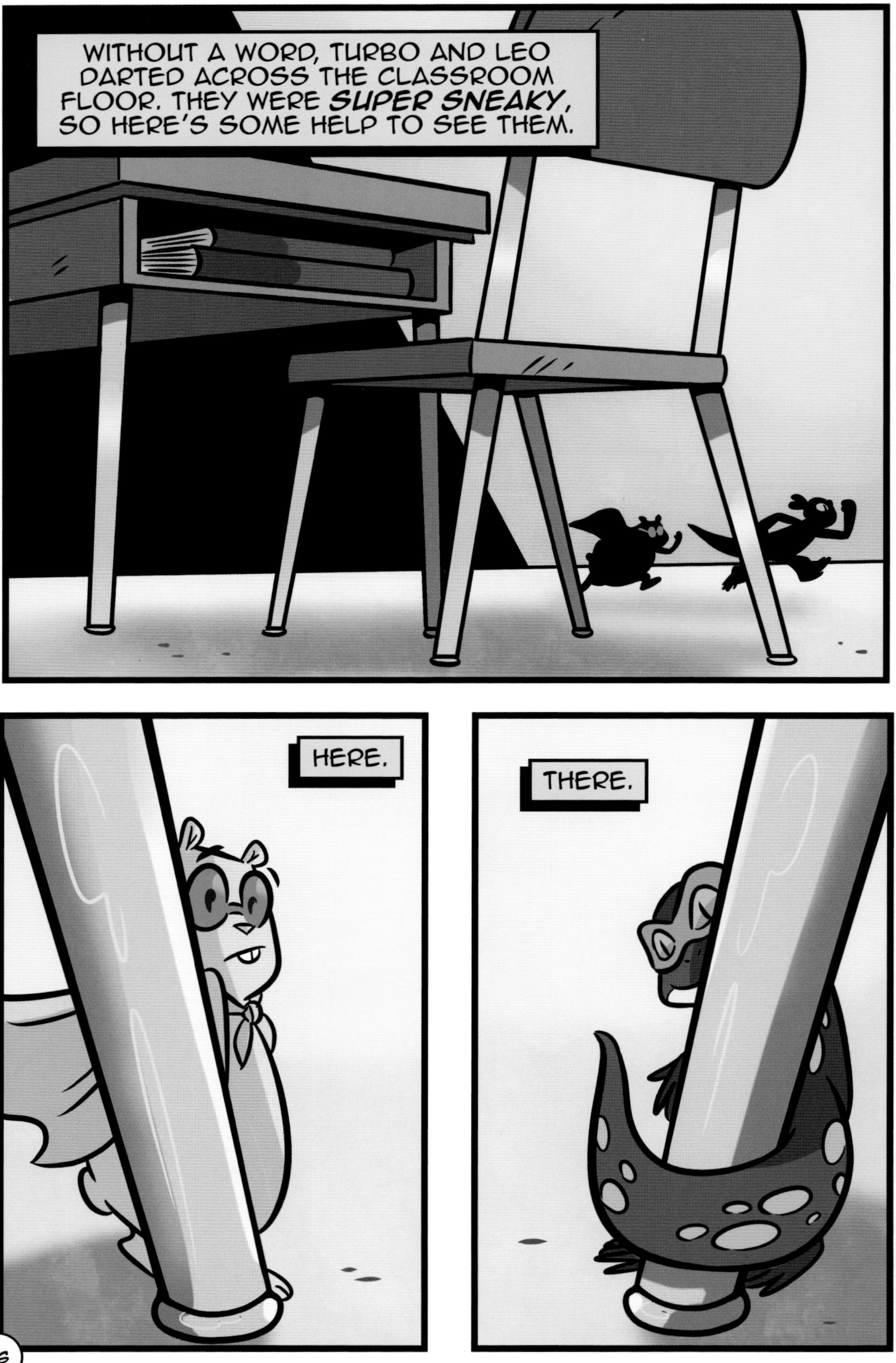
WITHOUT A WORD, TURBO AND LEO DARTED ACROSS THE CLASSROOM FLOOR. THEY WERE SUPER SNEAKY, SO HERE'S SOME HELP TO SEE THEM.
HERE.
THERE.

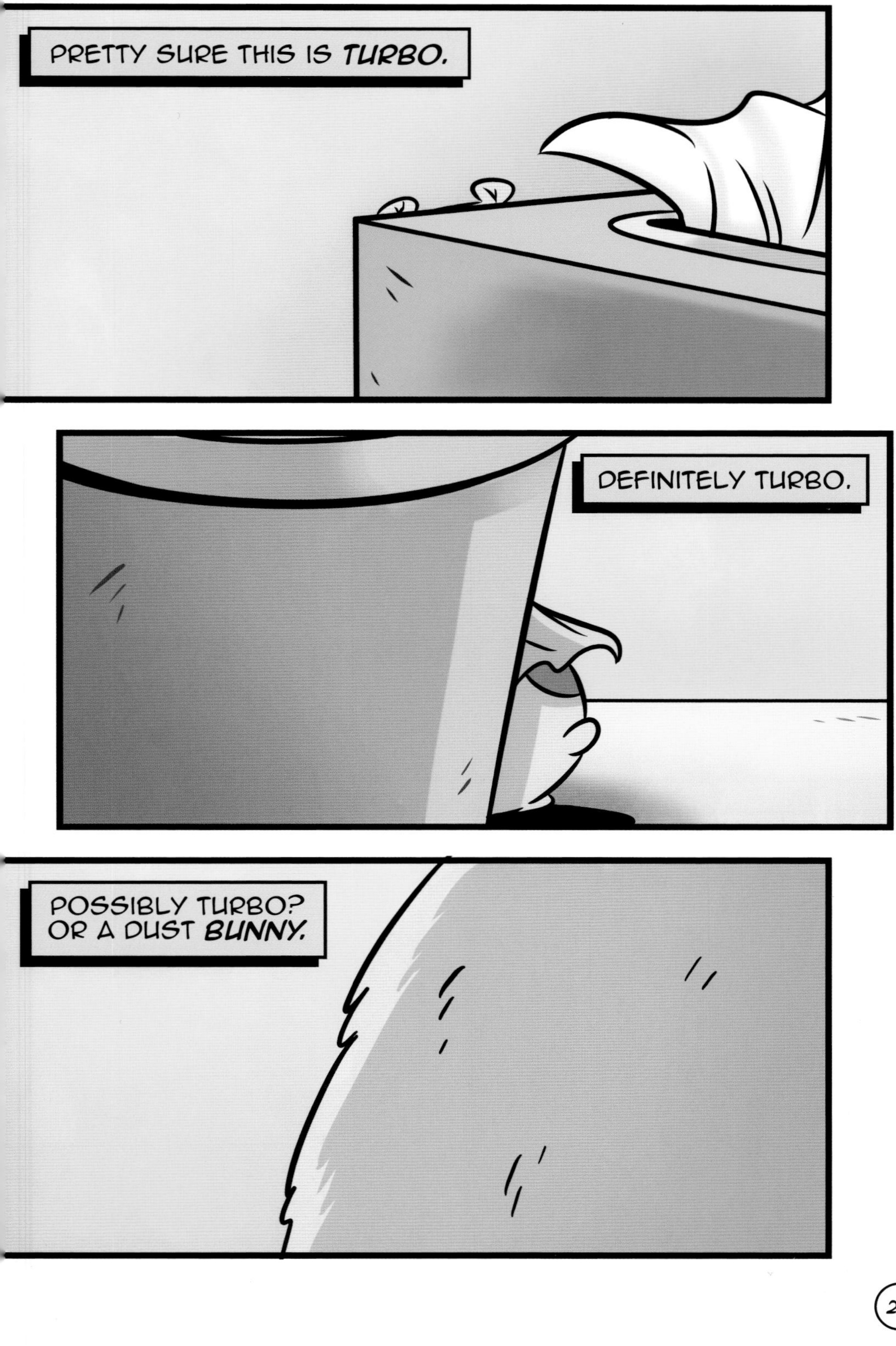
PRETTY SURE THIS IS *TURBO.*
DEFINITELY TURBO.
POSSIBLY TURBO? OR A DUST *BUNNY.*

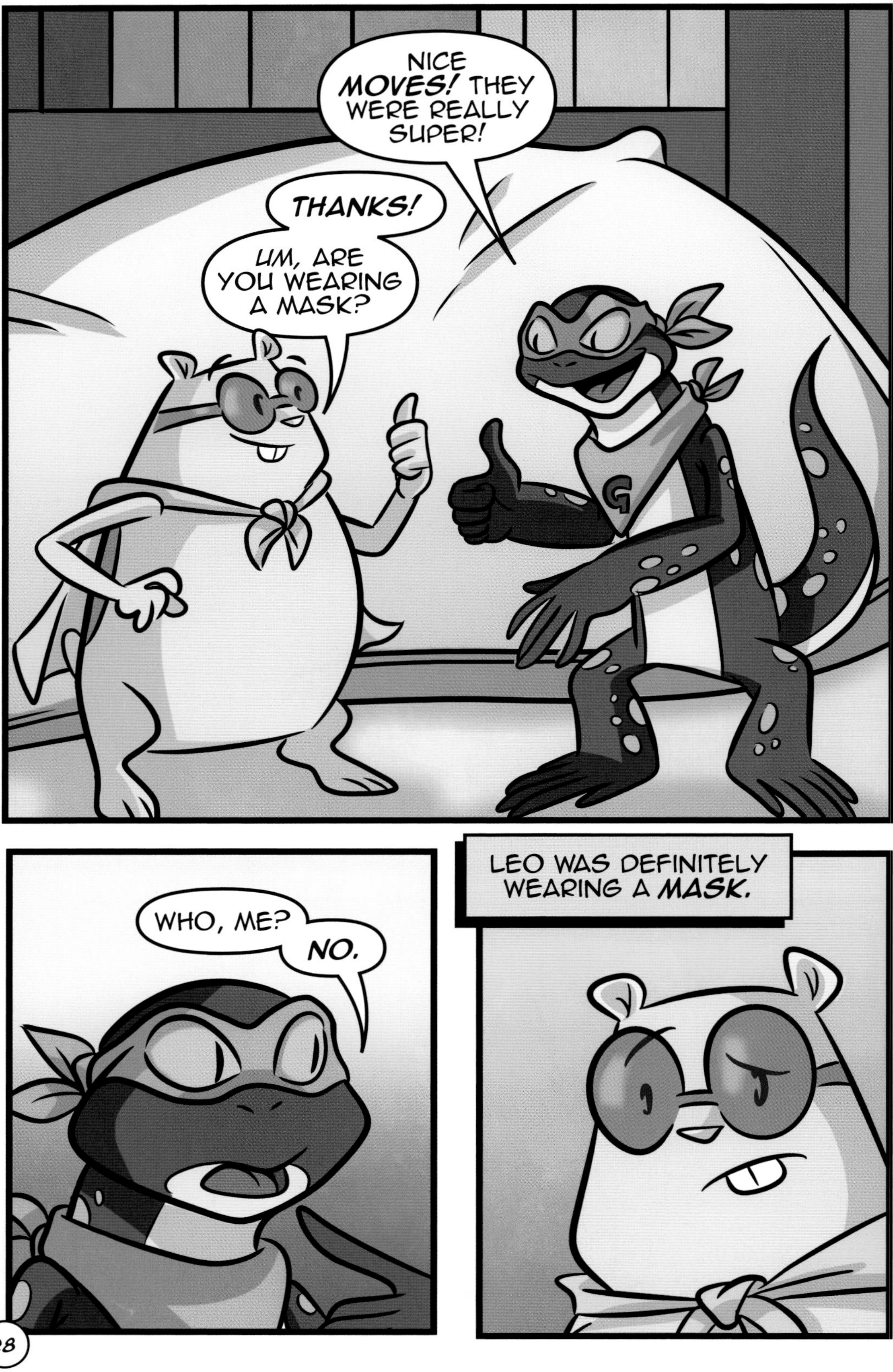
NICE *MOVES!* THEY WERE REALLY SUPER!
THANKS!
UM, ARE YOU WEARING A MASK?
WHO, ME?
NO.
LEO WAS DEFINITELY WEARING A *MASK.*

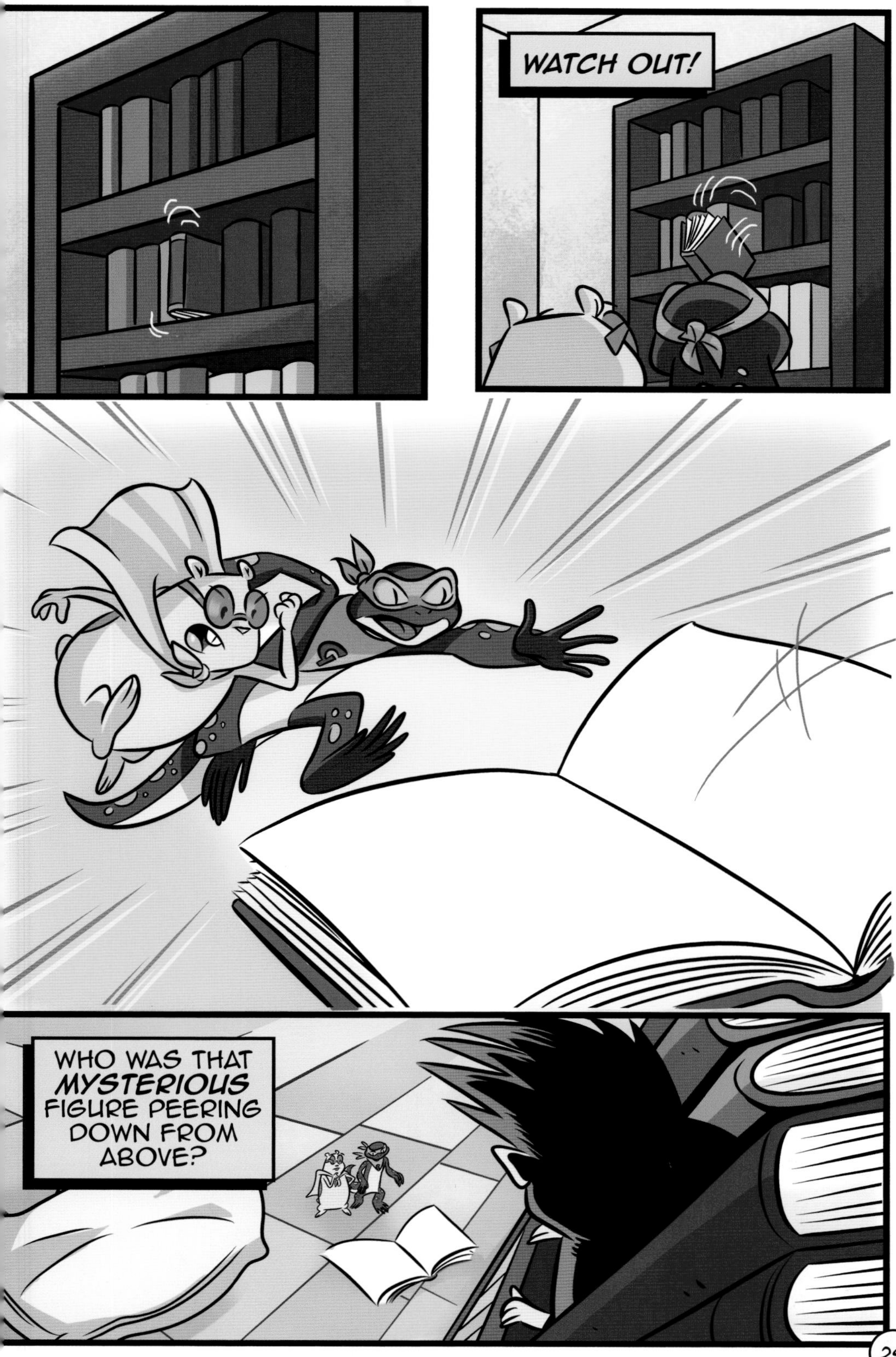
WATCH OUT!
WHO WAS THAT MYSTERIOUS FIGURE PEERING DOWN FROM ABOVE?

CHAPTER 3

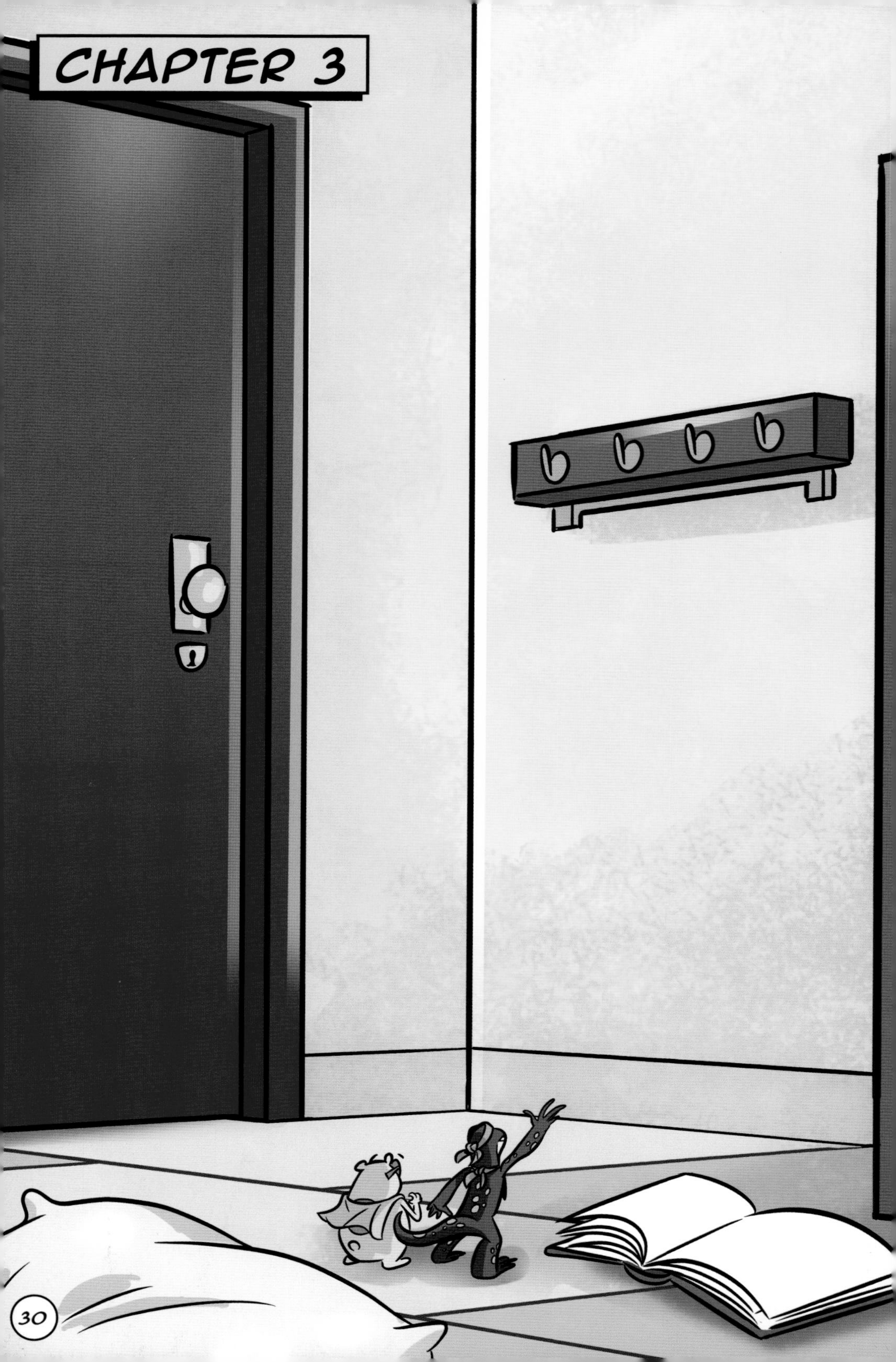

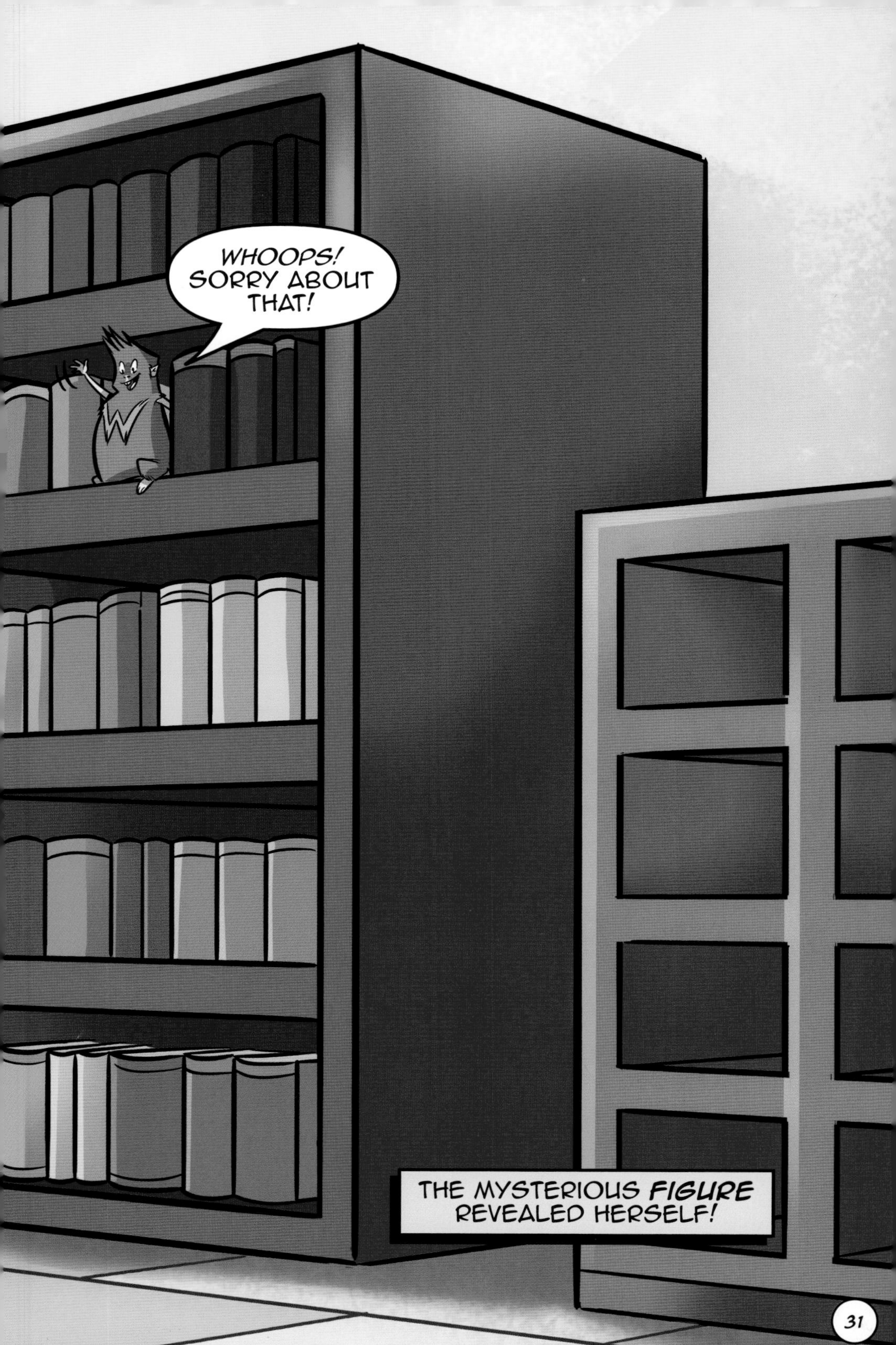
WHOOPS! SORRY ABOUT THAT!
THE MYSTERIOUS FIGURE REVEALED HERSELF!

HI, ANGELINA!

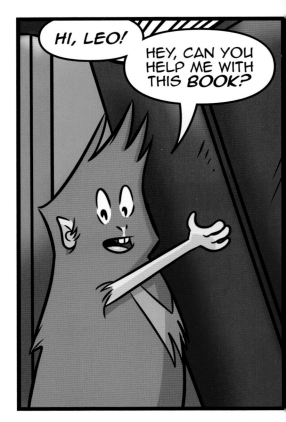

HI, LEO!

HEY, CAN YOU HELP ME WITH THIS *BOOK?*

SURE, BUT WHAT ARE YOU DOING IN CLASSROOM C?

I'VE *READ* ALL THE BOOKS IN CLASSROOM B. I NEED SOME NEW OPTIONS!

HUFF!!

PUFF!

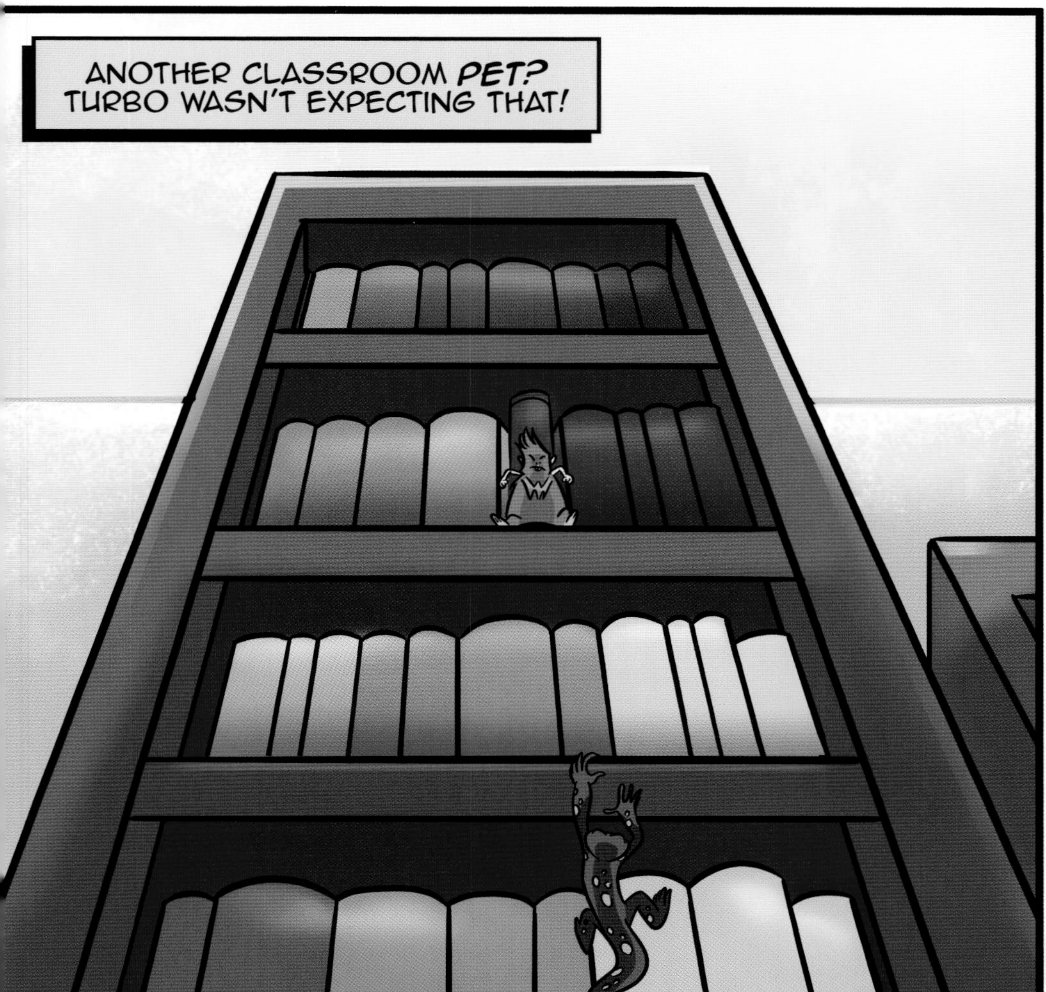
ANOTHER CLASSROOM PET? TURBO WASN'T EXPECTING THAT!

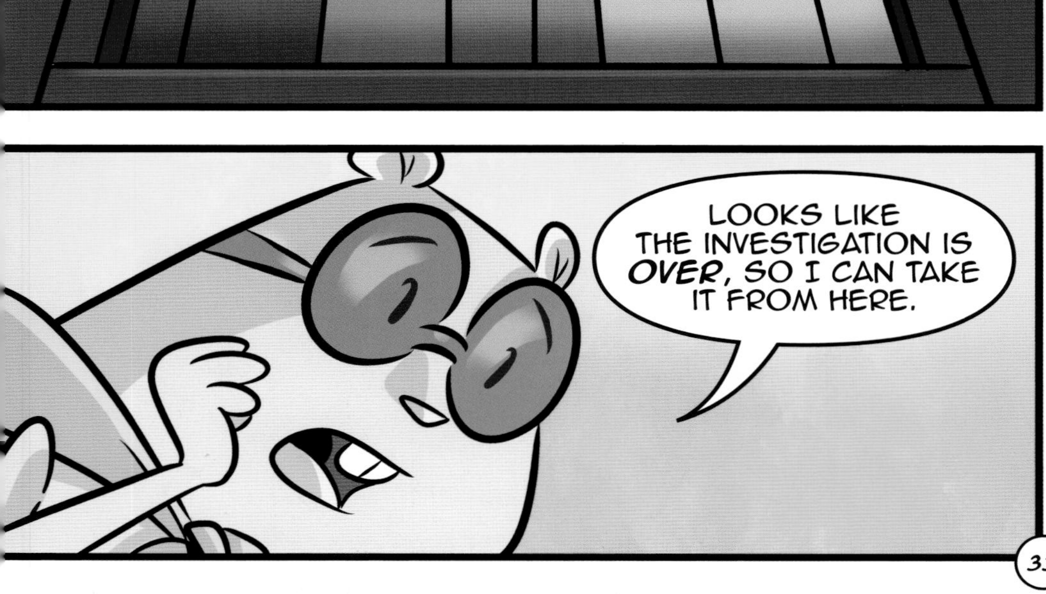
LOOKS LIKE THE INVESTIGATION IS OVER, SO I CAN TAKE IT FROM HERE.

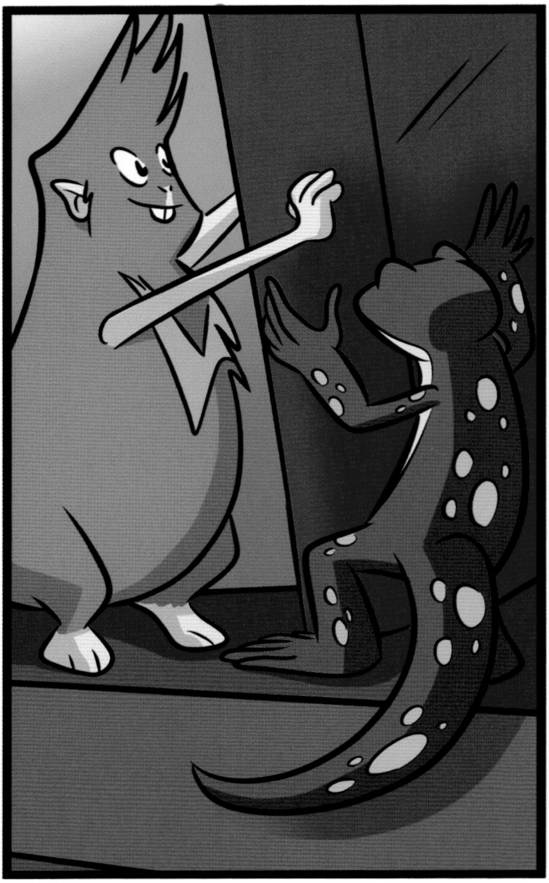

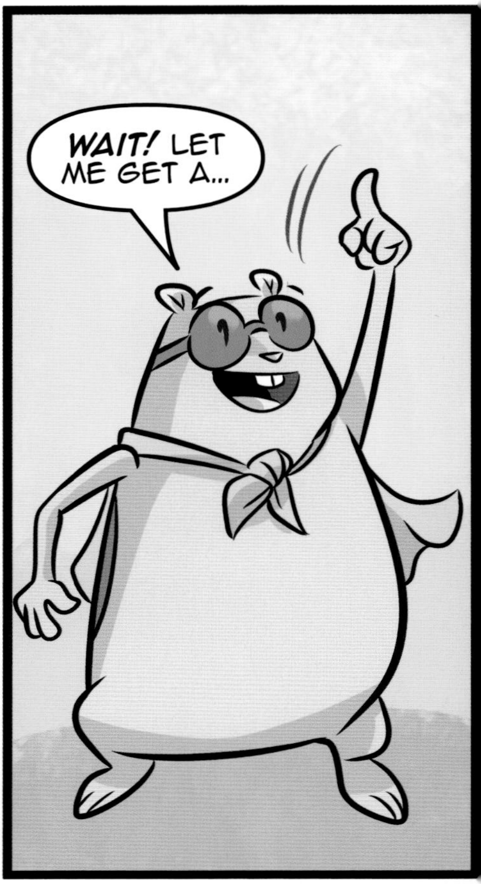
WAIT! LET ME GET A...

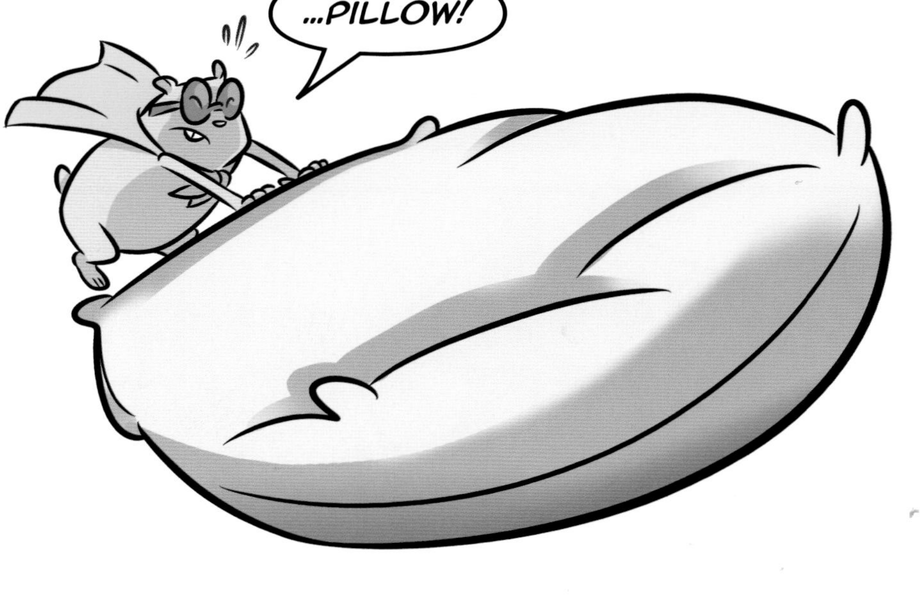
...PILLOW!

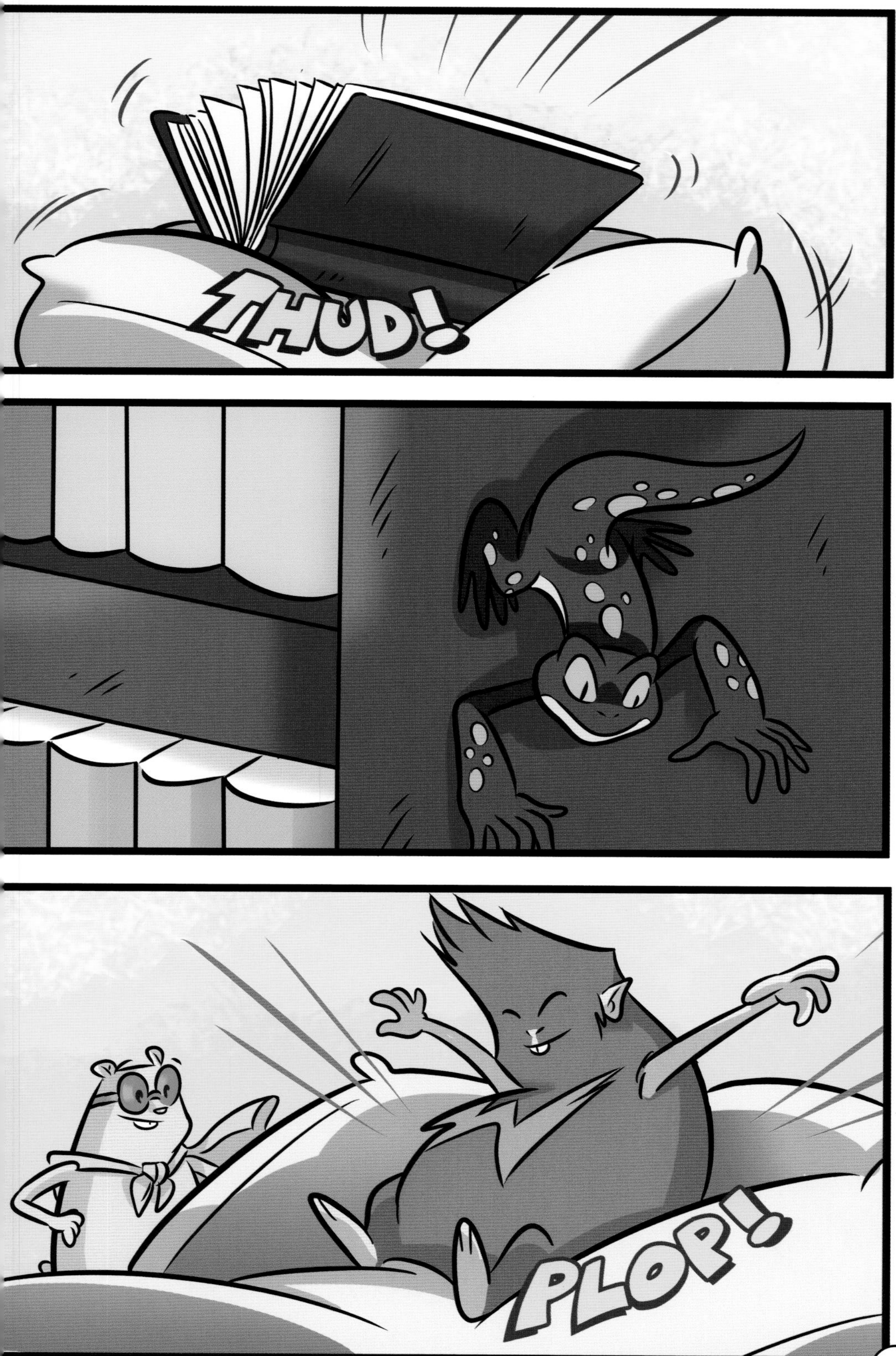
THUD!
PLOP!

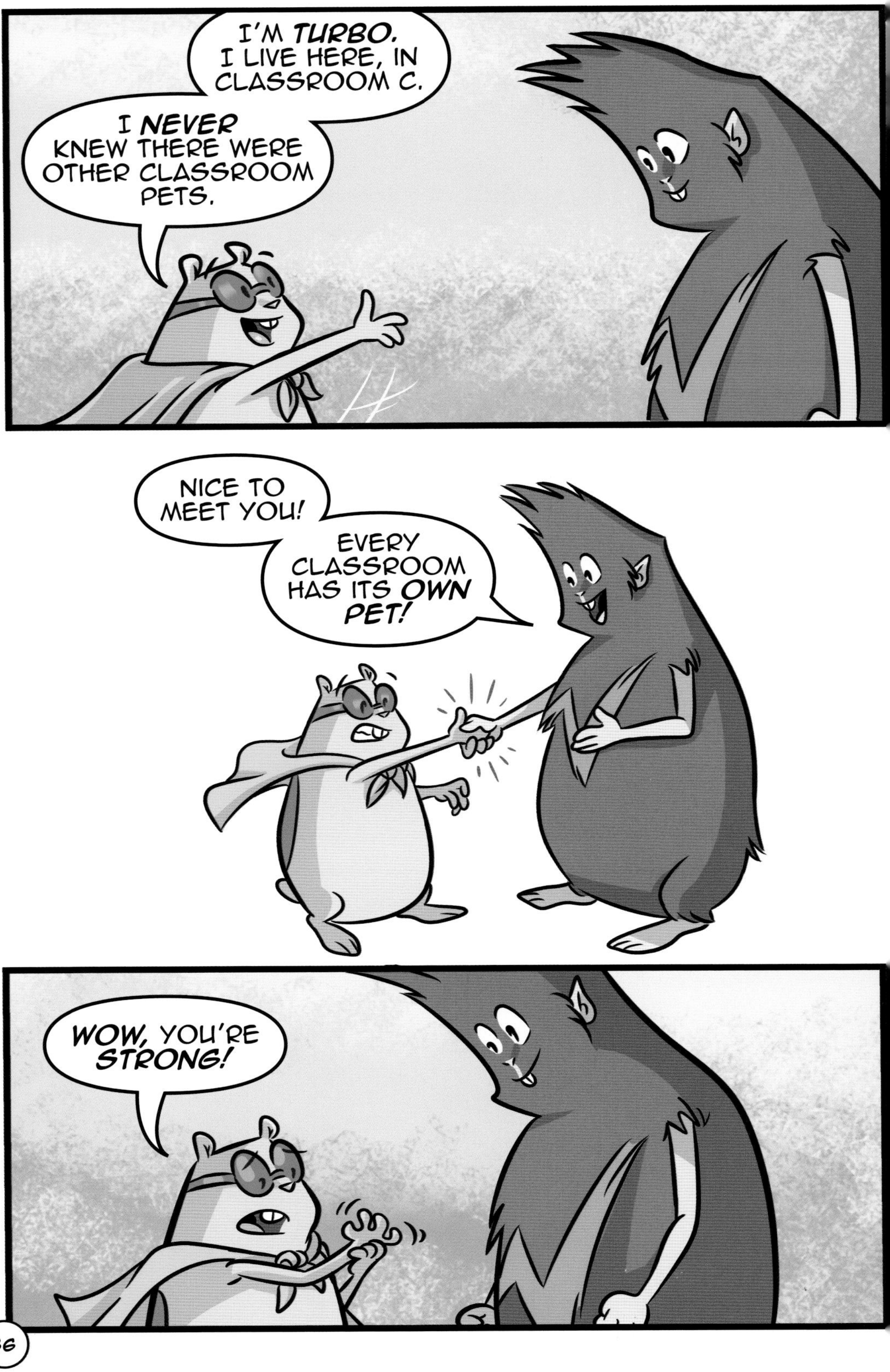
I'M TURBO. I LIVE HERE, IN CLASSROOM C.
I NEVER KNEW THERE WERE OTHER CLASSROOM PETS.
NICE TO MEET YOU!
EVERY CLASSROOM HAS ITS OWN PET!
WOW, YOU'RE STRONG!

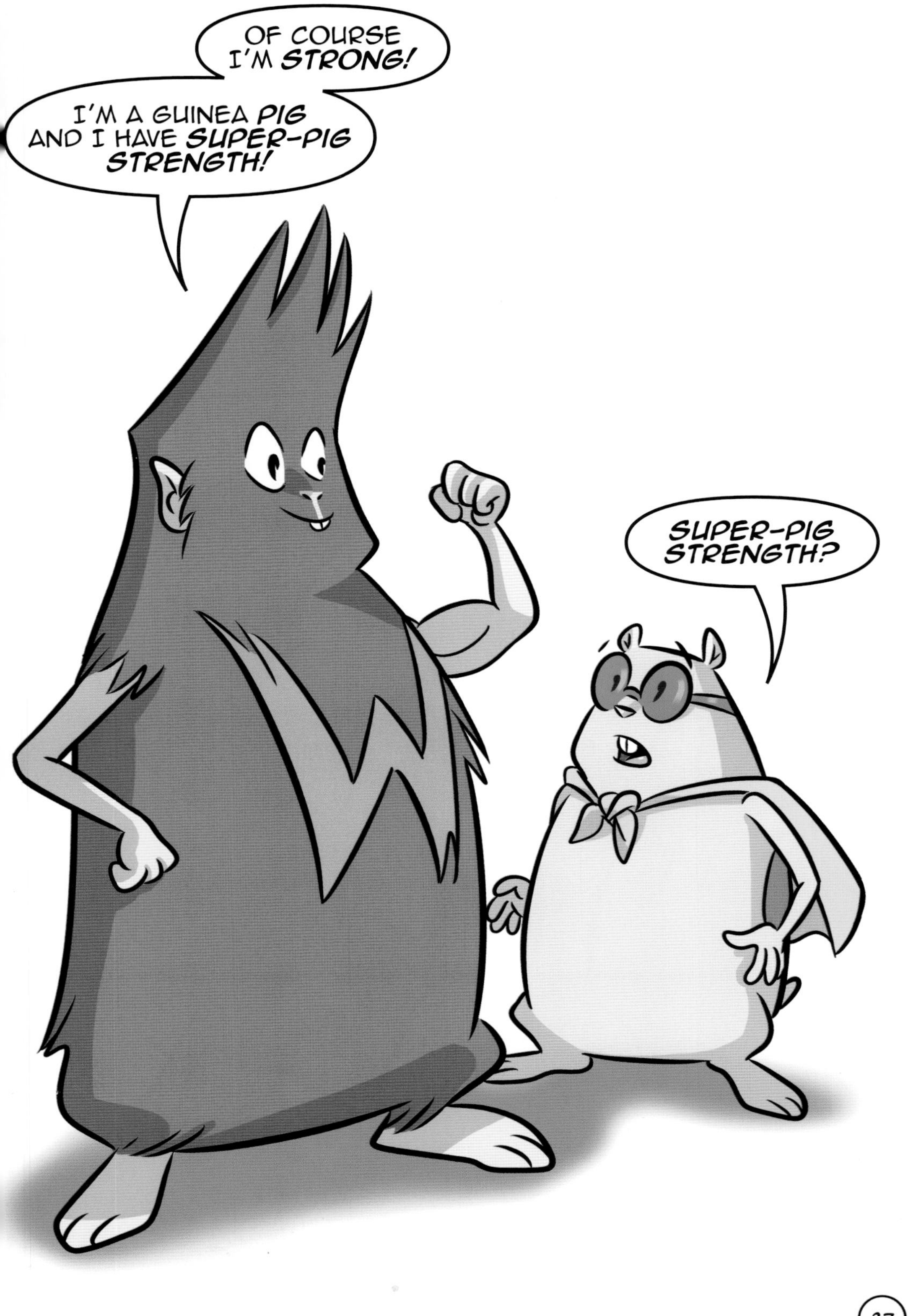
OF COURSE I'M STRONG!
I'M A GUINEA PIG AND I HAVE SUPER-PIG STRENGTH!
SUPER-PIG STRENGTH?

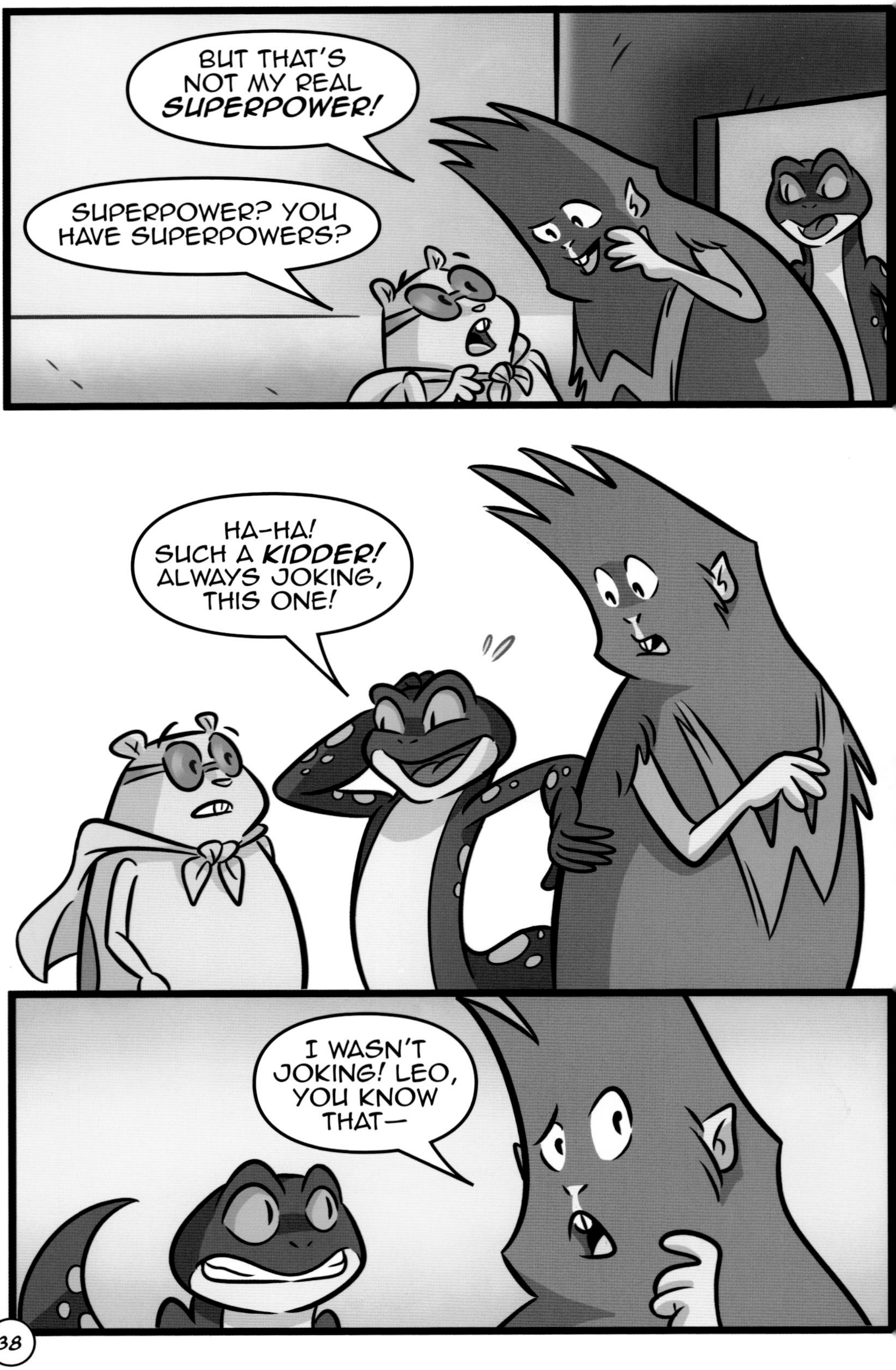
BUT THAT'S NOT MY REAL SUPERPOWER!
SUPERPOWER? YOU HAVE SUPERPOWERS?
HA-HA! SUCH A KIDDER! ALWAYS JOKING, THIS ONE!
I WASN'T JOKING! LEO, YOU KNOW THAT—

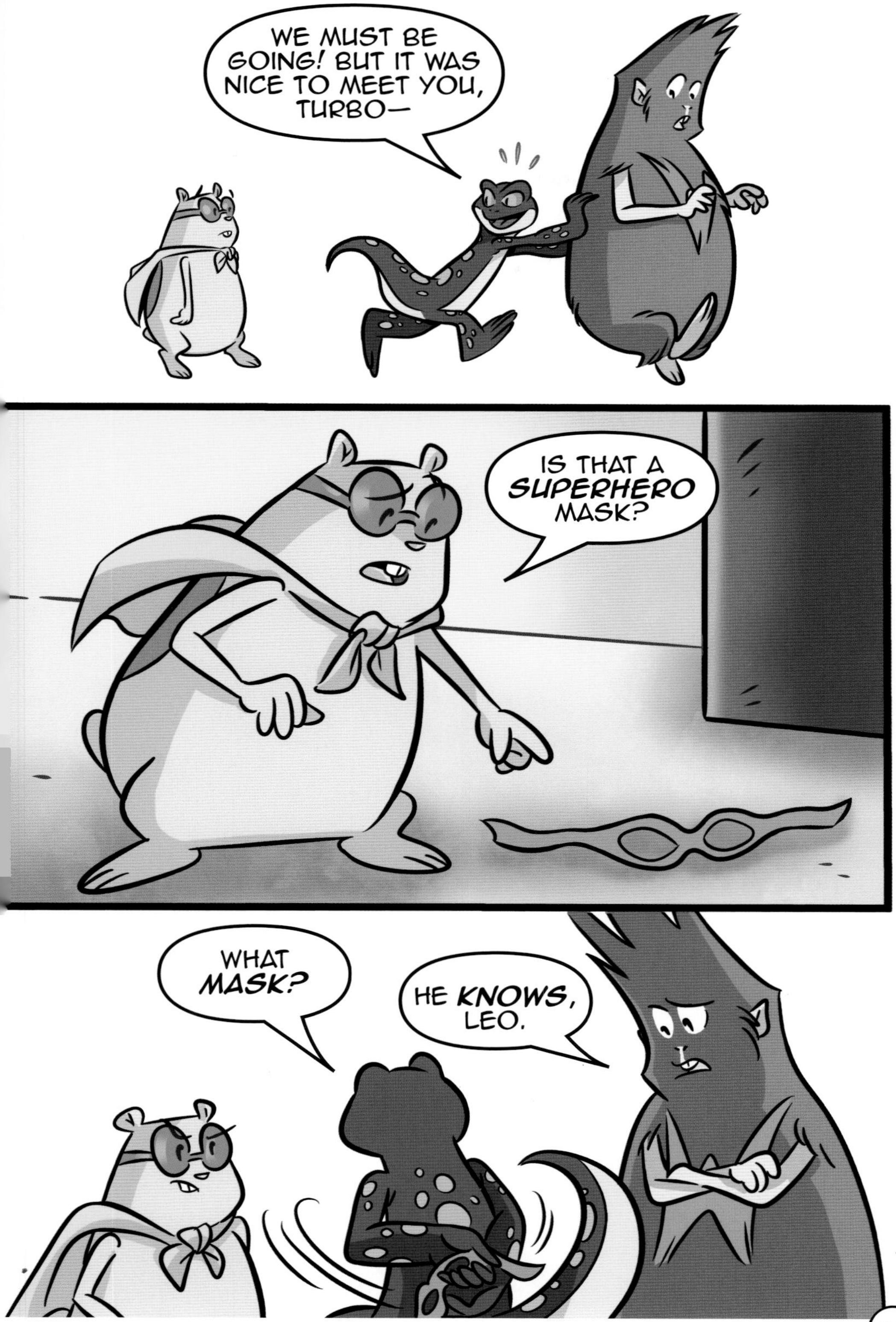
WE MUST BE GOING! BUT IT WAS NICE TO MEET YOU, TURBO—
IS THAT A *SUPERHERO* MASK?
WHAT *MASK?*
HE *KNOWS*, LEO.

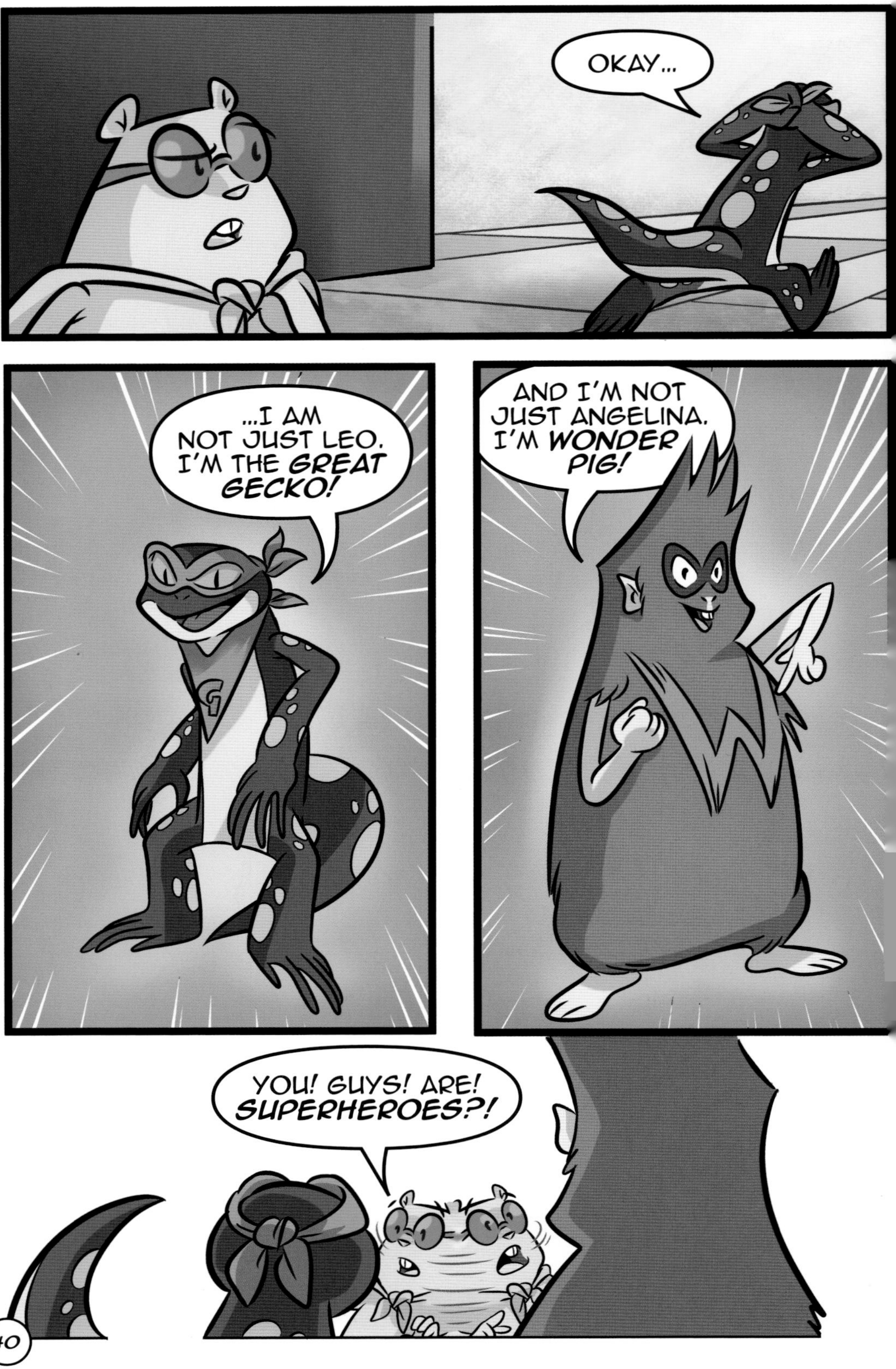
OKAY...
...I AM NOT JUST LEO. I'M THE GREAT GECKO!
AND I'M NOT JUST ANGELINA. I'M WONDER PIG!
YOU! GUYS! ARE! SUPERHEROES?!

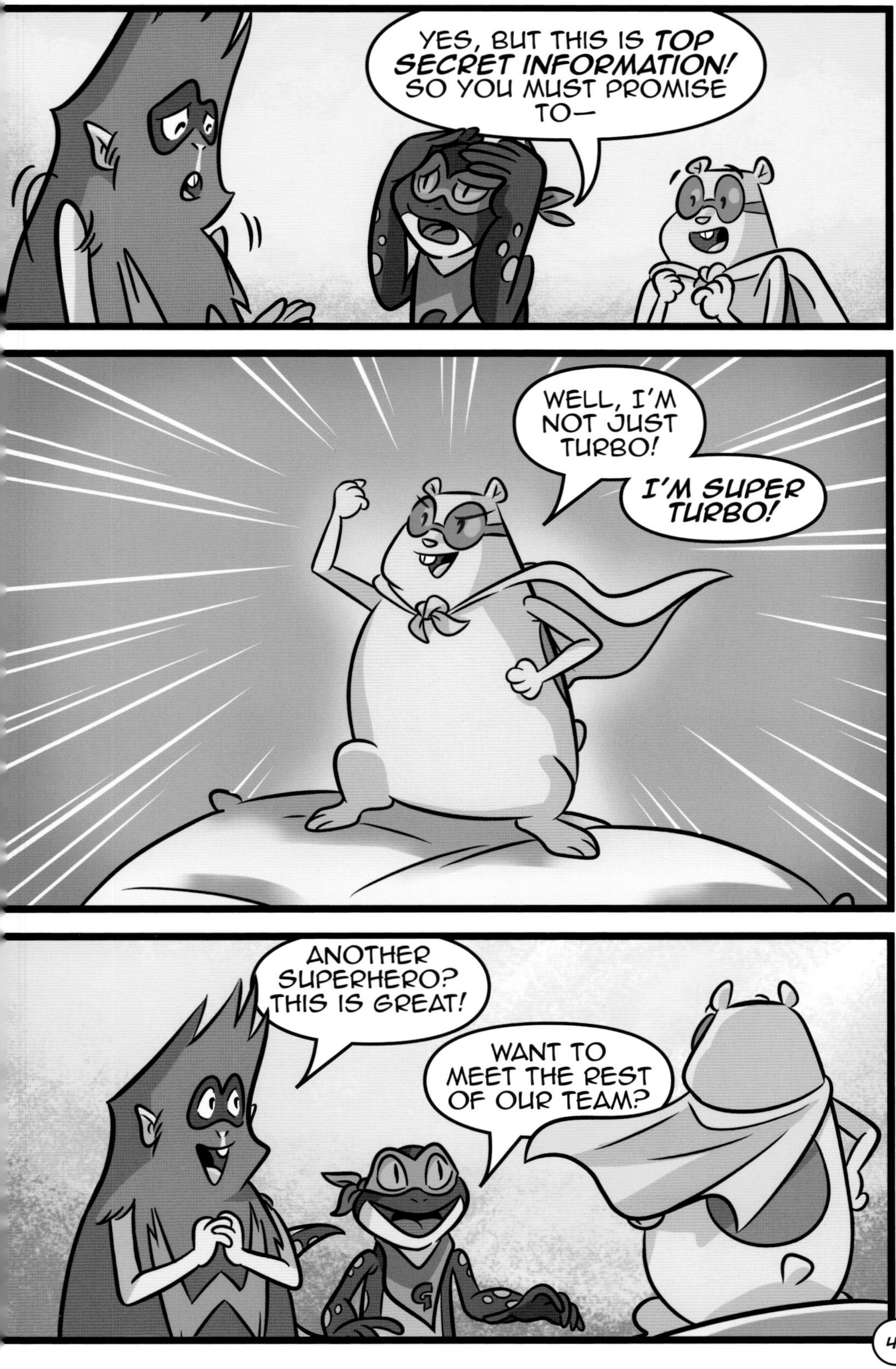
YES, BUT THIS IS TOP SECRET INFORMATION! SO YOU MUST PROMISE TO—
WELL, I'M NOT JUST TURBO!
I'M SUPER TURBO!
ANOTHER SUPERHERO? THIS IS GREAT!
WANT TO MEET THE REST OF OUR TEAM?

CHAPTER 4

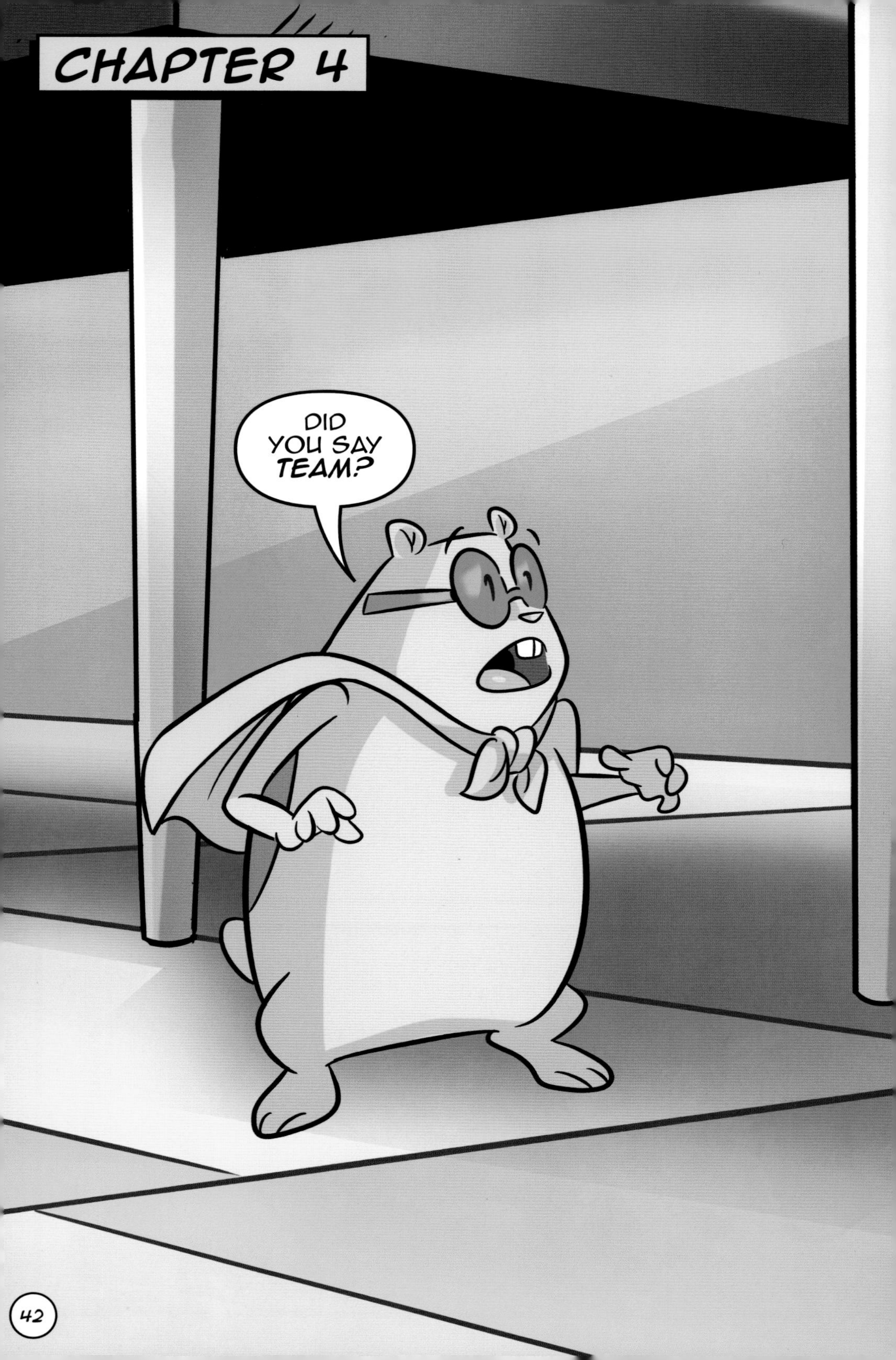
DID YOU SAY TEAM?

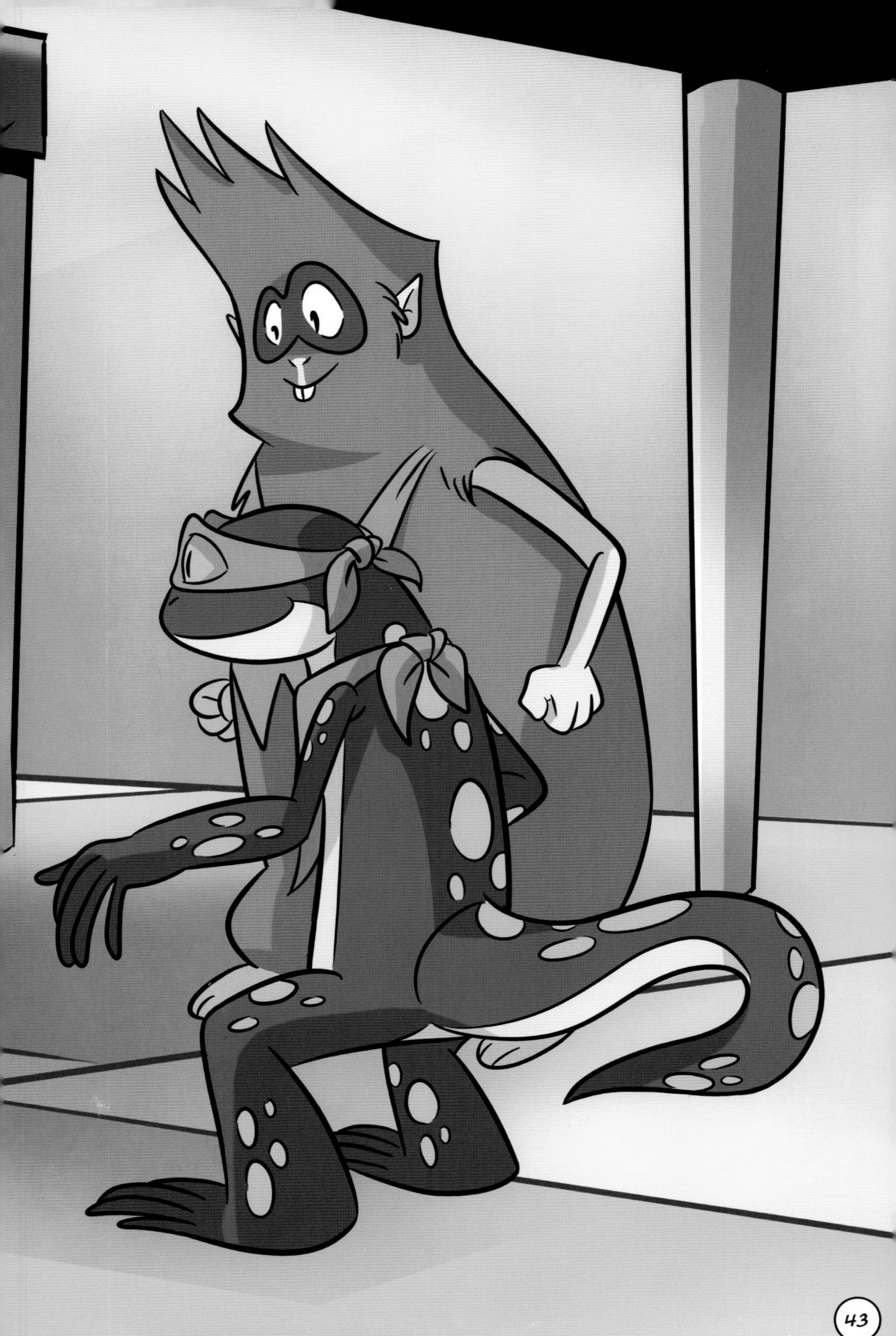

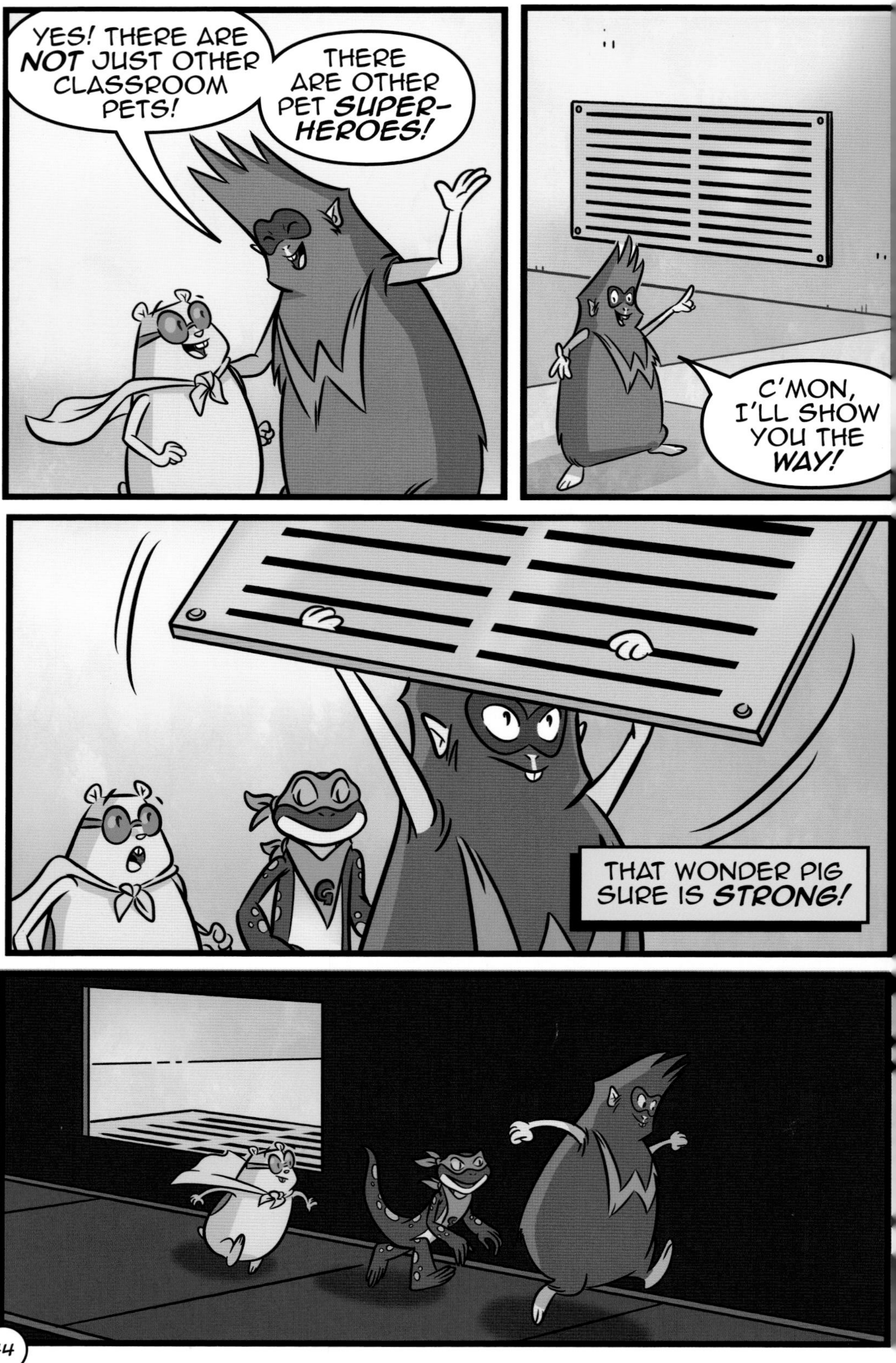

YES! THERE ARE NOT JUST OTHER CLASSROOM PETS!
THERE ARE OTHER PET SUPER-HEROES!
C'MON, I'LL SHOW YOU THE WAY!
THAT WONDER PIG SURE IS STRONG!

SUPERSTRONG!

HI, CLEVER!

MEET OUR NEW FRIEND, *SUPER TURBO!*

HE'S THE PET *PROTECTOR* OF CLASSROOM C!

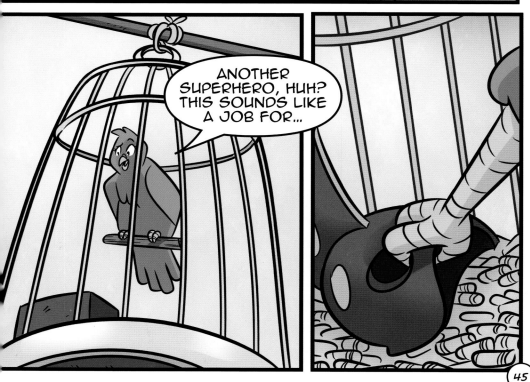

ANOTHER SUPERHERO, HUH? THIS SOUNDS LIKE A JOB FOR...

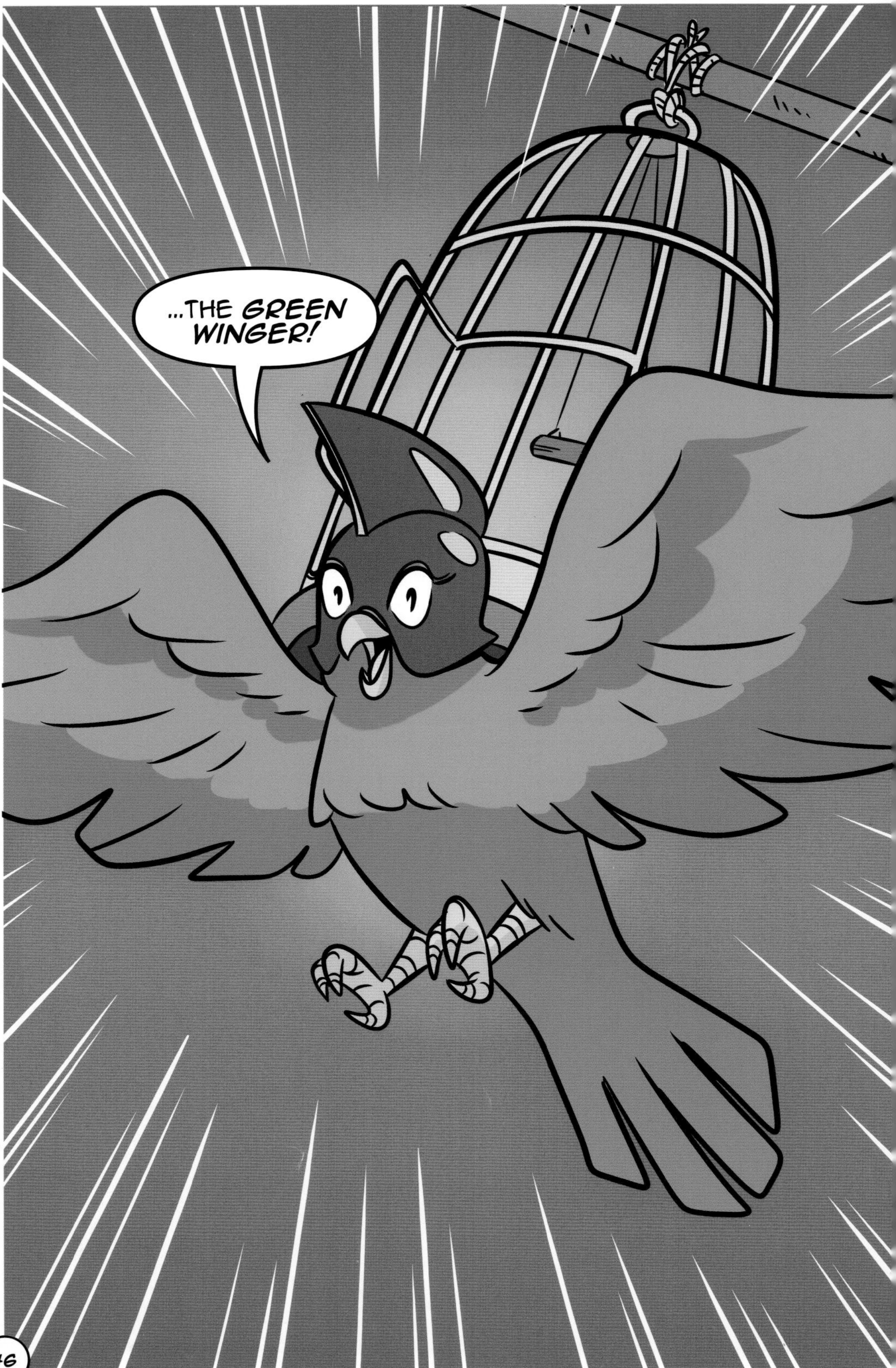
...THE GREEN WINGER!

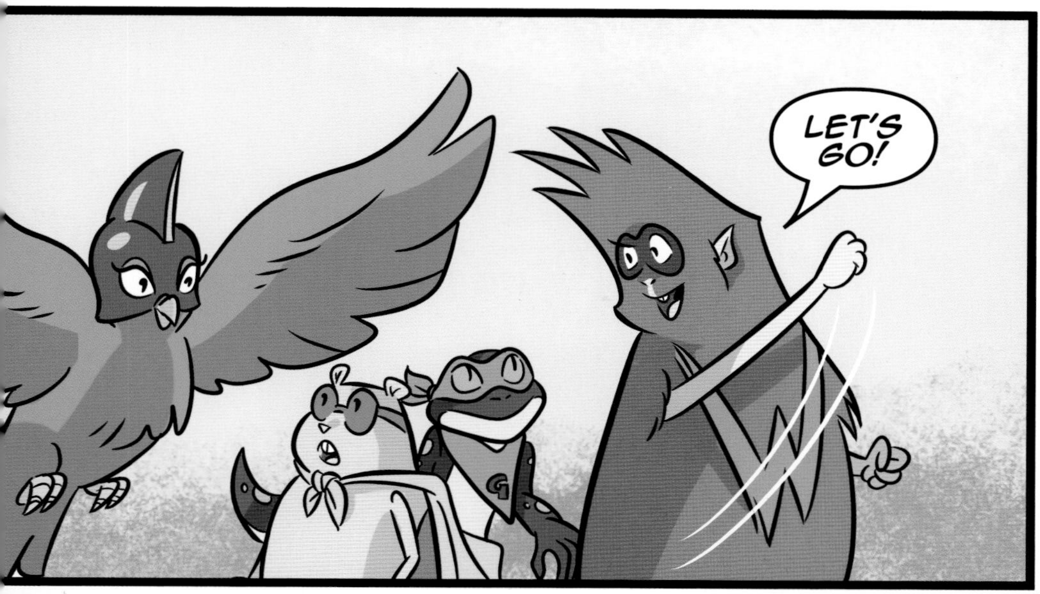
LET'S GO!

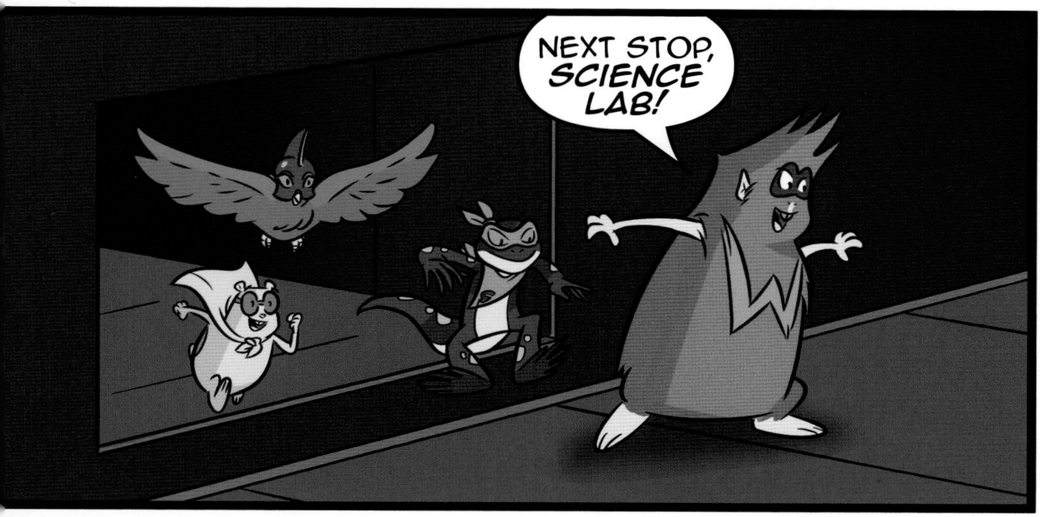
NEXT STOP, SCIENCE LAB!

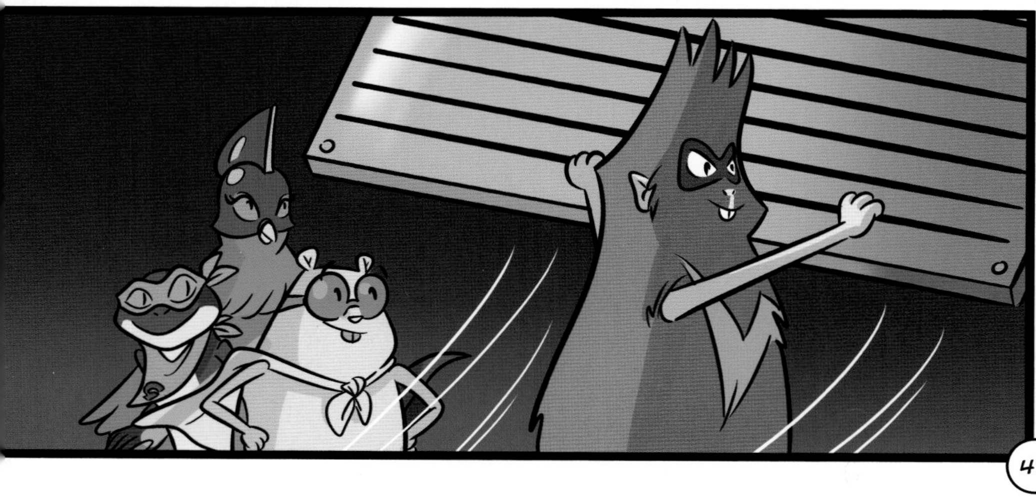

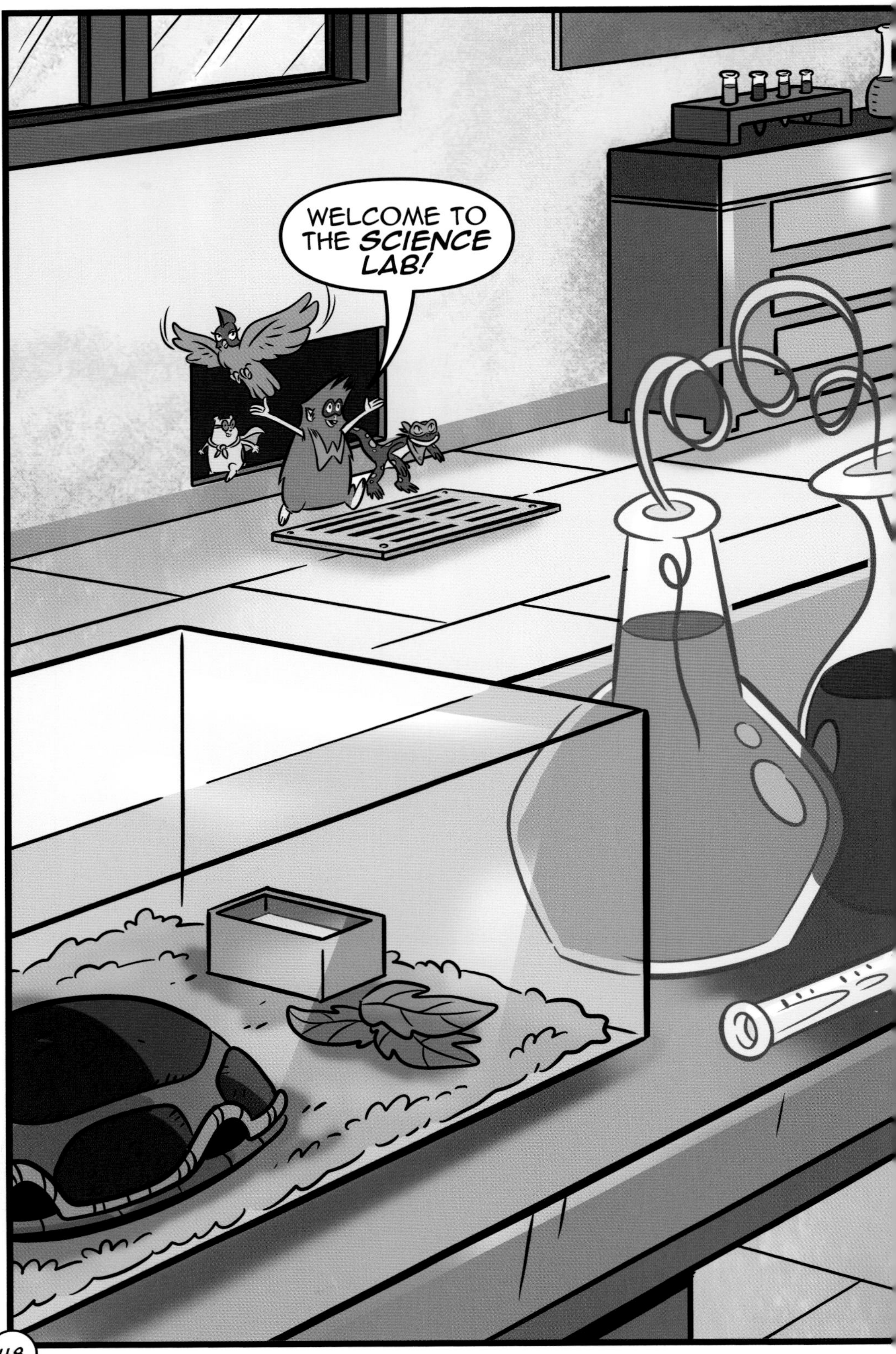
WELCOME TO THE *SCIENCE LAB!*

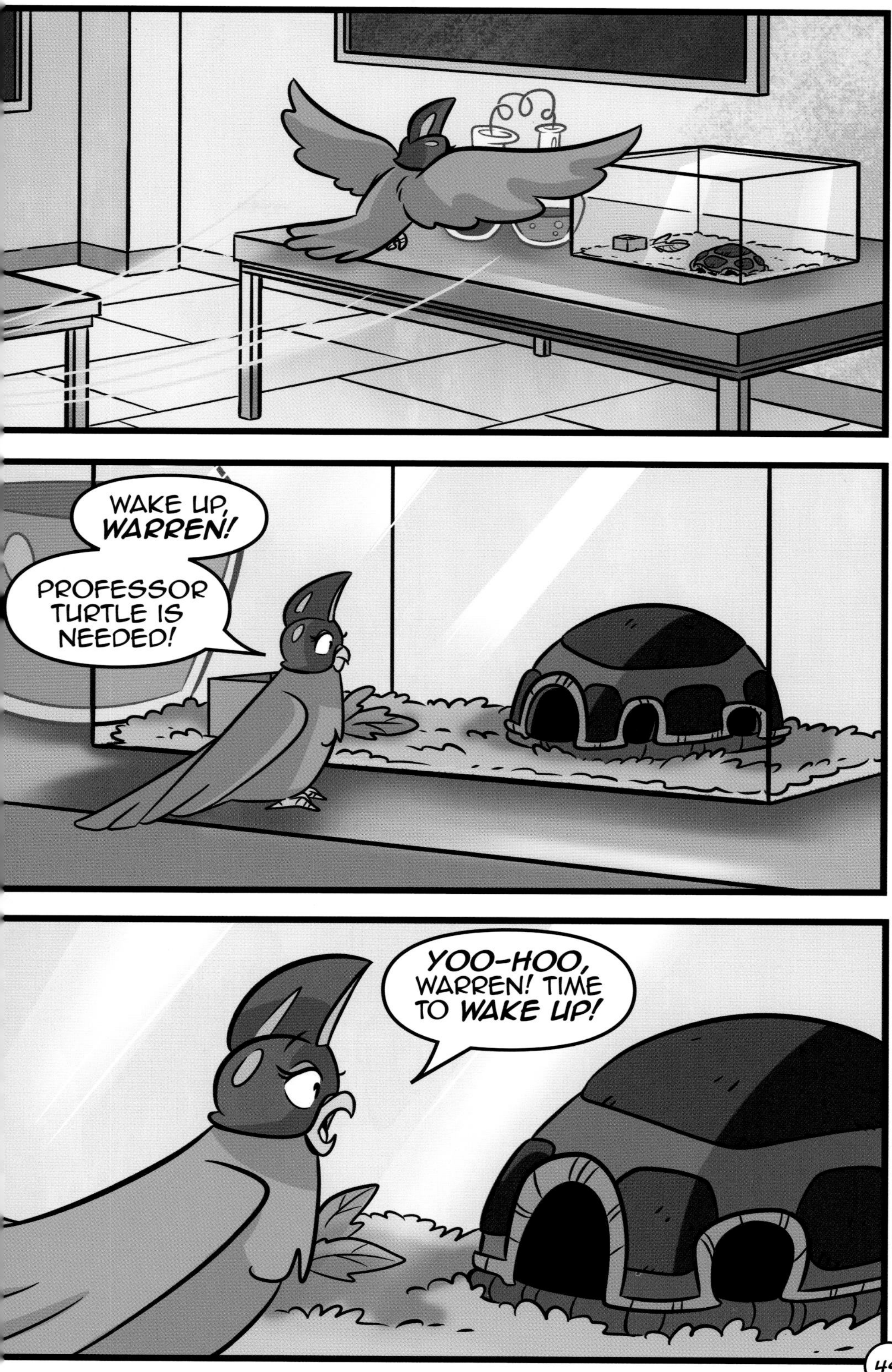
WAKE UP, WARREN!
PROFESSOR TURTLE IS NEEDED!
YOO-HOO, WARREN! TIME TO WAKE UP!

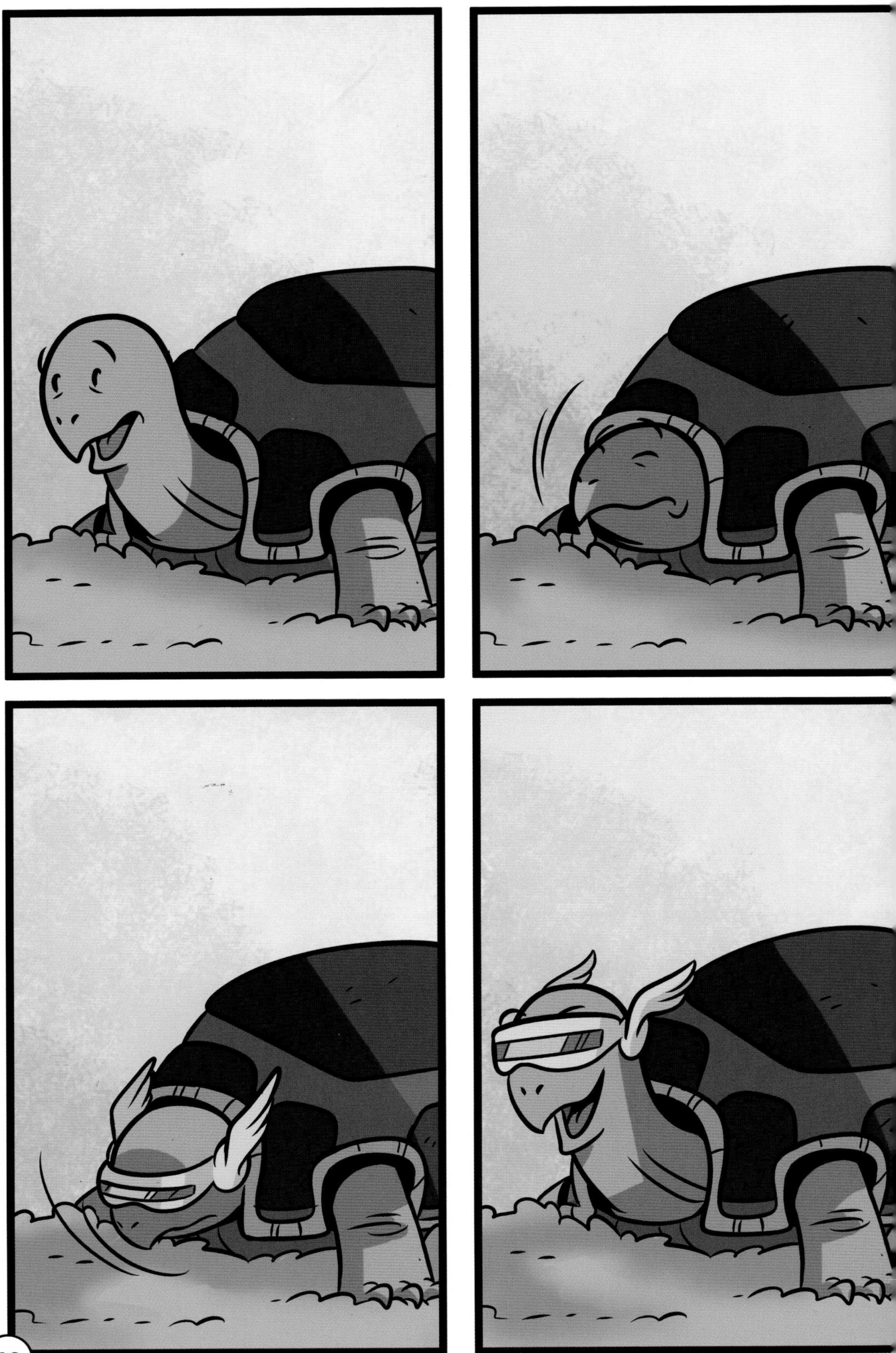

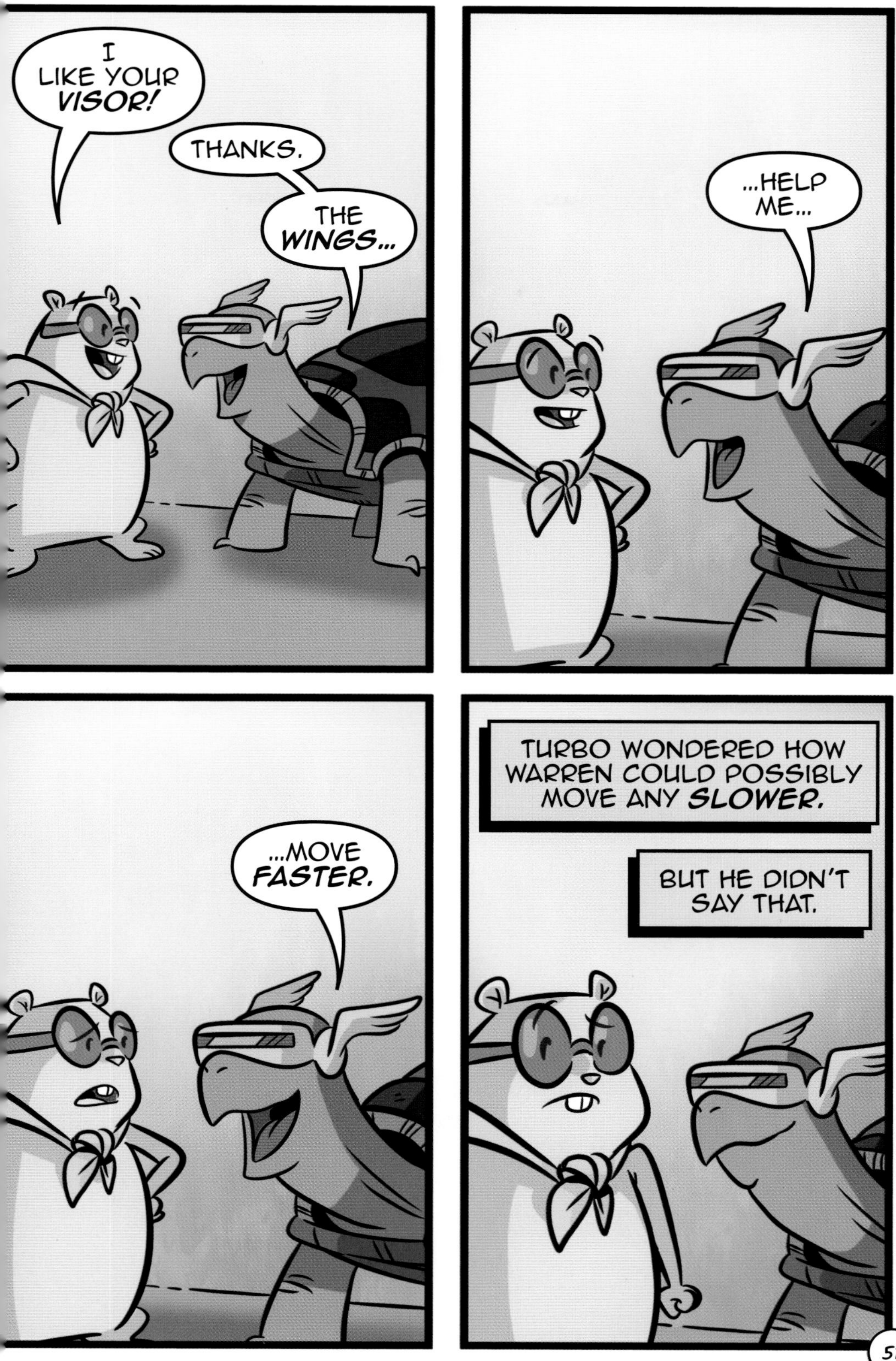
I LIKE YOUR VISOR!
THANKS.
THE WINGS...
...HELP ME...
...MOVE FASTER.
TURBO WONDERED HOW WARREN COULD POSSIBLY MOVE ANY SLOWER.
BUT HE DIDN'T SAY THAT.

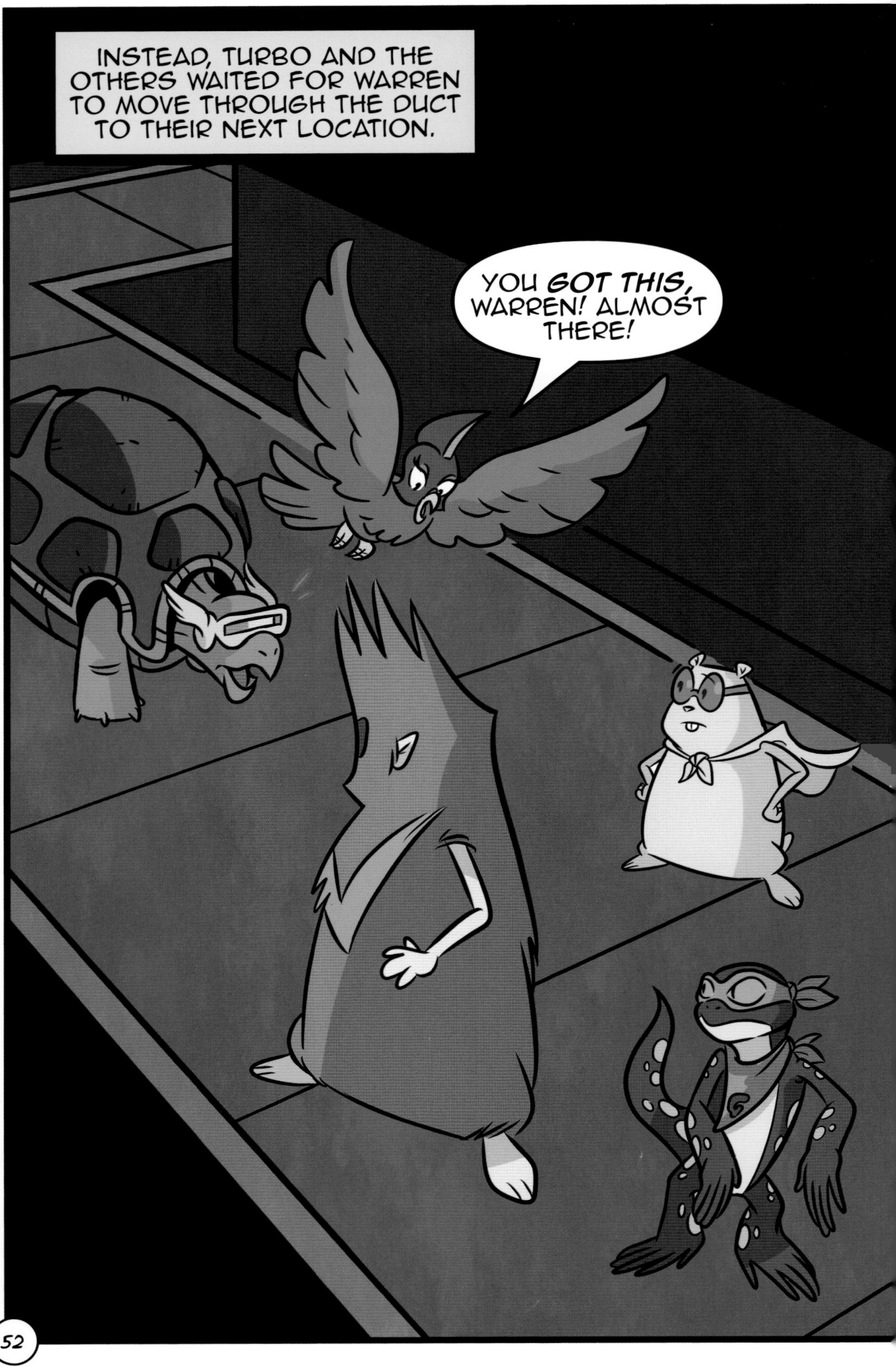
INSTEAD, TURBO AND THE OTHERS WAITED FOR WARREN TO MOVE THROUGH THE DUCT TO THEIR NEXT LOCATION.
YOU *GOT THIS*, WARREN! ALMOST THERE!

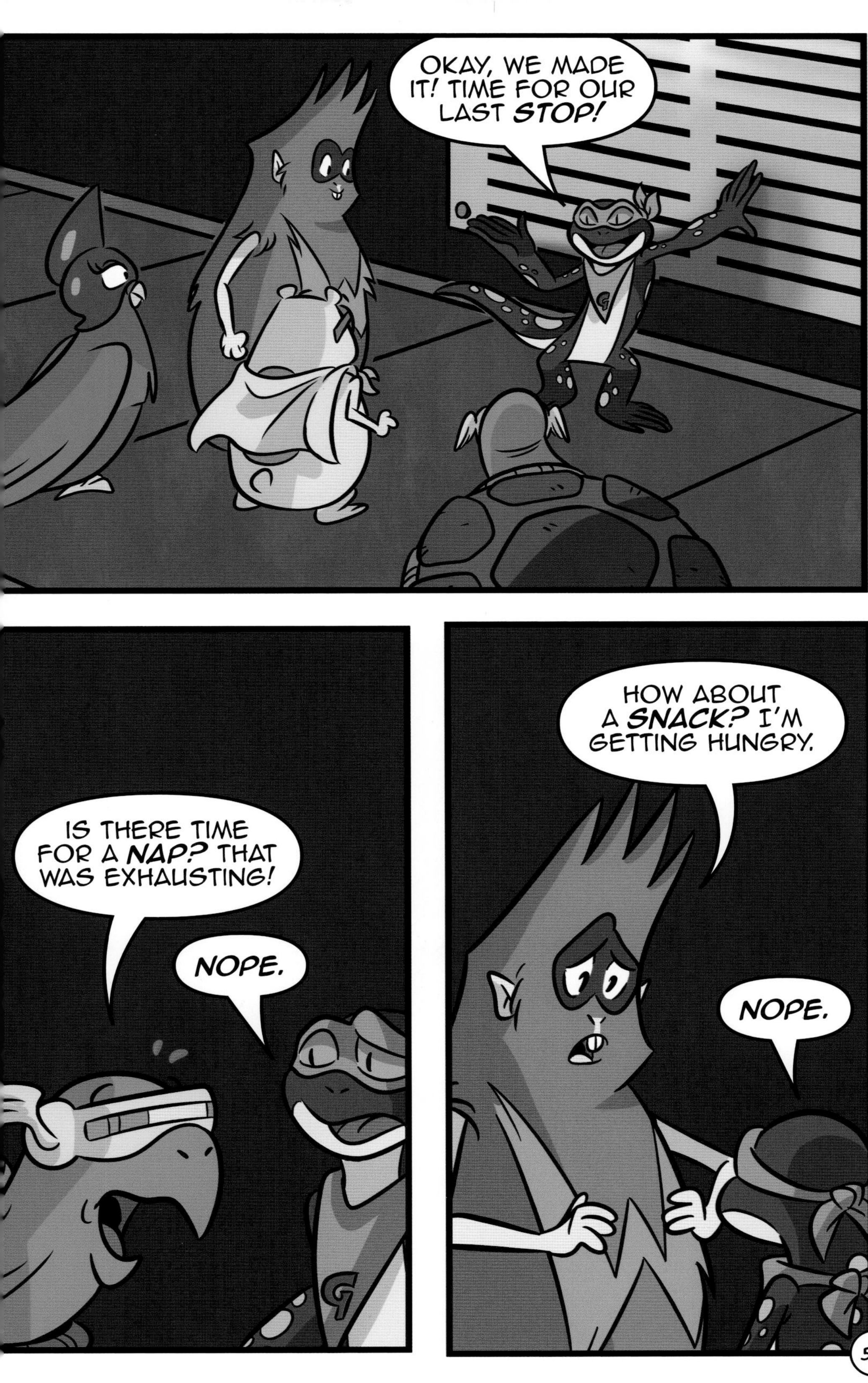

OKAY, WE MADE IT! TIME FOR OUR LAST STOP!
HOW ABOUT A SNACK? I'M GETTING HUNGRY.
IS THERE TIME FOR A NAP? THAT WAS EXHAUSTING!
NOPE.
NOPE.

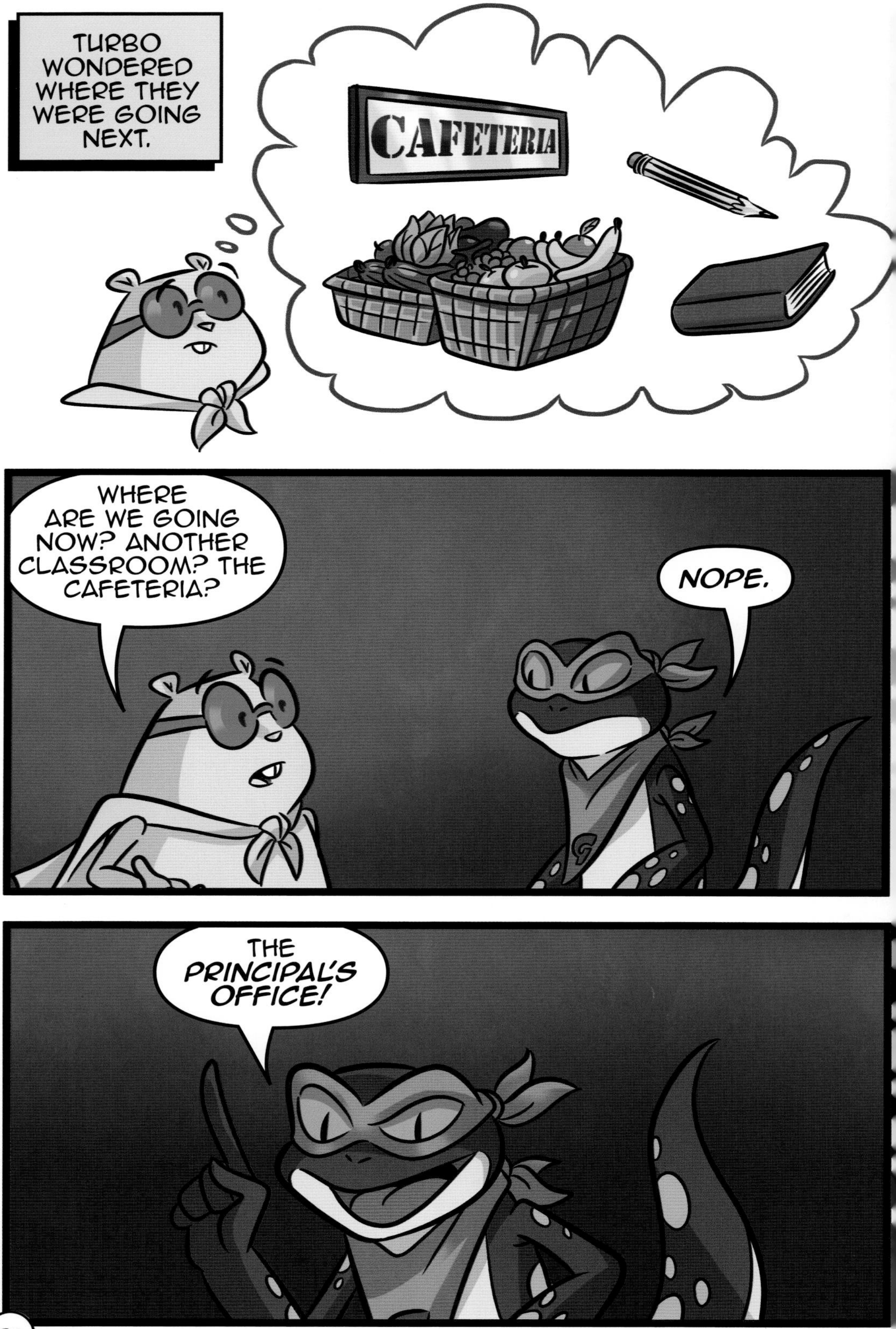
TURBO WONDERED WHERE THEY WERE GOING NEXT.
CAFETERIA
WHERE ARE WE GOING NOW? ANOTHER CLASSROOM? THE CAFETERIA?
NOPE.
THE PRINCIPAL'S OFFICE!

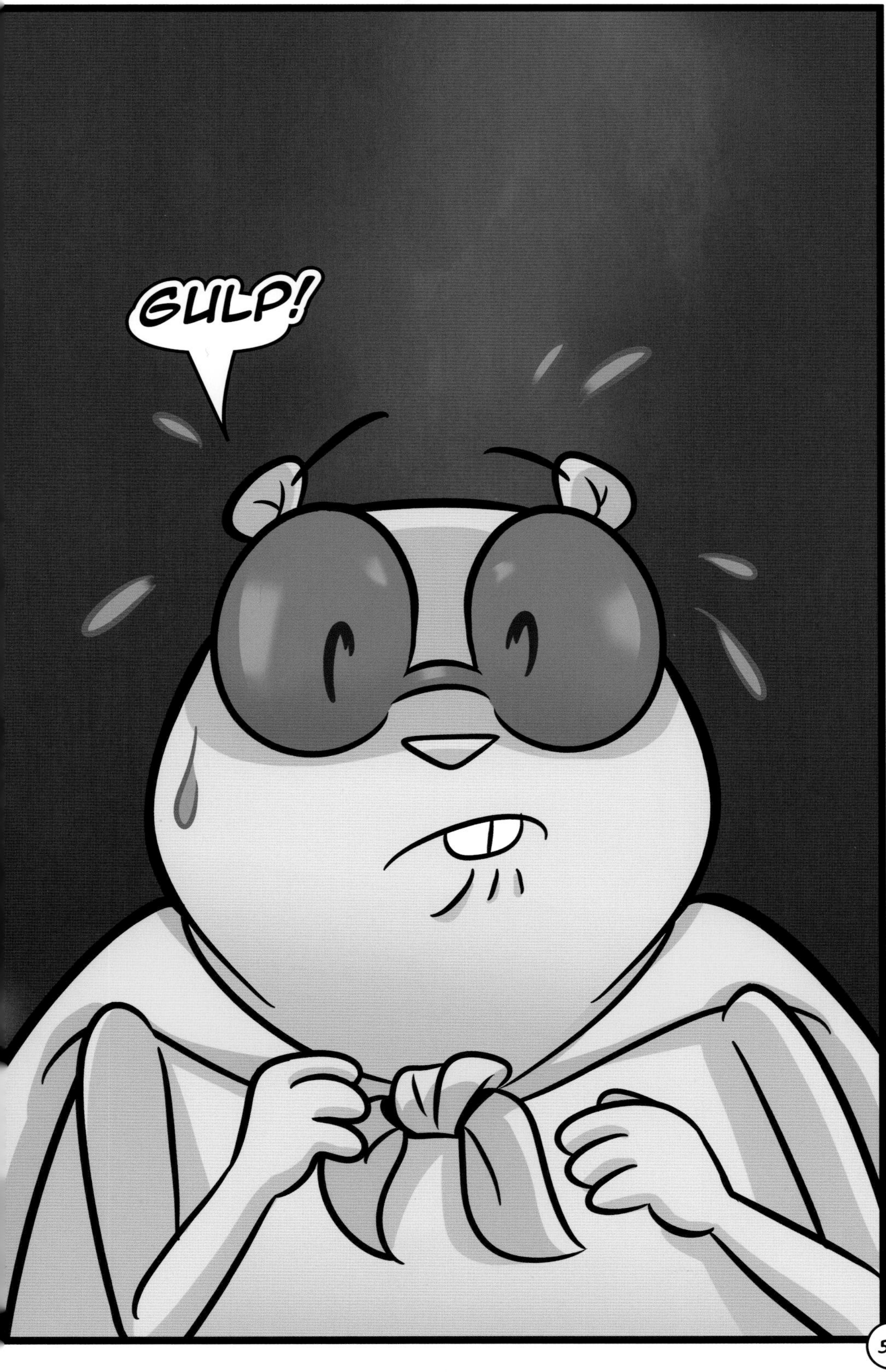
GULP!

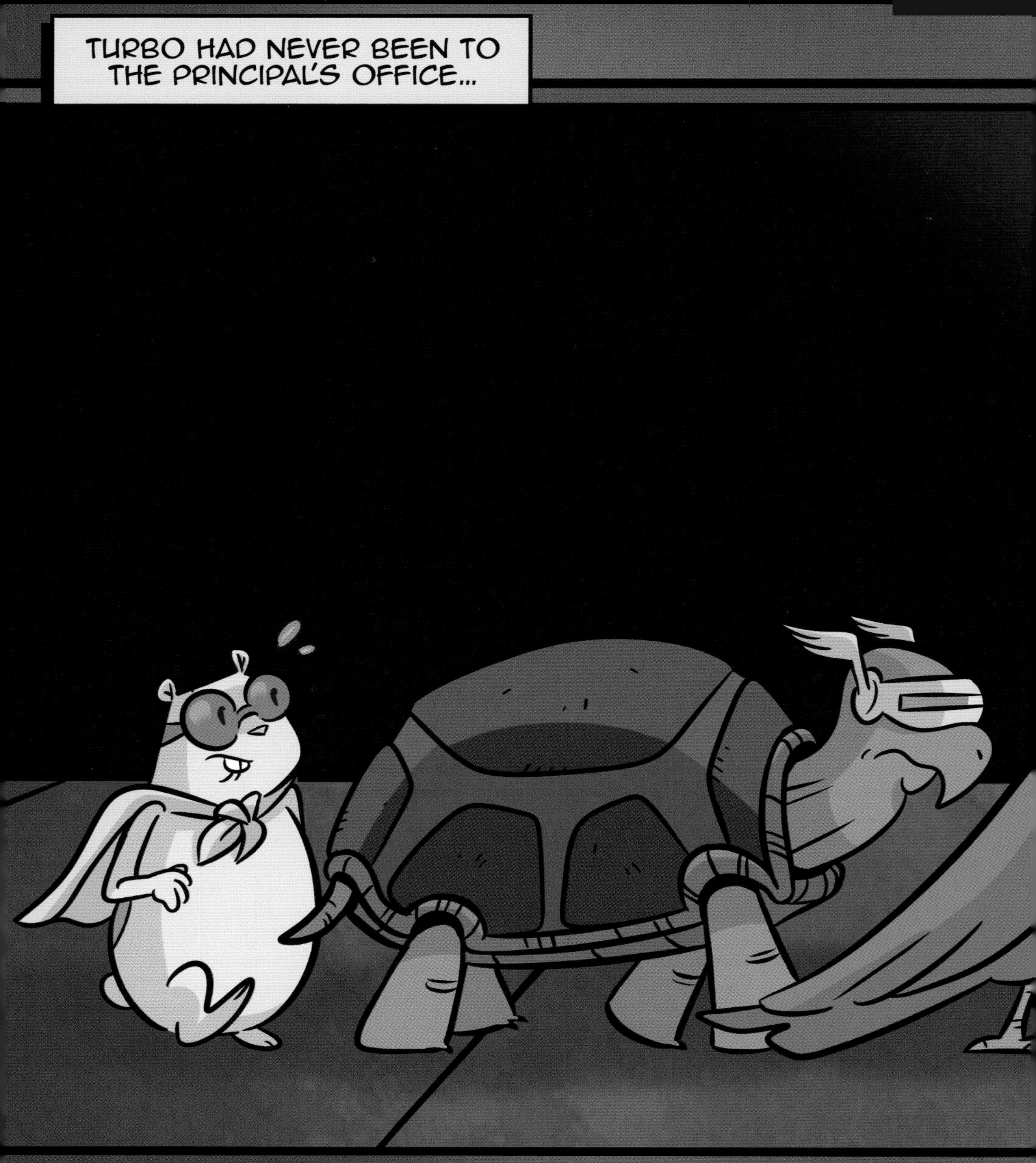
TURBO HAD NEVER BEEN TO THE PRINCIPAL'S OFFICE...

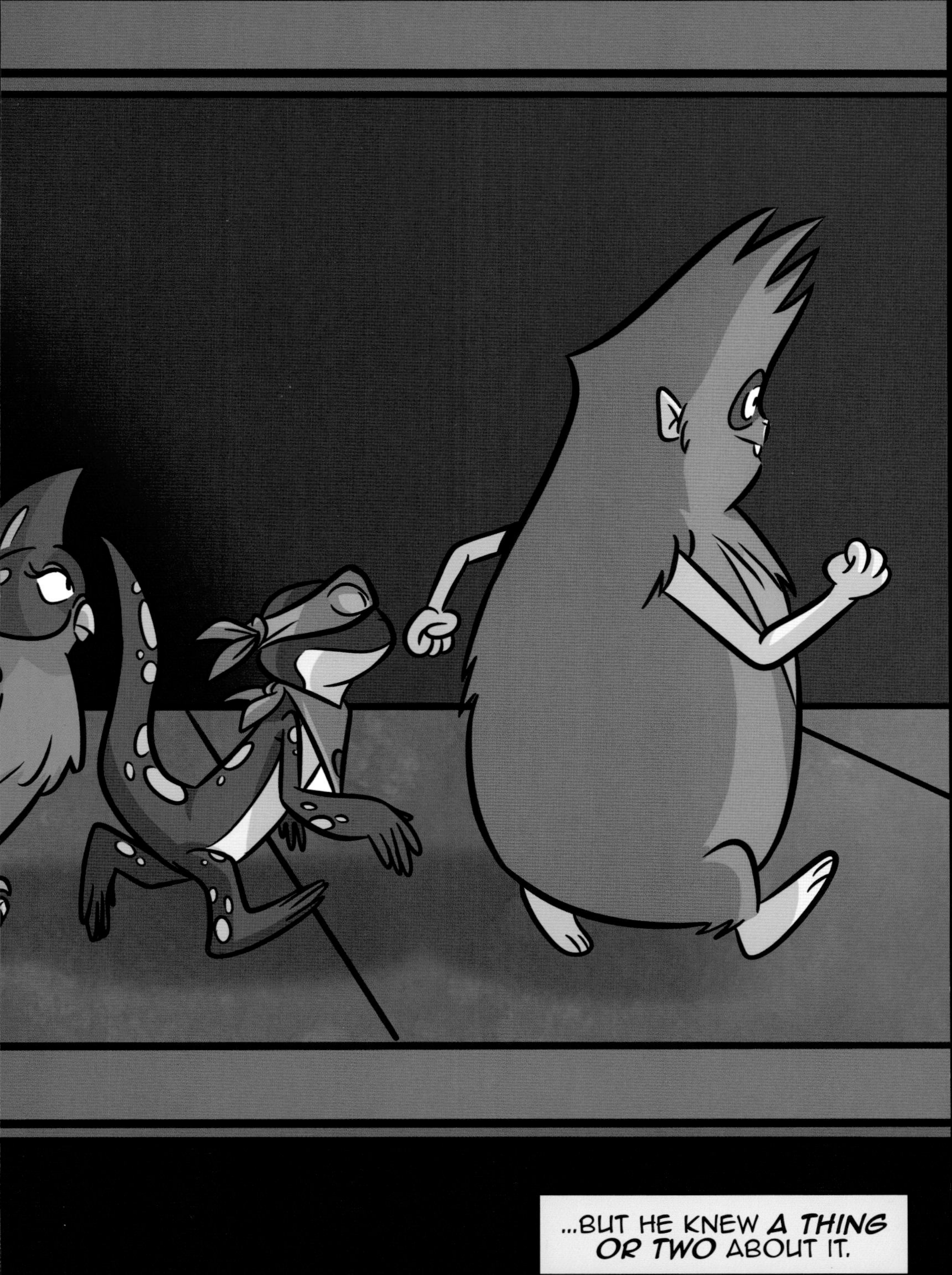
...BUT HE KNEW **A THING OR TWO** ABOUT IT.

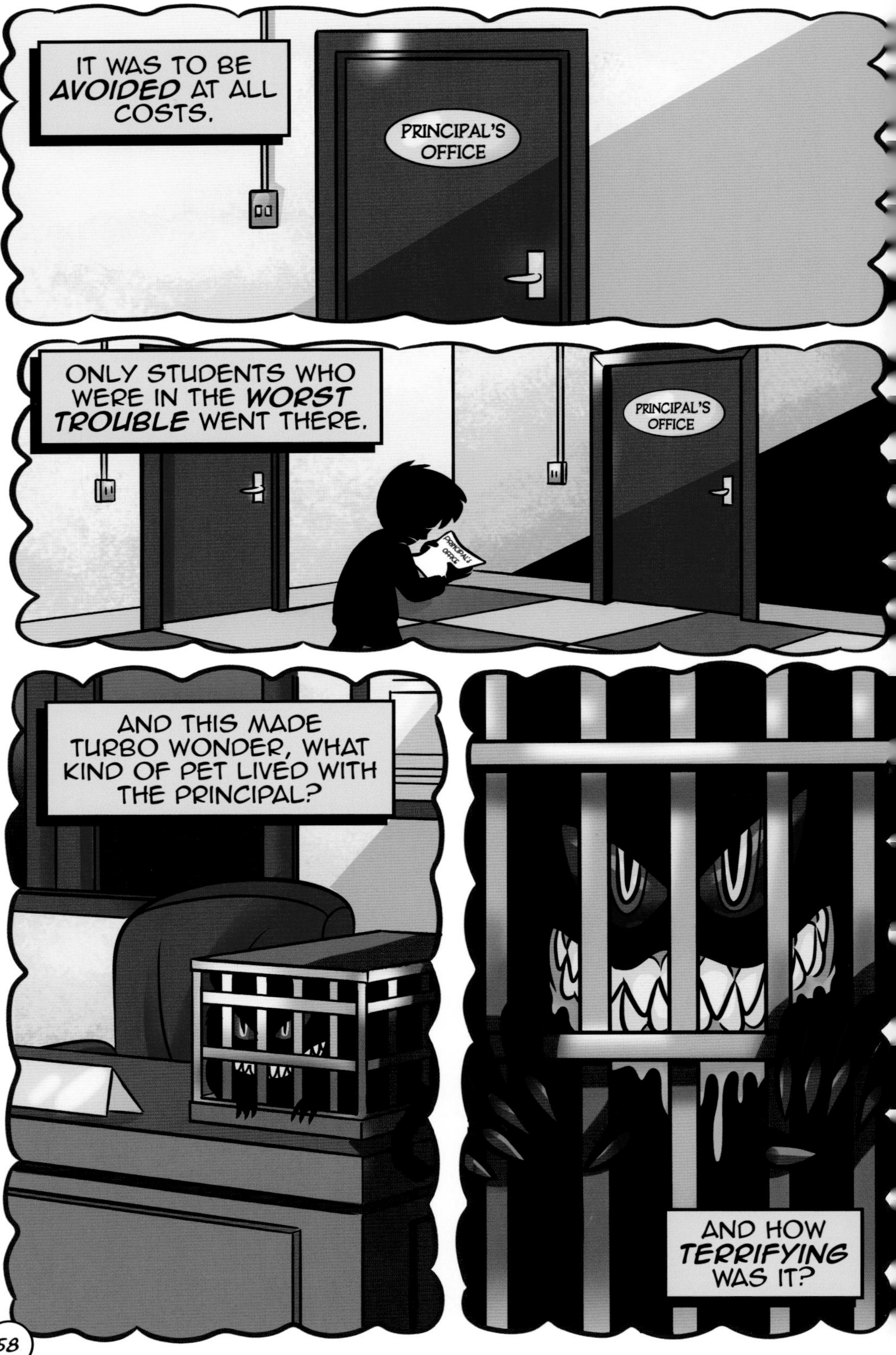
IT WAS TO BE *AVOIDED* AT ALL COSTS.
PRINCIPAL'S OFFICE
ONLY STUDENTS WHO WERE IN THE *WORST TROUBLE* WENT THERE.
PRINCIPAL'S OFFICE
AND THIS MADE TURBO WONDER, WHAT KIND OF PET LIVED WITH THE PRINCIPAL?
AND HOW *TERRIFYING* WAS IT?

I ACTUALLY WASN'T WORRIED THAT IT WAS TERRIFYING, BUT NOW I AM!

SO, UM, WHO LIVES HERE?

YOU'LL SEE!

IT WAS **DARK** IN THE PRINCIPAL'S OFFICE.

TURBO SQUINTED AND SAW A **CAGE** WITH METAL BARS, SIMILAR TO **HIS** CAGE.

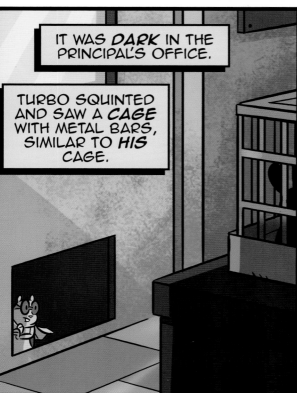

WE DON'T SAY "CAGE." WE SAY "**PALACE**," REMEMBER?

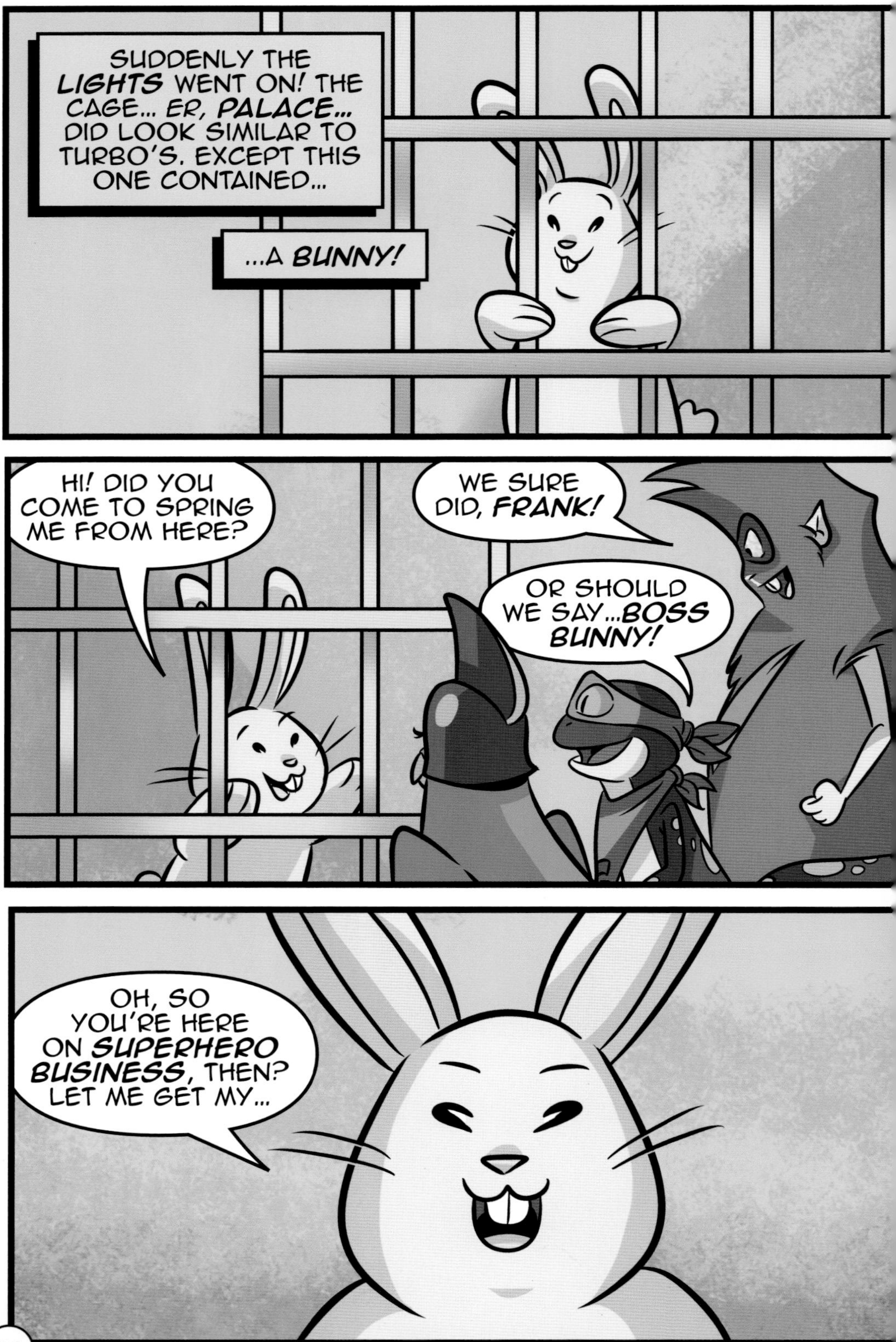
SUDDENLY THE *LIGHTS* WENT ON! THE CAGE... ER, *PALACE*... DID LOOK SIMILAR TO TURBO'S. EXCEPT THIS ONE CONTAINED...
...A *BUNNY!*
HI! DID YOU COME TO SPRING ME FROM HERE?
WE SURE DID, *FRANK!*
OR SHOULD WE SAY...*BOSS BUNNY!*
OH, SO YOU'RE HERE ON *SUPERHERO BUSINESS*, THEN? LET ME GET MY...

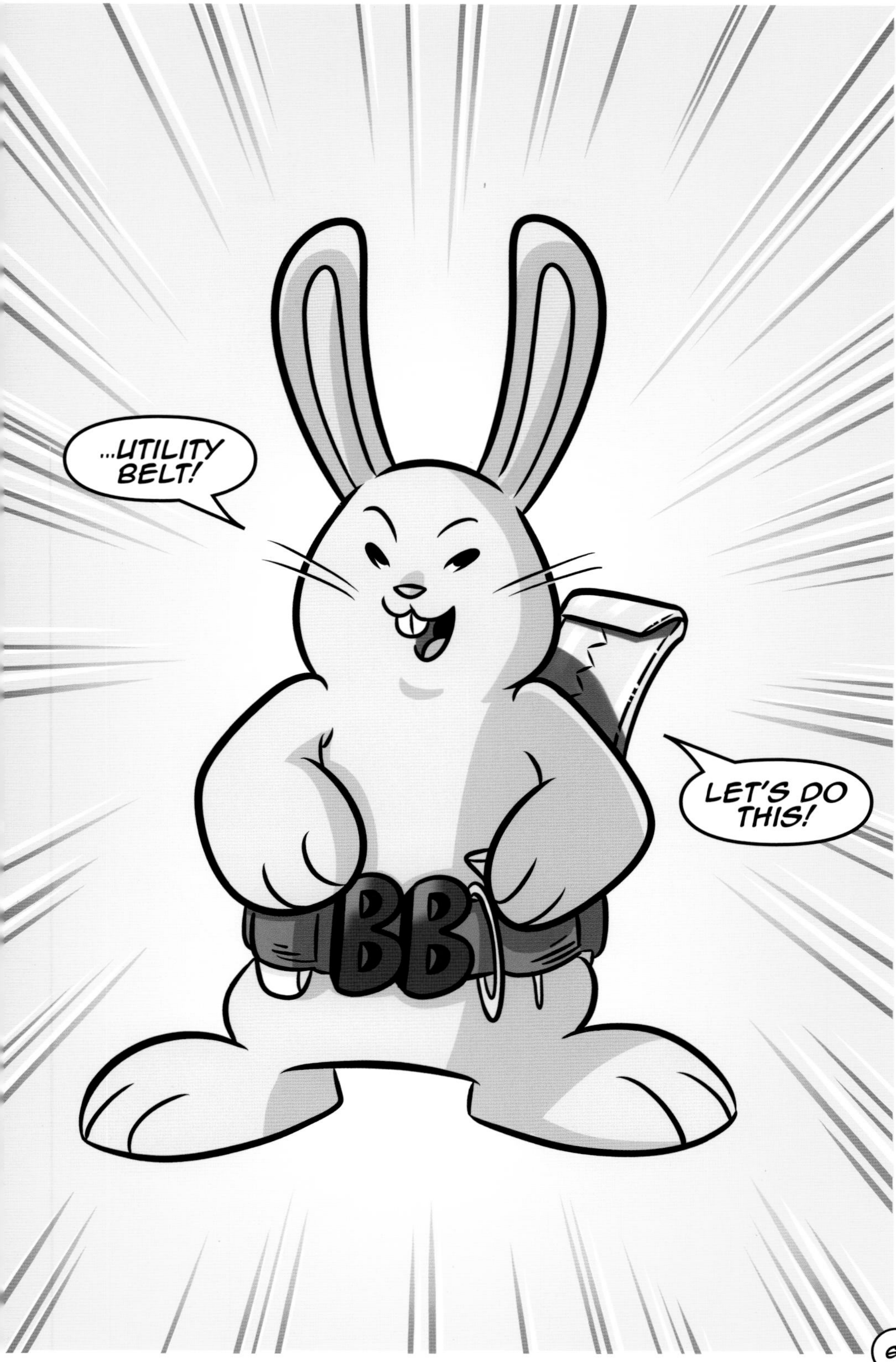
...UTILITY BELT!
BB
LET'S DO THIS!

AND WITH THAT, TURBO'S NEW FRIENDS SPRANG INTO *ACTION*.

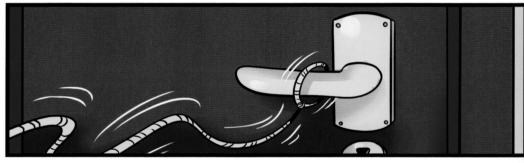

EVERYONE WAS HELPING...EXCEPT FOR TURBO.

HE JUST *WATCHED*.

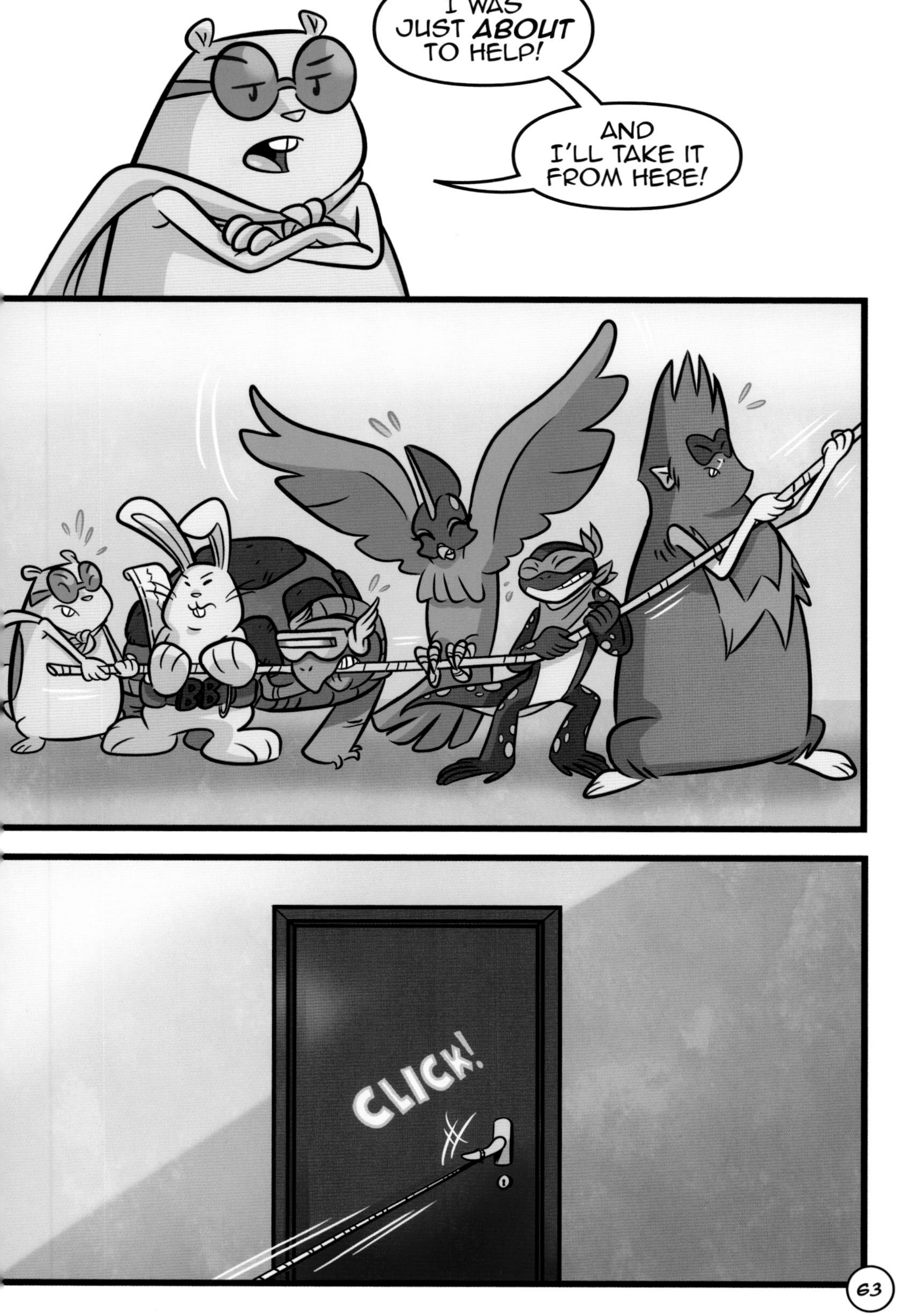
I WAS JUST ABOUT TO HELP!
AND I'LL TAKE IT FROM HERE!
CLICK!

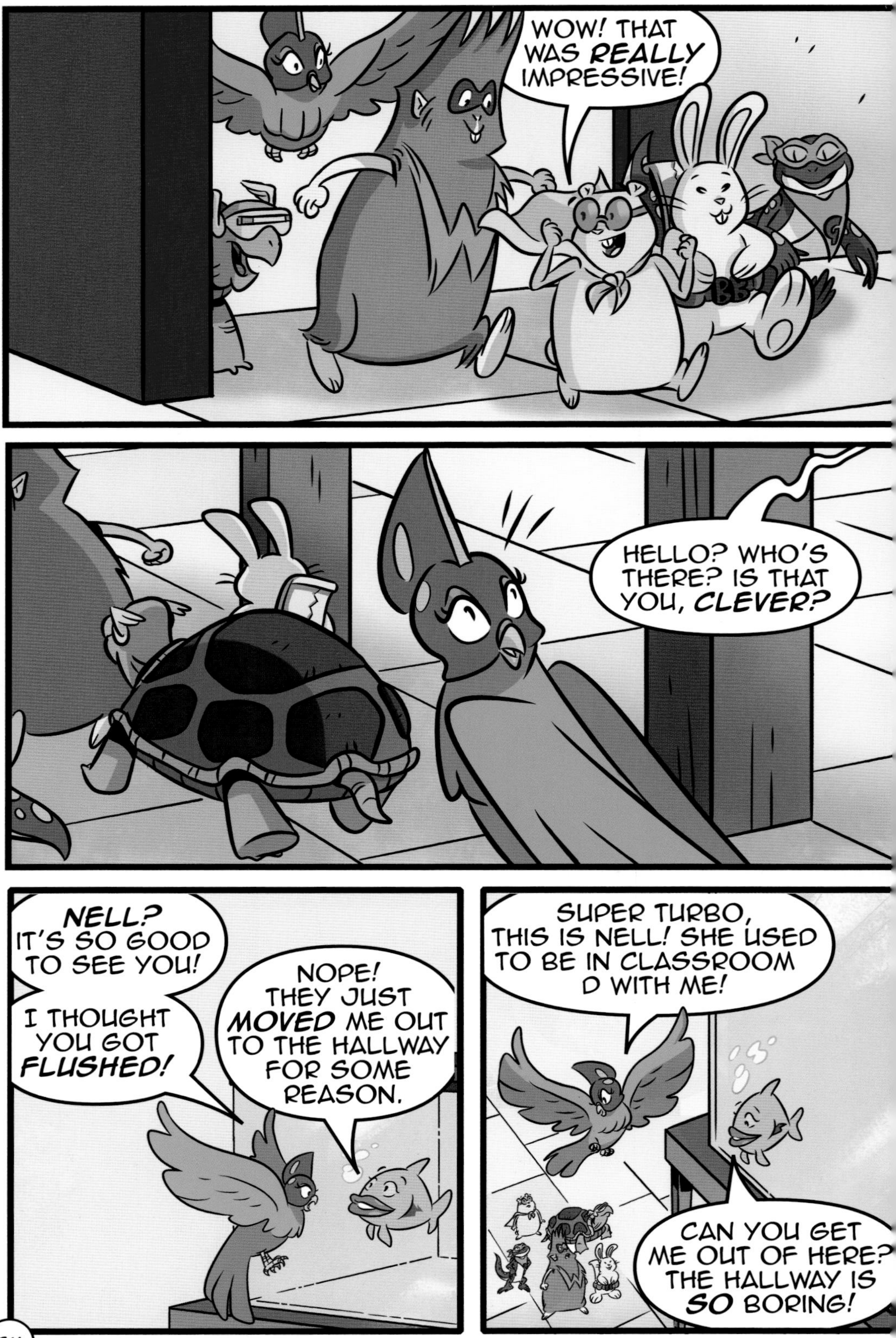

WOW! THAT WAS REALLY IMPRESSIVE!
BB
HELLO? WHO'S THERE? IS THAT YOU, CLEVER?
NELL? IT'S SO GOOD TO SEE YOU!
I THOUGHT YOU GOT FLUSHED!
NOPE! THEY JUST MOVED ME OUT TO THE HALLWAY FOR SOME REASON.
SUPER TURBO, THIS IS NELL! SHE USED TO BE IN CLASSROOM D WITH ME!
CAN YOU GET ME OUT OF HERE? THE HALLWAY IS SO BORING!

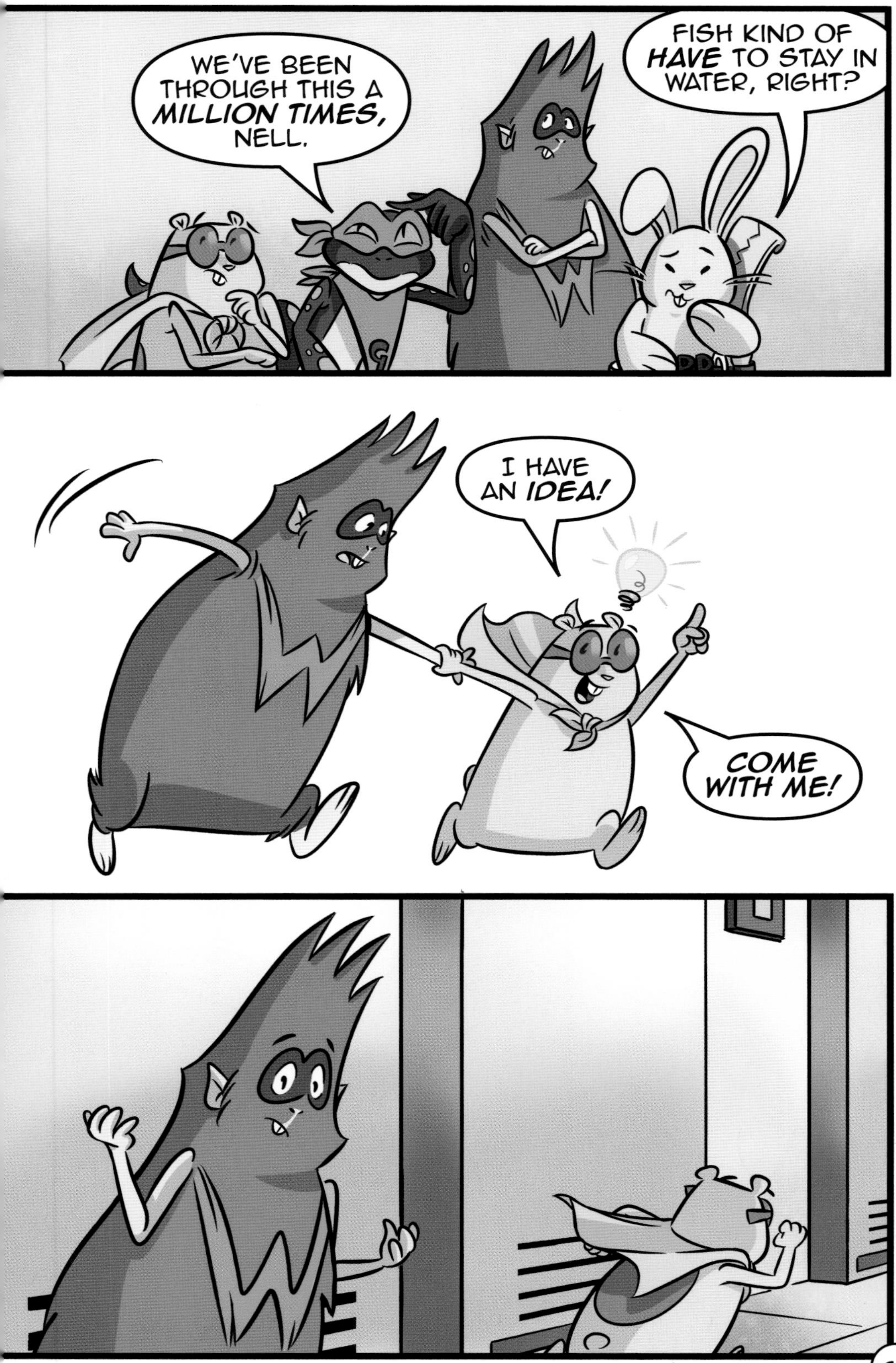
WE'VE BEEN THROUGH THIS A MILLION TIMES, NELL.
FISH KIND OF HAVE TO STAY IN WATER, RIGHT?
I HAVE AN IDEA!
COME WITH ME!

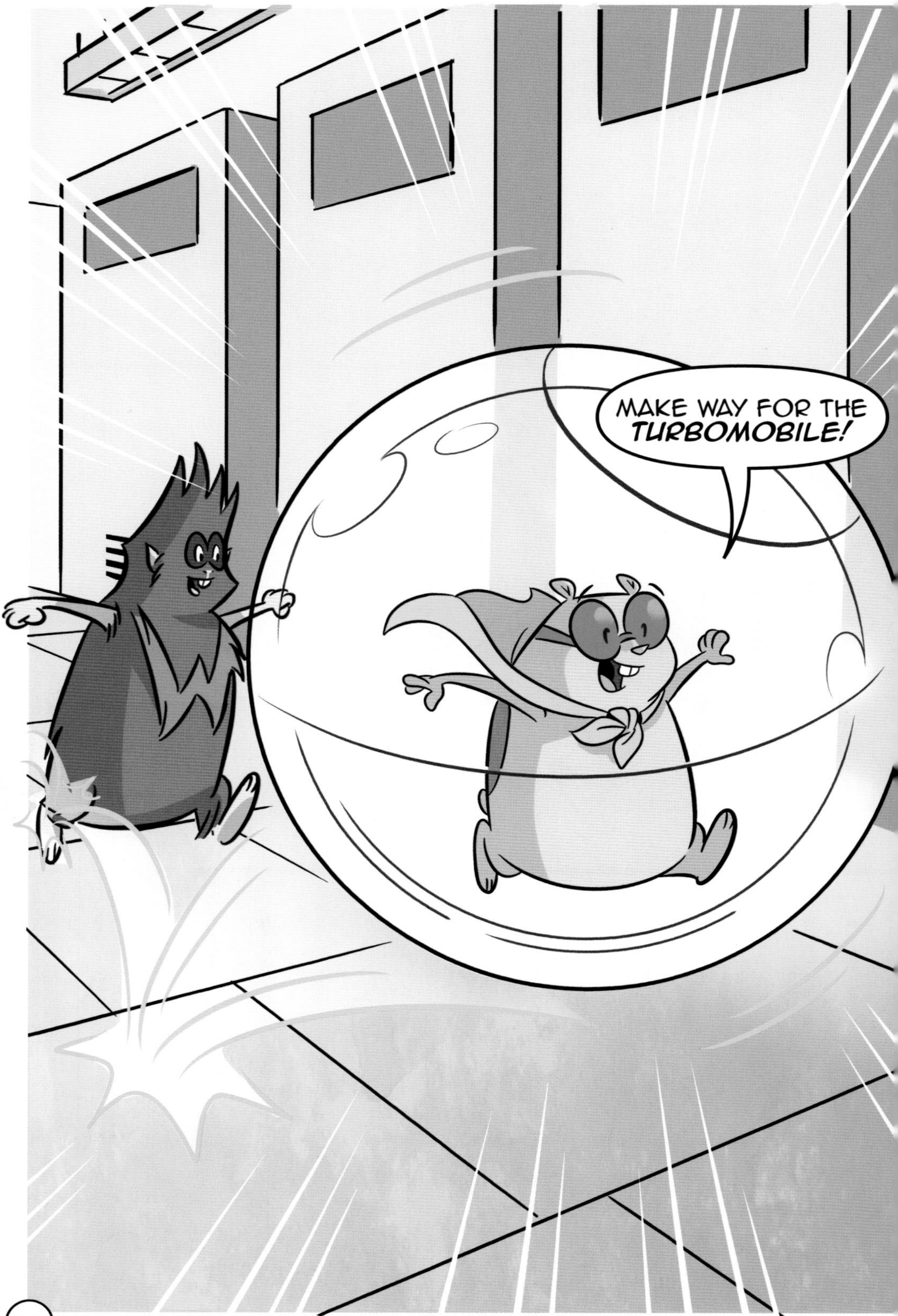
MAKE WAY FOR THE *TURBOMOBILE!*

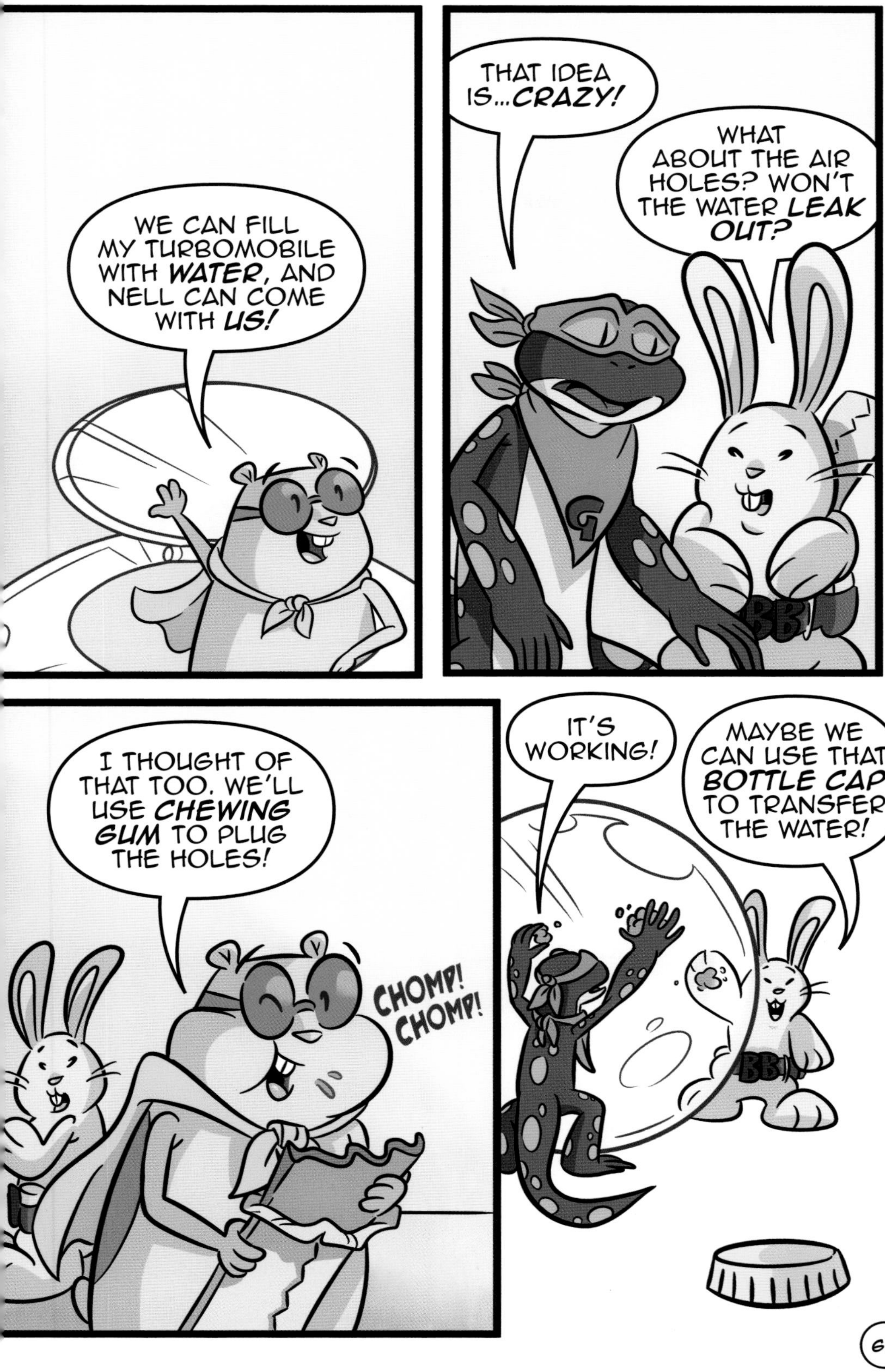
WE CAN FILL MY TURBOMOBILE WITH **WATER**, AND NELL CAN COME WITH **US!**
THAT IDEA IS...**CRAZY!**
WHAT ABOUT THE AIR HOLES? WON'T THE WATER **LEAK OUT?**
I THOUGHT OF THAT TOO. WE'LL USE **CHEWING GUM** TO PLUG THE HOLES!
CHOMP! CHOMP!
IT'S WORKING!
MAYBE WE CAN USE THAT **BOTTLE CAP** TO TRANSFER THE WATER!

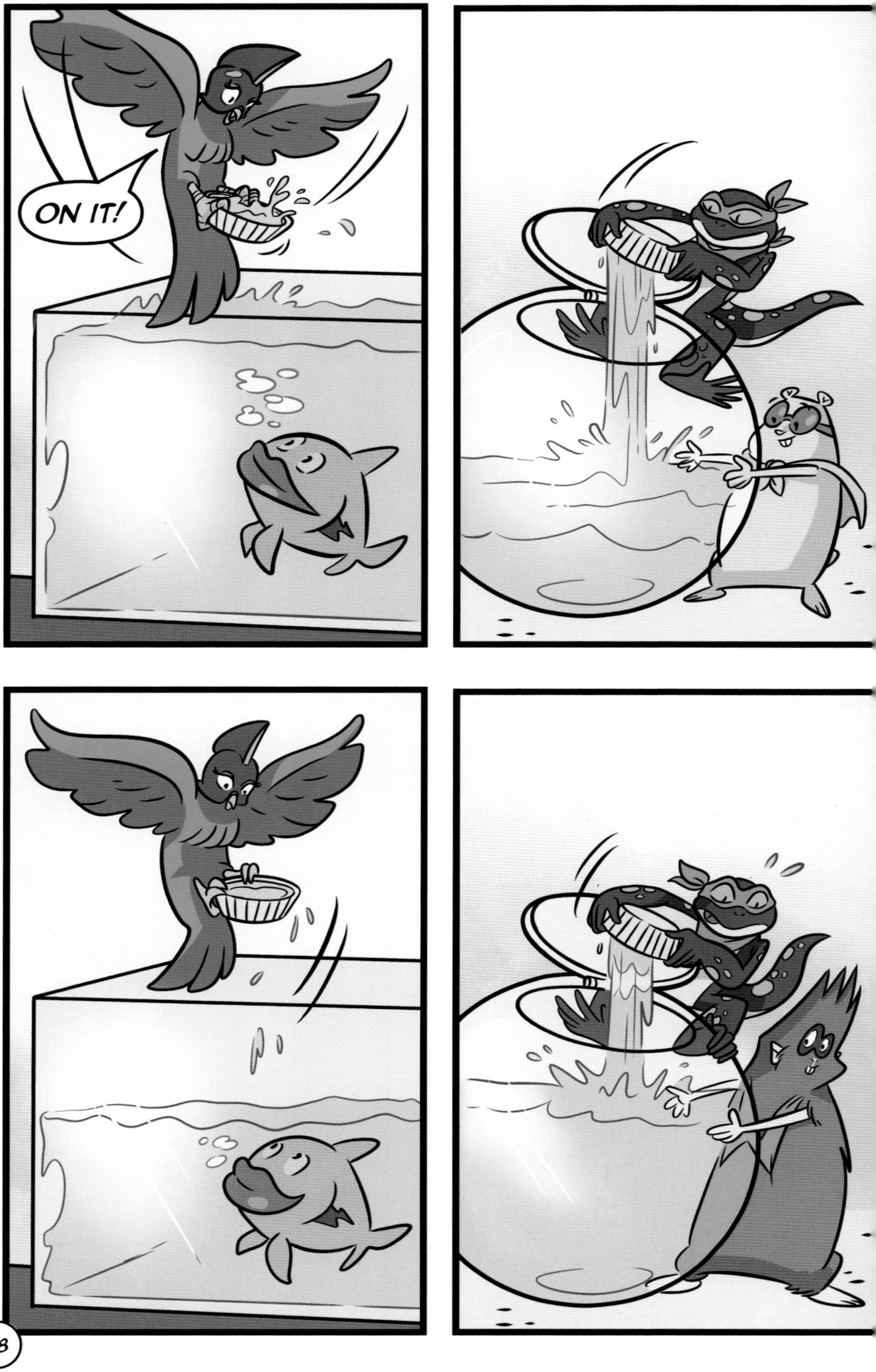
ON IT!

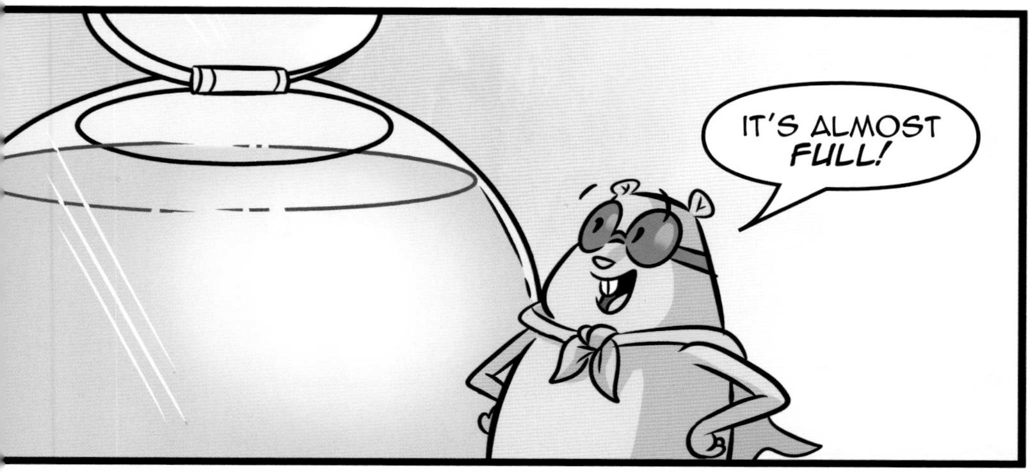
IT'S ALMOST FULL!

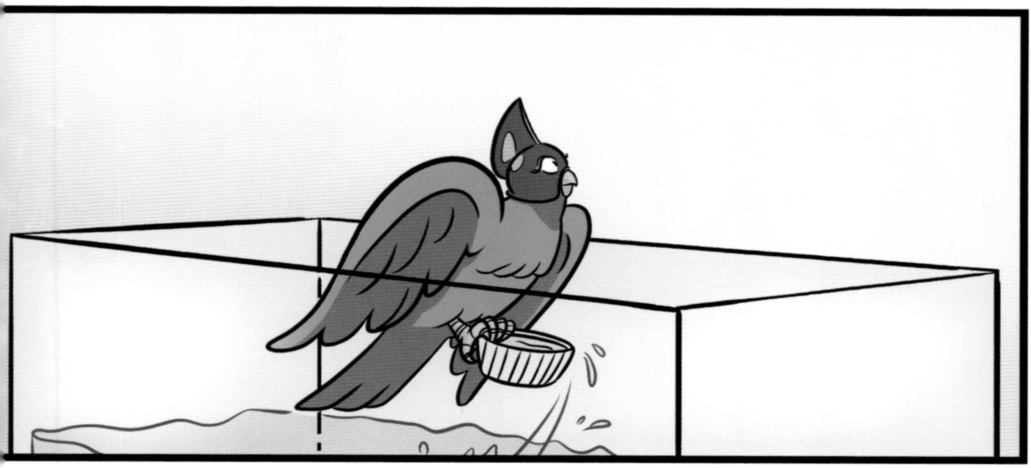

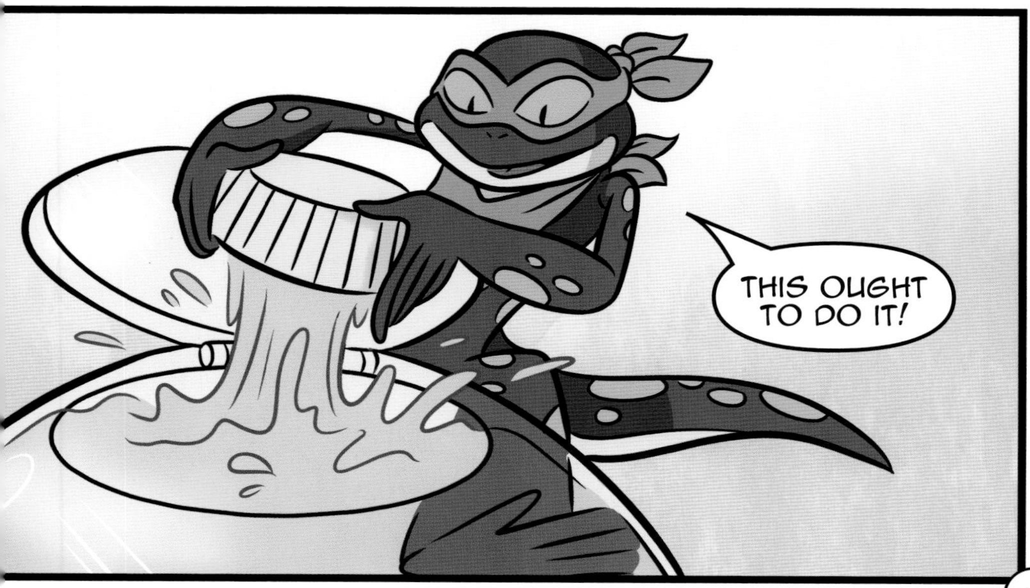
THIS OUGHT TO DO IT!

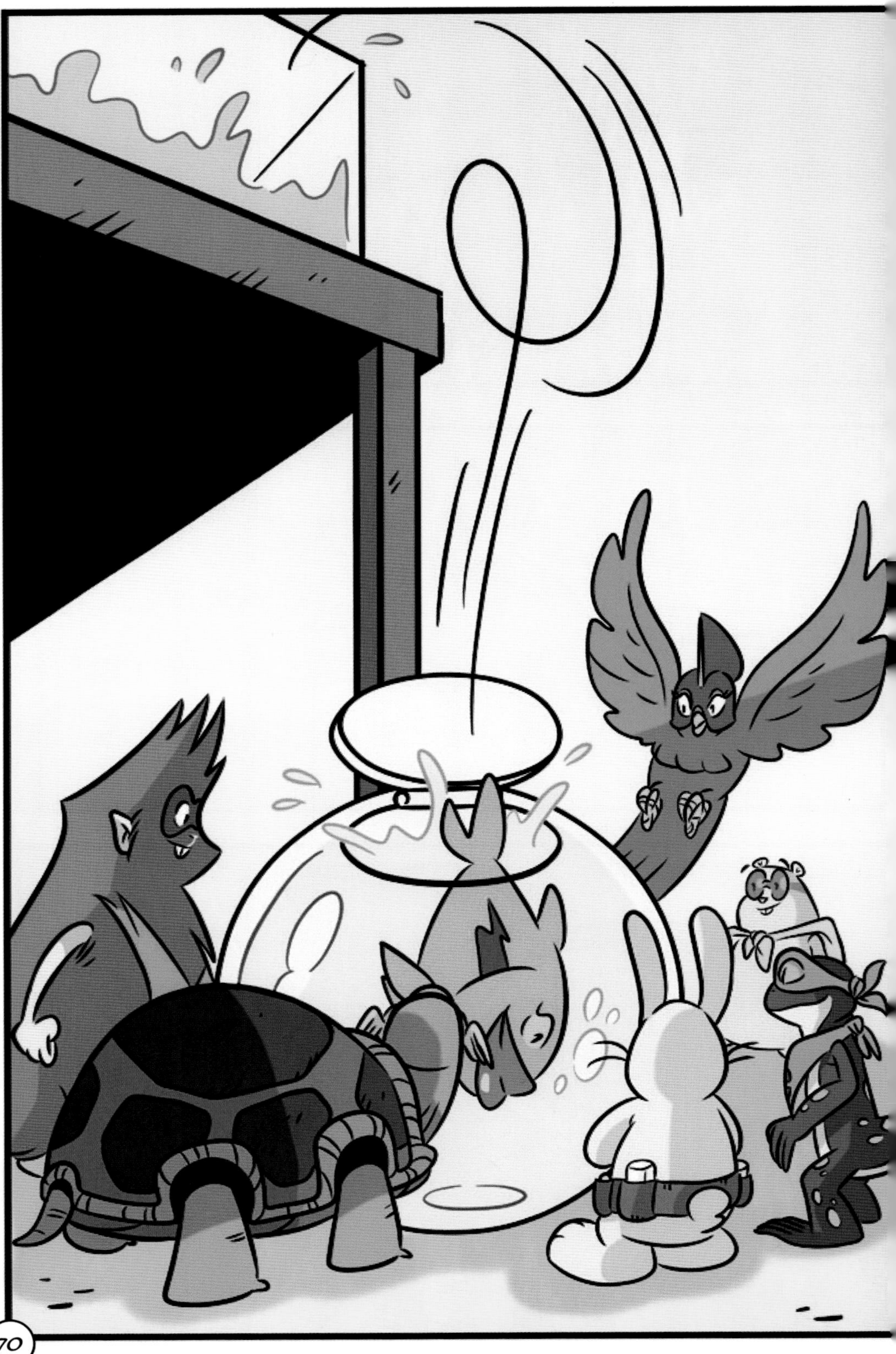

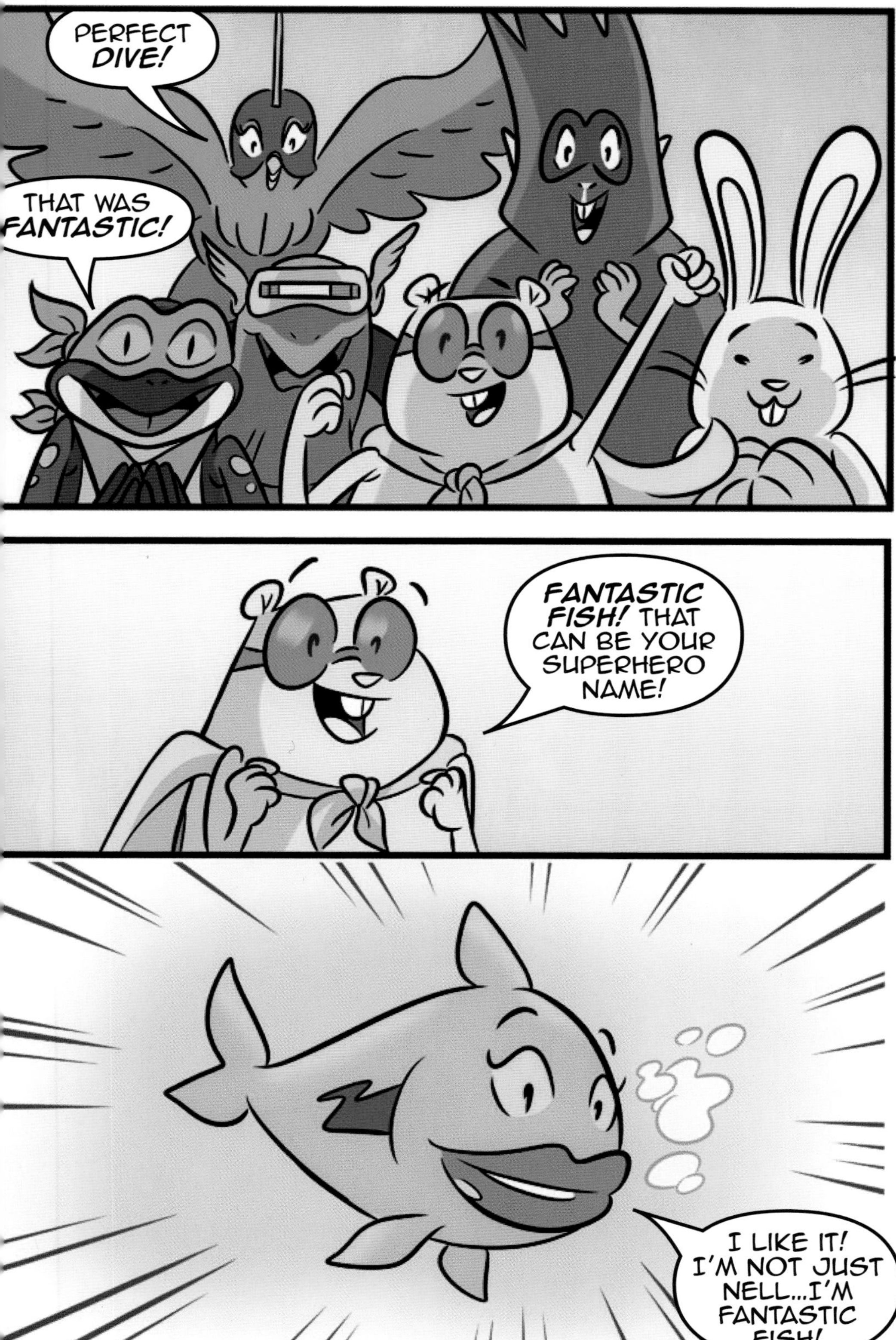
PERFECT DIVE!
THAT WAS FANTASTIC!
FANTASTIC FISH! THAT CAN BE YOUR SUPERHERO NAME!
I LIKE IT! I'M NOT JUST NELL...I'M FANTASTIC FISH!

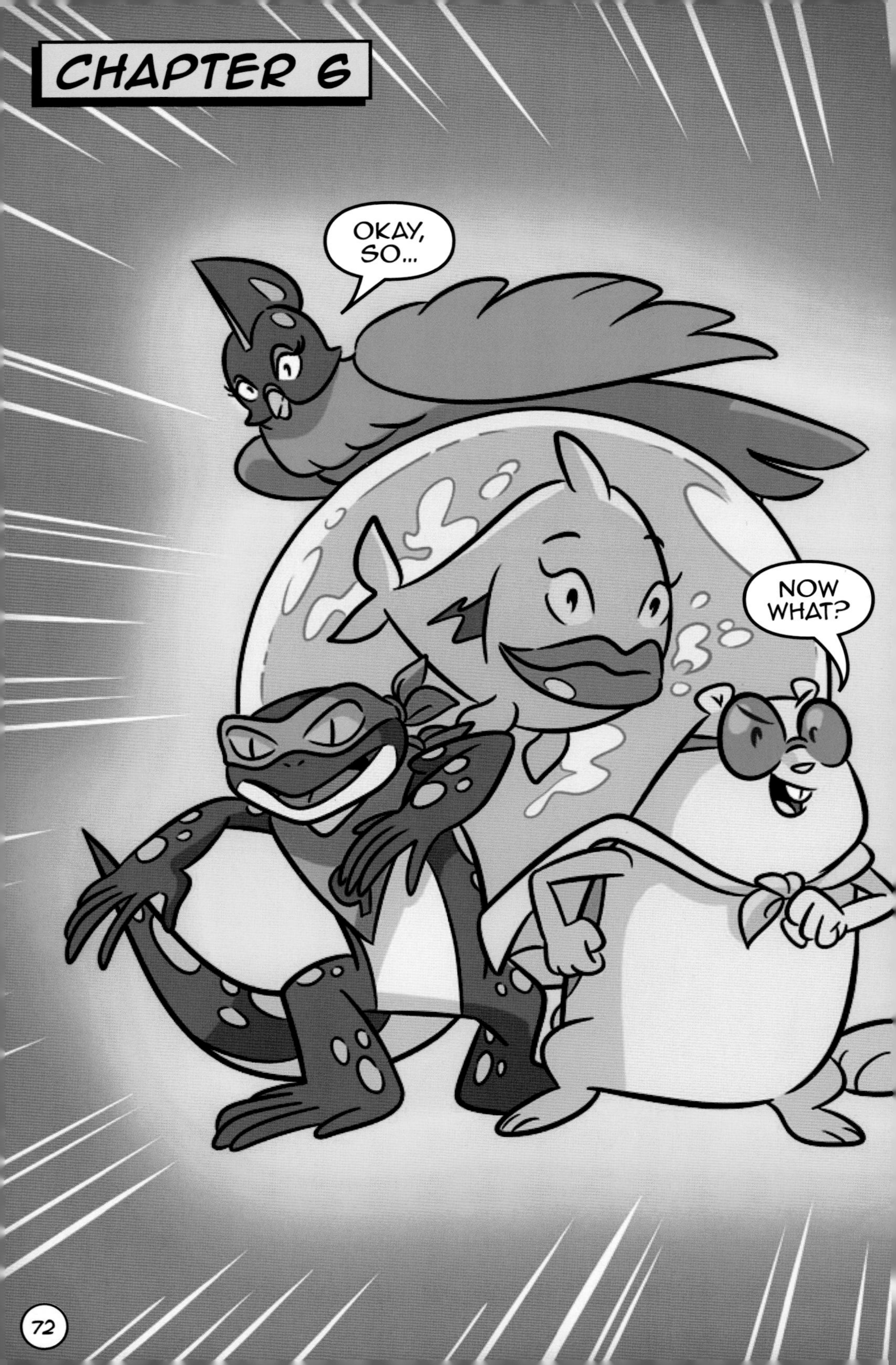
CHAPTER 6
OKAY, SO...
NOW WHAT?

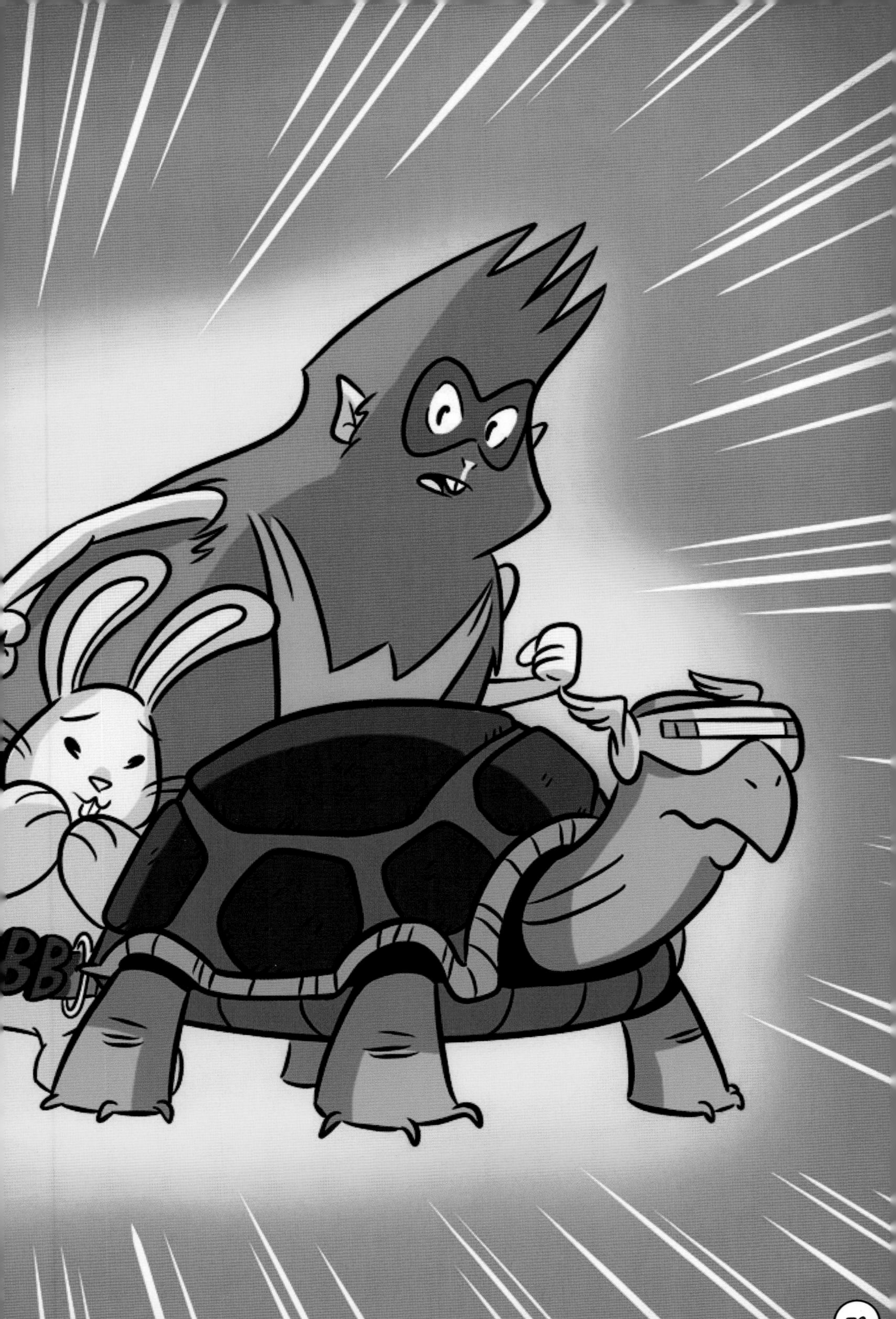

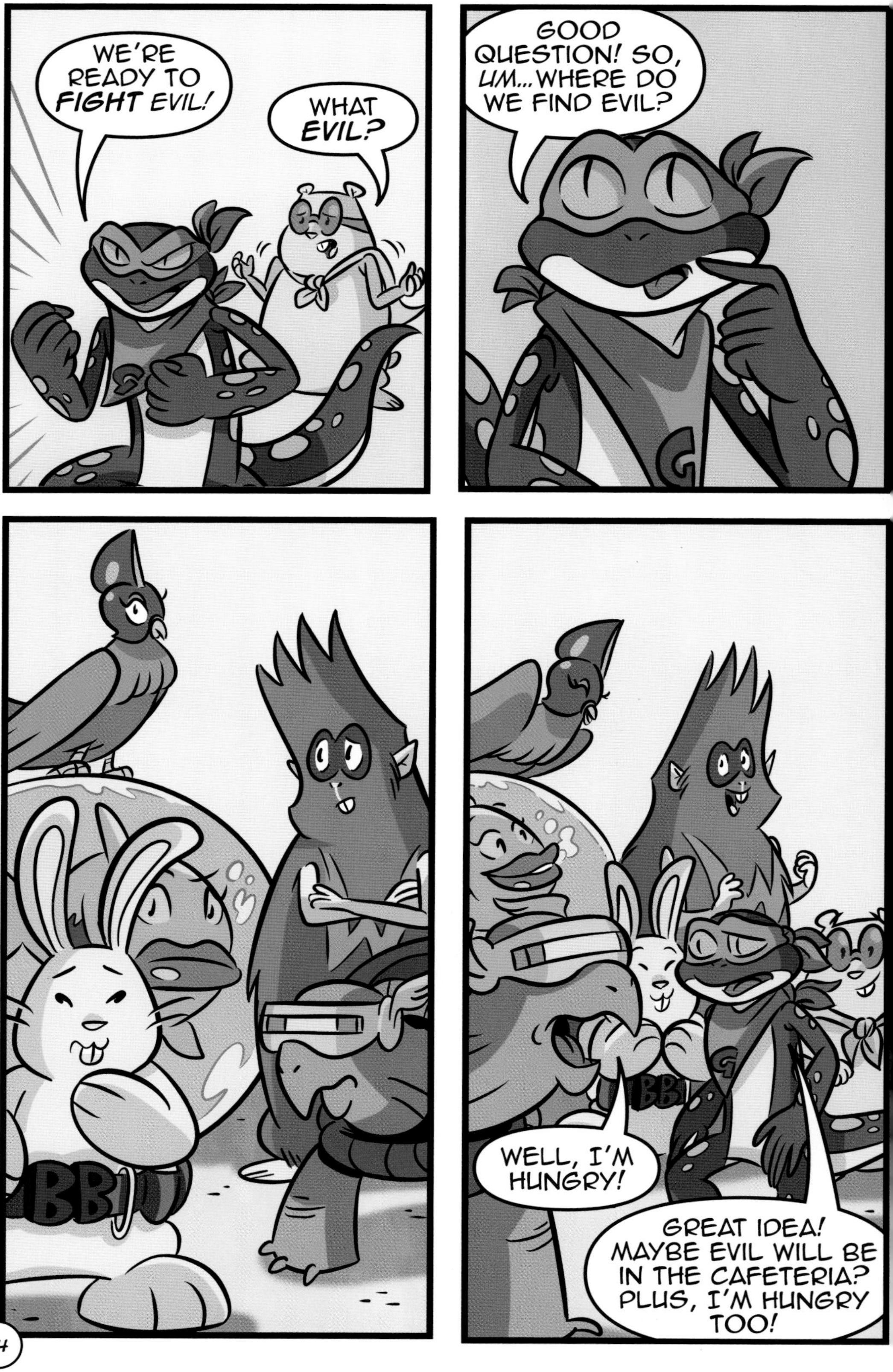
WE'RE READY TO *FIGHT* EVIL!
WHAT *EVIL?*
GOOD QUESTION! SO, *UM*...WHERE DO WE FIND EVIL?
WELL, I'M HUNGRY!
GREAT IDEA! MAYBE EVIL WILL BE IN THE CAFETERIA? PLUS, I'M HUNGRY TOO!

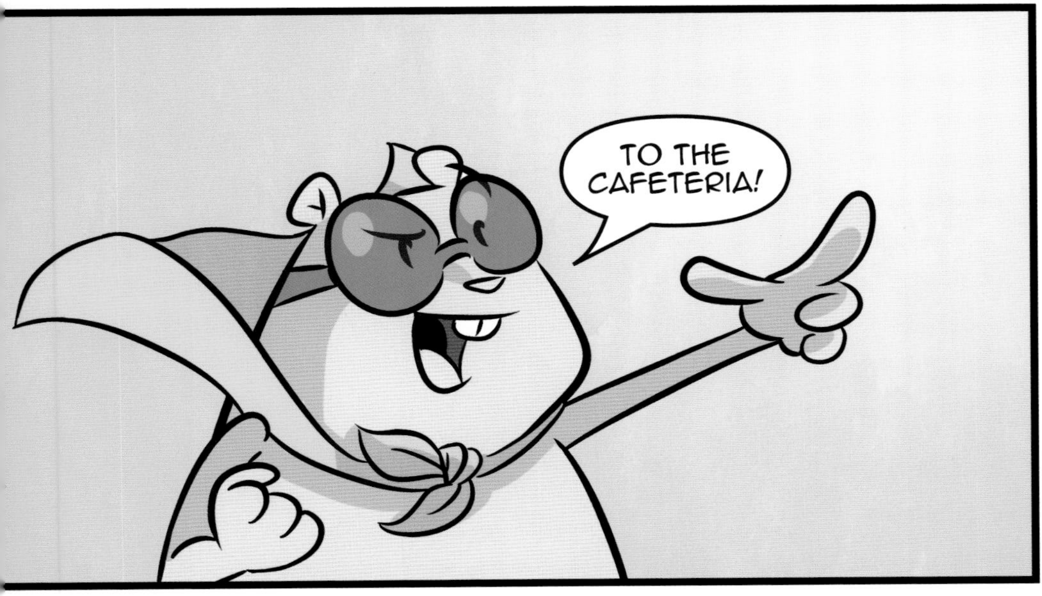
TO THE CAFETERIA!

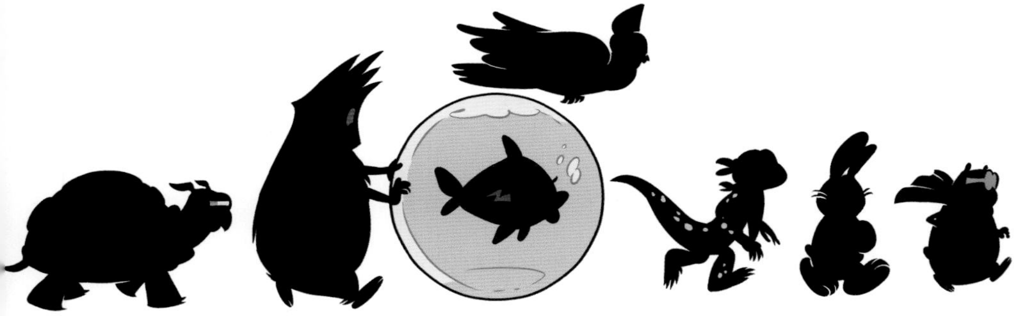

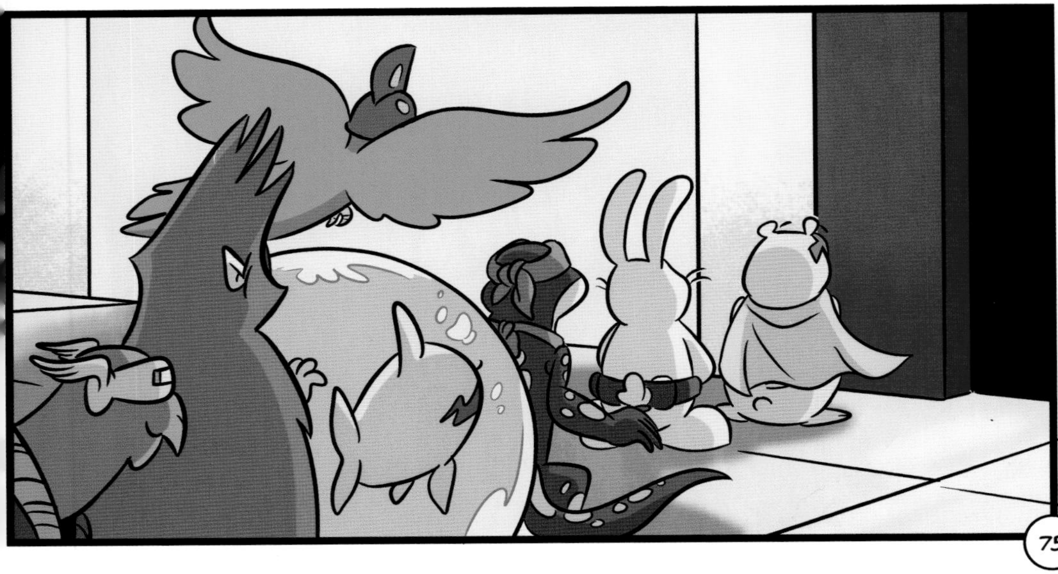

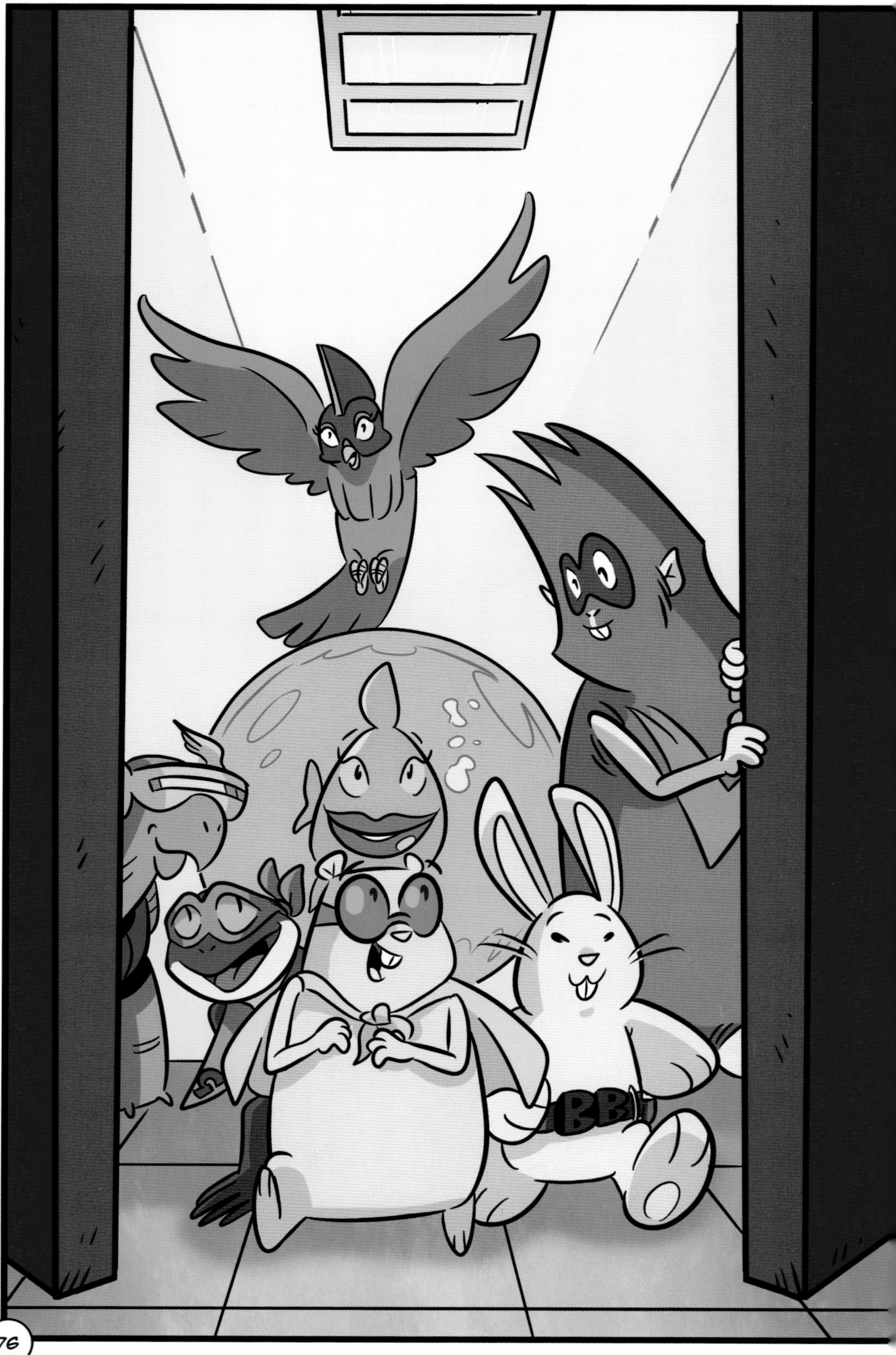
BB

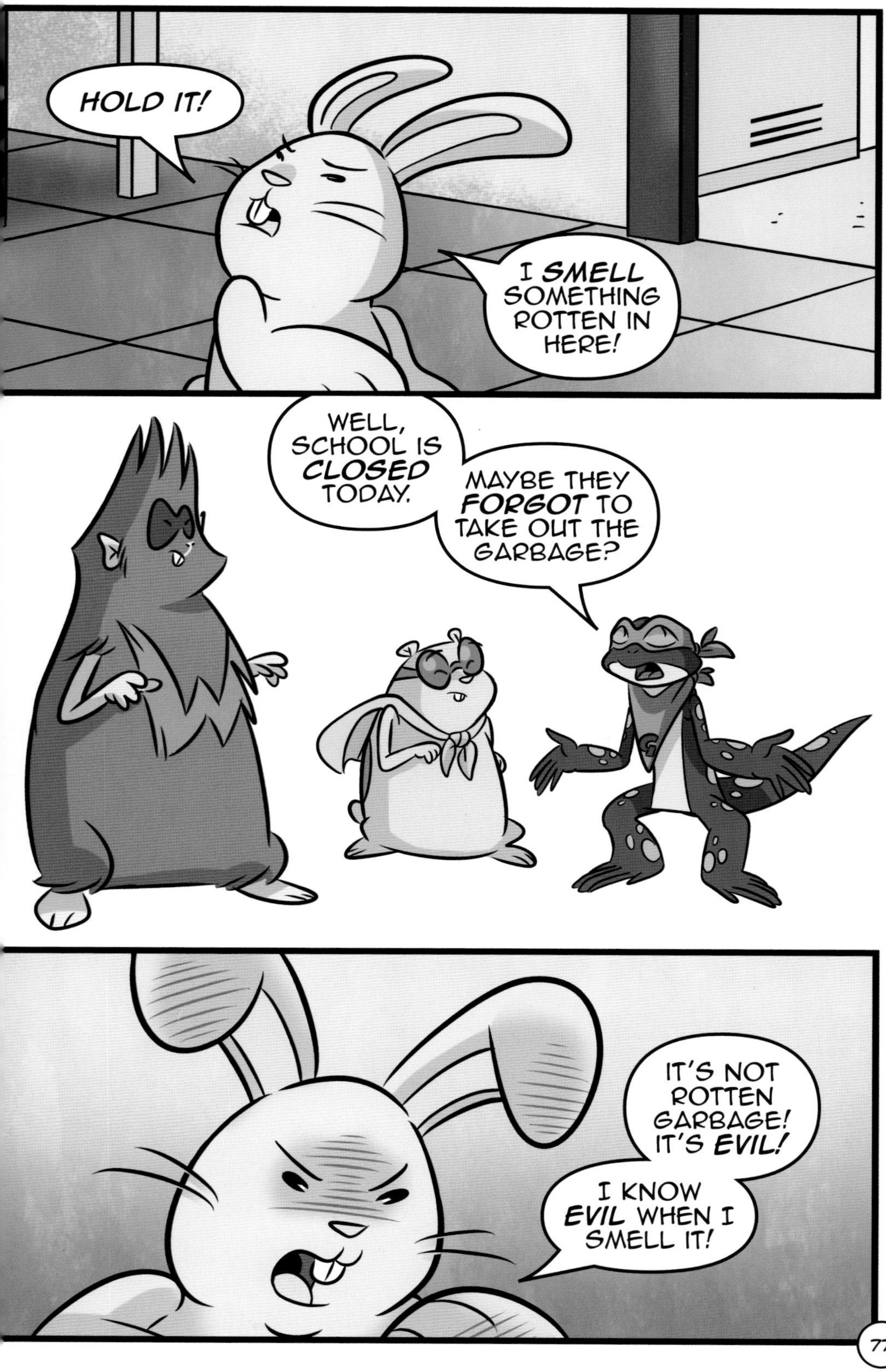
HOLD IT!
I SMELL SOMETHING ROTTEN IN HERE!
WELL, SCHOOL IS CLOSED TODAY.
MAYBE THEY FORGOT TO TAKE OUT THE GARBAGE?
IT'S NOT ROTTEN GARBAGE! IT'S EVIL!
I KNOW EVIL WHEN I SMELL IT!

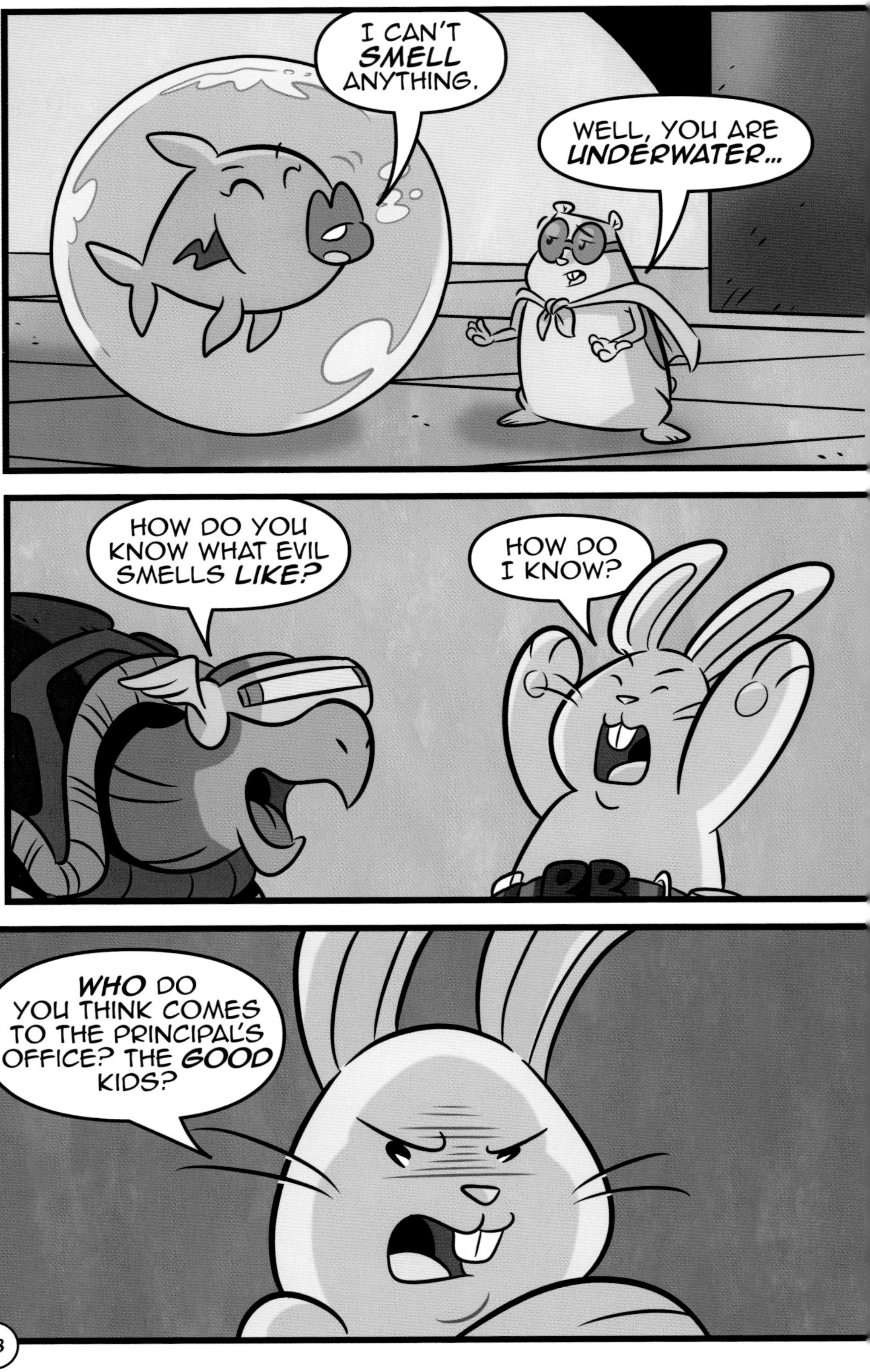
I CAN'T SMELL ANYTHING.
WELL, YOU ARE UNDERWATER...
HOW DO YOU KNOW WHAT EVIL SMELLS LIKE?
HOW DO I KNOW?
WHO DO YOU THINK COMES TO THE PRINCIPAL'S OFFICE? THE GOOD KIDS?

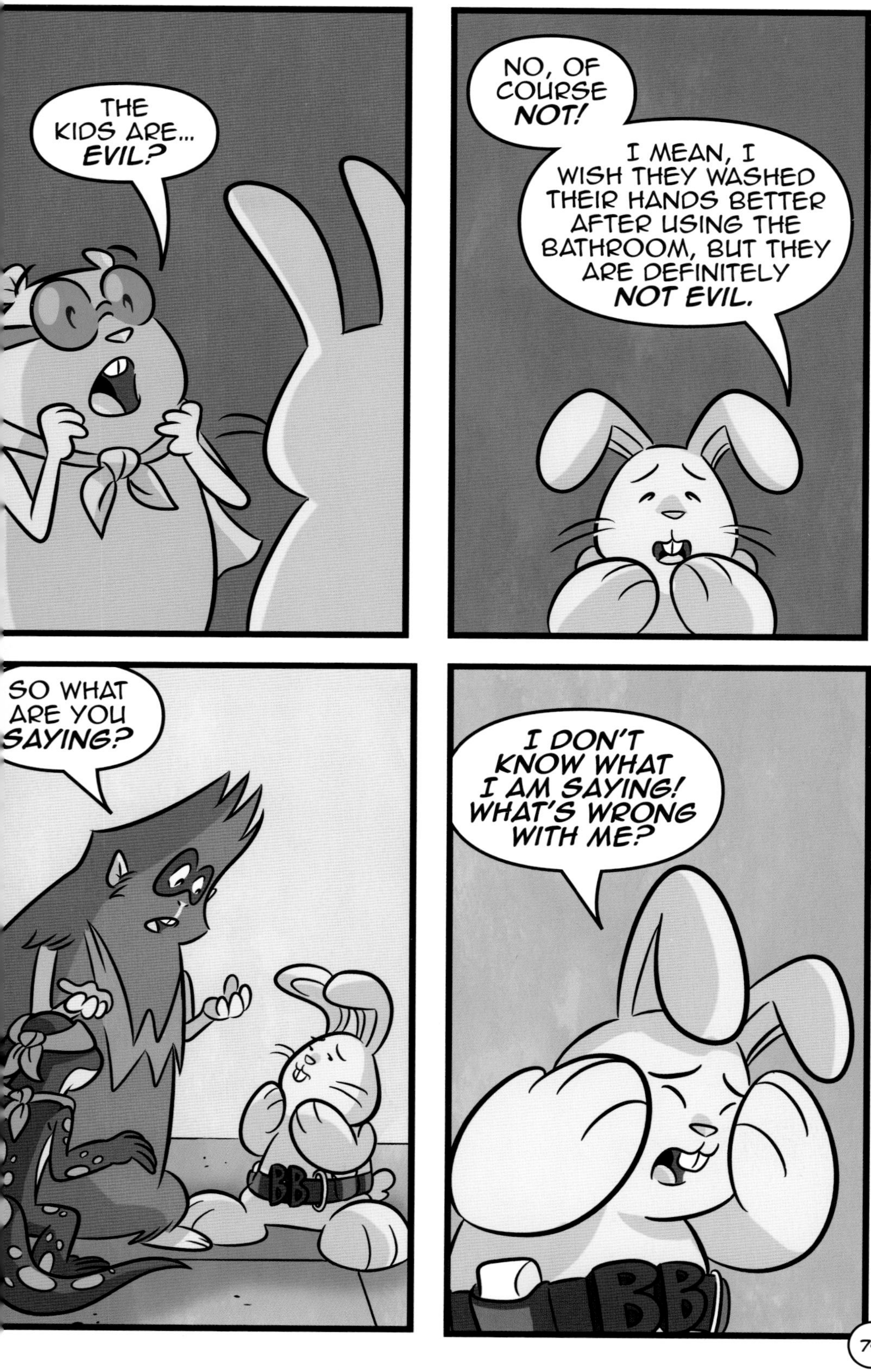
THE KIDS ARE... EVIL?
NO, OF COURSE NOT!
I MEAN, I WISH THEY WASHED THEIR HANDS BETTER AFTER USING THE BATHROOM, BUT THEY ARE DEFINITELY NOT EVIL.
SO WHAT ARE YOU SAYING?
I DON'T KNOW WHAT I AM SAYING! WHAT'S WRONG WITH ME?
BB
BB

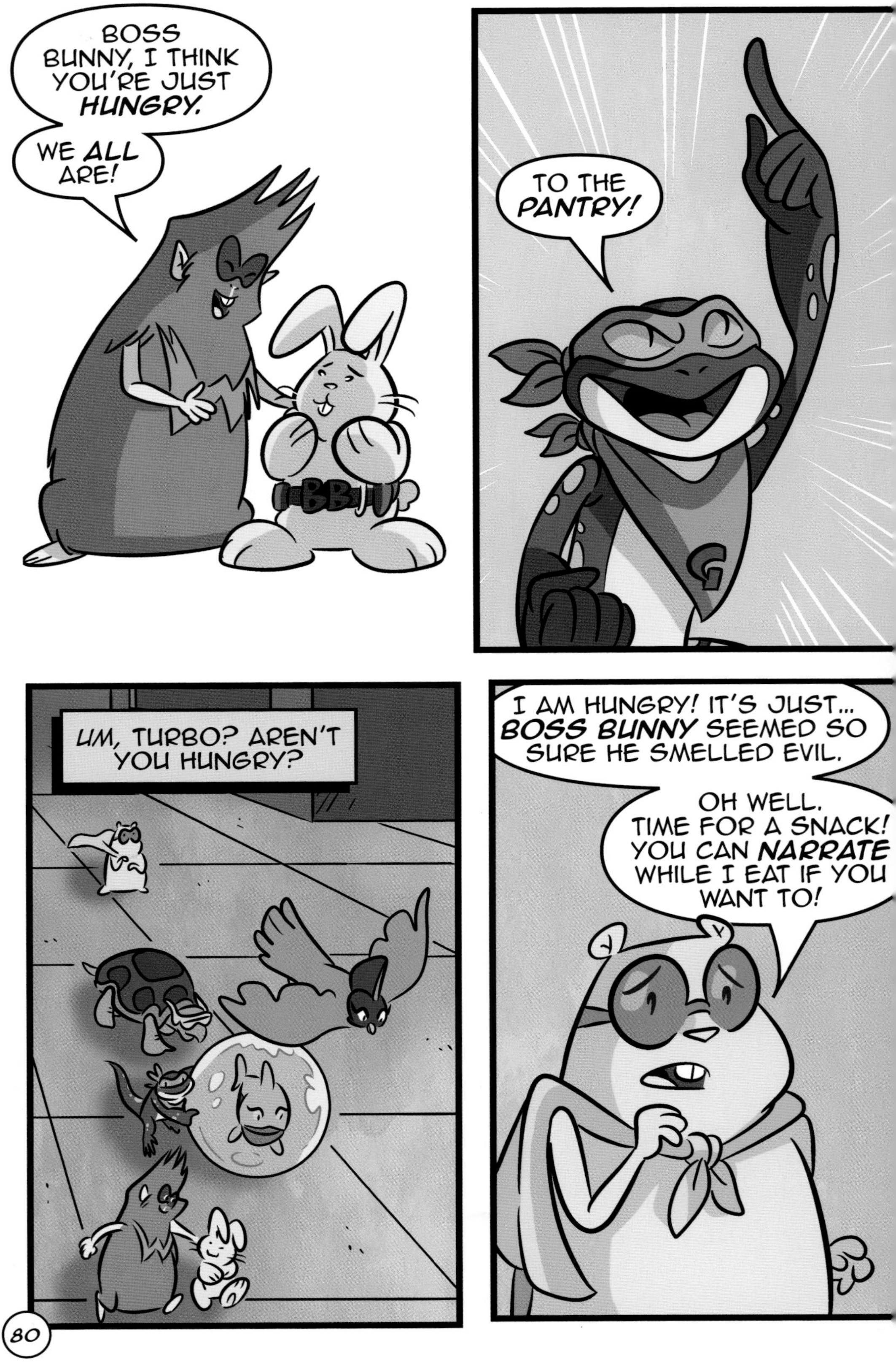
BOSS BUNNY, I THINK YOU'RE JUST HUNGRY.
WE ALL ARE!
TO THE PANTRY!
UM, TURBO? AREN'T YOU HUNGRY?
I AM HUNGRY! IT'S JUST... BOSS BUNNY SEEMED SO SURE HE SMELLED EVIL.
OH WELL. TIME FOR A SNACK! YOU CAN NARRATE WHILE I EAT IF YOU WANT TO!

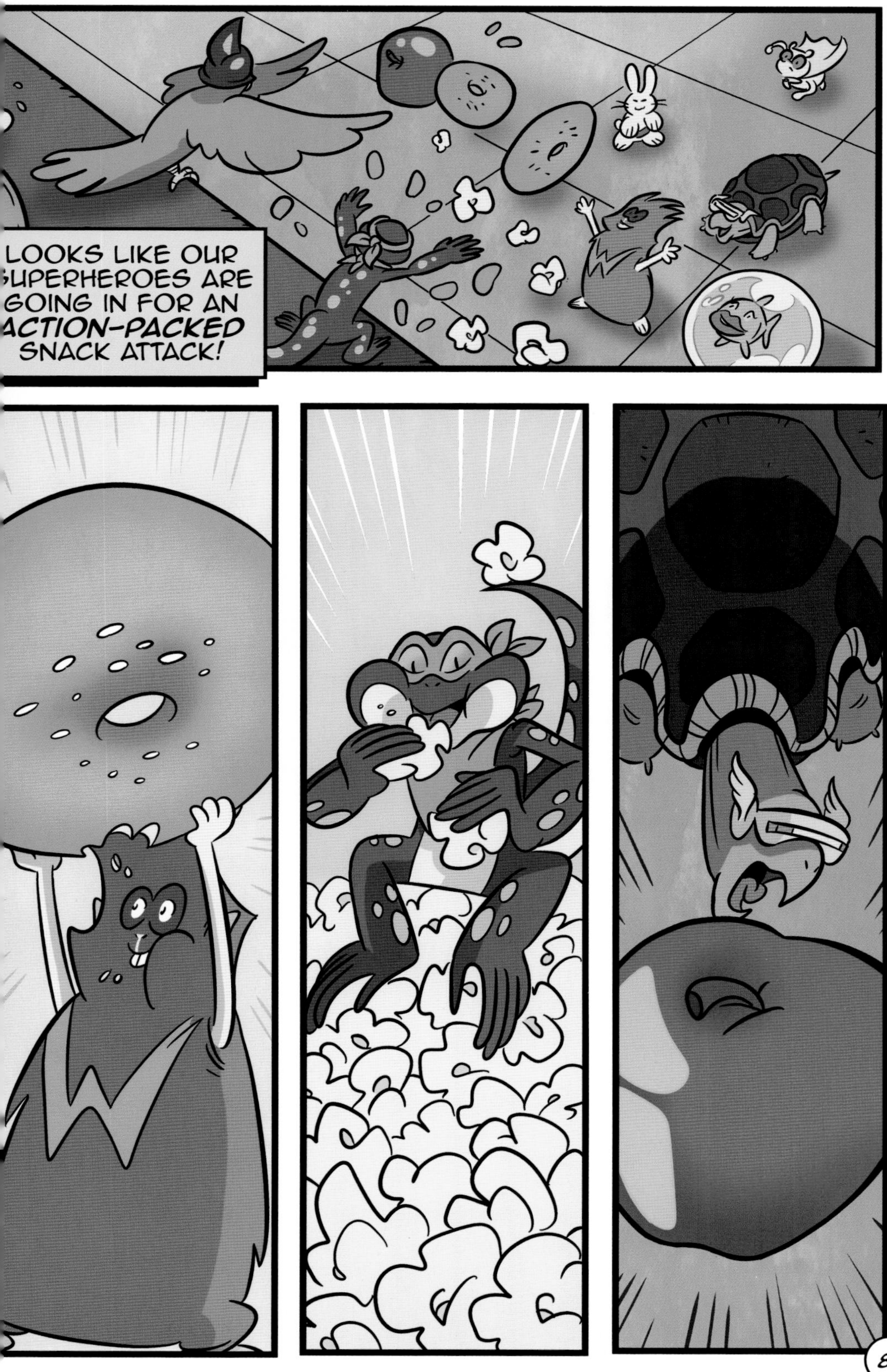
LOOKS LIKE OUR SUPERHEROES ARE GOING IN FOR AN ACTION-PACKED SNACK ATTACK!

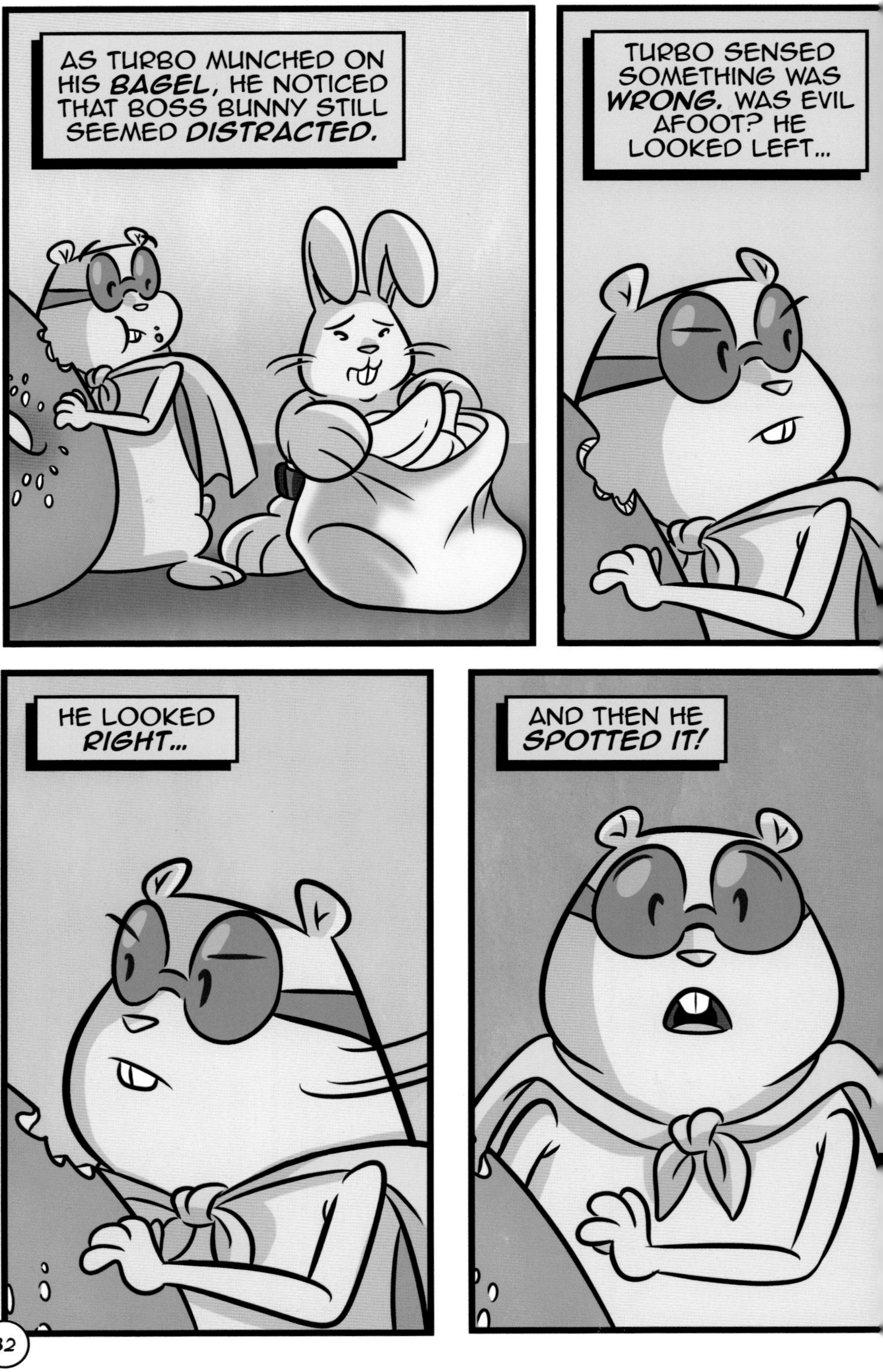
AS TURBO MUNCHED ON HIS BAGEL, HE NOTICED THAT BOSS BUNNY STILL SEEMED DISTRACTED.
TURBO SENSED SOMETHING WAS WRONG. WAS EVIL AFOOT? HE LOOKED LEFT...
HE LOOKED RIGHT...
AND THEN HE SPOTTED IT!

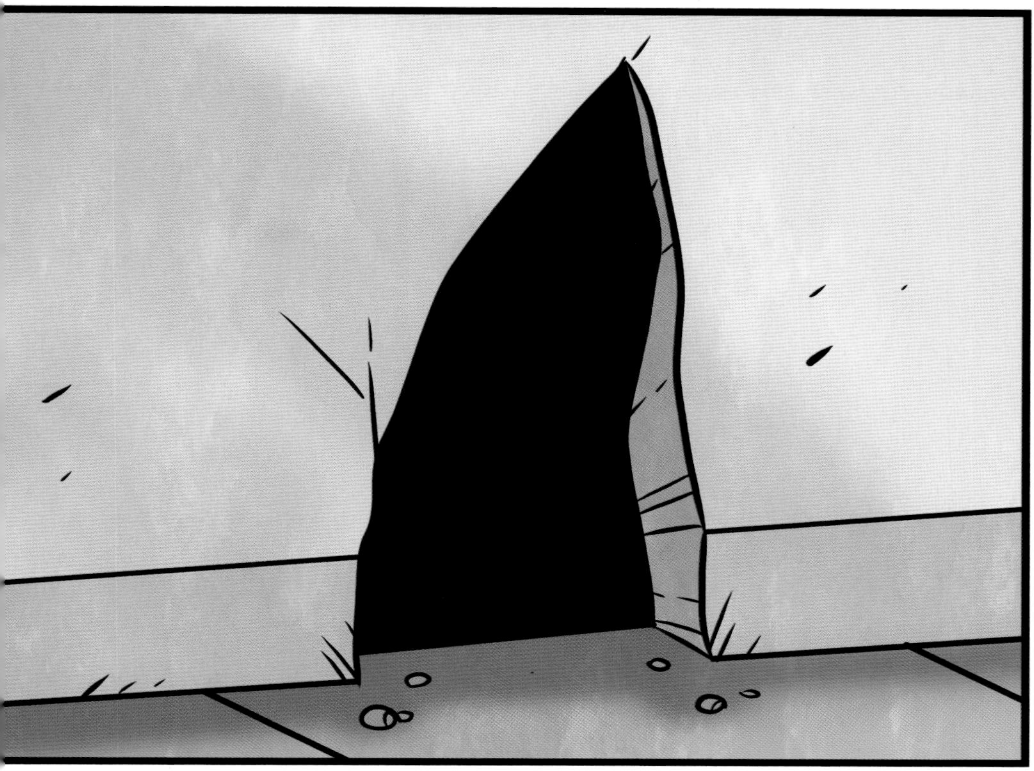

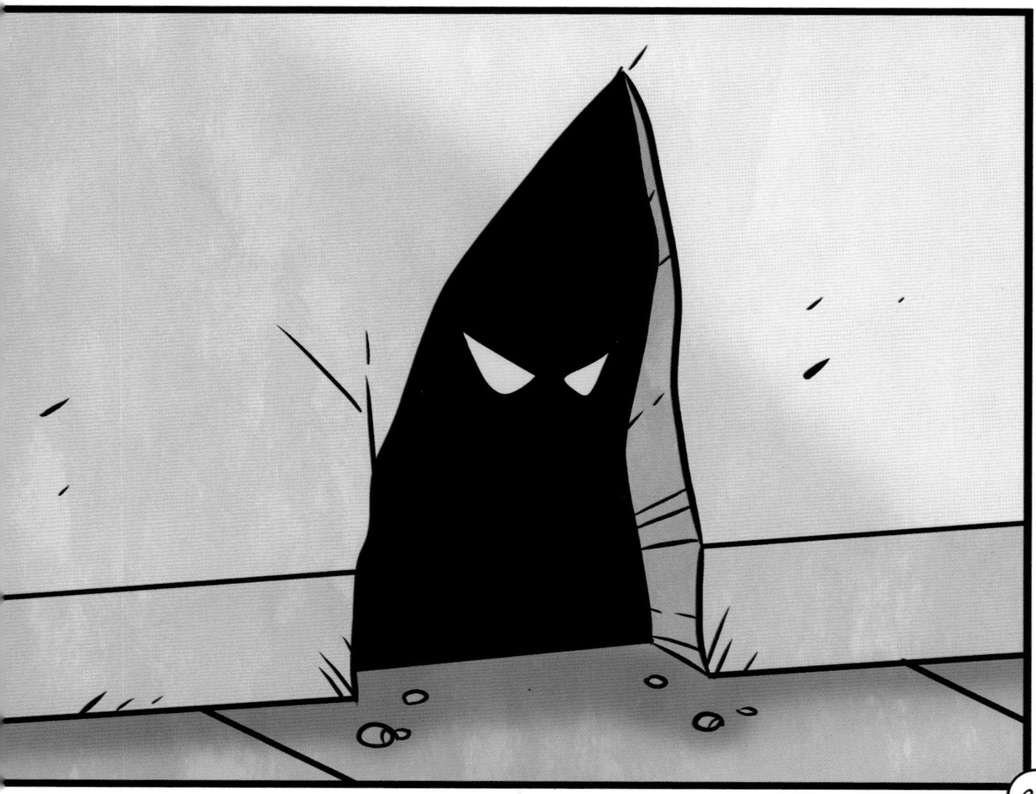

CHAPTER 7

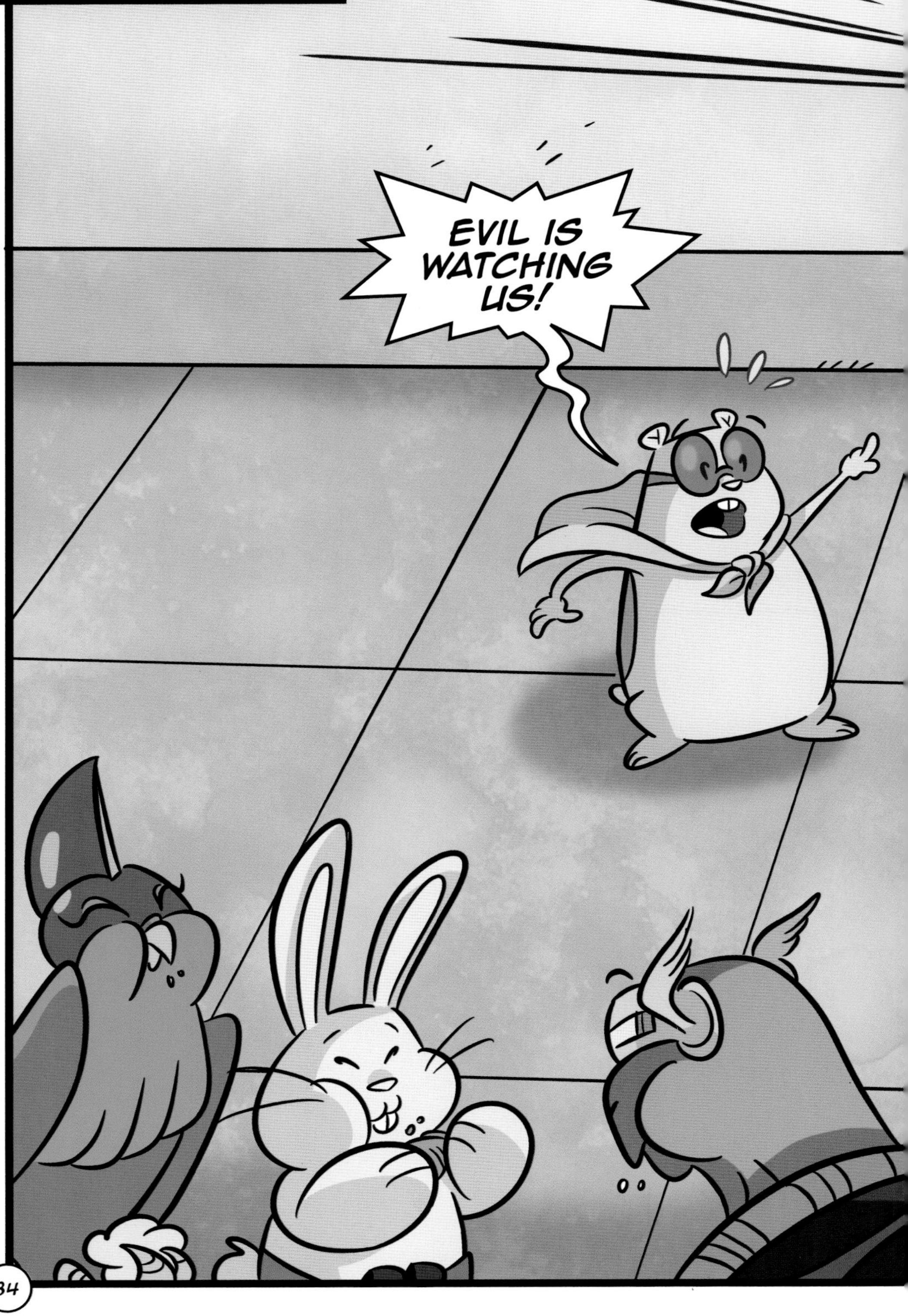
EVIL IS WATCHING US!

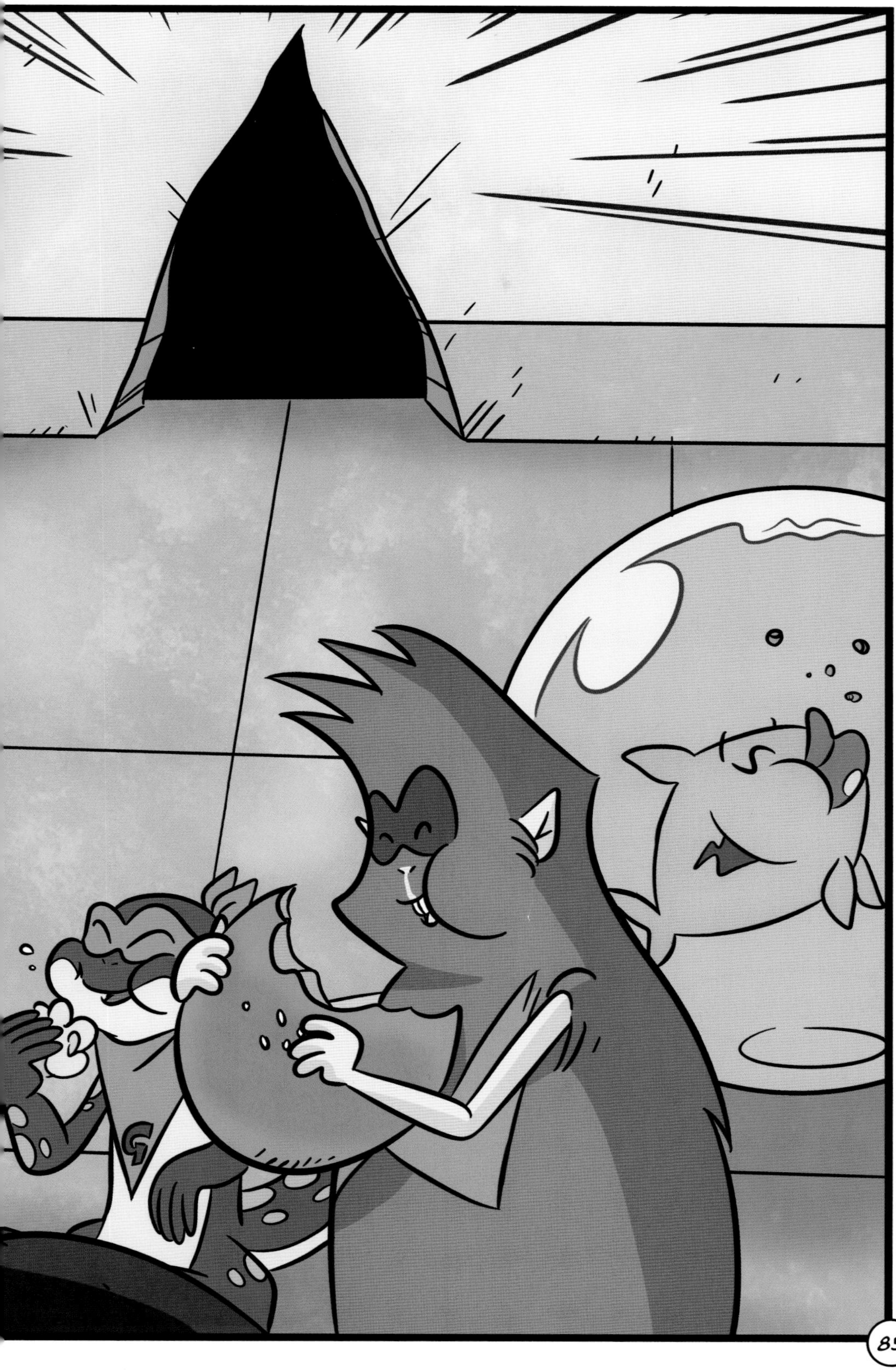

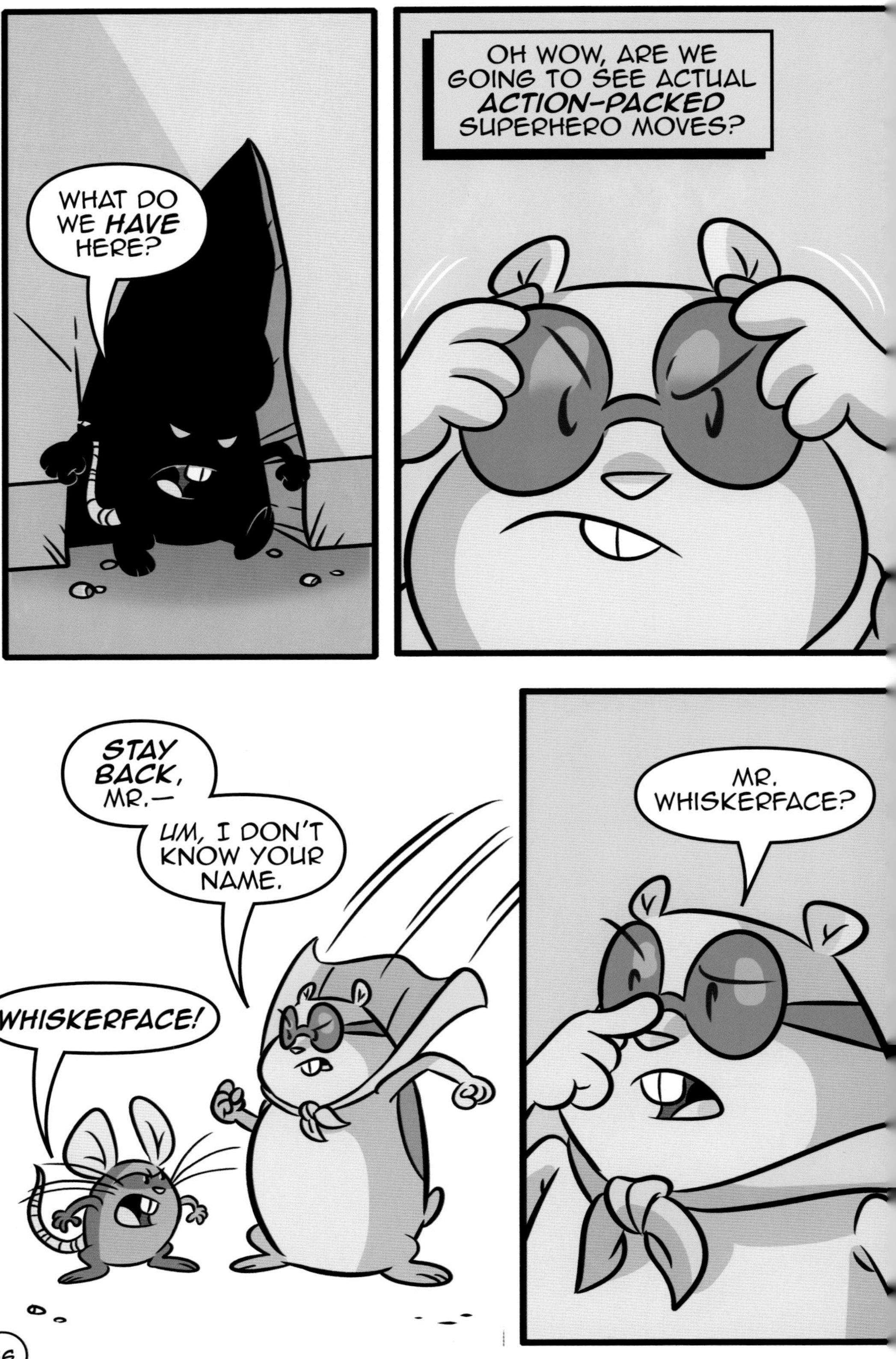
WHAT DO WE *HAVE* HERE?
OH WOW, ARE WE GOING TO SEE ACTUAL *ACTION-PACKED* SUPERHERO MOVES?
STAY BACK, MR.—
UM, I DON'T KNOW YOUR NAME.
WHISKERFACE!
MR. WHISKERFACE?

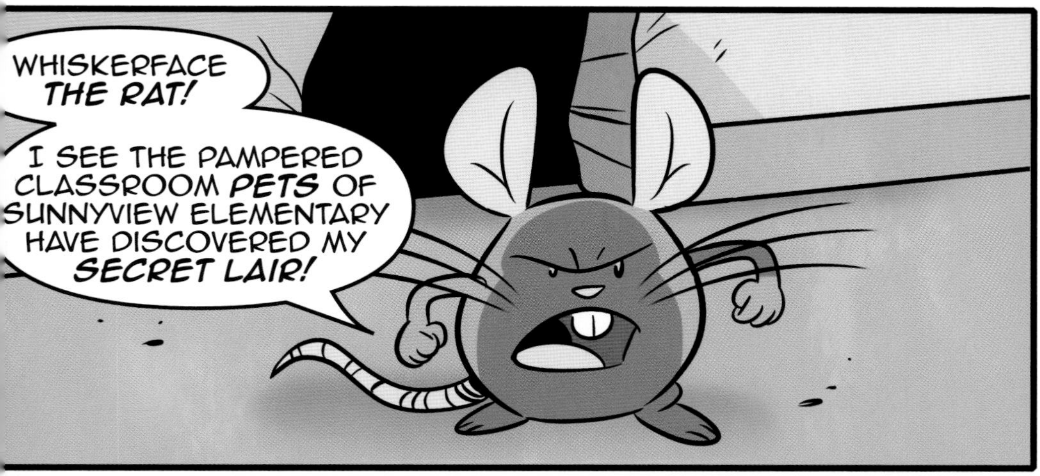
WHISKERFACE *THE RAT!*
I SEE THE PAMPERED CLASSROOM *PETS* OF SUNNYVIEW ELEMENTARY HAVE DISCOVERED MY *SECRET LAIR!*

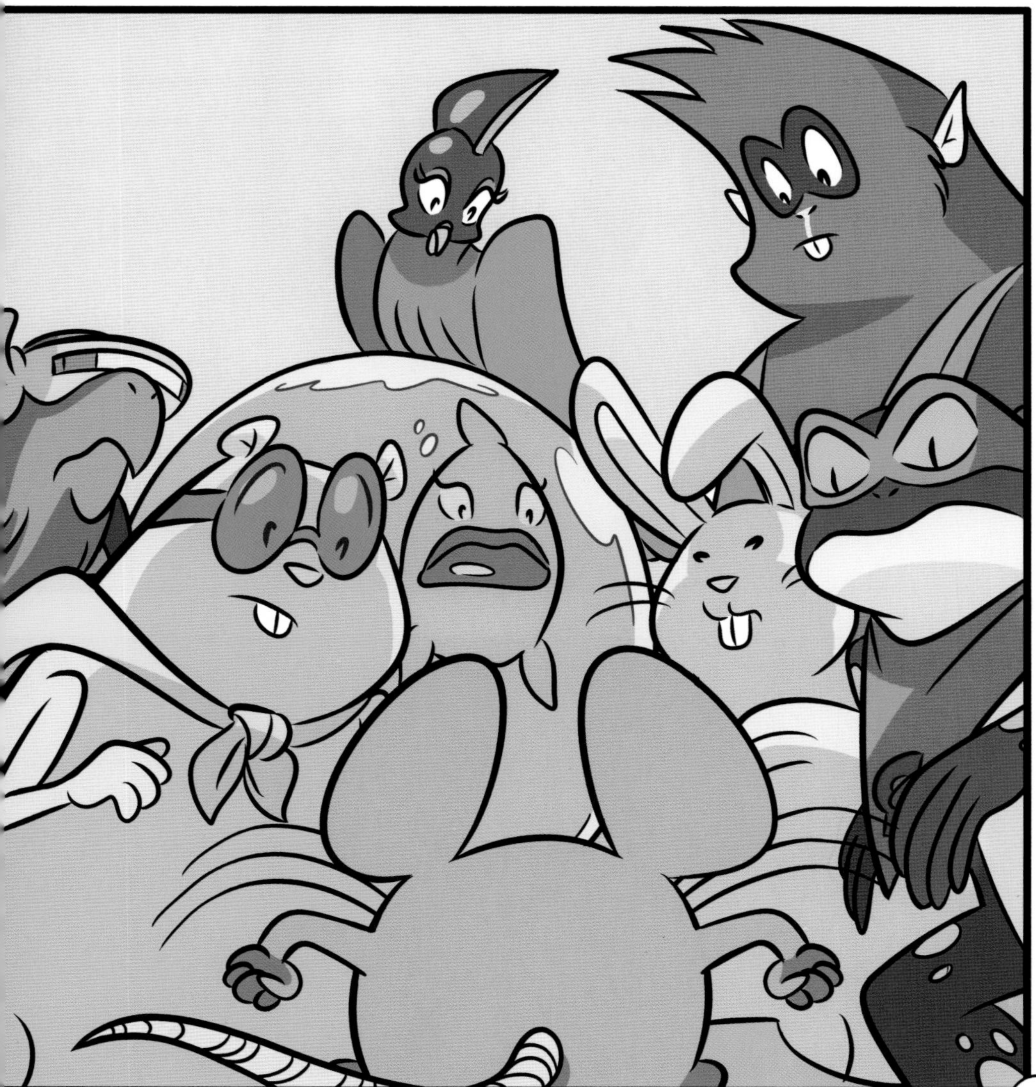

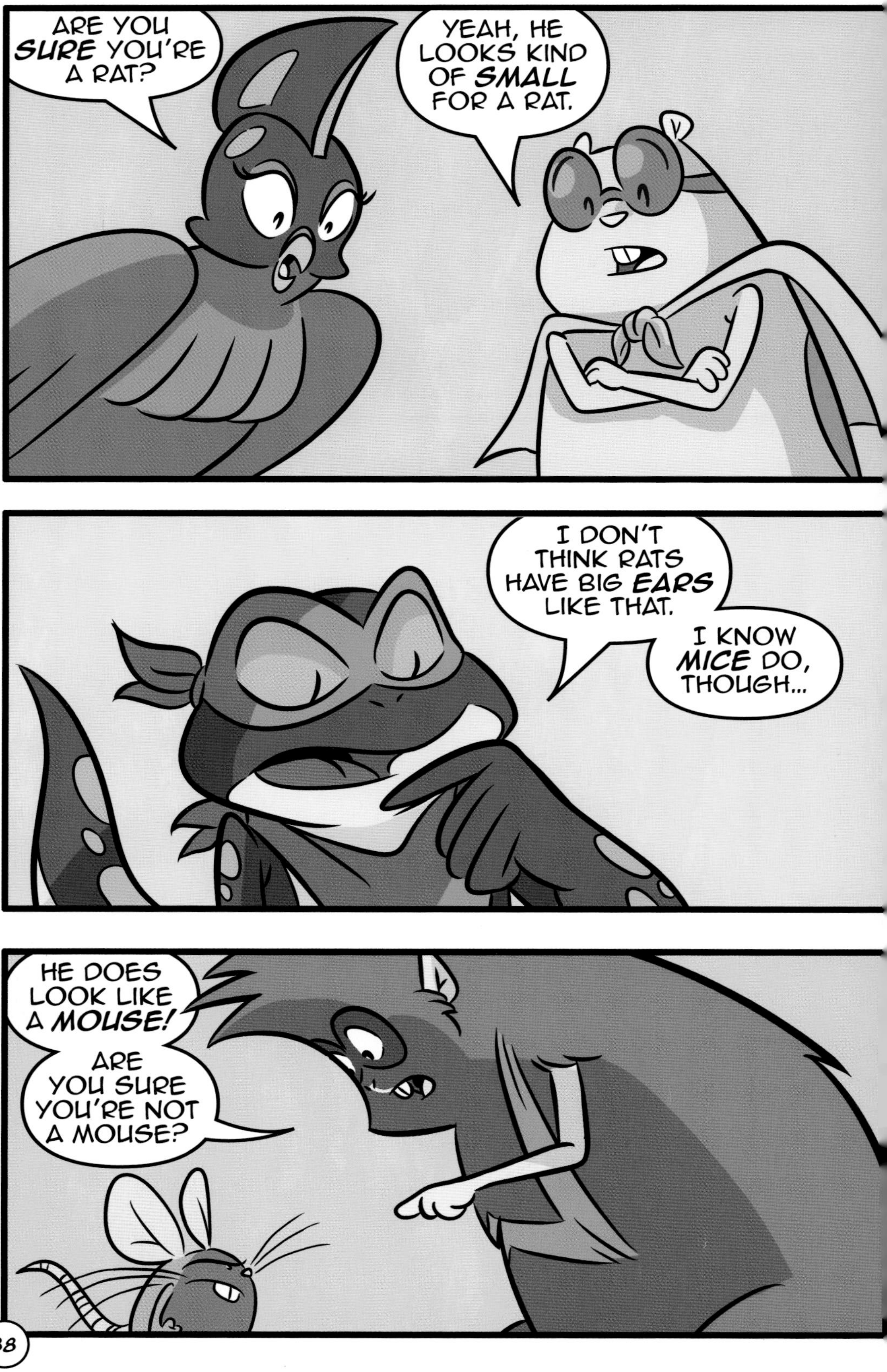
ARE YOU SURE YOU'RE A RAT?
YEAH, HE LOOKS KIND OF SMALL FOR A RAT.
I DON'T THINK RATS HAVE BIG EARS LIKE THAT.
I KNOW MICE DO, THOUGH...
HE DOES LOOK LIKE A MOUSE!
ARE YOU SURE YOU'RE NOT A MOUSE?

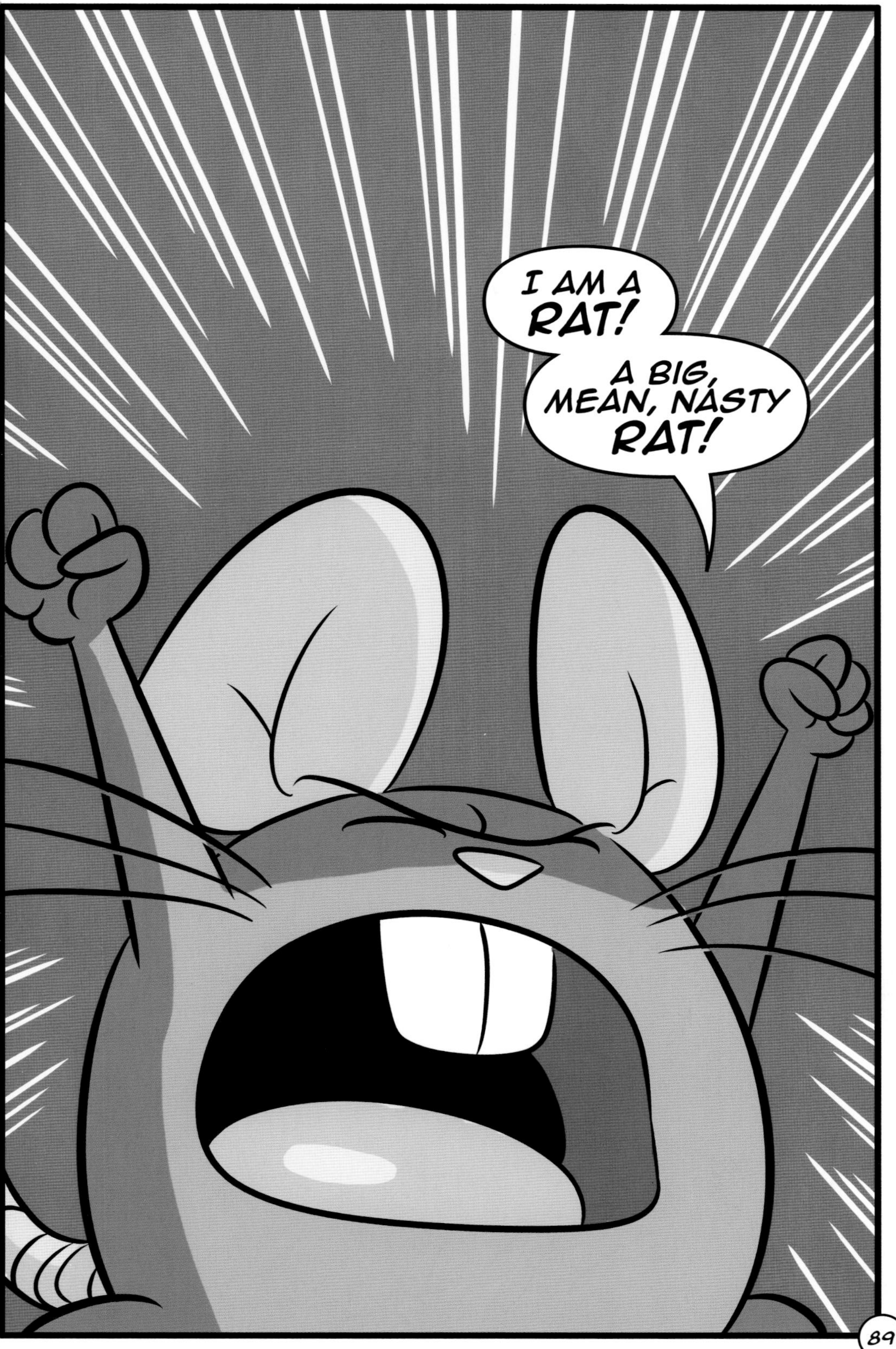
I AM A RAT!
A BIG, MEAN, NASTY RAT!

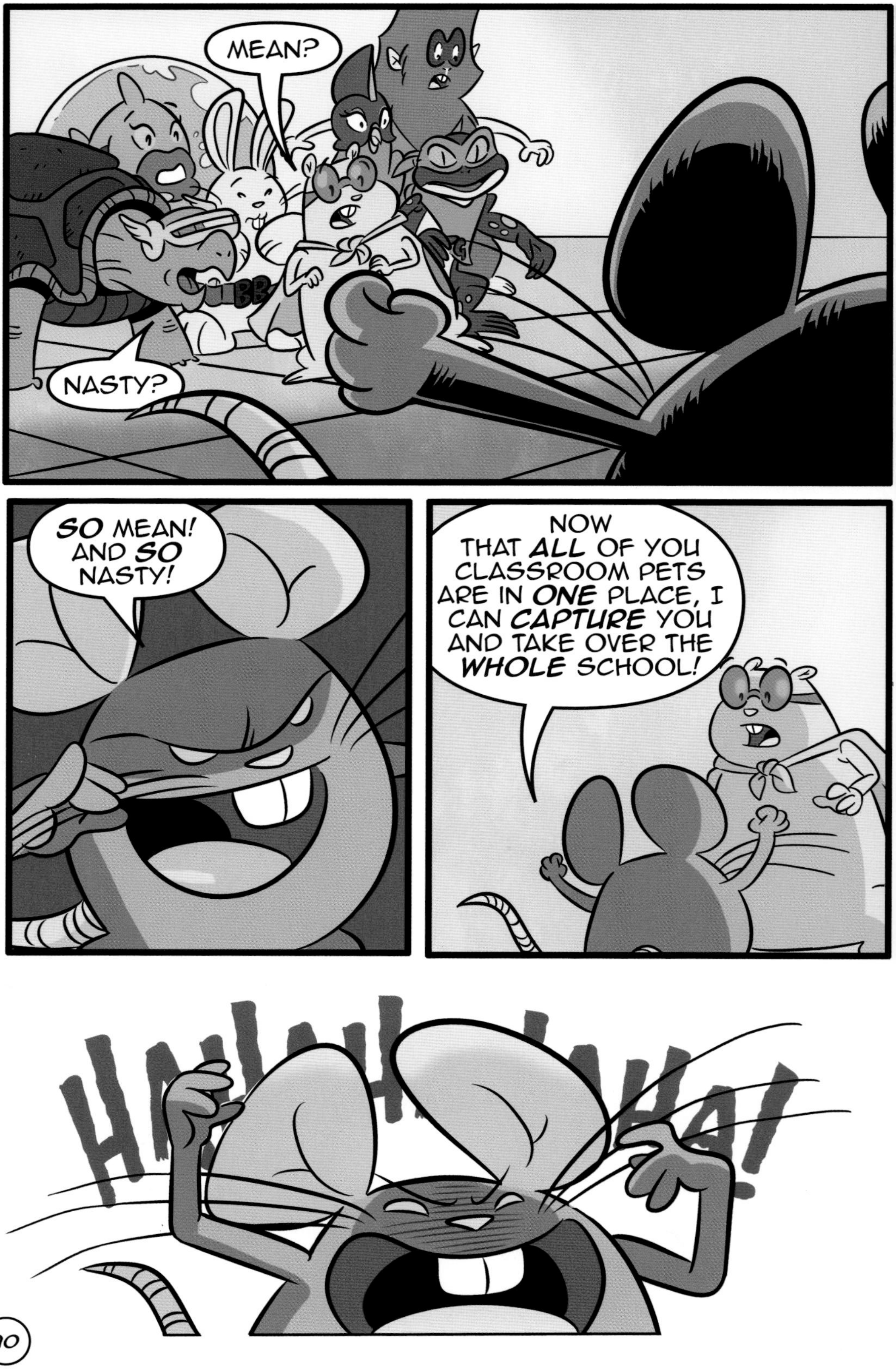
MEAN?
NASTY?
SO MEAN! AND SO NASTY!
NOW THAT ALL OF YOU CLASSROOM PETS ARE IN ONE PLACE, I CAN CAPTURE YOU AND TAKE OVER THE WHOLE SCHOOL!

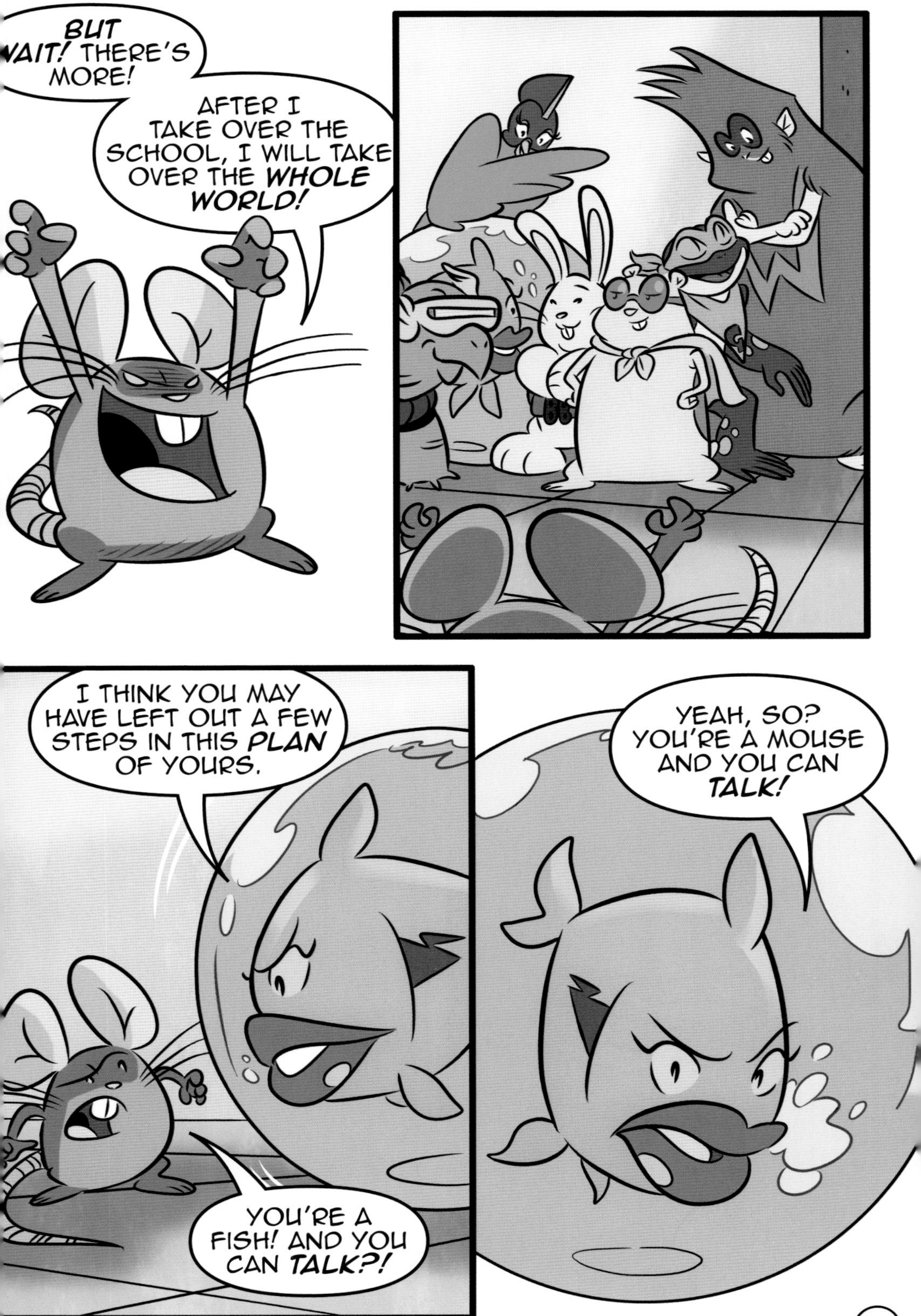
BUT WAIT! THERE'S MORE!
AFTER I TAKE OVER THE SCHOOL, I WILL TAKE OVER THE WHOLE WORLD!
I THINK YOU MAY HAVE LEFT OUT A FEW STEPS IN THIS PLAN OF YOURS.
YOU'RE A FISH! AND YOU CAN TALK?!
YEAH, SO? YOU'RE A MOUSE AND YOU CAN TALK!

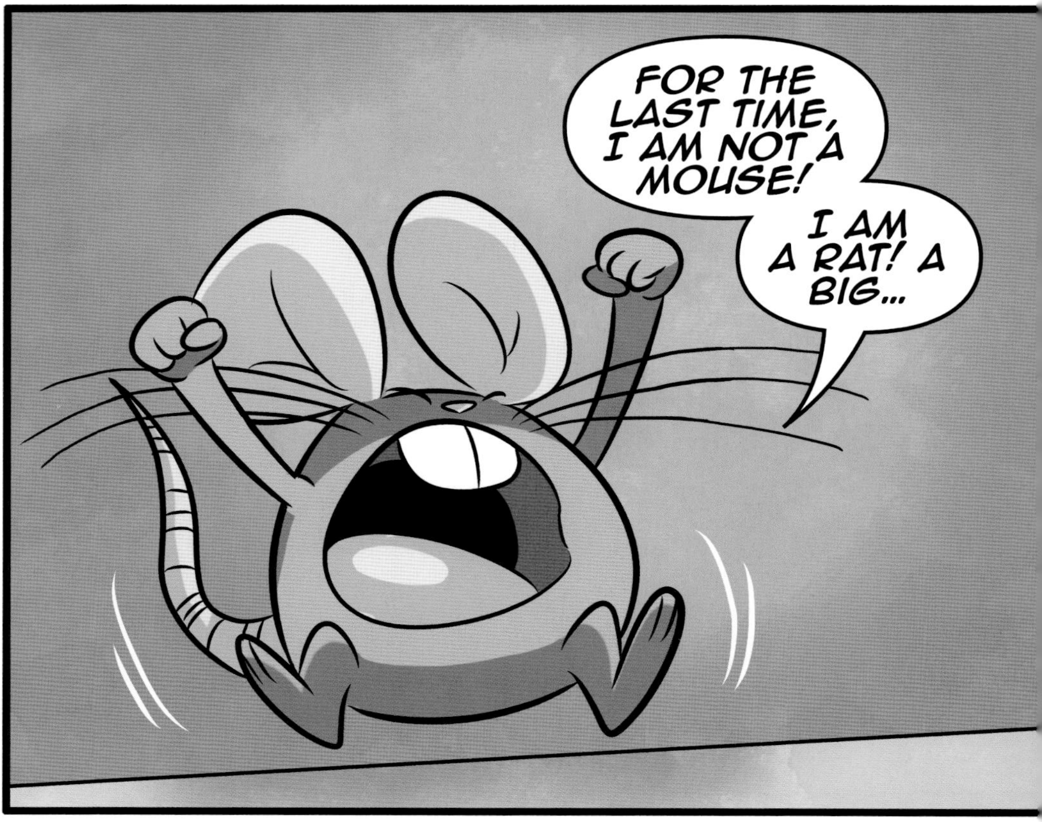
FOR THE LAST TIME, I AM NOT A MOUSE!
I AM A RAT! A BIG...

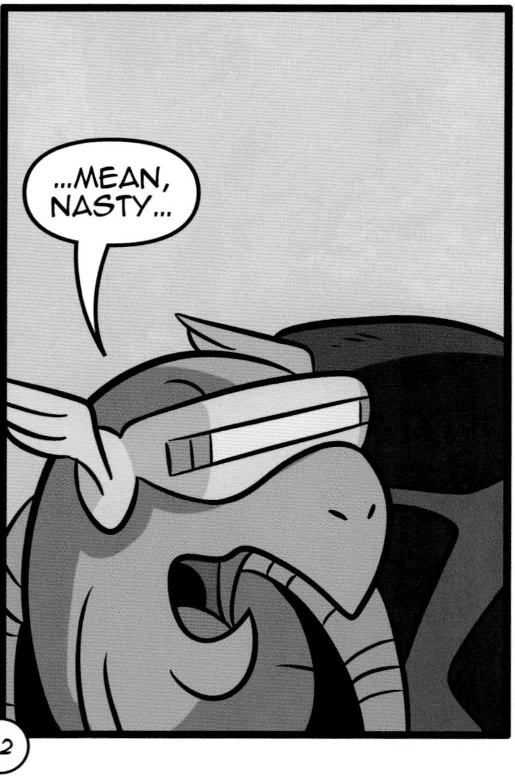
...MEAN, NASTY...

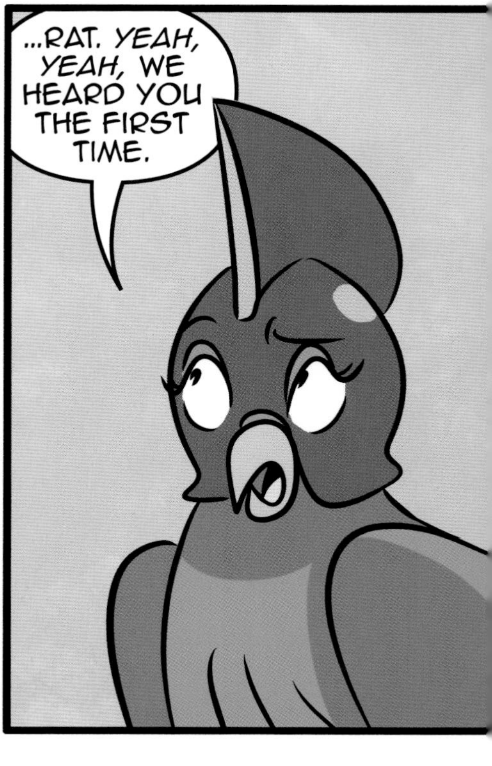
...RAT. YEAH, YEAH, WE HEARD YOU THE FIRST TIME.

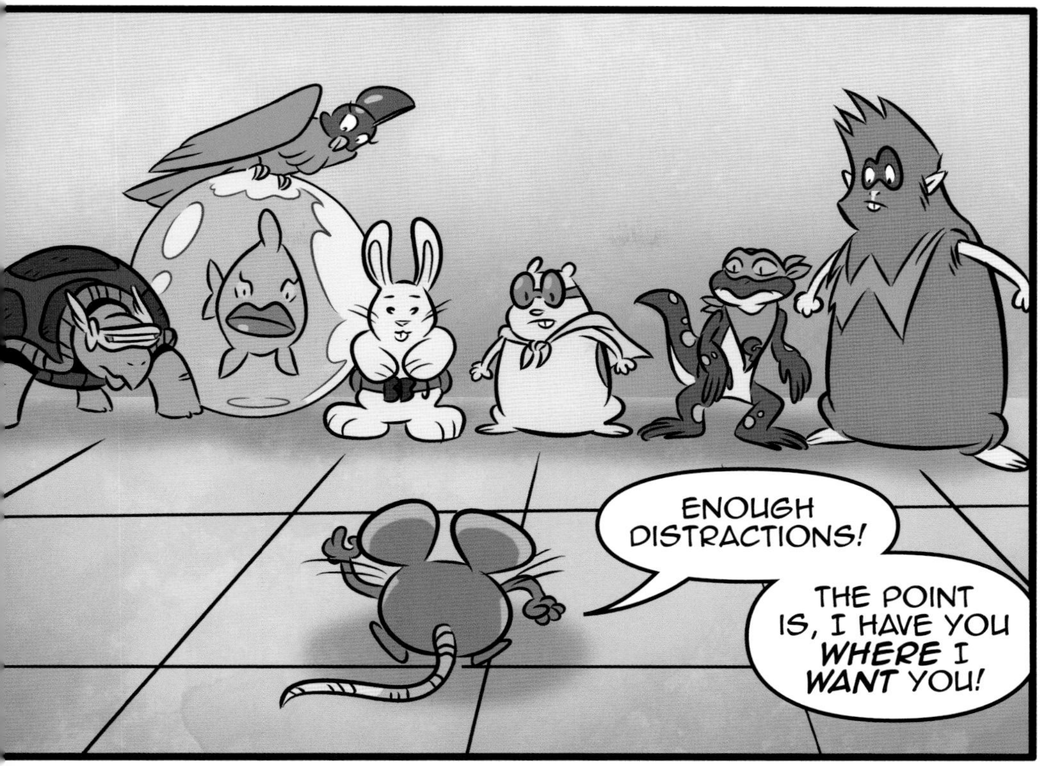
ENOUGH DISTRACTIONS!
THE POINT IS, I HAVE YOU *WHERE* I *WANT* YOU!
BB

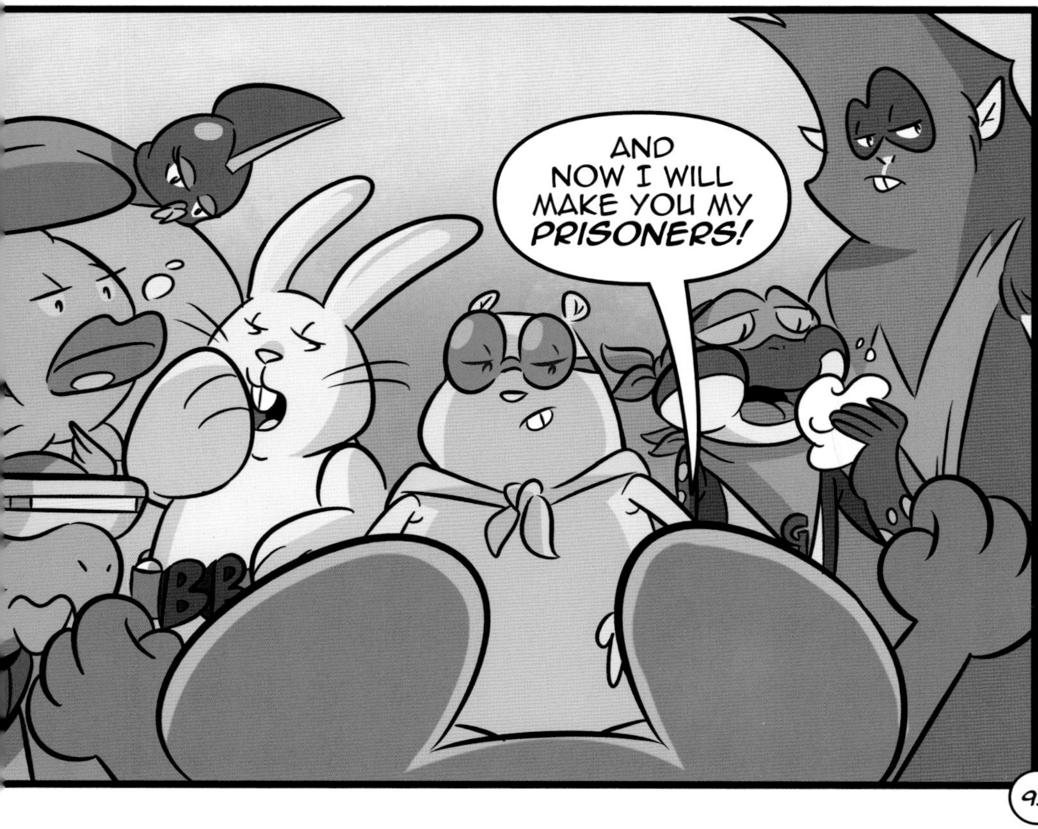
AND NOW I WILL MAKE YOU MY *PRISONERS!*
BB

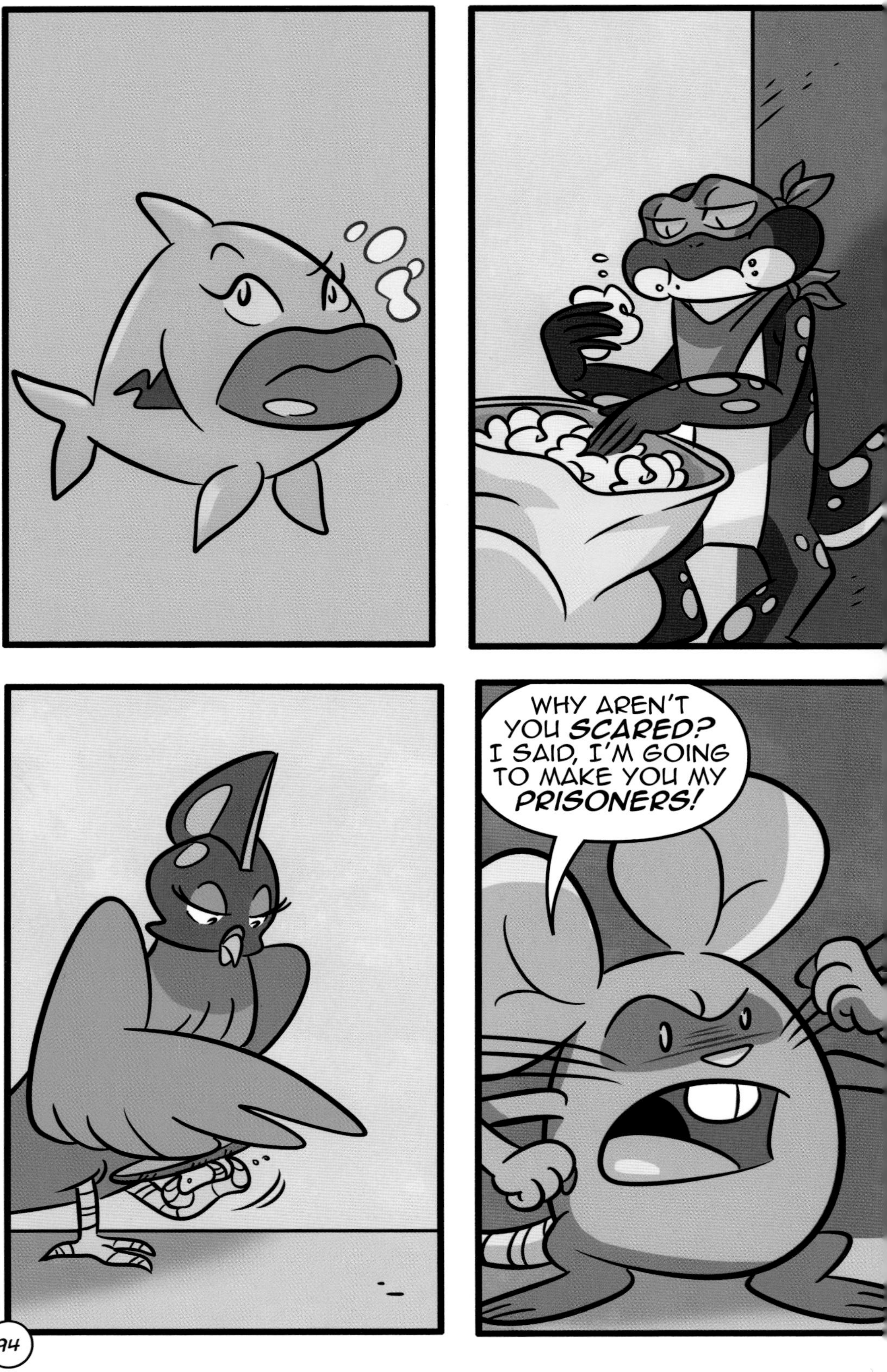
WHY AREN'T YOU *SCARED?* I SAID, I'M GOING TO MAKE YOU MY *PRISONERS!*

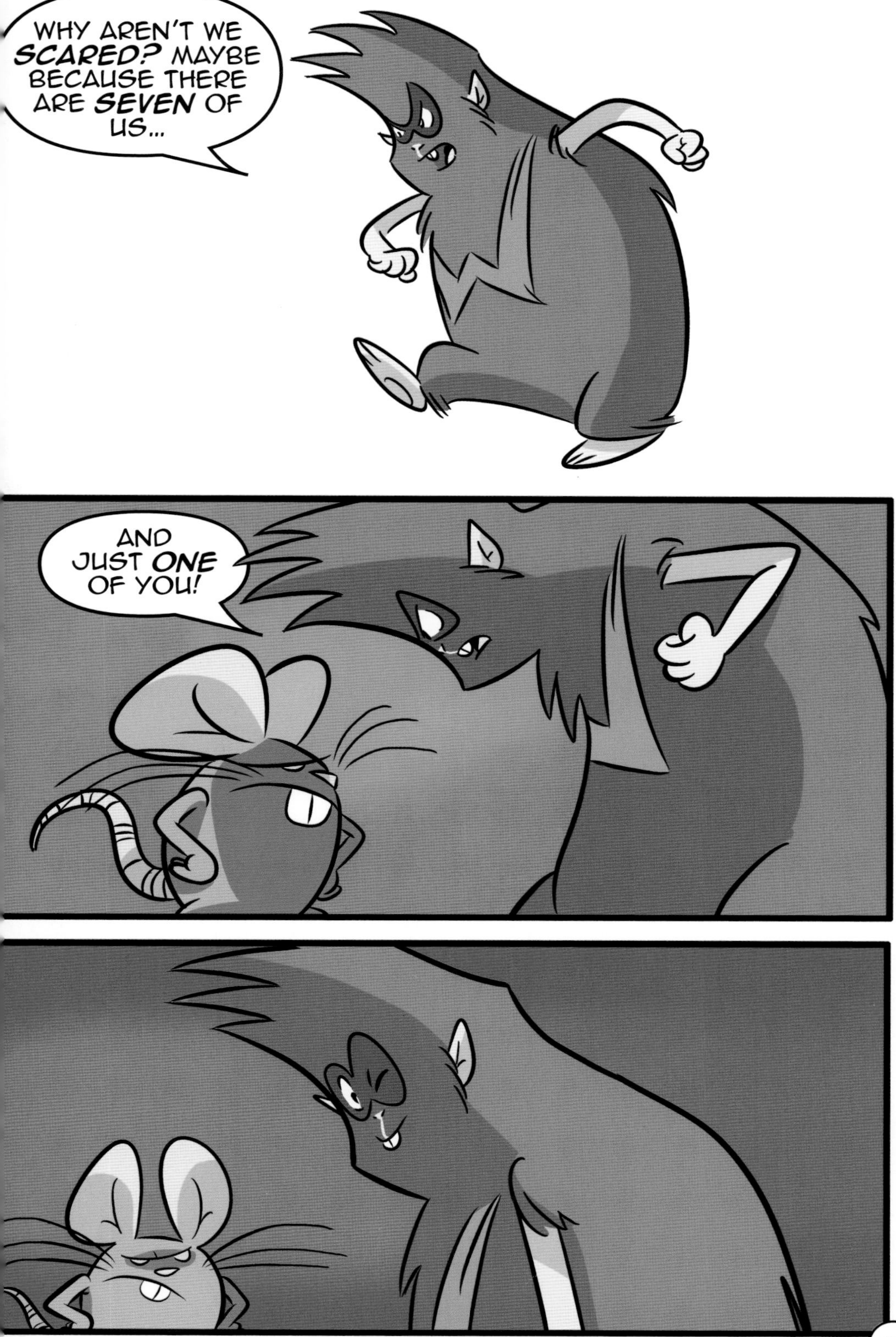
WHY AREN'T WE **SCARED?** MAYBE BECAUSE THERE ARE **SEVEN** OF US...
AND JUST **ONE** OF YOU!

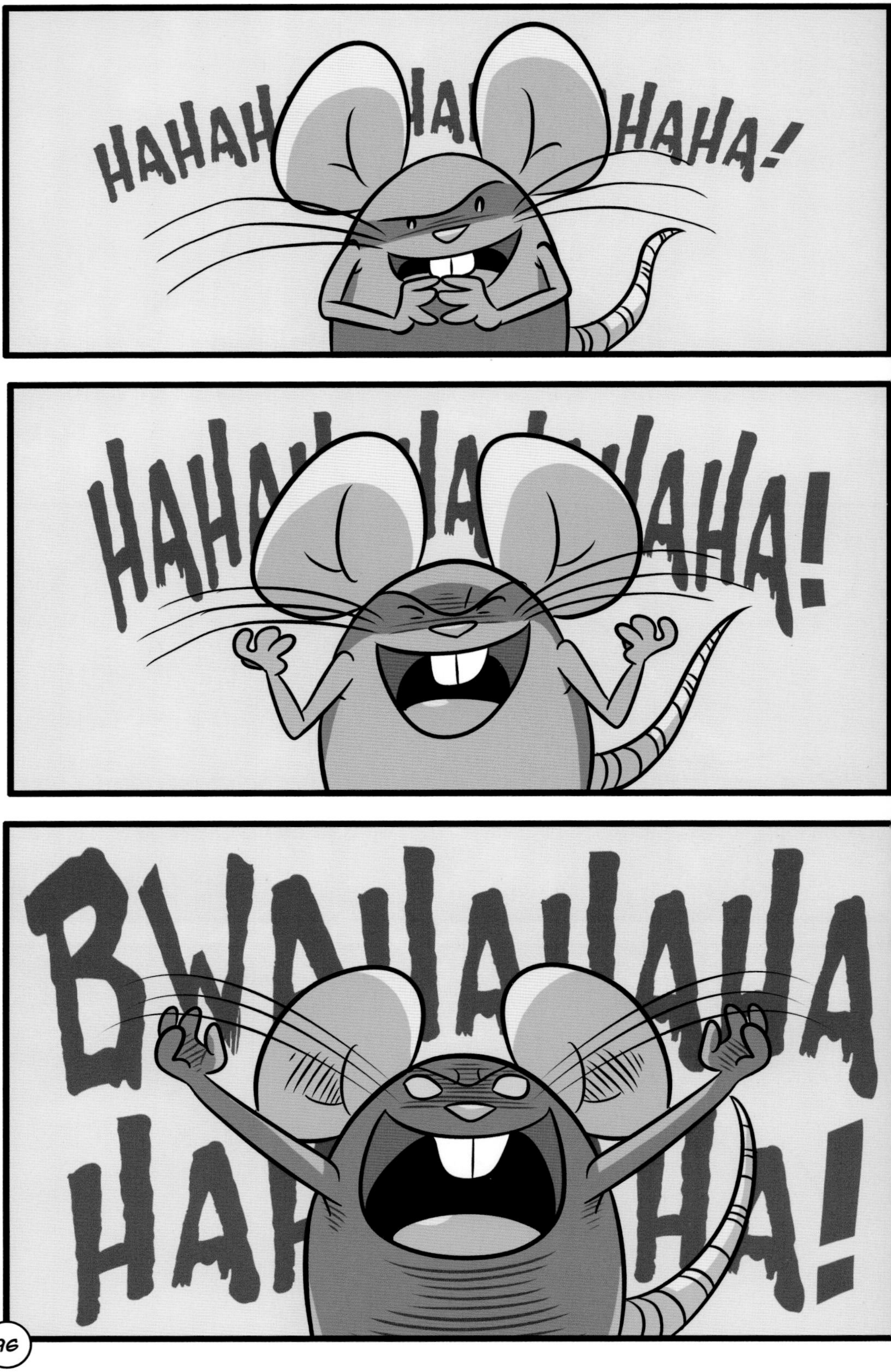
HAHAH
HA
HAHA!
HAHA
HA
HAHA!
BW
HA
HAHA!

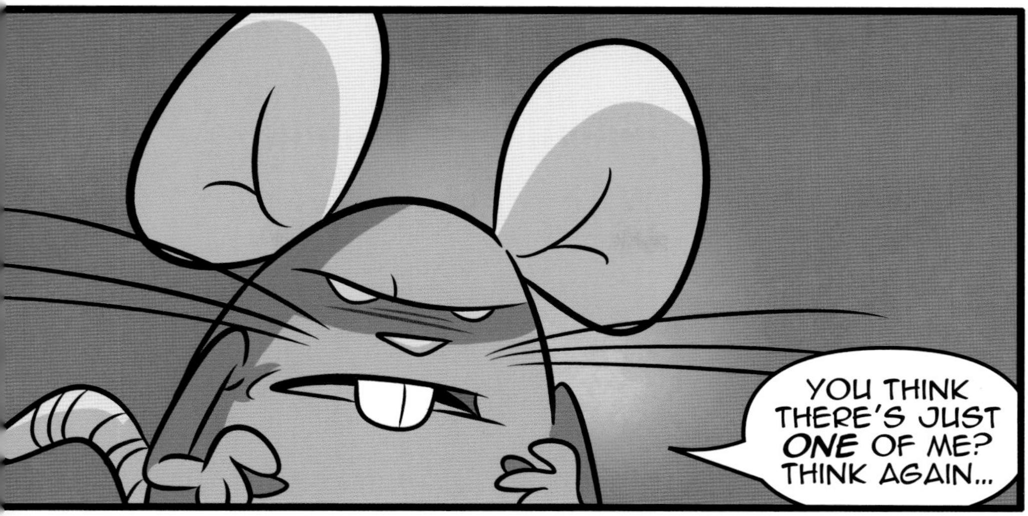
YOU THINK THERE'S JUST *ONE* OF ME? THINK AGAIN...

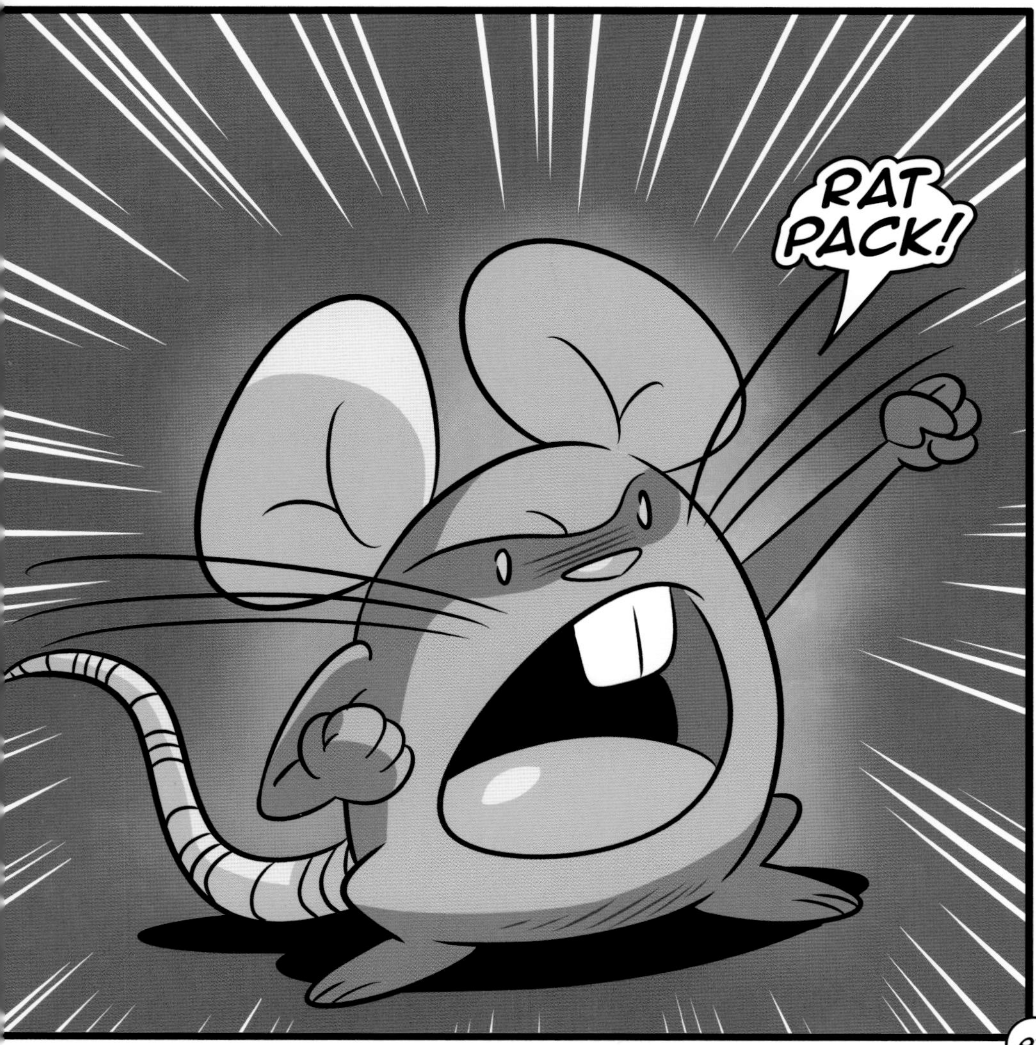
RAT PACK!

CHAPTER 8

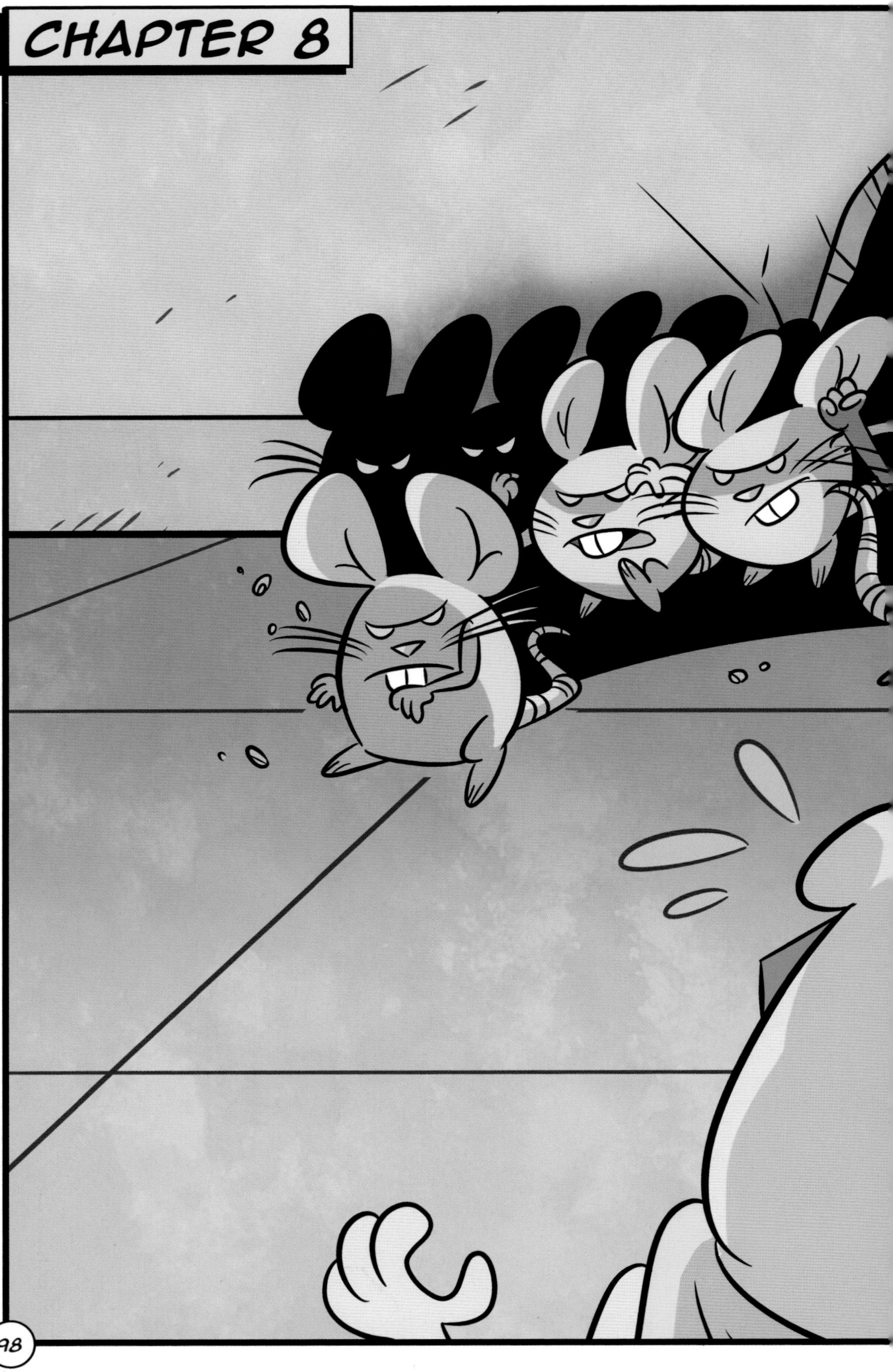

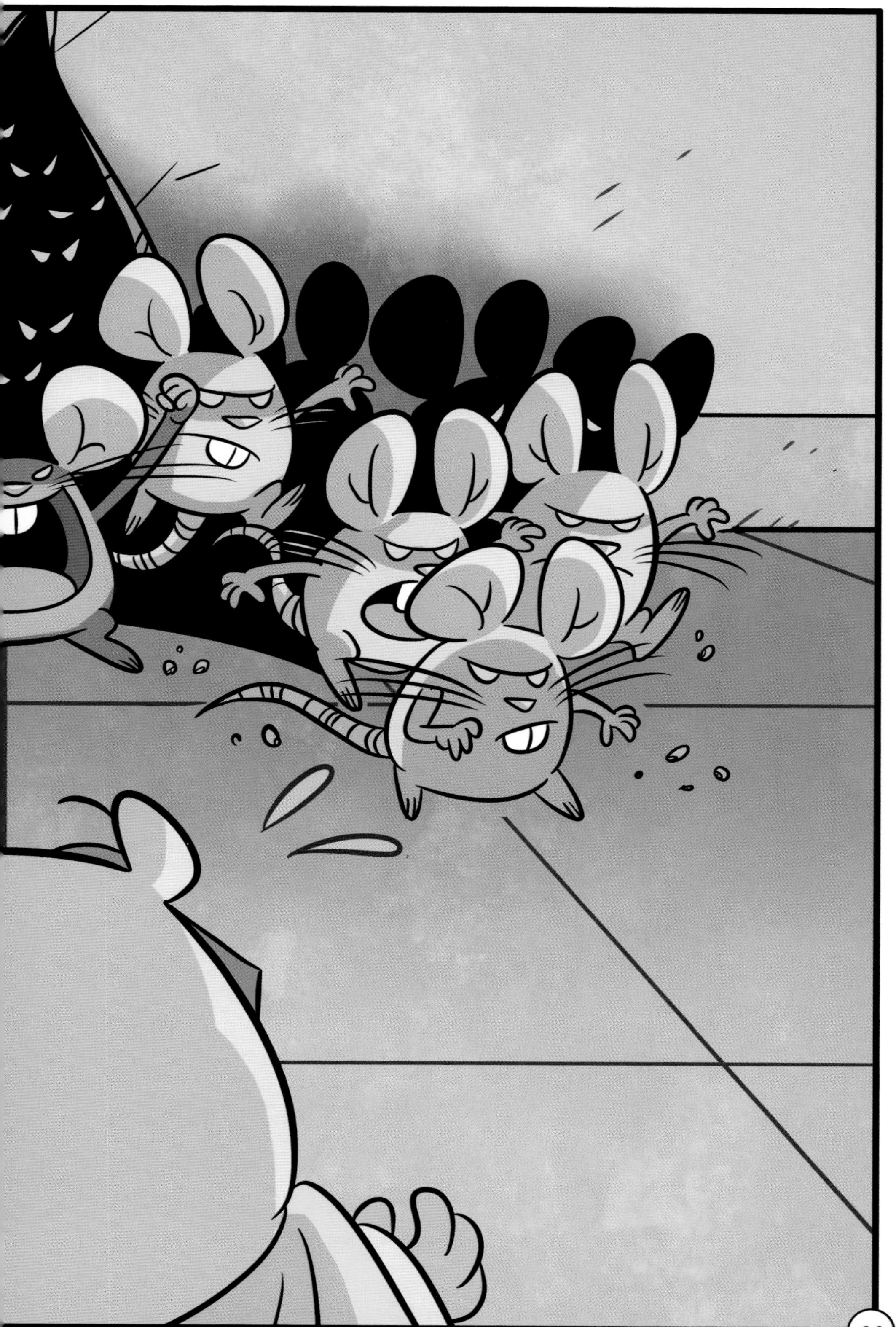

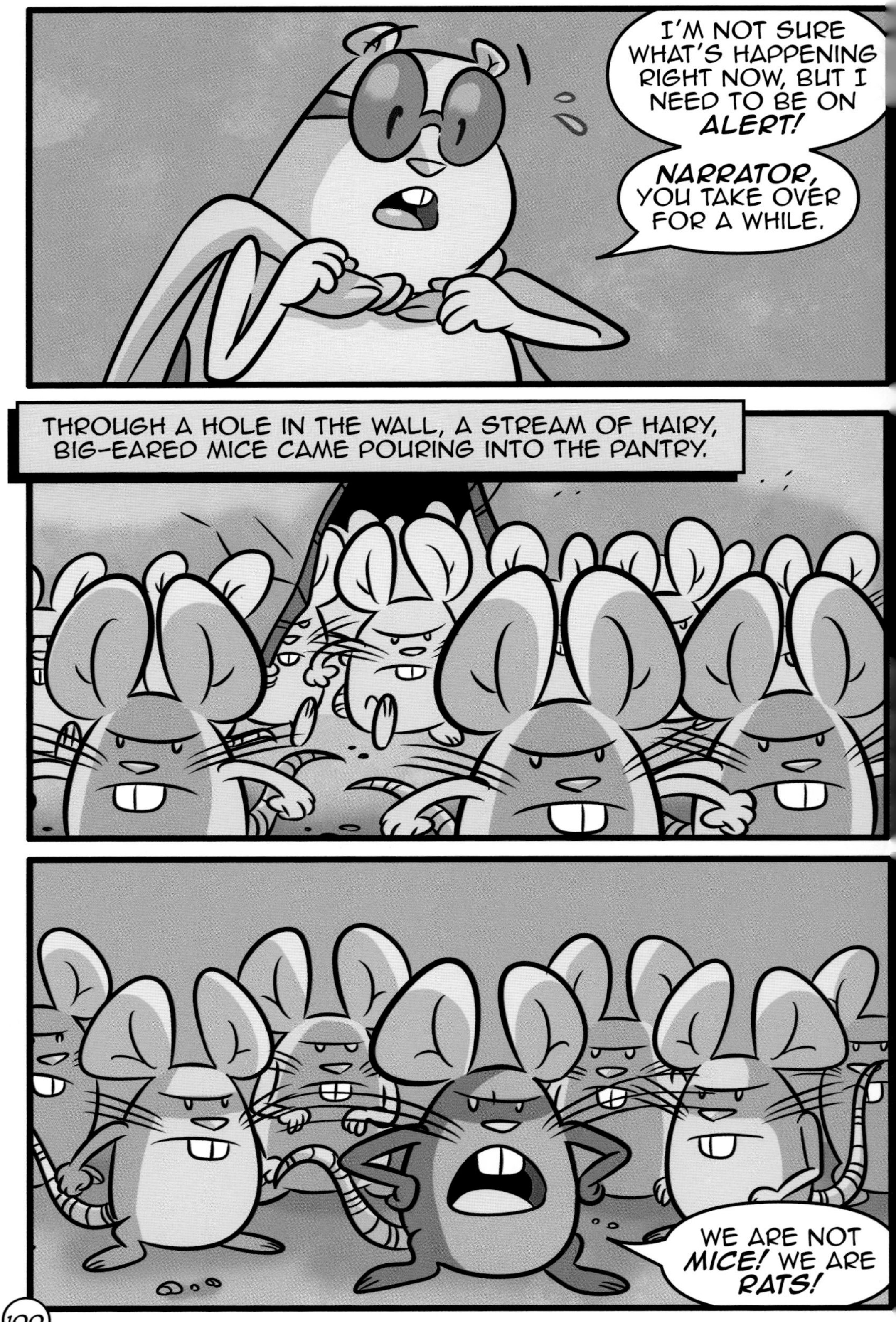
I'M NOT SURE WHAT'S HAPPENING RIGHT NOW, BUT I NEED TO BE ON ALERT!
NARRATOR, YOU TAKE OVER FOR A WHILE.
THROUGH A HOLE IN THE WALL, A STREAM OF HAIRY, BIG-EARED MICE CAME POURING INTO THE PANTRY.
WE ARE NOT MICE! WE ARE RATS!

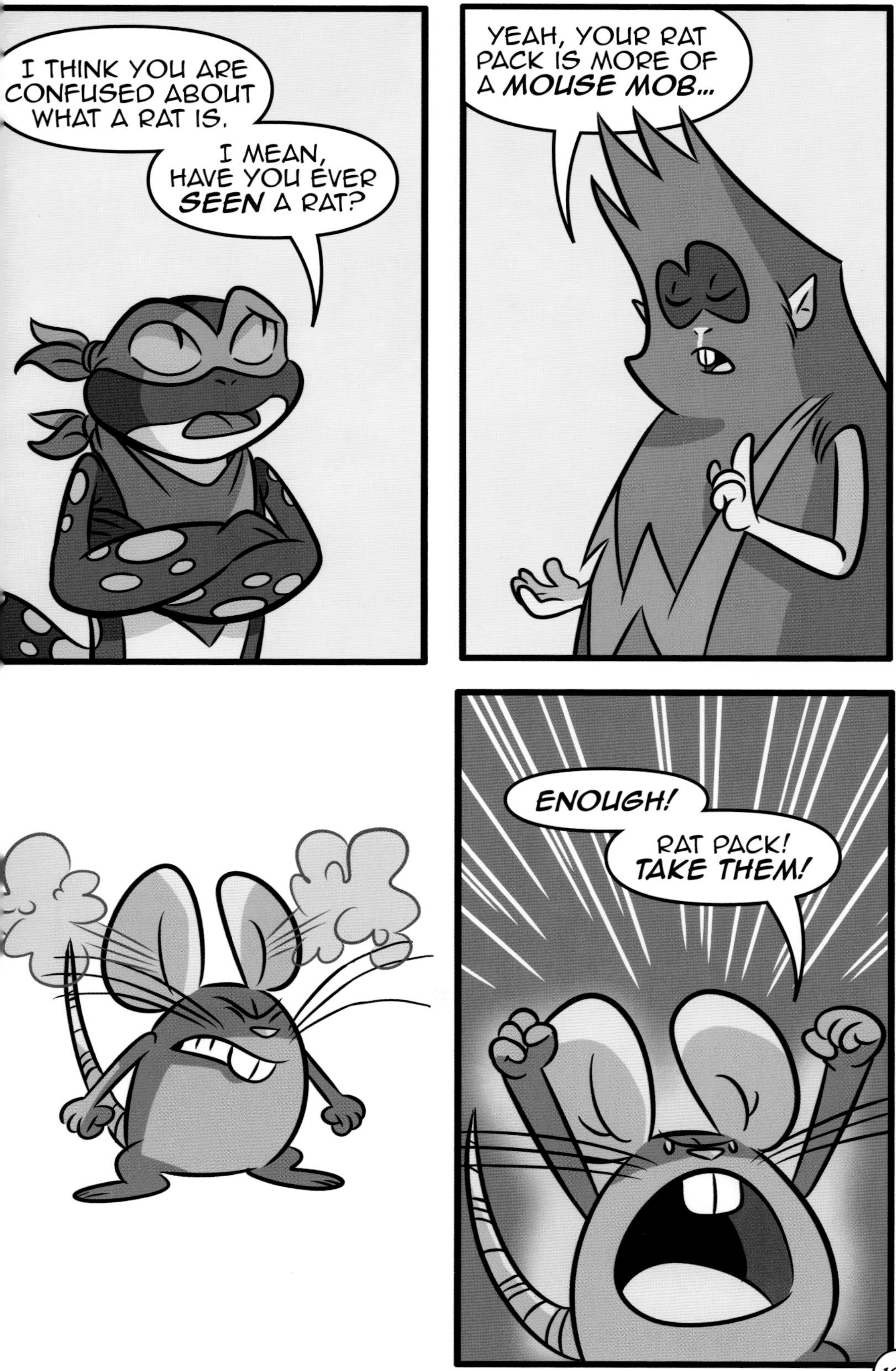
I THINK YOU ARE CONFUSED ABOUT WHAT A RAT IS.
I MEAN, HAVE YOU EVER *SEEN* A RAT?
YEAH, YOUR RAT PACK IS MORE OF A *MOUSE MOB*...
ENOUGH!
RAT PACK! *TAKE THEM!*

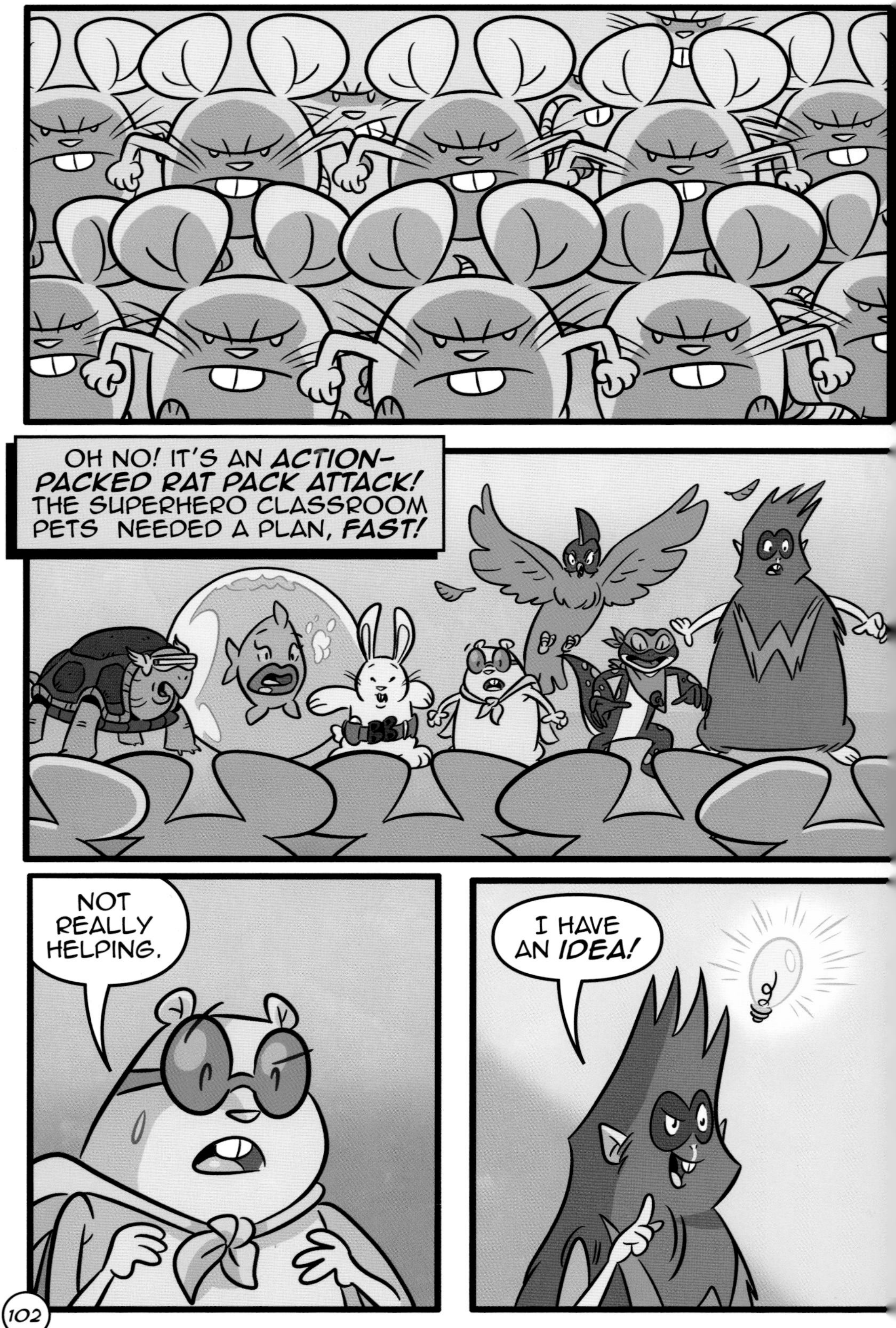

OH NO! IT'S AN *ACTION-PACKED RAT PACK ATTACK!* THE SUPERHERO CLASSROOM PETS NEEDED A PLAN, ***FAST!***
NOT REALLY HELPING.
I HAVE AN *IDEA!*

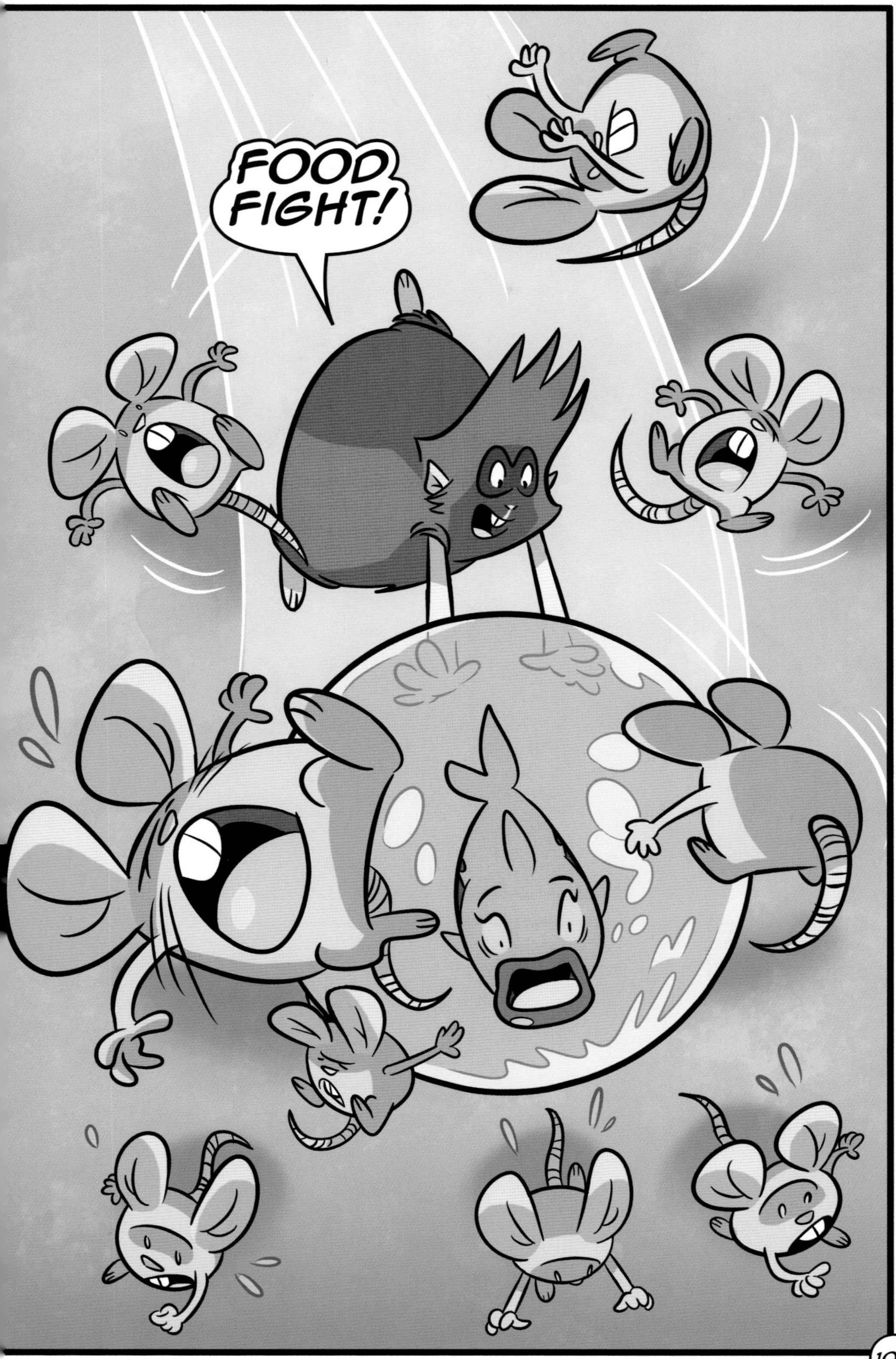
FOOD FIGHT!

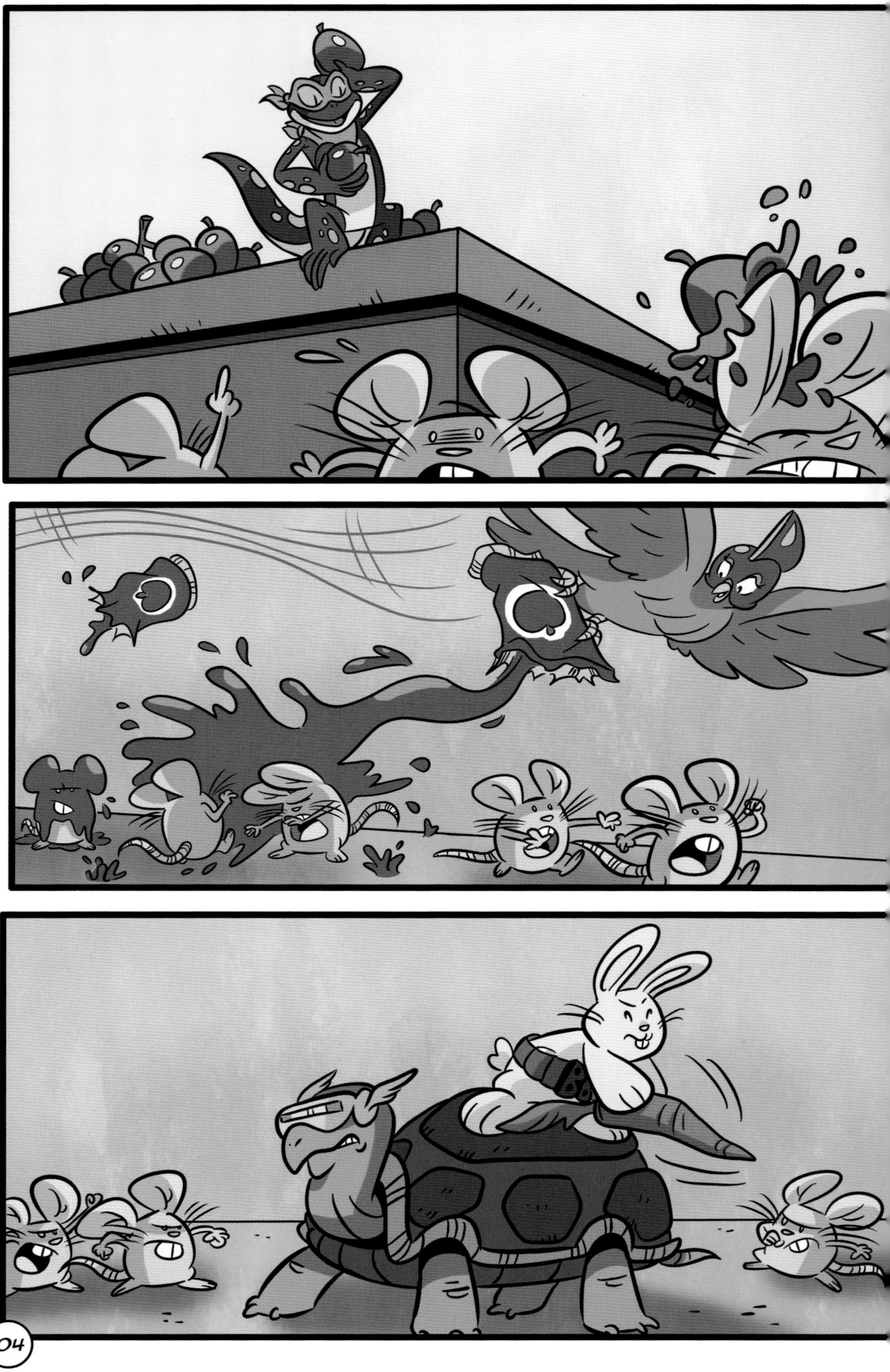

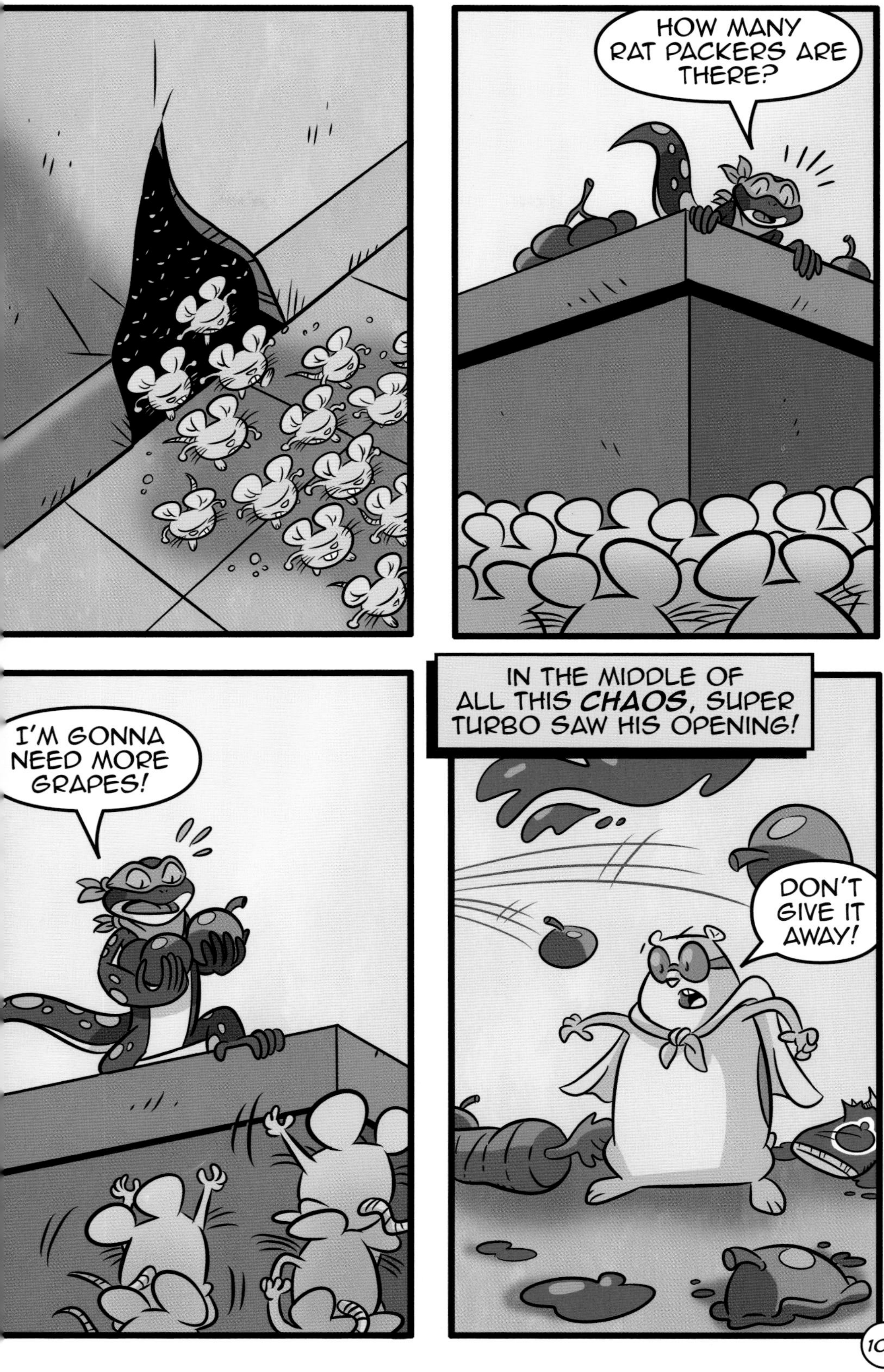
HOW MANY RAT PACKERS ARE THERE?
I'M GONNA NEED MORE GRAPES!
IN THE MIDDLE OF ALL THIS CHAOS, SUPER TURBO SAW HIS OPENING!
DON'T GIVE IT AWAY!

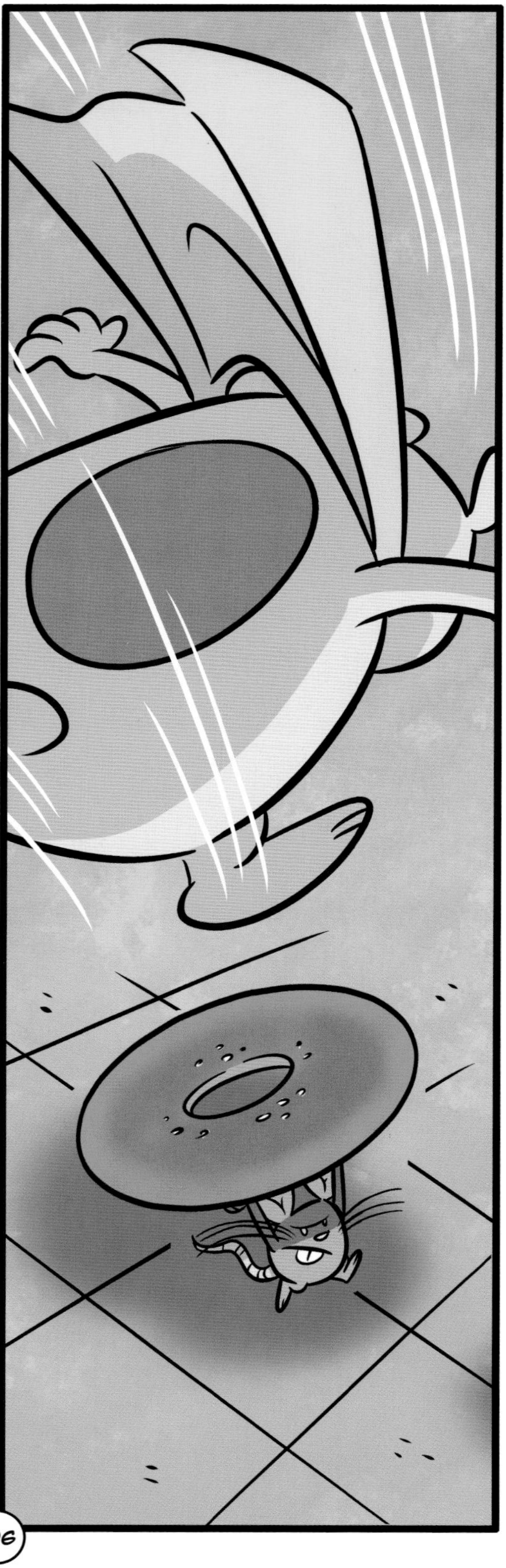

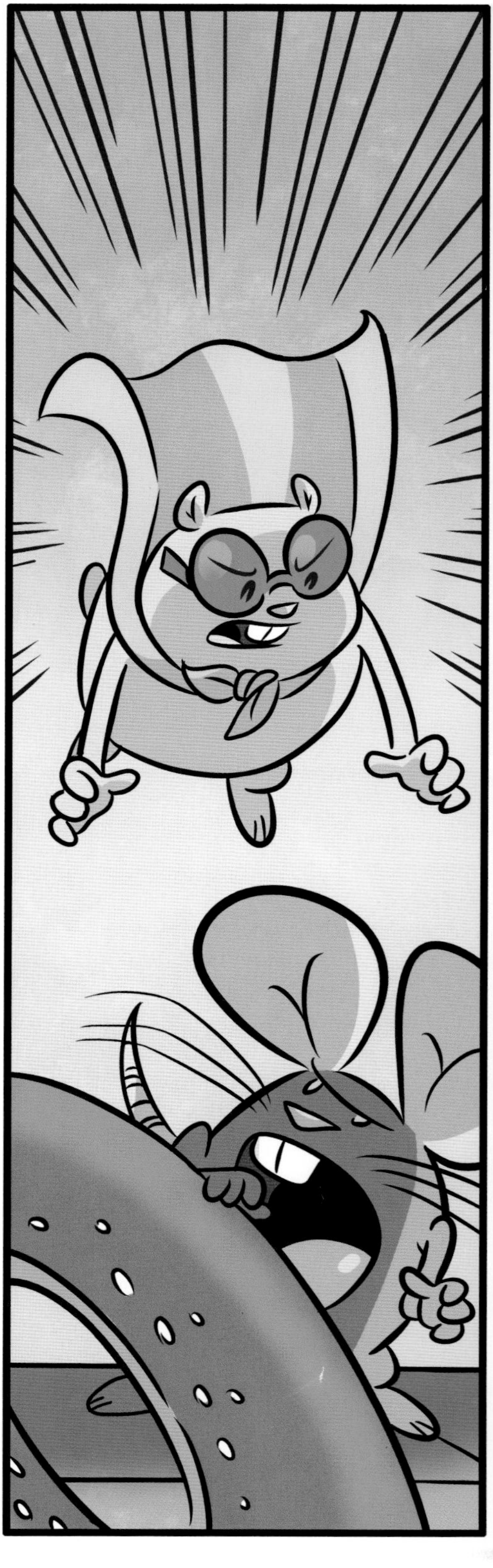

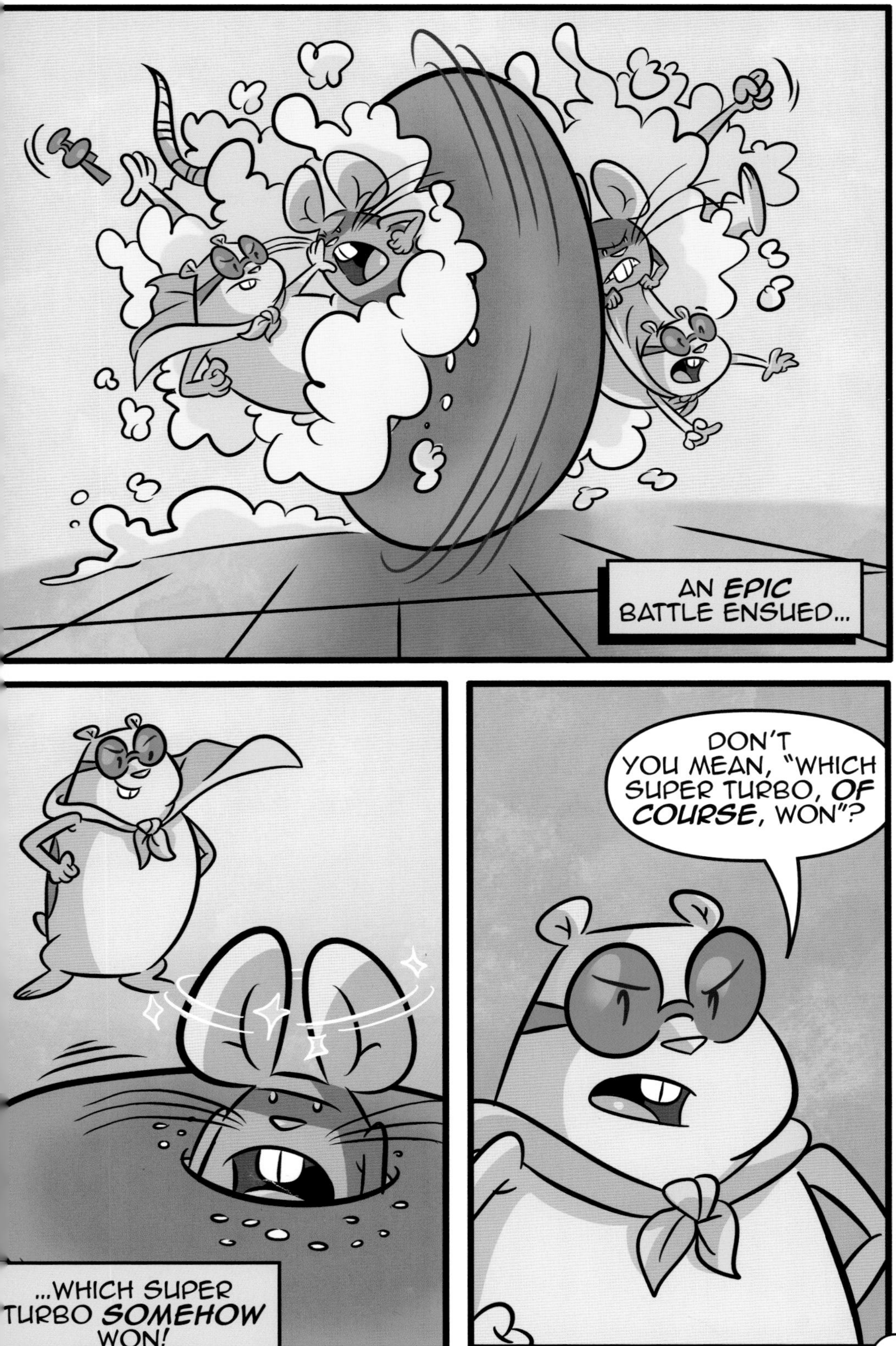
AN EPIC BATTLE ENSUED...
...WHICH SUPER TURBO SOMEHOW WON!
DON'T YOU MEAN, "WHICH SUPER TURBO, OF COURSE, WON"?

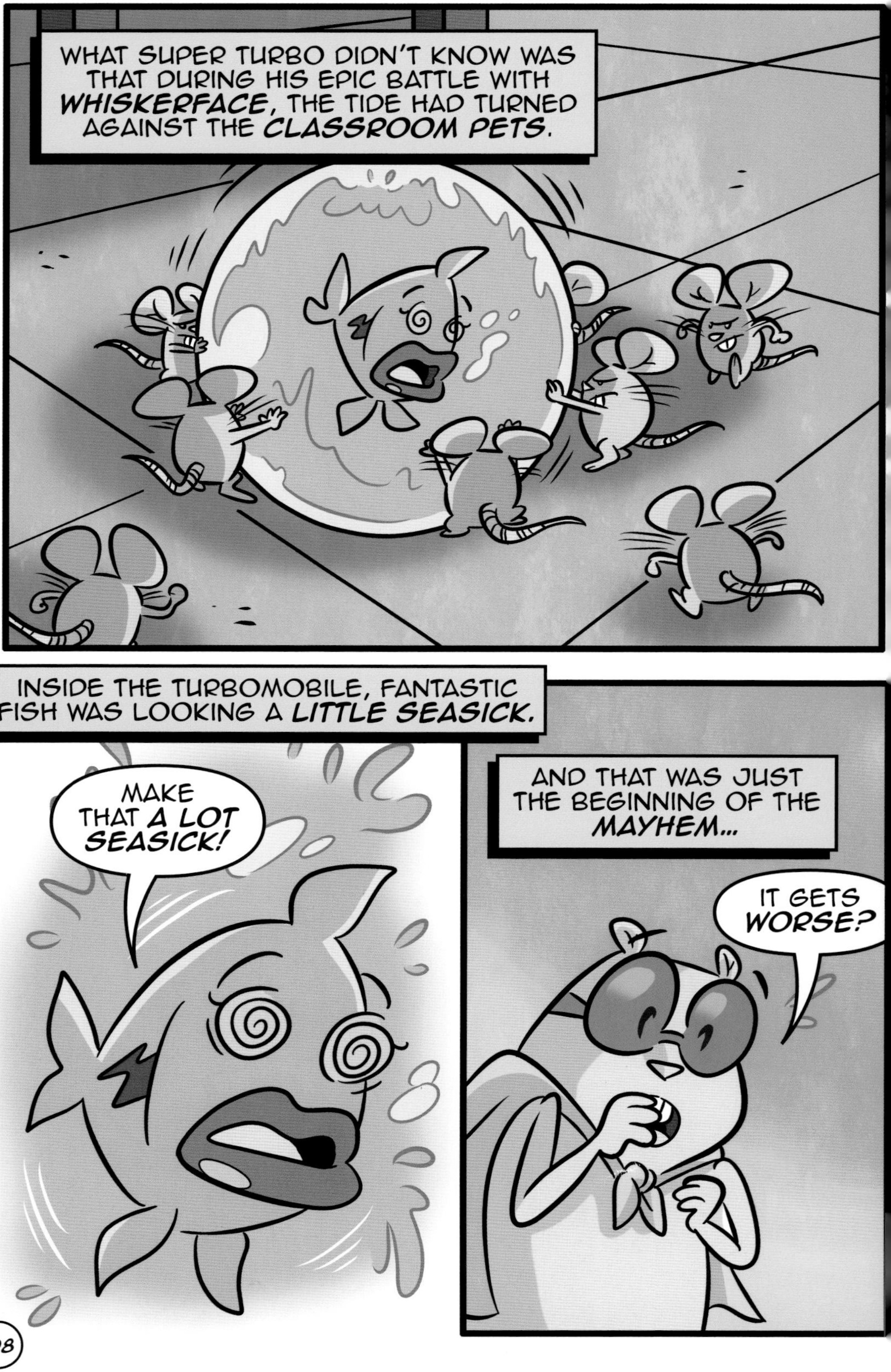
WHAT SUPER TURBO DIDN'T KNOW WAS THAT DURING HIS EPIC BATTLE WITH WHISKERFACE, THE TIDE HAD TURNED AGAINST THE CLASSROOM PETS.
INSIDE THE TURBOMOBILE, FANTASTIC FISH WAS LOOKING A LITTLE SEASICK.
MAKE THAT A LOT SEASICK!
AND THAT WAS JUST THE BEGINNING OF THE MAYHEM...
IT GETS WORSE?

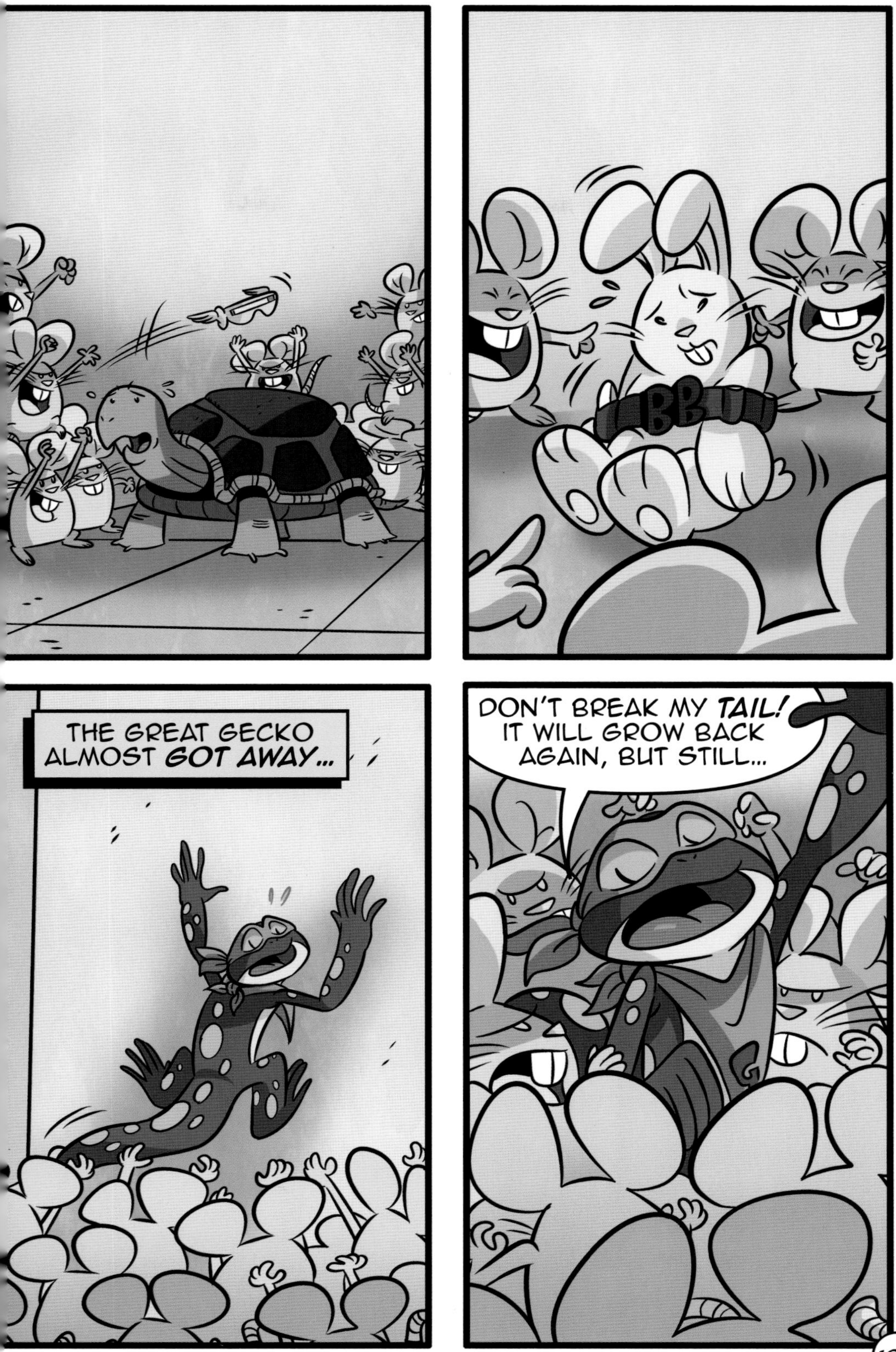
BB
THE GREAT GECKO ALMOST **GOT AWAY**...
DON'T BREAK MY ***TAIL!*** IT WILL GROW BACK AGAIN, BUT STILL...

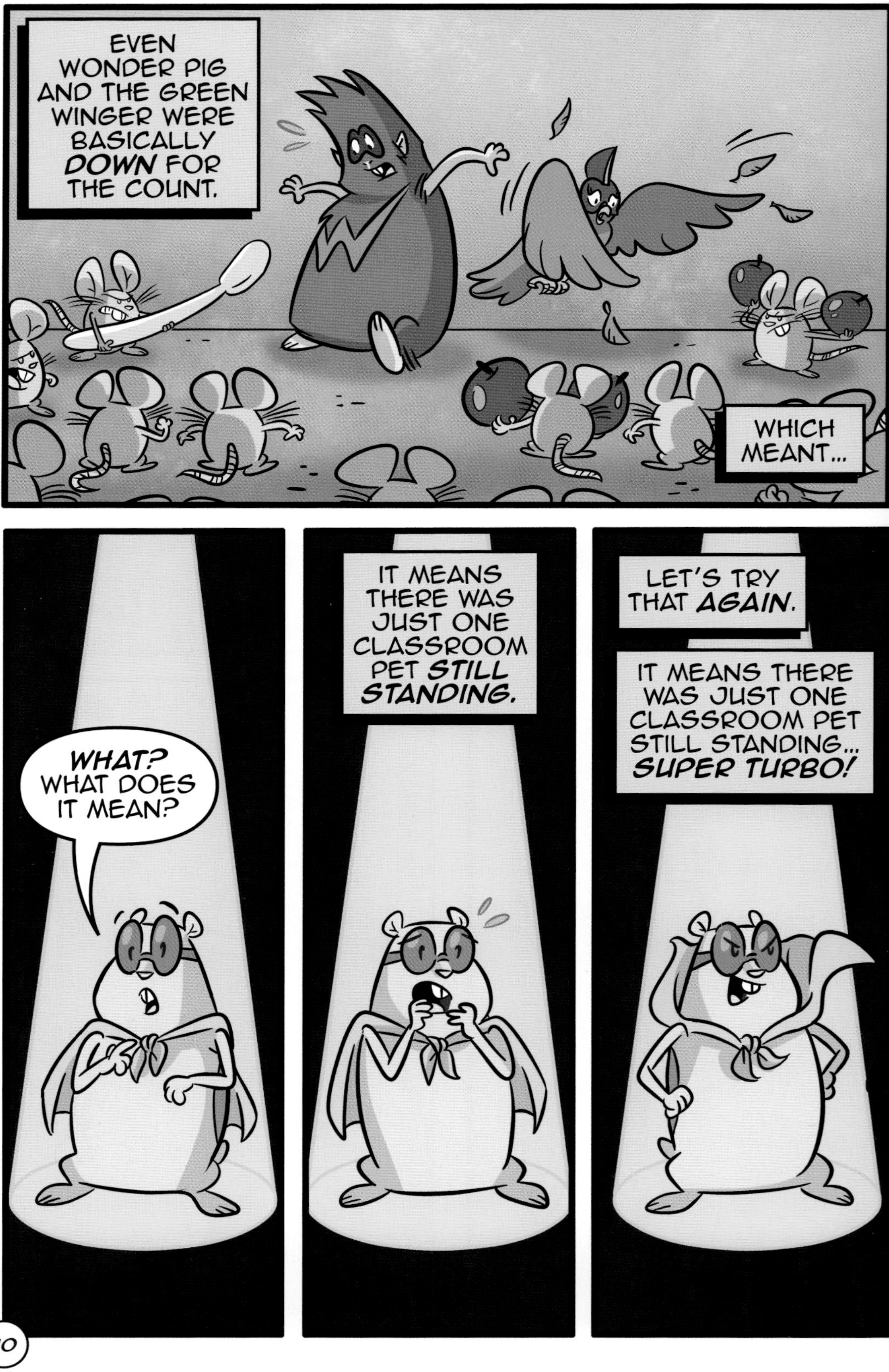
EVEN WONDER PIG AND THE GREEN WINGER WERE BASICALLY DOWN FOR THE COUNT.
WHICH MEANT...
WHAT? WHAT DOES IT MEAN?
IT MEANS THERE WAS JUST ONE CLASSROOM PET STILL STANDING.
LET'S TRY THAT AGAIN.
IT MEANS THERE WAS JUST ONE CLASSROOM PET STILL STANDING... SUPER TURBO!

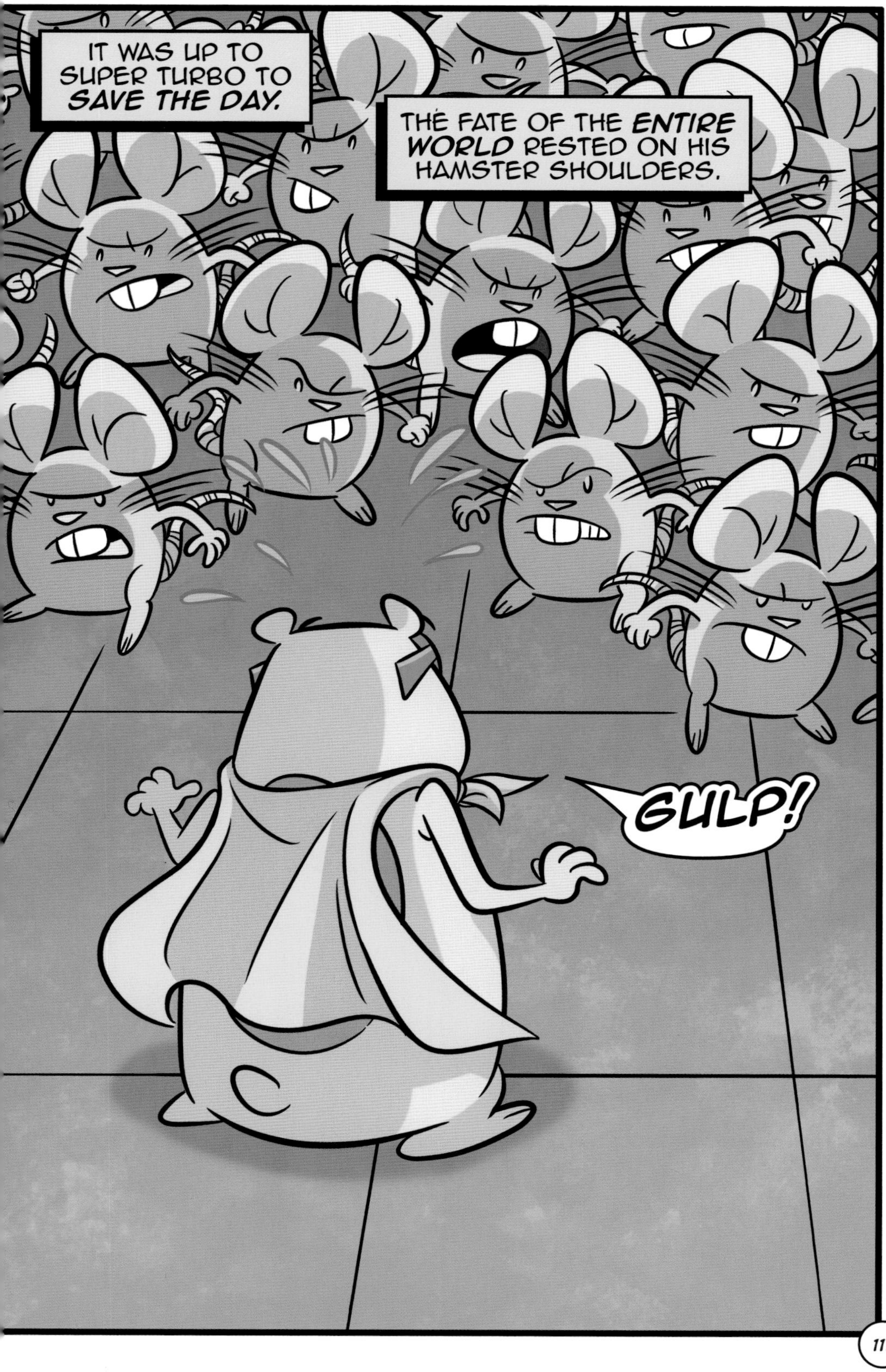
IT WAS UP TO SUPER TURBO TO *SAVE THE DAY.*
THE FATE OF THE *ENTIRE WORLD* RESTED ON HIS HAMSTER SHOULDERS.
GULP!

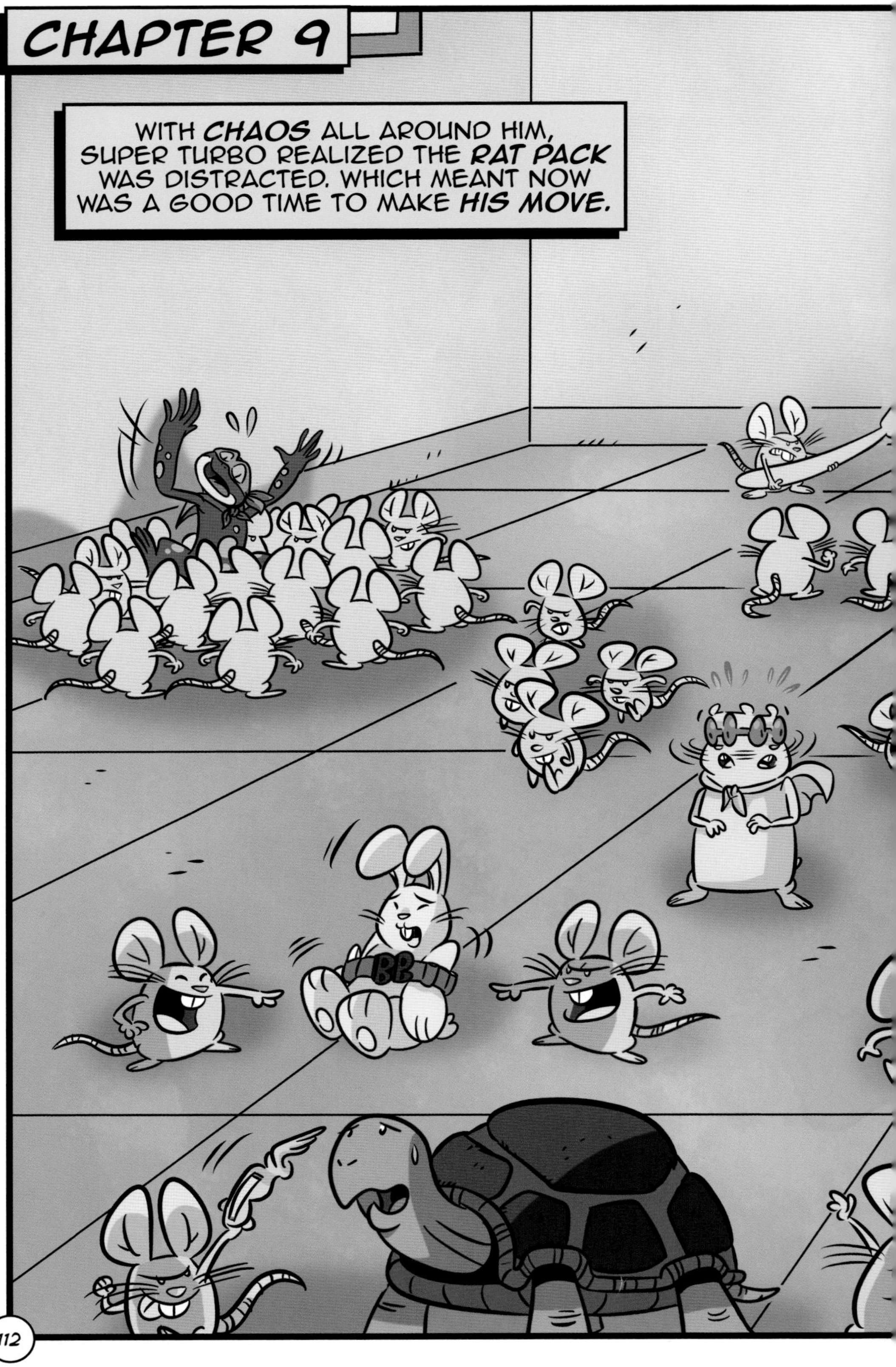
CHAPTER 9
WITH CHAOS ALL AROUND HIM, SUPER TURBO REALIZED THE RAT PACK WAS DISTRACTED. WHICH MEANT NOW WAS A GOOD TIME TO MAKE HIS MOVE.
BB

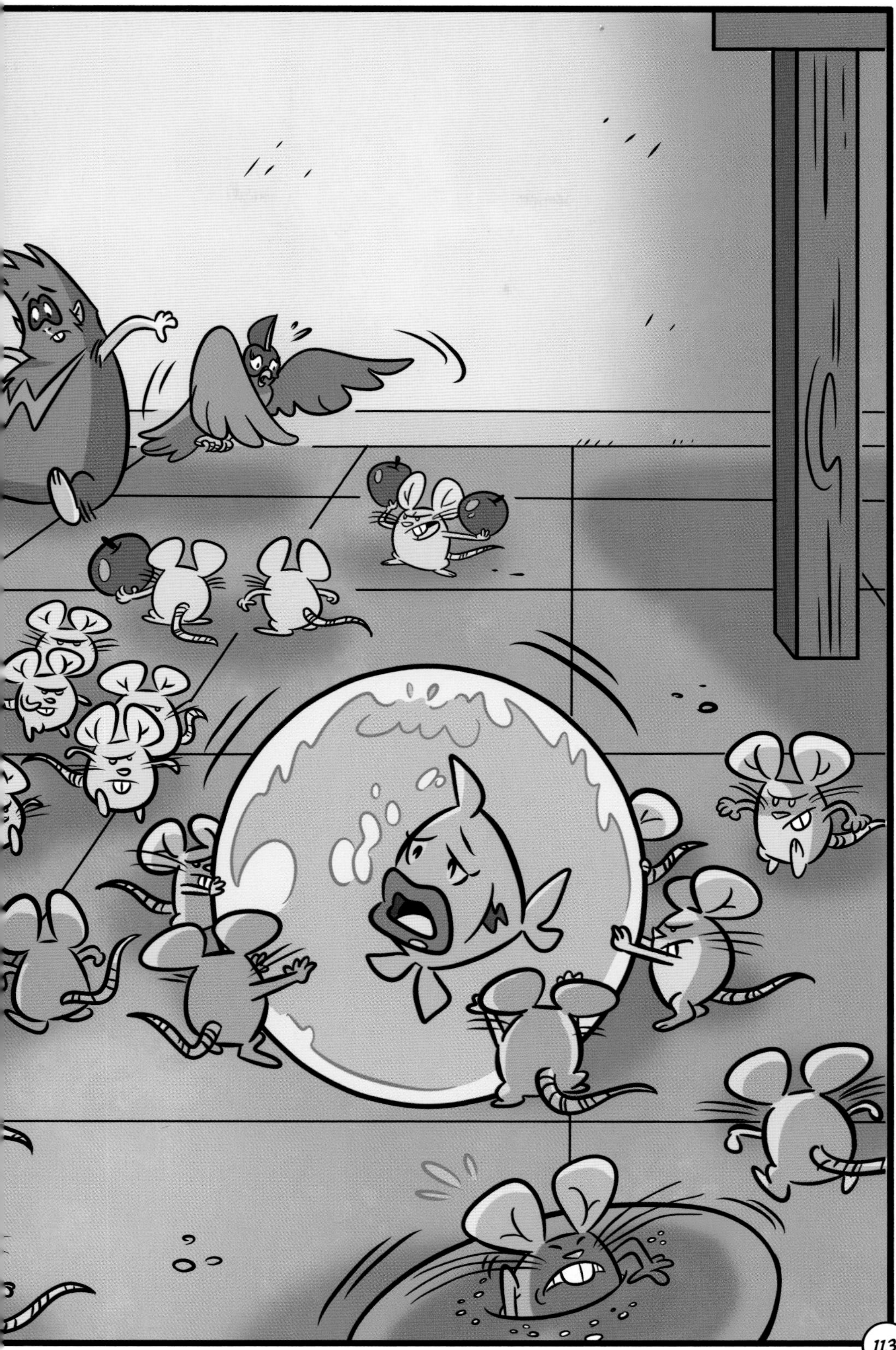

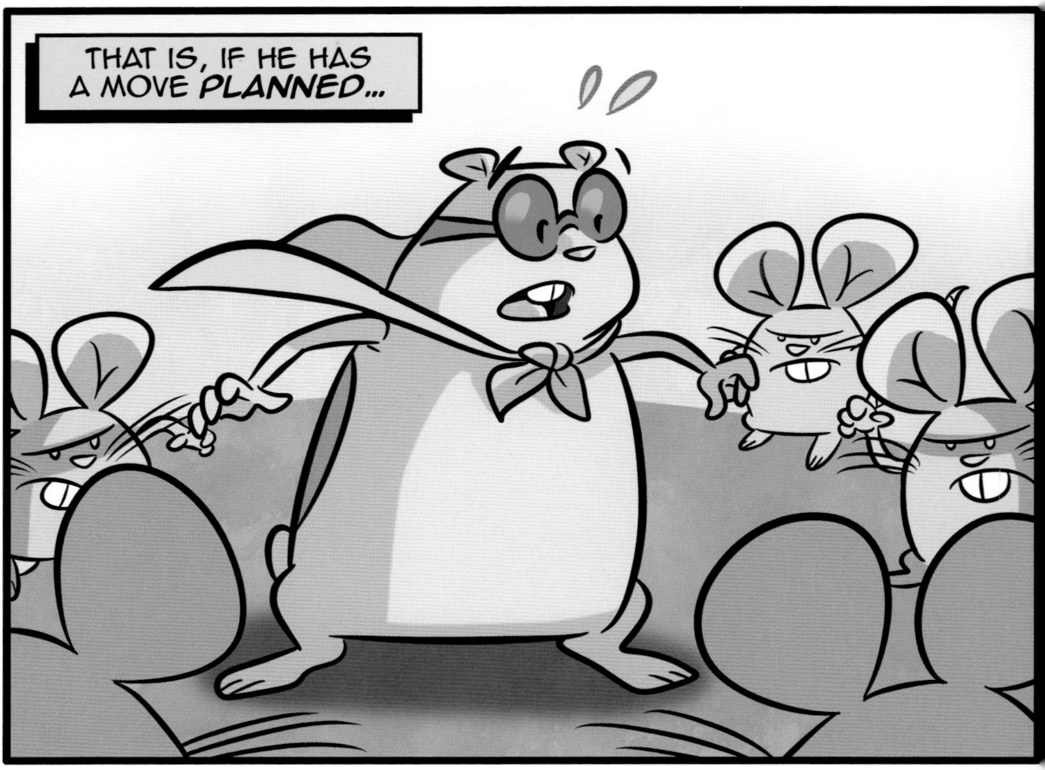
THAT IS, IF HE HAS A MOVE PLANNED...

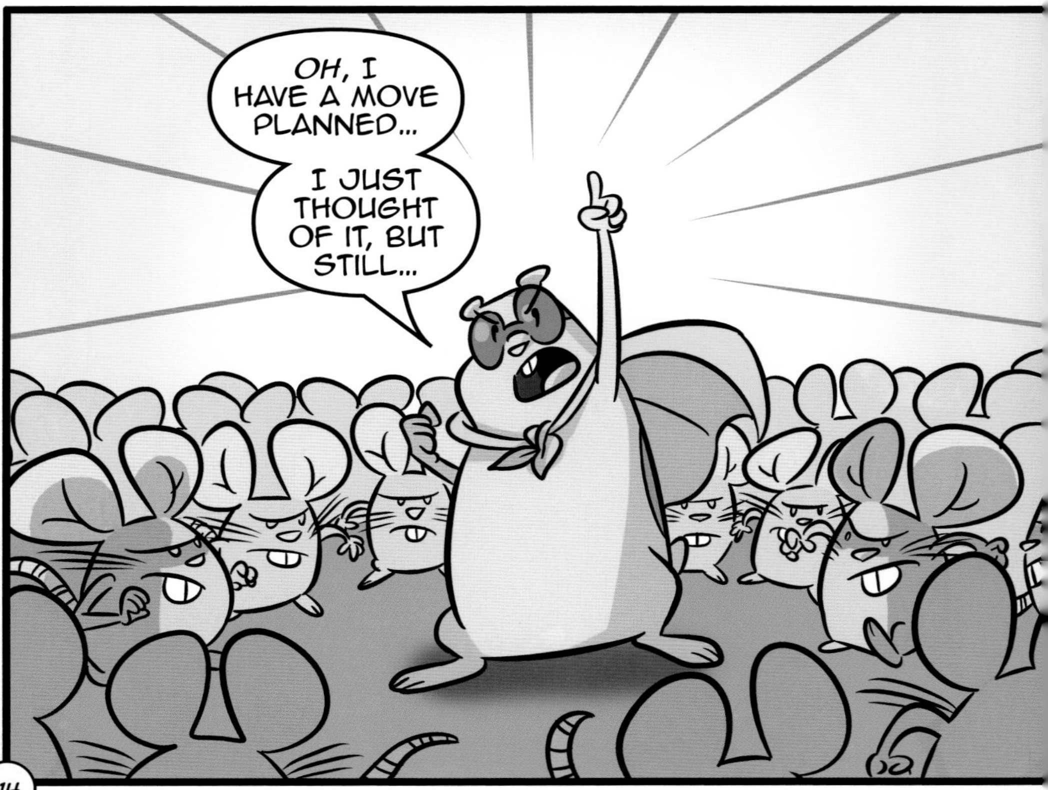
OH, I HAVE A MOVE PLANNED...
I JUST THOUGHT OF IT, BUT STILL...

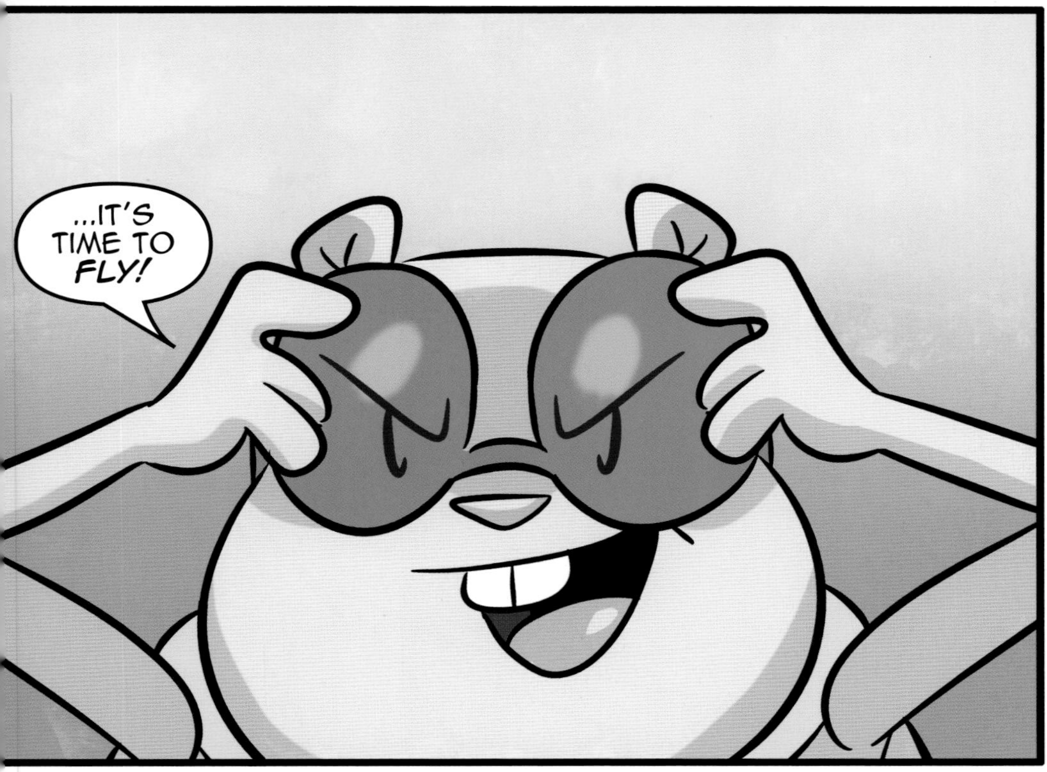
...IT'S TIME TO FLY!

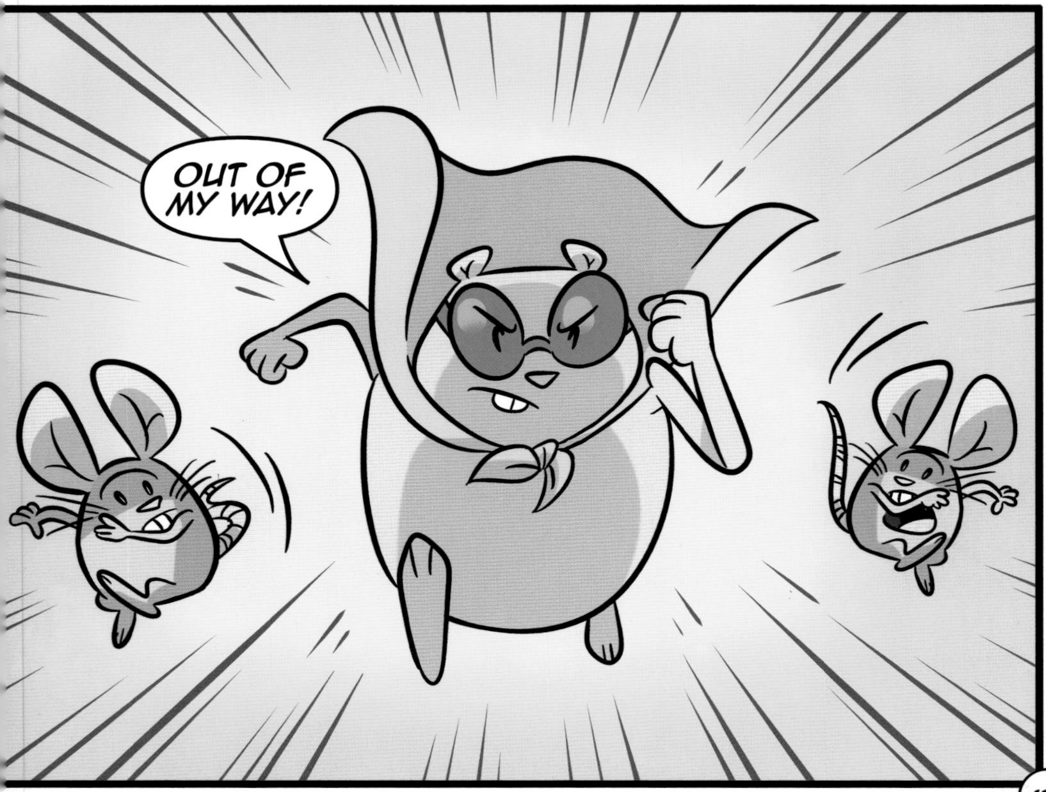
OUT OF MY WAY!

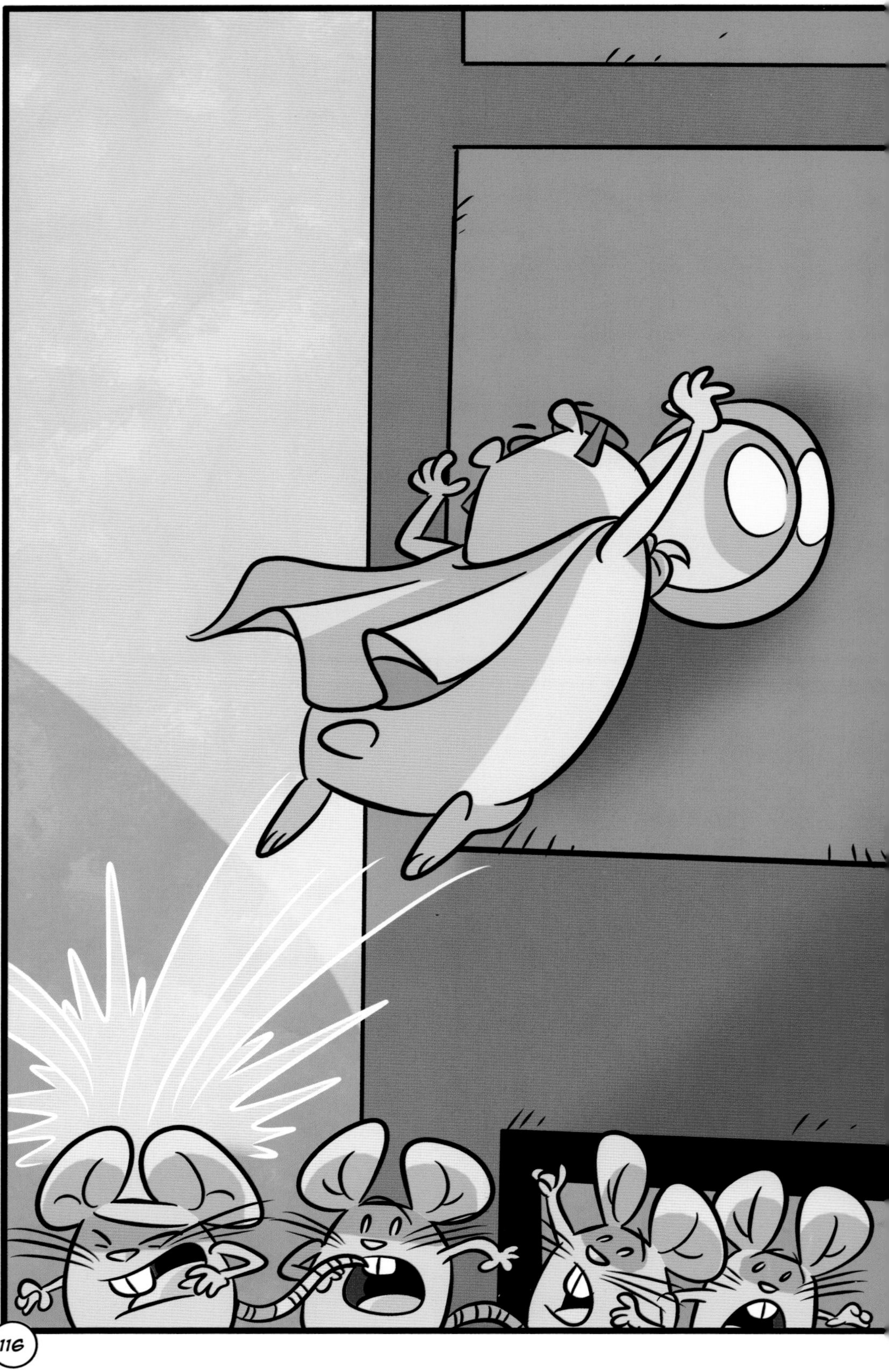

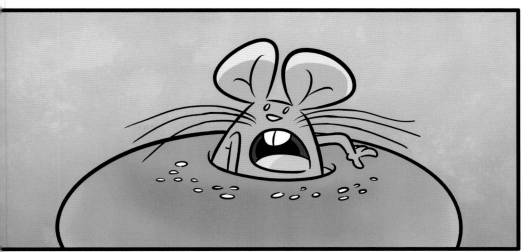

IS THAT *FLYING*, THOUGH? OR JUST REALLY GOOD *JUMPING*?

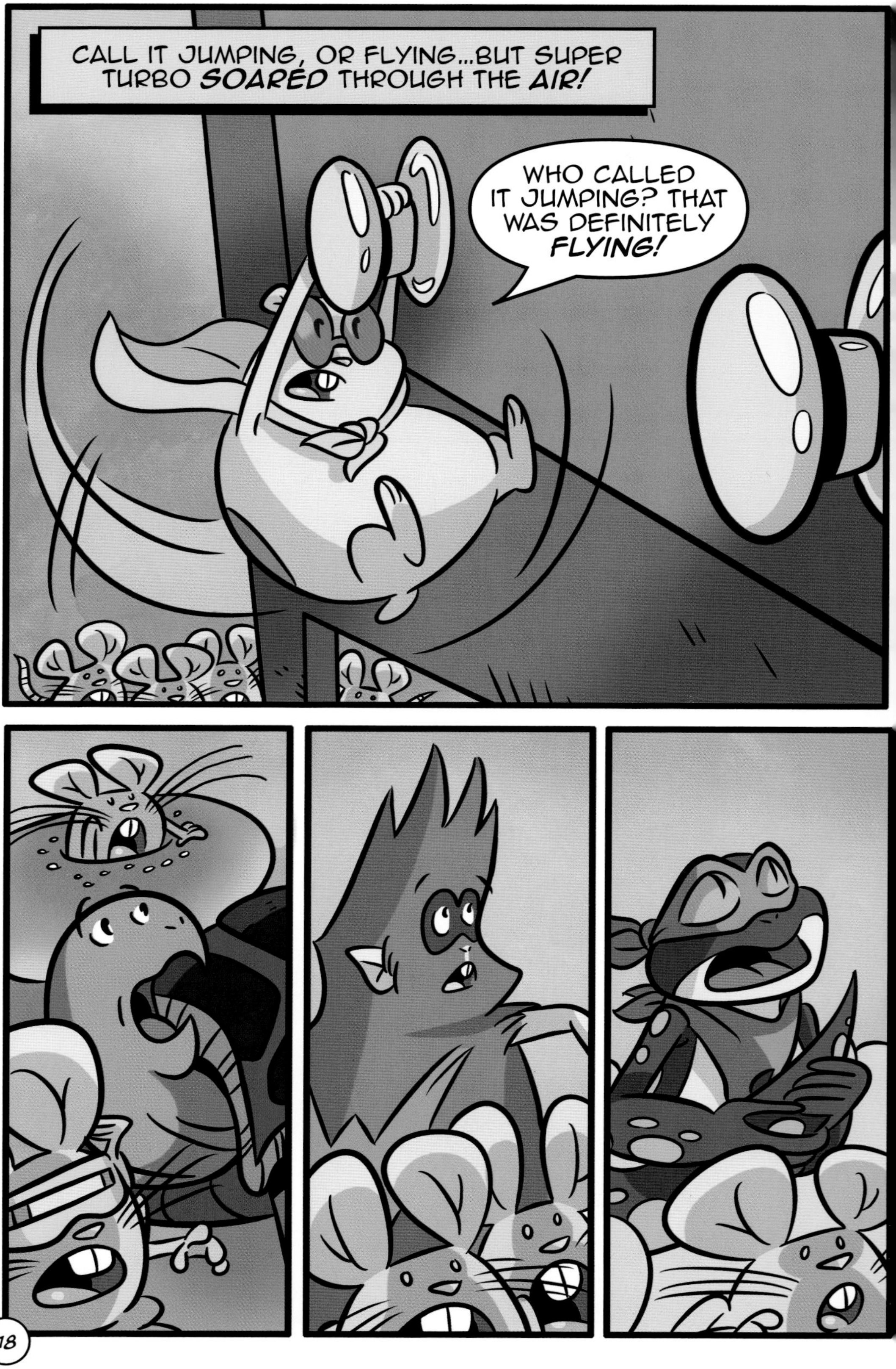
CALL IT JUMPING, OR FLYING...BUT SUPER TURBO SOARED THROUGH THE AIR!
WHO CALLED IT JUMPING? THAT WAS DEFINITELY FLYING!

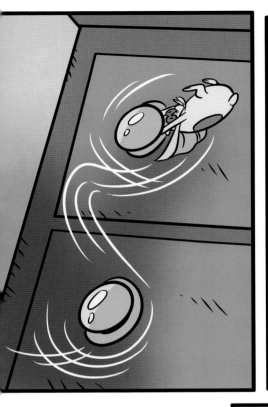
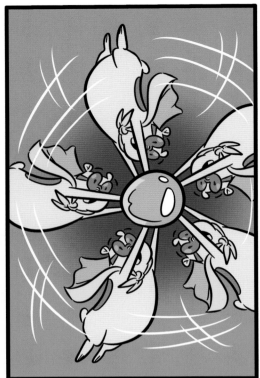

HE MADE IT! MAYBE...?

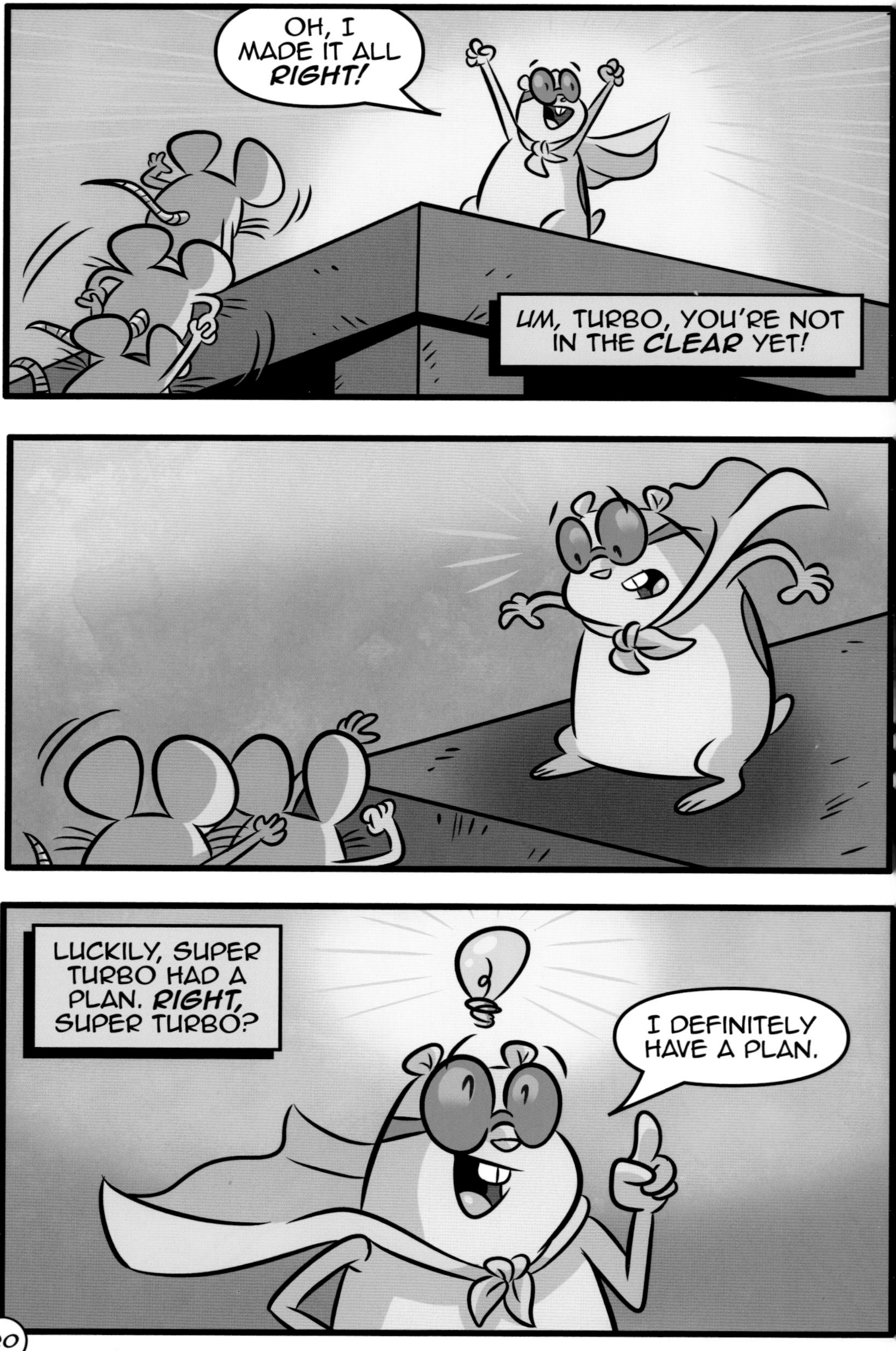
OH, I MADE IT ALL RIGHT!
UM, TURBO, YOU'RE NOT IN THE CLEAR YET!
LUCKILY, SUPER TURBO HAD A PLAN. RIGHT, SUPER TURBO?
I DEFINITELY HAVE A PLAN.

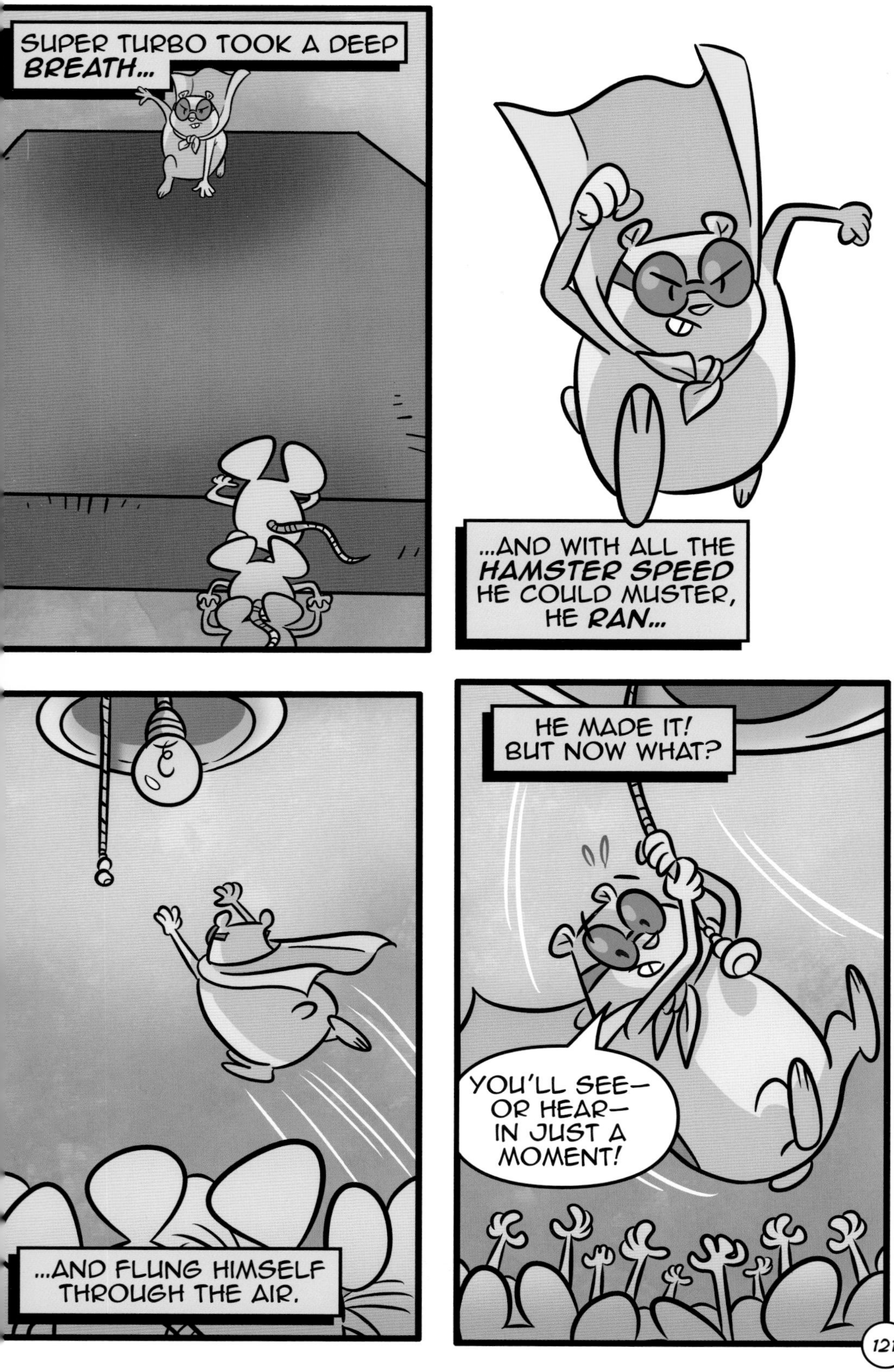
SUPER TURBO TOOK A DEEP BREATH...
...AND WITH ALL THE HAMSTER SPEED HE COULD MUSTER, HE RAN...
...AND FLUNG HIMSELF THROUGH THE AIR.
HE MADE IT! BUT NOW WHAT?
YOU'LL SEE— OR HEAR— IN JUST A MOMENT!

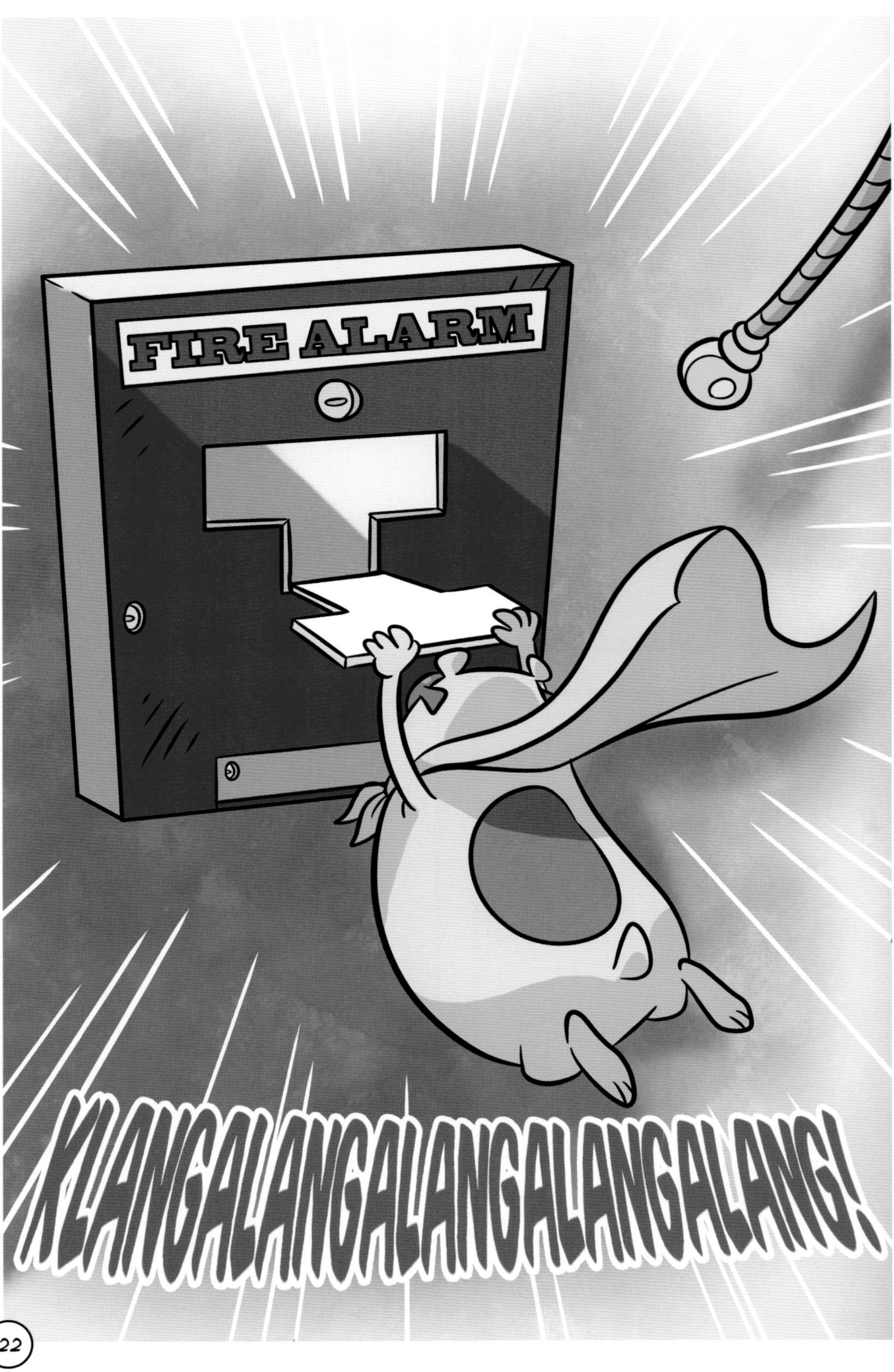
FIRE ALARM
KLANGALANGALANGALANGALANG!

THE FIRE ALARM WAS LOUD, ESPECIALLY TO THE EVIL RATS OF THE RAT PACK, WITH THEIR GIANT *MOUSE EARS!*

KLANGALANGALANGALANGALANG!

THEY HAVE MOUSE EARS BECAUSE THEY ARE *MICE!*

THE *NOISE* WAS TOO MUCH AND THE RAT PACK *RETREATED.*

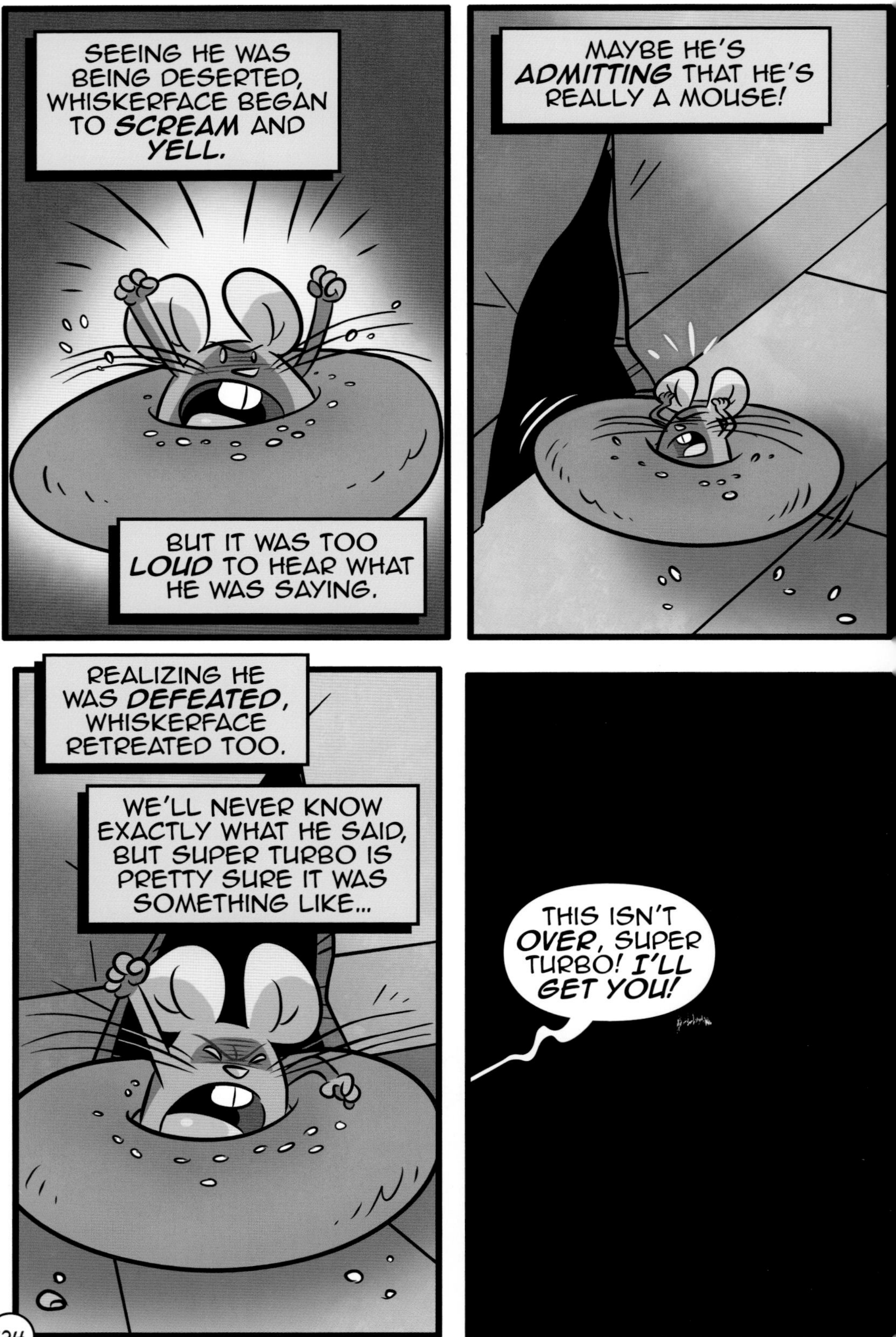

SEEING HE WAS BEING DESERTED, WHISKERFACE BEGAN TO *SCREAM* AND *YELL.*
BUT IT WAS TOO *LOUD* TO HEAR WHAT HE WAS SAYING.
MAYBE HE'S *ADMITTING* THAT HE'S REALLY A MOUSE!
REALIZING HE WAS *DEFEATED*, WHISKERFACE RETREATED TOO.
WE'LL NEVER KNOW EXACTLY WHAT HE SAID, BUT SUPER TURBO IS PRETTY SURE IT WAS SOMETHING LIKE...
THIS ISN'T *OVER*, SUPER TURBO! *I'LL GET YOU!*

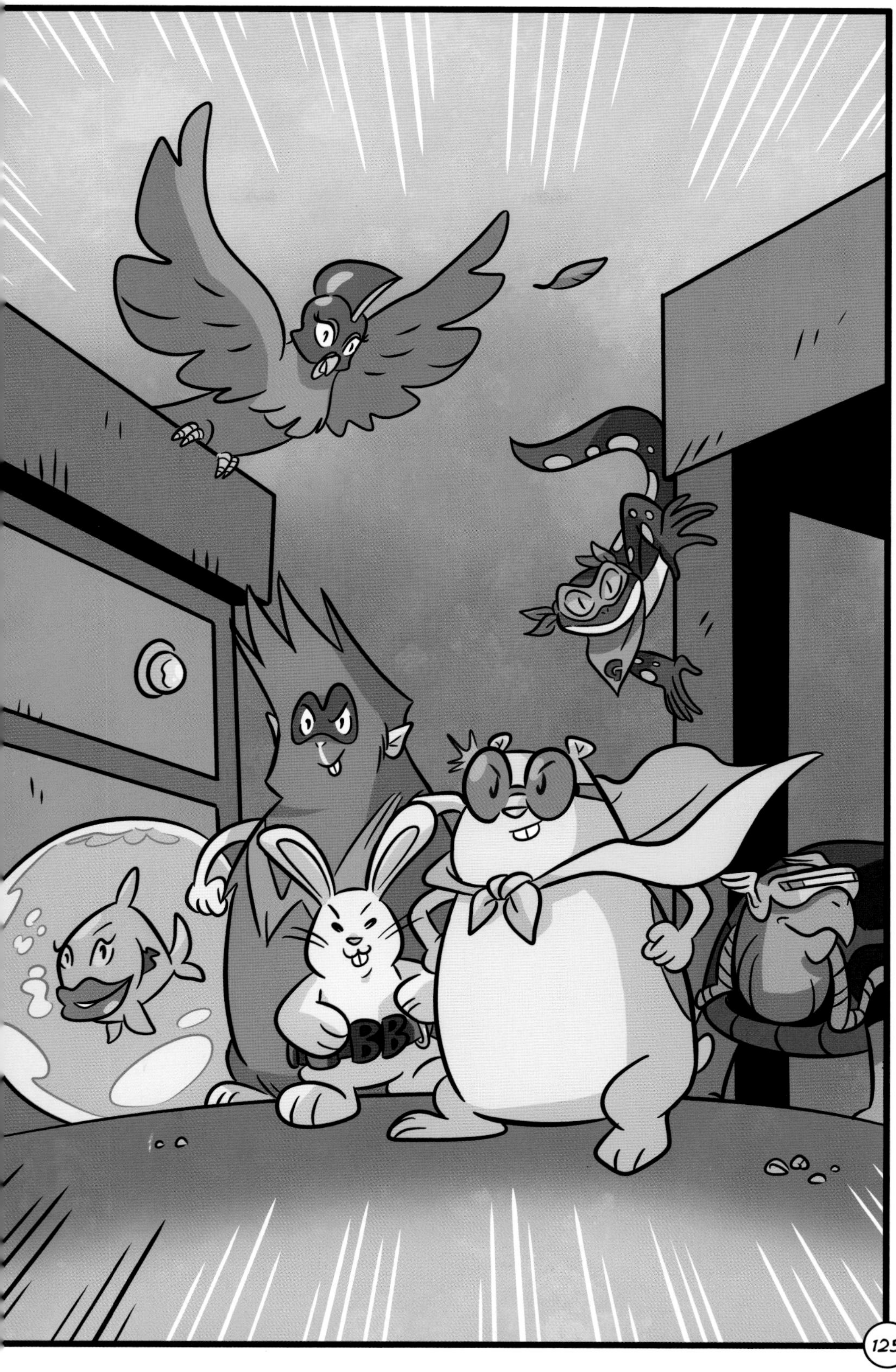
BB

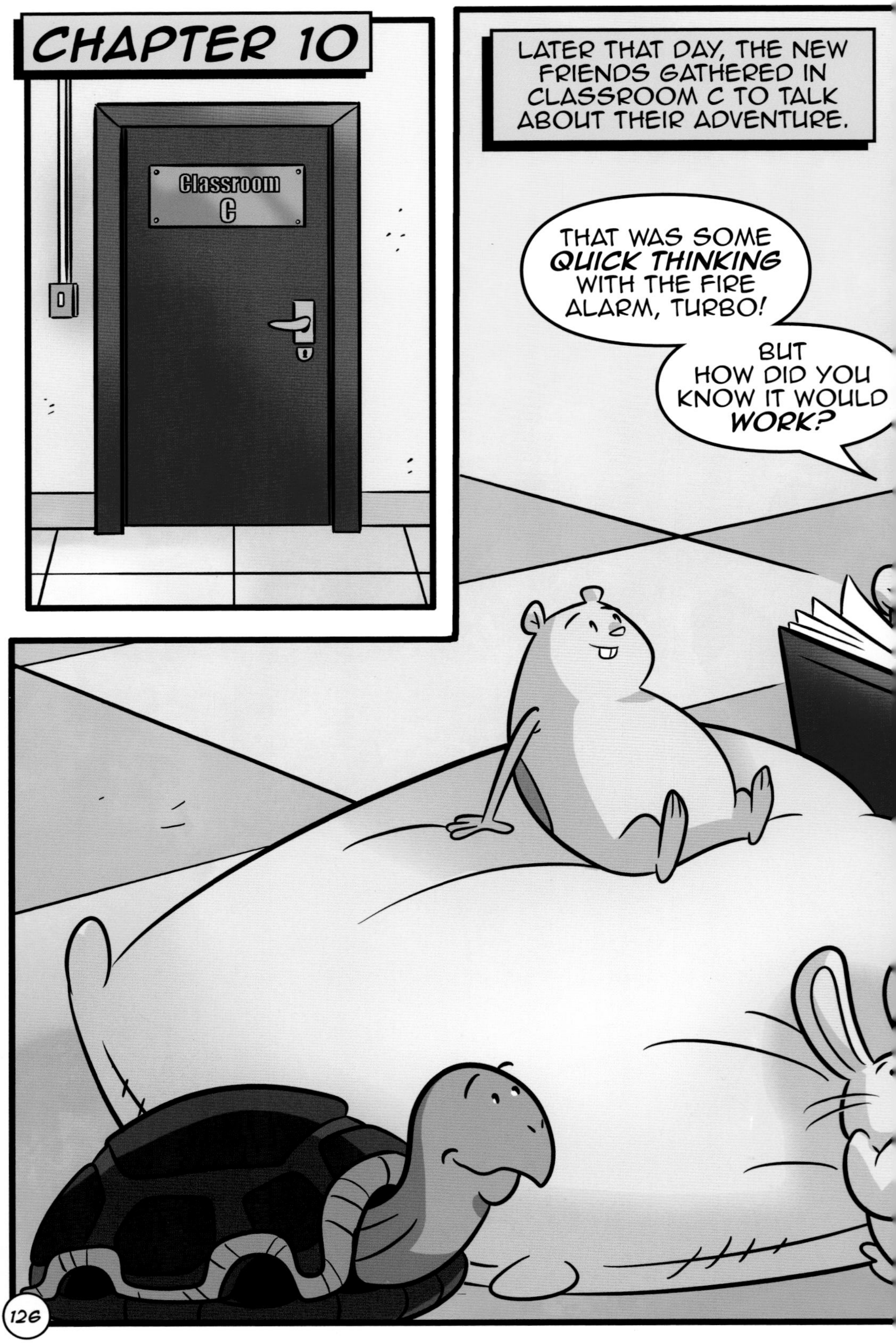
CHAPTER 10
Classroom C
LATER THAT DAY, THE NEW FRIENDS GATHERED IN CLASSROOM C TO TALK ABOUT THEIR ADVENTURE.
THAT WAS SOME QUICK THINKING WITH THE FIRE ALARM, TURBO!
BUT HOW DID YOU KNOW IT WOULD WORK?

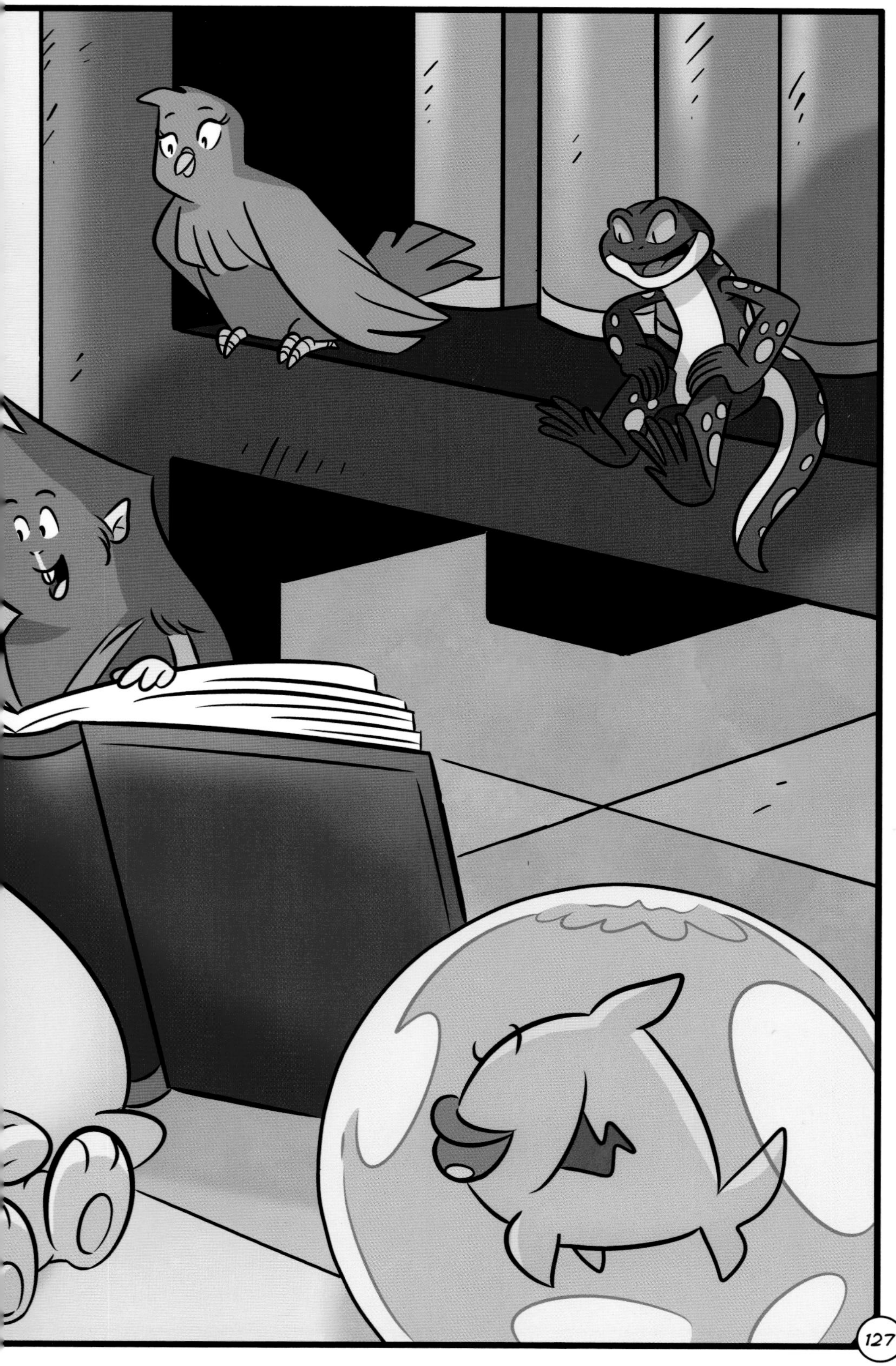

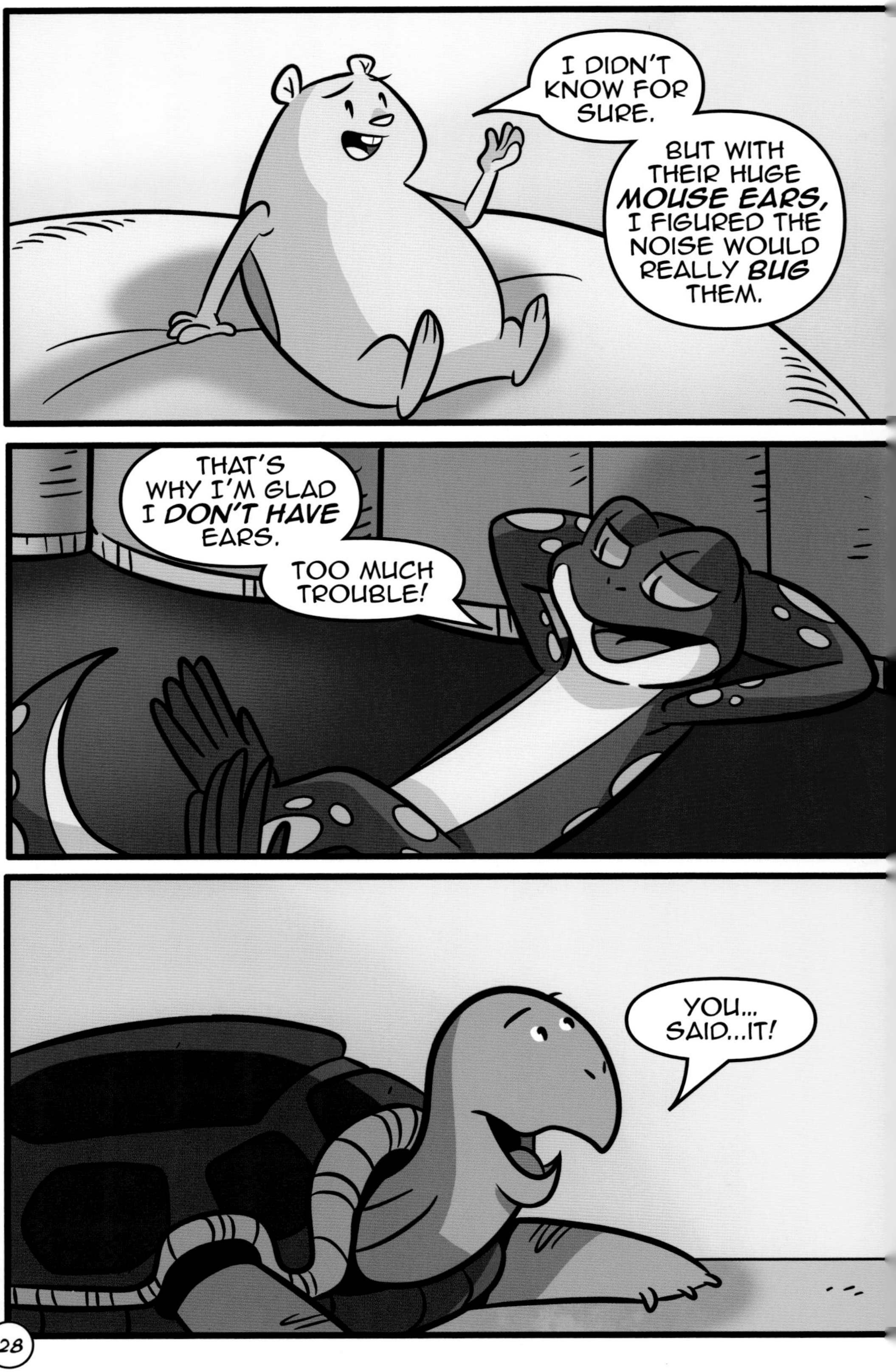
I DIDN'T KNOW FOR SURE.
BUT WITH THEIR HUGE ***MOUSE EARS,*** I FIGURED THE NOISE WOULD REALLY ***BUG*** THEM.
THAT'S WHY I'M GLAD I ***DON'T HAVE*** EARS.
TOO MUCH TROUBLE!
YOU... SAID...IT!

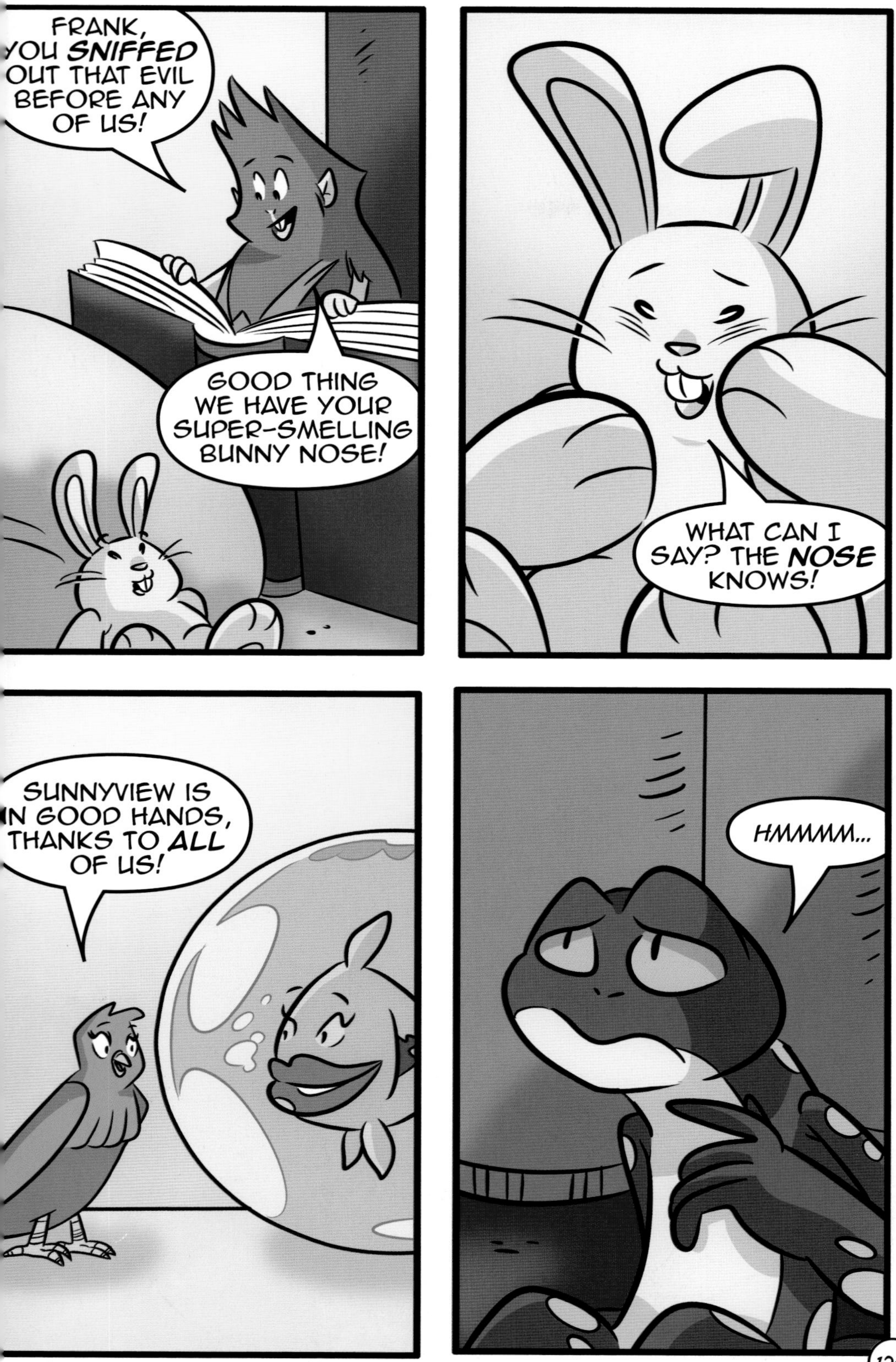
FRANK, YOU **SNIFFED** OUT THAT EVIL BEFORE ANY OF US!
GOOD THING WE HAVE YOUR SUPER-SMELLING BUNNY NOSE!
WHAT CAN I SAY? THE **NOSE** KNOWS!
SUNNYVIEW IS IN GOOD HANDS, THANKS TO **ALL** OF US!
HMMMM...

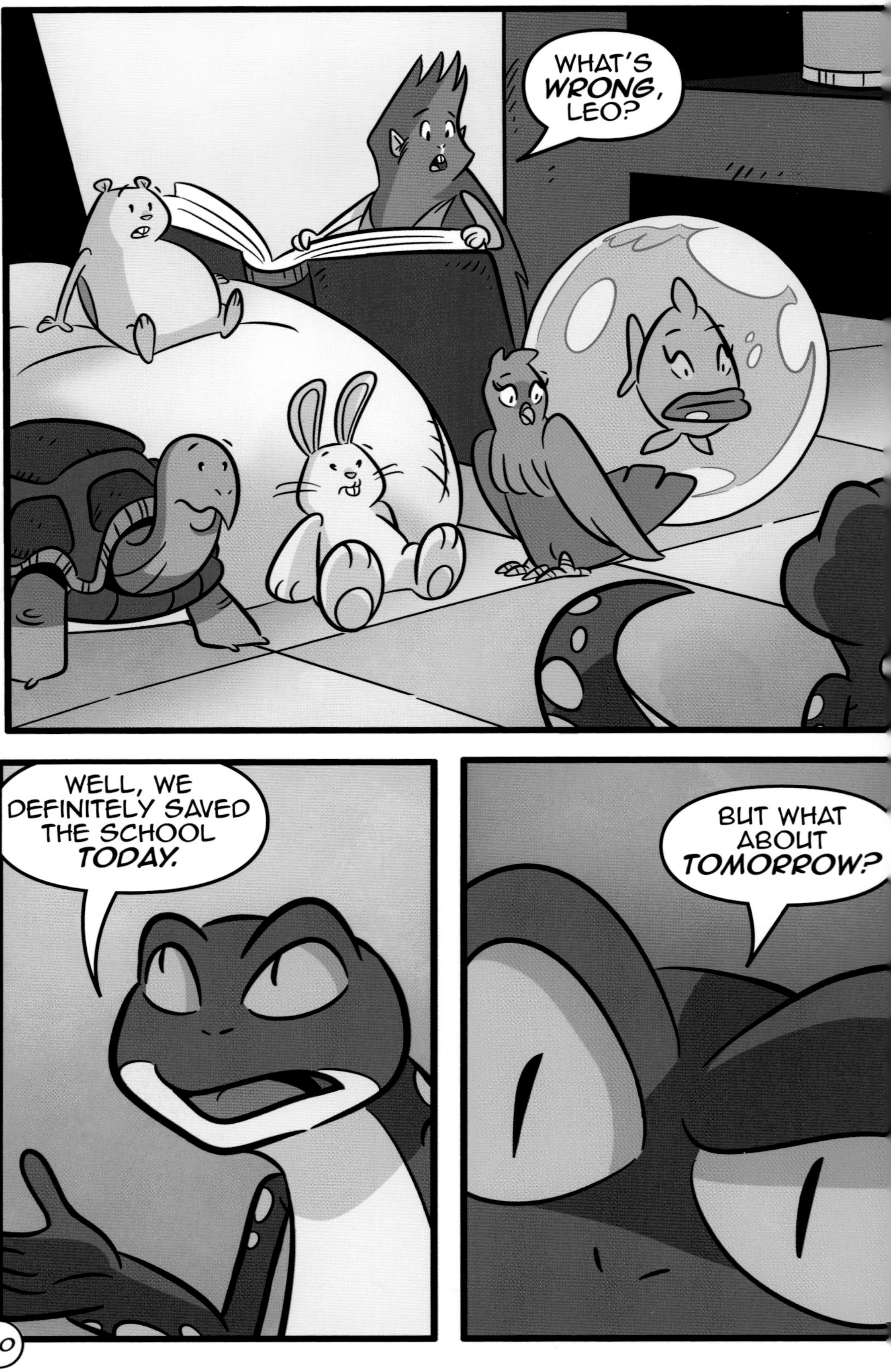
WHAT'S WRONG, LEO?
WELL, WE DEFINITELY SAVED THE SCHOOL TODAY.
BUT WHAT ABOUT TOMORROW?

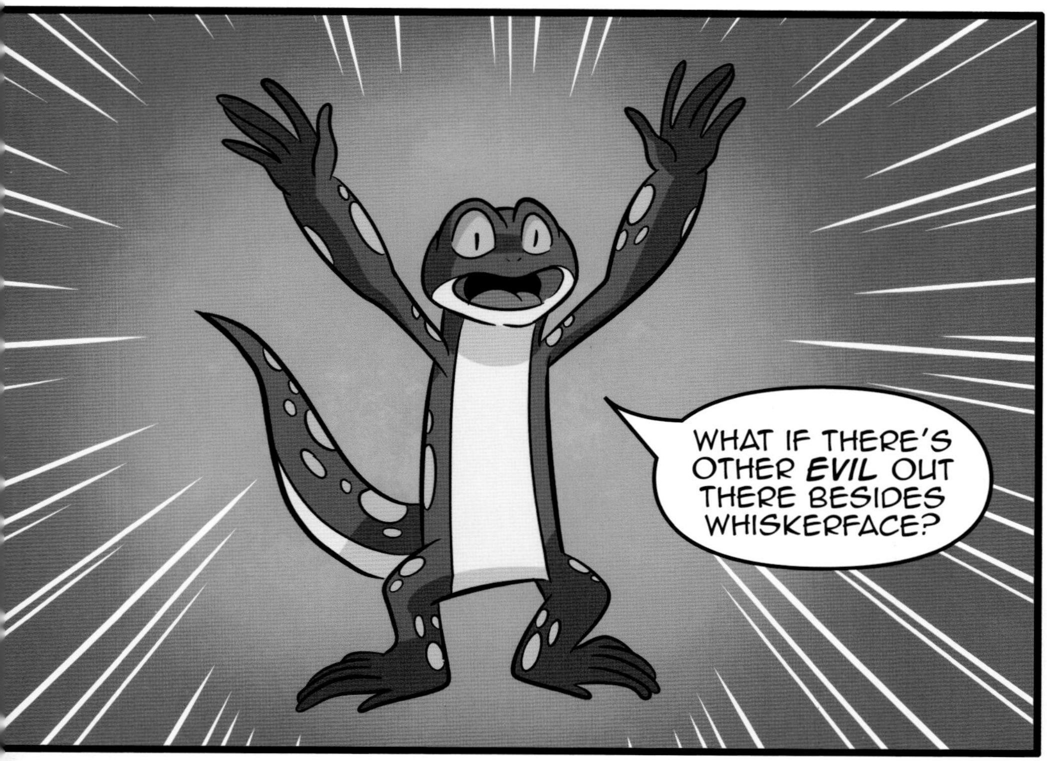
WHAT IF THERE'S OTHER EVIL OUT THERE BESIDES WHISKERFACE?

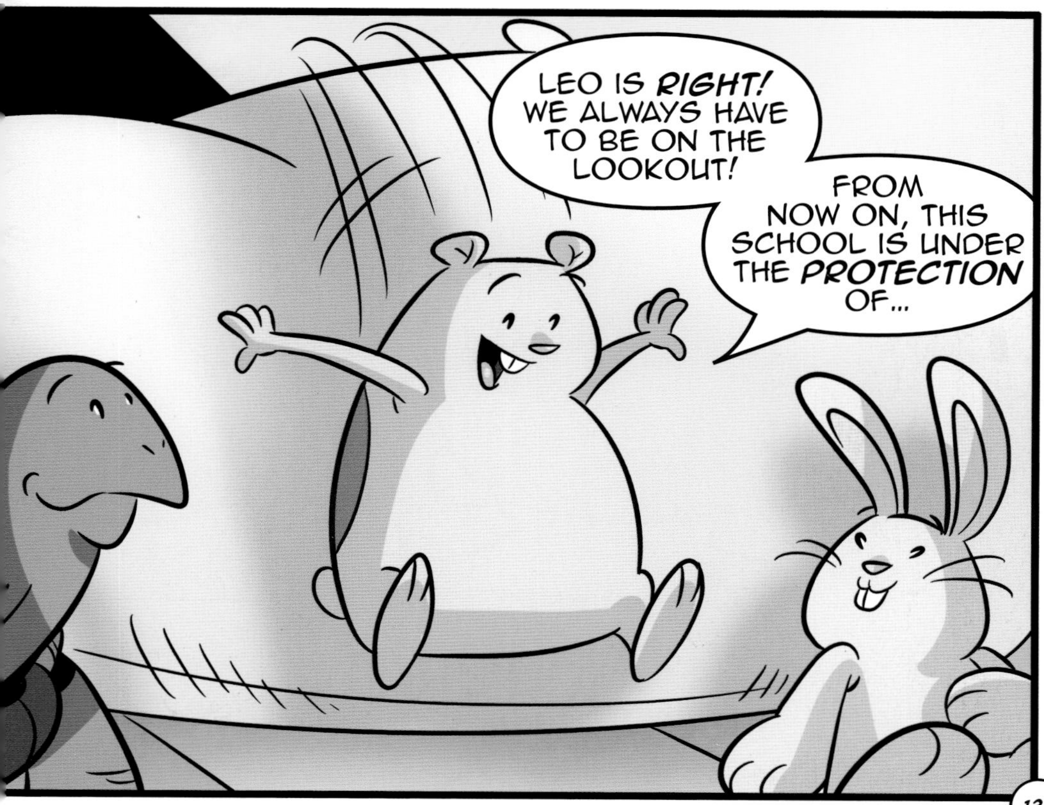
LEO IS RIGHT! WE ALWAYS HAVE TO BE ON THE LOOKOUT!
FROM NOW ON, THIS SCHOOL IS UNDER THE PROTECTION OF...

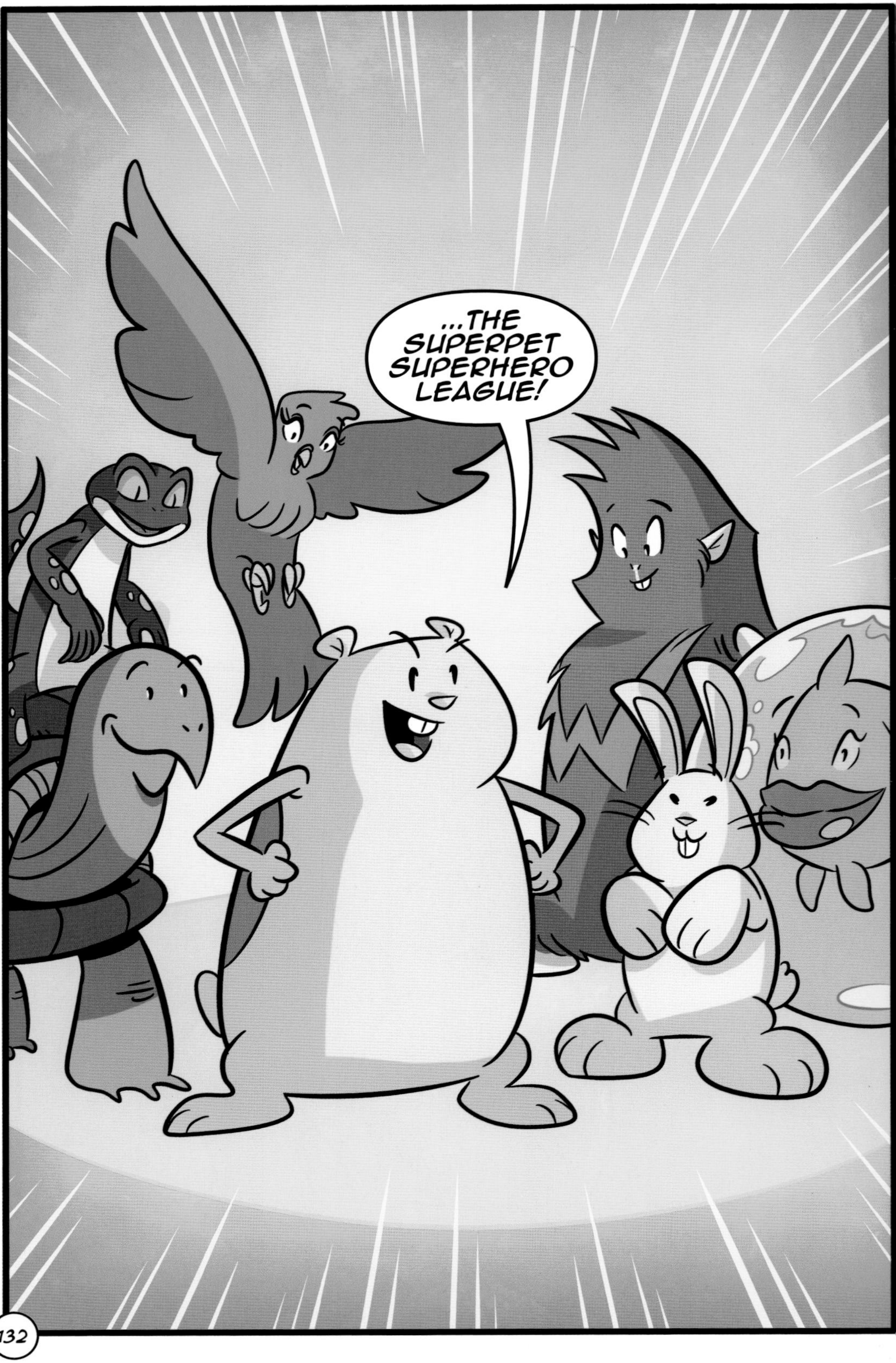
...THE SUPERPET SUPERHERO LEAGUE!

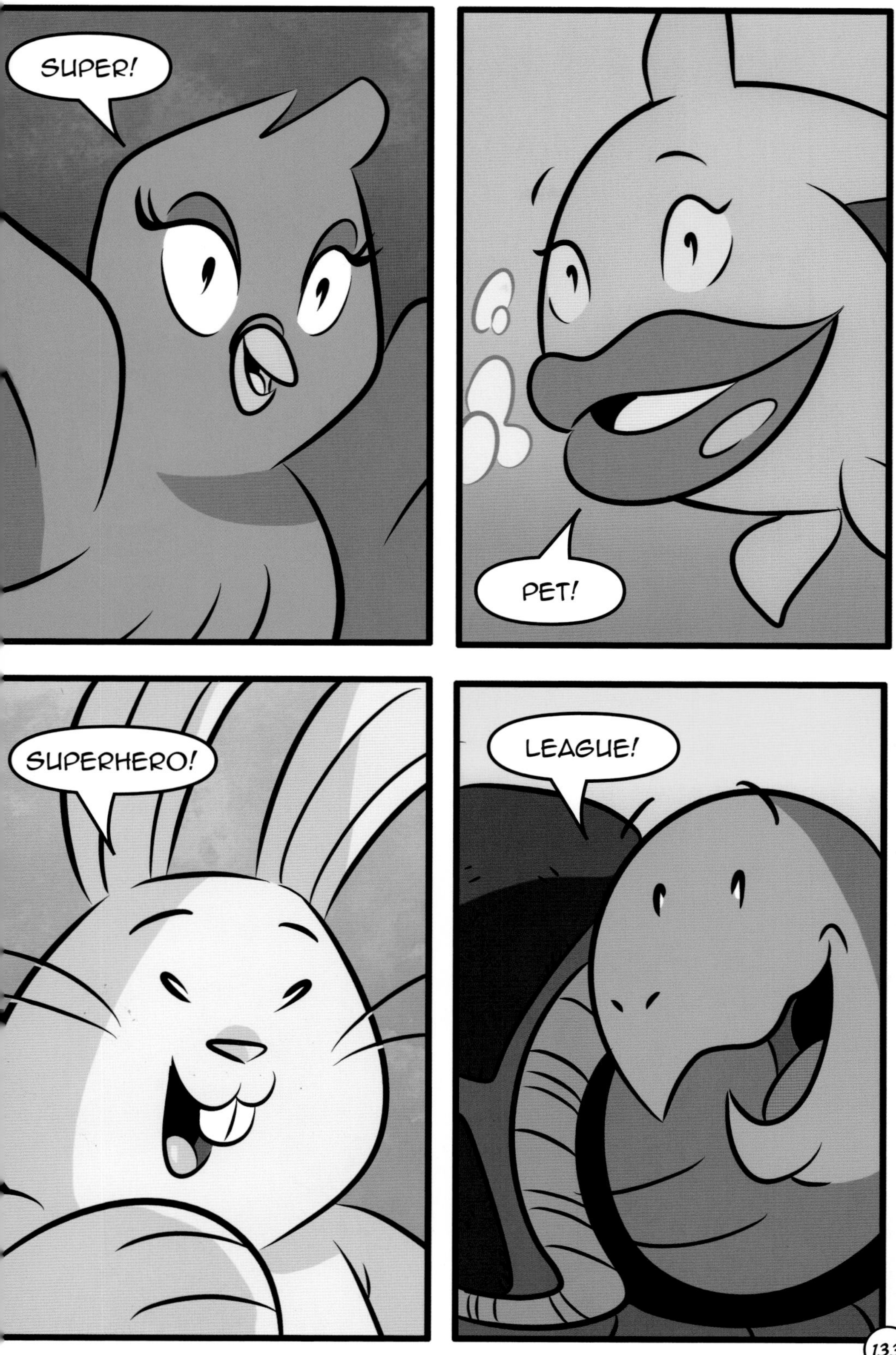
SUPER!
PET!
SUPERHERO!
LEAGUE!

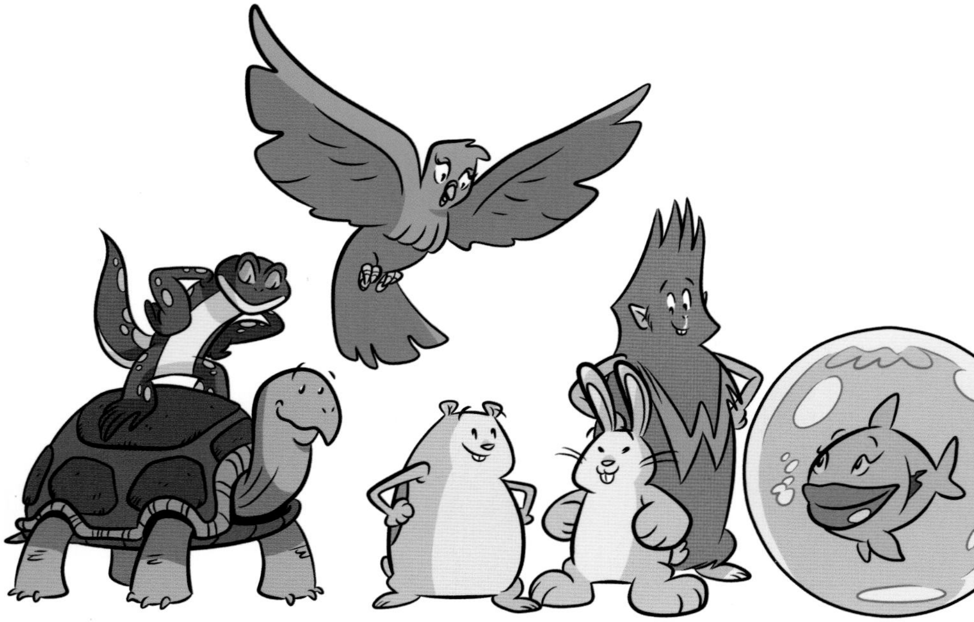

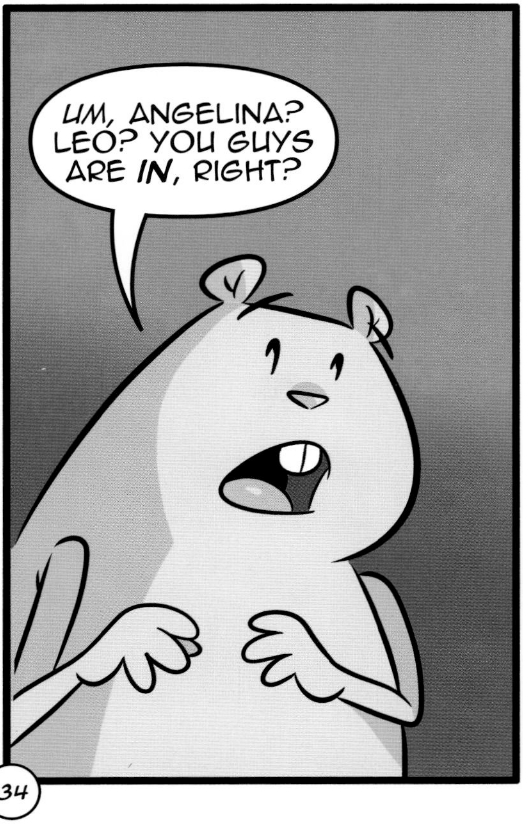
UM, ANGELINA? LEO? YOU GUYS ARE *IN*, RIGHT?

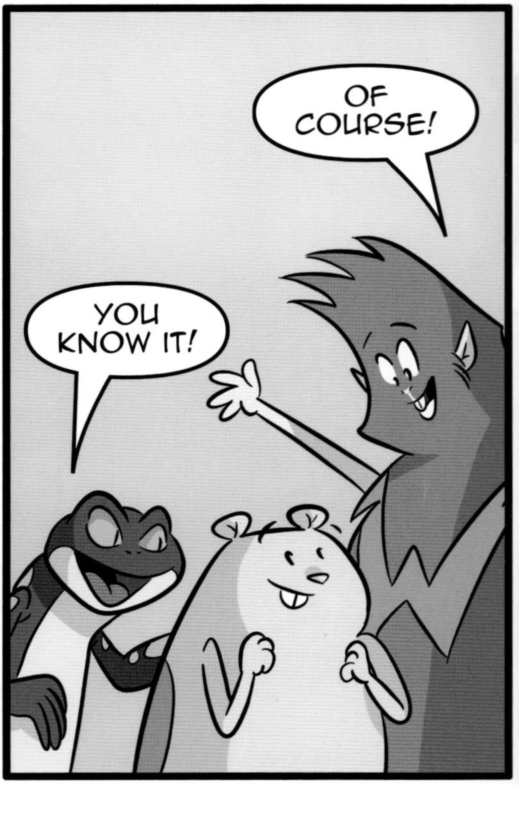
OF COURSE!
YOU KNOW IT!

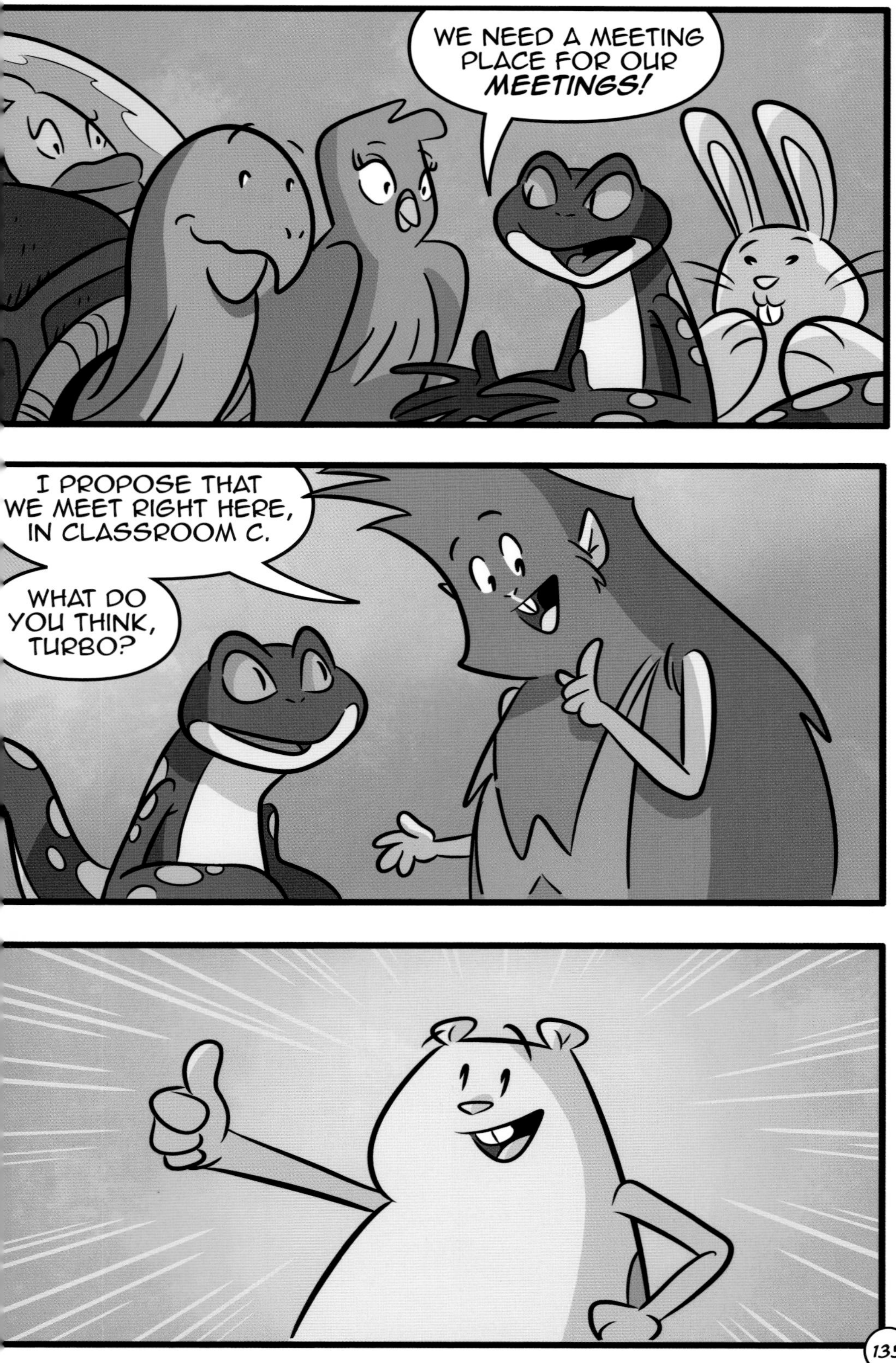
WE NEED A MEETING PLACE FOR OUR *MEETINGS!*
I PROPOSE THAT WE MEET RIGHT HERE, IN CLASSROOM C.
WHAT DO YOU THINK, TURBO?

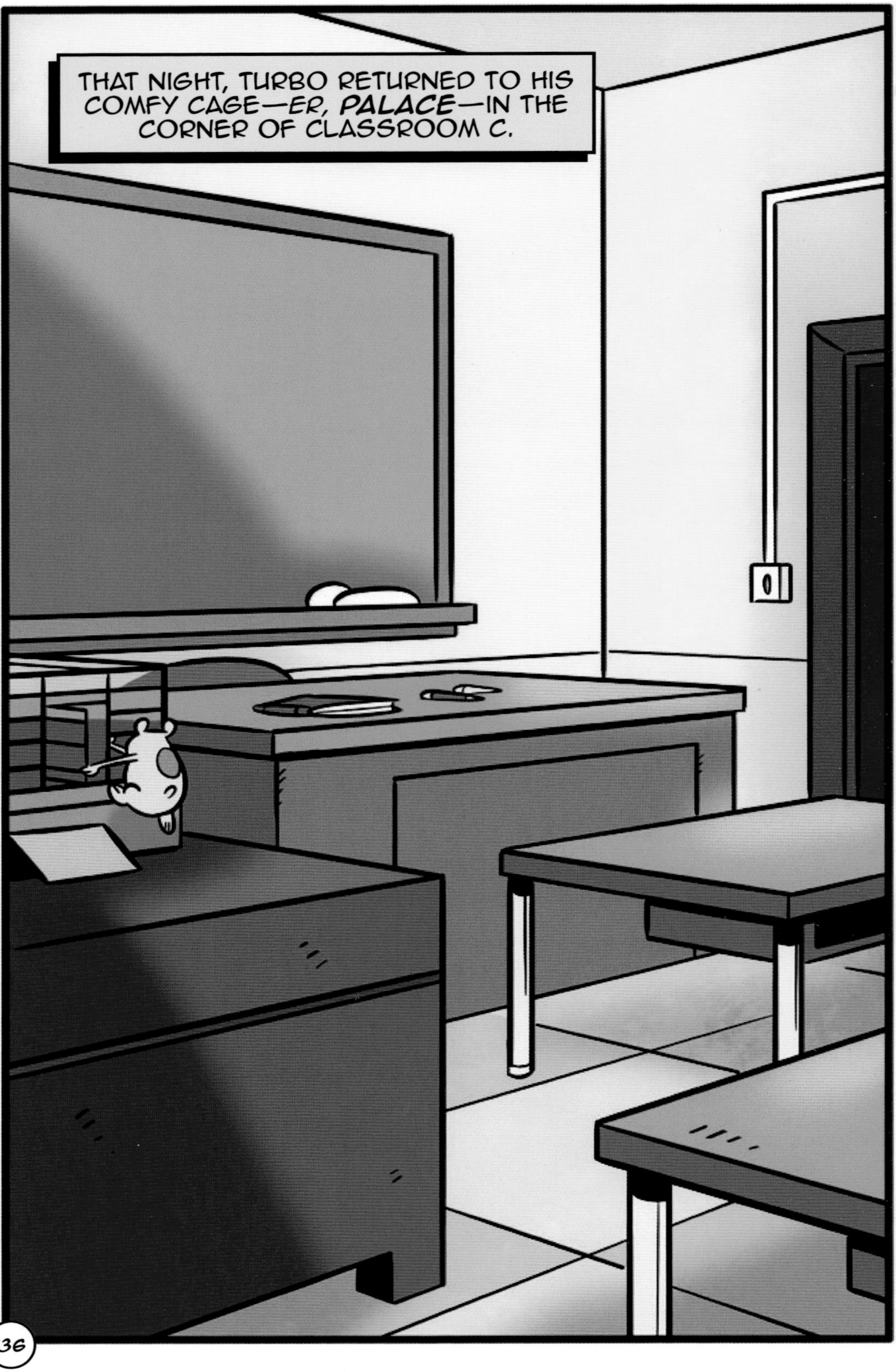
THAT NIGHT, TURBO RETURNED TO HIS COMFY CAGE—ER, ***PALACE***—IN THE CORNER OF CLASSROOM C.

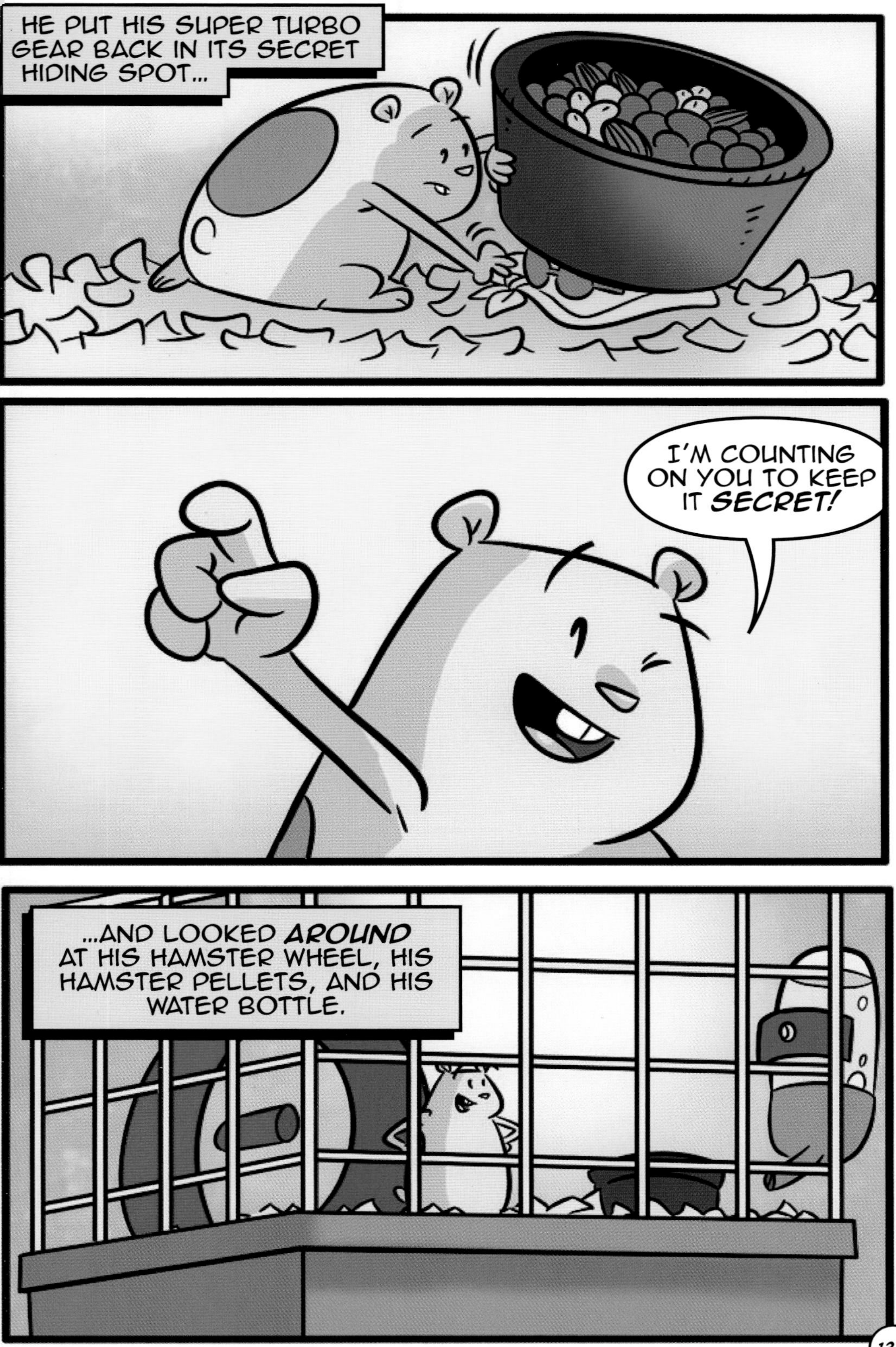
HE PUT HIS SUPER TURBO GEAR BACK IN ITS SECRET HIDING SPOT...
I'M COUNTING ON YOU TO KEEP IT *SECRET!*
...AND LOOKED ***AROUND*** AT HIS HAMSTER WHEEL, HIS HAMSTER PELLETS, AND HIS WATER BOTTLE.

TOMORROW, SCHOOL WOULD BE BACK IN SESSION.

FOR ALL THE STUDENTS AND TEACHERS, IT WOULD BE NO DIFFERENT FROM ANY OTHER DAY. BUT WE KNOW IT WILL *NEVER* BE THE SAME.

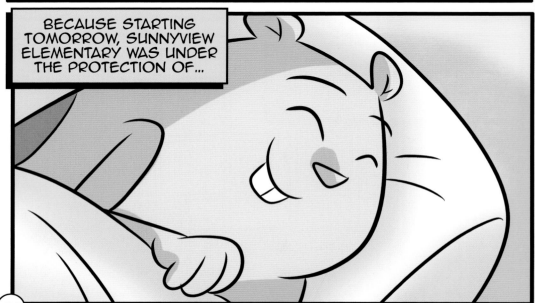

BECAUSE STARTING TOMORROW, SUNNYVIEW ELEMENTARY WAS UNDER THE PROTECTION OF...

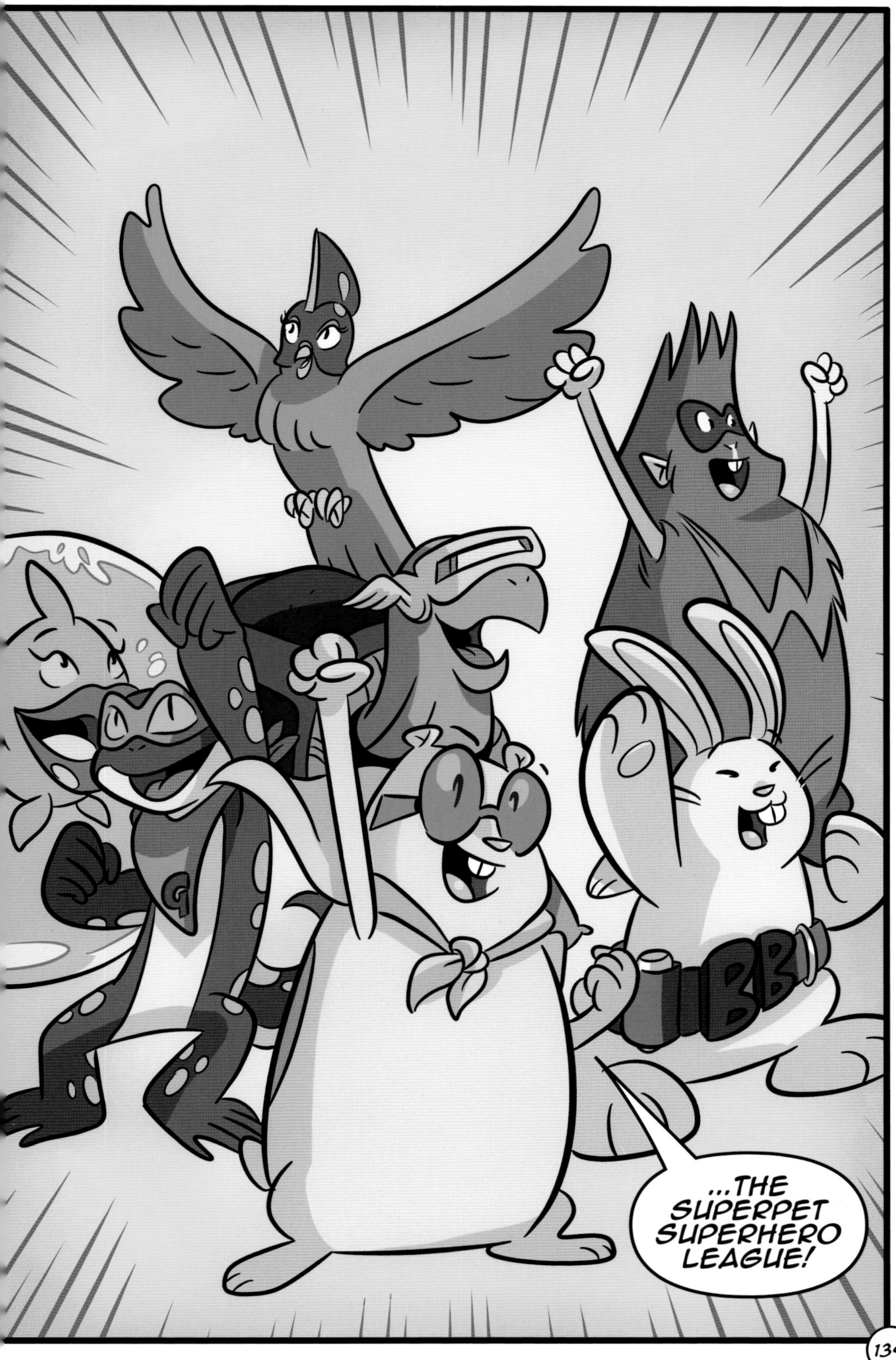
...THE
SUPERPET
SUPERHERO
LEAGUE!

CAN'T GET ENOUGH OF THE

SUPERPET SUPERHERO LEAGUE?

CHECK OUT THEIR NEXT ADVENTURE...

Graphic Novel
SUPER TURBO
VS. THE FLYING NINJA SQUIRRELS

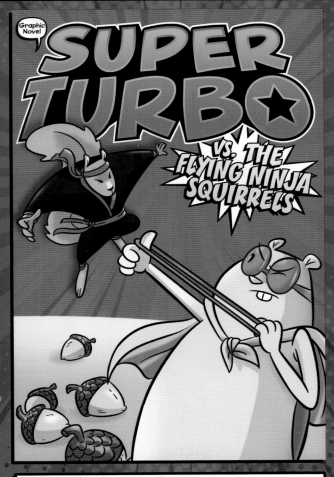

TURN THE PAGE FOR A SNEAK PEEK...

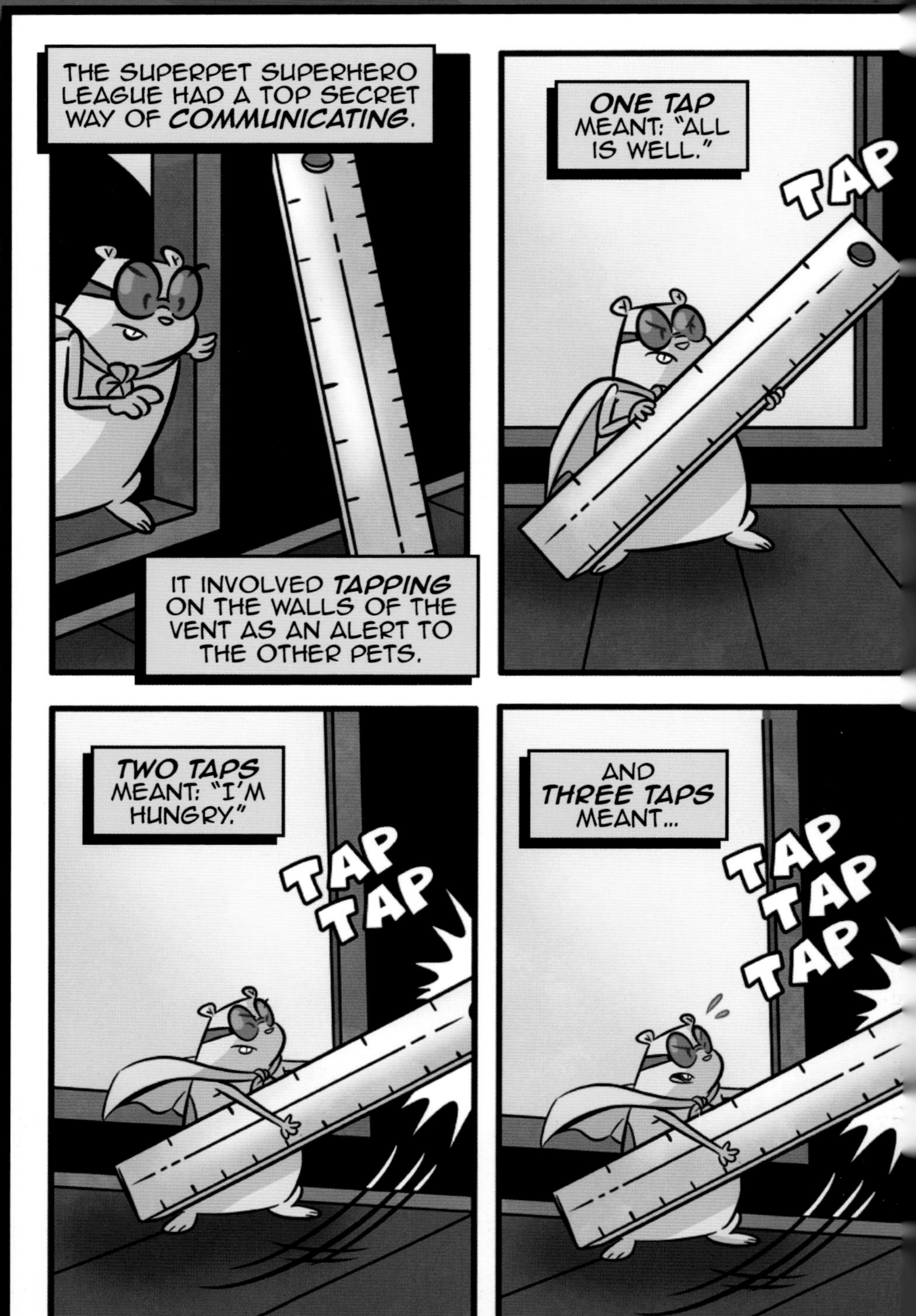

THE SUPERPET SUPERHERO LEAGUE HAD A TOP SECRET WAY OF COMMUNICATING.
IT INVOLVED TAPPING ON THE WALLS OF THE VENT AS AN ALERT TO THE OTHER PETS.
ONE TAP MEANT: "ALL IS WELL."
TAP
TWO TAPS MEANT: "I'M HUNGRY."
TAP
TAP
AND THREE TAPS MEANT...
TAP
TAP
TAP

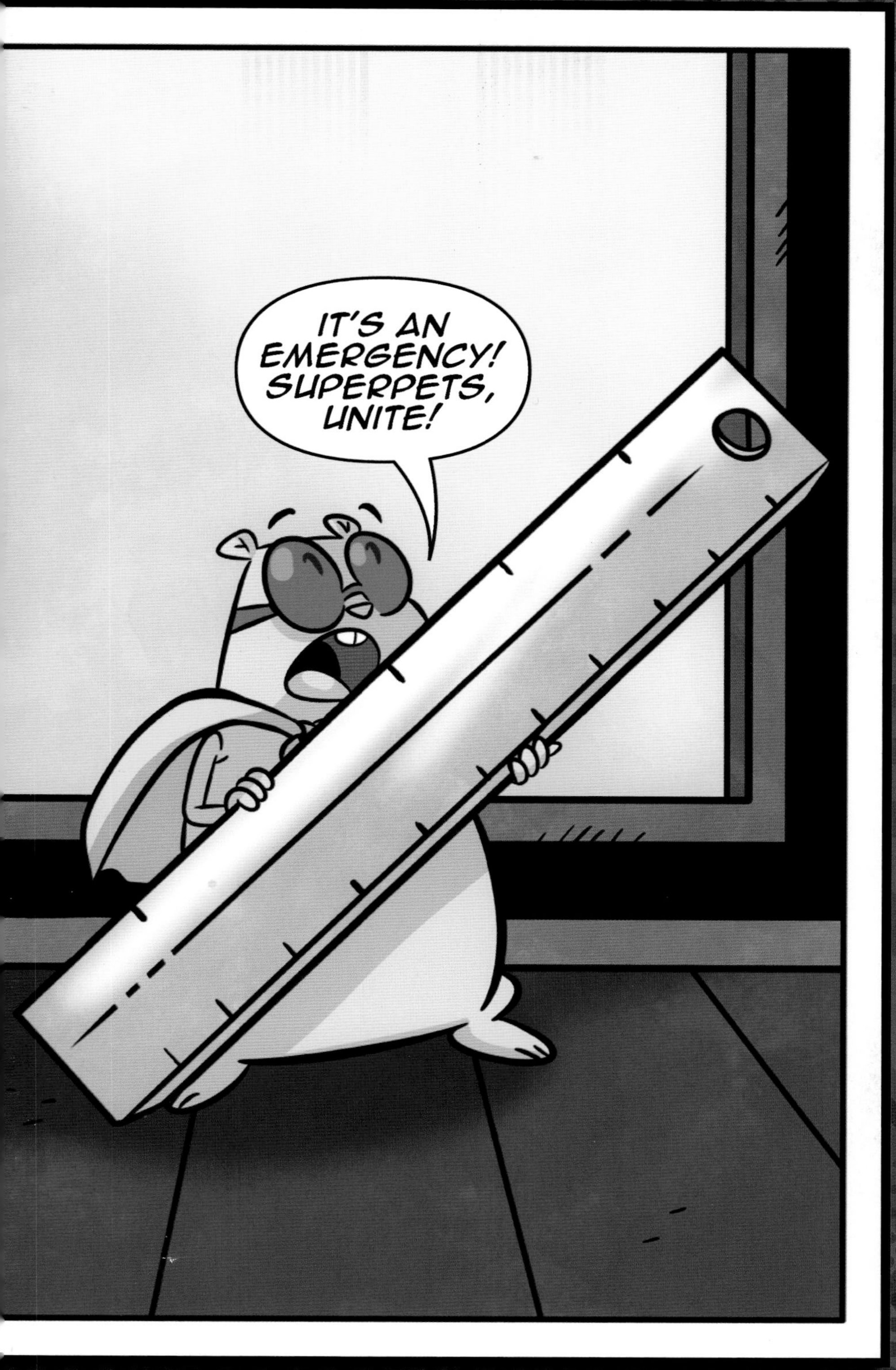
IT'S AN EMERGENCY! SUPERPETS, UNITE!